Stephen White is a clinical psychologist and the author of the Alan Gregory series of psychological thrillers. He lives in Colorado with his wife and son, where he is at work on his next novel. His previous novels available from Sphere are *Warning Signs*, *The Best Revenge*, *Blinded* and *Missing Persons*.

STEPHEN WHITE

KILL ME

A NOVEL

sphere

SPHERE

First published in the US by Dutton,
a member of the Penguin Group (USA) Inc.
This paperback edition published in 2007 by Sphere

Copyright © Stephen W. White 2006

The moral right of the author has been asserted.

A CIP catalogue record for this book
is available from the British Library.

ISBN-13: 978-0-7515-3629-4
ISBN-10: 0-7515-3629-6

Typeset in Sabon by M Rules
Printed and bound in Great Britain by
Clays Ltd, St Ives plc

Sphere
An imprint of
Little, Brown Book Group
Brettenham House
Lancaster Place
London WC2E 7EN

A Member of the Hatchette Livre Group of Companies

www.littlebrown.co.uk

for my mother

KILL ME

His Story

It started simply enough.

Progress Notes—1st session
Pt is a 44 yr old mwm in nad c/ only vague complaints.
Dx: ? ? Has apparent fatigue. Irritability. Anxiety? R/O:
296.82/309.24
Impression: Pt is smart, elusive, sarcastic. Goals unclear. Trust?
Rx Plan: Short term? Confront resistance, est. trust. Long
term? TWT.

AG

I was his clinical psychologist. I scribbled those notes after our first session.

I ended up treating him—the "married white male in no apparent distress"—for three weeks. In therapy-years, that's an eye blink.

What was I treating him for? I didn't have an answer to the diagnostic question until the last time I saw him. That first day I was ruling out Atypical Depression and Adjustment Disorder with Anxiety. They were both safe guesses.

Why all the doubt? Because I'm no clinical genius. And because patients lie. Anyone who has been doing healthcare for more than a week knows the feeling,

3

the nagging sense that something a patient is saying doesn't ring quite true.

The establish-trust part of my treatment plan was pro forma. "TWT"? That's my shorthand for time-will-tell. In therapy I typically wait things out. As days pass, untruths become unimportant or untruths become truths of a different species.

It turned out that he didn't have time and that I never appreciated how crucial the answer to the question of why he was in psychotherapy was going to turn out to be. All I knew back then was that there were pieces that felt incomplete.

Usually, early in therapy, that wouldn't be important.

That's what I thought this time, too.

Until the end.

The end changed everything.

PART I

My Story

PROLOGUE

I was about to downshift.

The motor of the old 911 purred only inches behind my ears, its tenor pulse as familiar to me as the treble of my wife's laugh. I couldn't be a hundred percent sure, but I thought I'd also sensed the telltale progression of airy metallic pings that would be the sign that my first true love was coming down with a little valve clatter.

She'd been prone to it her entire life, but still, *damn.*

It didn't take long for reality—my peculiar reality—to descend and for *damn* to morph into *it doesn't really matter.*

The car and I were old lovers; I'd owned her, or she'd owned me, for almost a third of my forty-two years. Neither of us was a virgin when we got together. She'd been assembled by others' hands way back in 1988 and I didn't fondle her wheel or feather her pedals for the first time until 1993, just shy of my thirtieth birthday.

The Porsche and I were gobbling up concrete in the fast lane of Colorado's Interstate 70 right where it begins to climb dramatically into the Rocky Mountain foothills from the table plateaus below Morrison. After an initial long rising straightaway and then a gentle, almost ninety-degree arc that completes a surgical slice through the spine of a Front Range hogback, the freeway suddenly stops messing around and shouts at drivers to take notice, that they've really, truly entered some legendary hills.

Fat bends in the road hug the contour of the soaring mountain and as those curves begin to meld into an ever sharper incline, under-endowed cars struggle to maintain their speed. Fully laden big rigs drift over toward the right shoulder where they fight the steep rise in elevation with the resolve of tortoises. They're slowing not because they want to, but because the gravitational reality of Colorado's main route into the Rocky Mountains offers them no alternative.

I was coming up on that first long right-angle curve, the one just before the highway transects the hogback. That's the spot where I was about to downshift.

A man standing on the bluff above the Morrison exit near Red Rocks caught my eye. Why? Probably because of all the recent news about the sniper. But this guy was too obvious to seem dangerous, and I didn't see a rifle in his hands. He was a man wearing a baseball cap and a fleece jacket, alone on the side of the road. He was leaning forward and gazing over the westbound lanes, his elbows resting on a fence, his right hand pressing a mobile phone to his ear. For the second or two that I spotted him above me he didn't seem to move a muscle. He was staring down at the traffic, seemingly mesmerized by us all.

He was, I decided, probably a plainclothes cop doing surveillance for the damn I-70 sniper.

I downshifted into third as I zoomed past him and shot toward the upcoming climb with a fresh boost of torque and enough raw power and confidence to soar past anybody or anything that might be blocking my path on the curving ascent ahead.

The interstate flattens out for a prolonged stretch prior to the brash incline of Floyd Hill. Buffalo Bill's grave and the Chief Hosa campground come and go. Exits weave off toward the mountain suburbs of Genesee and Evergreen. As I passed those landmarks my wheeled love held eighty, and joyfully toyed with ninety. For me and the German girl with the perfect body and the motor to match, the mountain curves and passes were mere playthings. And that moment, that day, I was trying to let it all be about the driving; I barely noticed any of the scenery flying by. In fact, the only reason I recalled seeing the Evergreen exit at all was because on the overpass I spotted another man standing with yet another cell phone to his ear.

More law enforcement? I wondered. *Odd.*

For half an eye blink, just before I flashed below him, I could have sworn the man was pointing at my car or gesturing toward me with his free hand, but I wiped the image out of my consciousness by letting myself be consumed for an instant with the juvenile fantasy that the bridge was the finish line and I was an Earnhardt cousin raising a fist skyward at the checkered flag at Daytona.

A third man. A third cell phone.

No overpass the third time.

This man was a little farther down the road, near the top of the hill where Highway 65 joins up with the freeway. A white Escalade was parked on the right shoulder, hood up in the air, emergency blinkers pulsing. The man I spotted—I was looking for guys near the road by then—stood at the rear of the SUV, and he, of course, had a cell phone to his ear. As I passed by I could see him talking, and nodding. His eyes, I thought, seemed to be tracking my red Porsche's progress as his neck rotated to follow me down the road.

Nodding.

First? A simple, *huh*? Followed by an *uh-oh*.

Then came the *damn*.
Could this be it?
Could it?

I've never known what the next section of I-70, the one just west of El Rancho, is called, but I always figured that it had to have a name. It's the kind of stretch of road that over the years should have earned a nefarious handle. Something like the "Death Drop" would have been appropriate.

The girl from Stuttgart and I were cresting the El Rancho hill above that long, steep downhill section of highway. The lanes that stretch out below teeter on the edge of an almost straight ridge as it descends at an acute angle into the rocky canyons along Clear Creek. To the right, off the downhill shoulder of the road, is a cliff. How high is the cliff? Too high. Lots of air. From the concrete lanes drivers can't even see how far they'd soar if they misjudged their way on that side of the interstate.

It's just as well. It isn't a survivable fall.

Experienced truckers find low gears in order to spare their brakes on this stretch of 70, and their crawling rigs almost always clog the right two lanes on the downhill side. The slope is steep enough that inexperienced mountain drivers, and even some experienced ones, see their carefully modulated seventy miles per hour become eighty-five or ninety or even ninety-five before they figure out exactly what effect gravity is having on their control of their cars. I knew from dozens—hell, hundreds—of prior journeys along the route that I could count on a stream of red brake lights flashing on in front of me as drivers fought to harness the sudden increase in speed foisted upon them during their descent.

I also knew that at the bottom of the long downhill a constellation of geographic features and design complications conspired to further confound the drivers who were already struggling with the gravitational challenges of the cruel section of road. Within the space of a few hundred yards at the bottom of the hill, the posted speed limit was suddenly reduced from seventy-five to fifty, Highway 6 merged into I-70, the number of westbound lanes decreased from four to three and then suddenly to two, and—and—a not-so-subtle wall of rough granite a few hundred feet high insisted that the roadway make an abrupt change in course almost ninety degrees to the west. For the half mile or so that came next, the narrowed path hugged the radically curving outlines of Clear Creek. Towering granite walls loomed overhead on both sides.

Despite the upcoming hazards I wasn't foreseeing a need to tap my girl's brakes on the downhill. History told me that the Porsche and I could dodge the trucks and weave past the slower cars regardless of how many lanes were available. The Carrera and I only needed one lane for ourselves, we didn't need all of it, and we needed it only briefly. The posted speed limit was inconsequential to me; taking a highway curve at eighty miles an hour that pedestrian cars took at fifty meant nothing to me and my little fräulein.

We were both designed for it, regardless of what the highway engineers and the Colorado State Patrol might think to the contrary.

I first noticed the flatbed truck when I was in the fast lane about a quarter of the way down the hill below El Rancho. The rig—it had a tall cab and an extended, stake-lined open bed that was filled with neat rows of fifty-gallon metal drums—was in front of me a couple of lanes over, nearing the halfway point of the long descent. It appeared to me that the driver of the truck was making a rookie mistake, moving into the lane adjacent to mine to try to pass a couple of tractor-trailers crawling hub-to-hub in the

11

two far-right lanes. The computer in my head immediately organized the equation: The eighteen-wheelers were in low gear going, maybe, twenty miles per hour. I was doing eighty-five, ninety. The open-bed truck had accelerated to something in the vicinity of thirty-five or forty to pass the bigger trucks. In the left two lanes in front of me, five or six smaller vehicles dotted the highway between me and the converging rigs.

The cars, SUVs, and pickup trucks were cruising downhill at various speeds between sixty and eighty.

The skill of the drivers? I decided that the safest thing for me was to assume that the other drivers sucked.

The algebra wasn't complicated: Would the flatbed truck with the oil drums finish passing the tractor-trailers and vacate its current lane before the cluster of cars and pickups in front of me were forced to squeeze together into the fast lane—the one smack in front of me—to avoid the temporary blockade caused by the three big trucks descending in consort down below?

It was going to be close, I decided.

Without any further deliberation my right foot shifted slightly at the ankle, the base of my big toe prepared to find purchase on the brake pedal, my left foot lifted up off the floor and hovered above the pad of the clutch, and the base of the palm of my right hand found the trailing edge of the gear shift, readying for the motion necessary to flick the smooth knob from fourth gear back down into third.

As I eased off on the accelerator and the rpm wound down, I once again heard the unwelcome melody of tinny clatter from the valves.

Got to tune you, baby girl. Got to tune you up.

It's the thinking that we don't try to do but that our magical brains do anyway that distinguishes the human animal from the machines we build. We can teach our machines to solve problems and even to ponder the value of various innovative solutions, but we haven't yet figured out how to teach the machines to recognize novel problems that will ultimately require us to use other machines to help us find solutions. For now, at least, that's still the stuff of humanity.

Unbidden by me, that's exactly what my mind was busy doing in the next few milliseconds as it changed effortlessly from the consideration of the algebra of gravity, variable speeds, crappy drivers, available lanes, and currently present vehicles, into the consideration of the calculus of a problem set that included an entirely novel set of variables: three men on cell phones watching traffic at three different locations on the same small stretch of Colorado interstate, constricted flow on a historically dangerous downhill section of highway, and an open-bed truck that was lined with seemingly innocuous big black drums.

My brain's assessment of those facts was confounded by one brand-new piece of information that it threw into the problem set: Big, rectangular red lights were beaming on each side of the back of the flatbed truck that was transporting the big metal drums.

The truck driver was hitting his brakes.

Wow.

I reached an instant, terrifying conclusion: The truck wasn't accelerating to pass the two tractor-trailers. It was braking to stay even with them.

Why?

My mind chose to take the developing conundrum one step further, instinctively including a seemingly extraneous variable in its calculation: the y variable, the variable that I'd been consciously adding into almost every novel problem set that had crossed my path over the past few days.

The y variable was the small matter of the standing commitment from the Death Angels.

How to precisely weight the y variable had been proving to be a tough thing for me to figure, primarily because the people charged with implementing the y variable had proven to be an imaginative bunch. Before I was even consciously aware that I actually had the acute new problem—the driving-down-this-hill and surviving this apparent Death Angels assault problem—I was actively struggling with the chronic dilemma I'd had since Adam left Providence, which was the whole general Death Angel survival problem.

The novel problem? The current assault? I read it this way: Over the last ten minutes or so I had apparently been driving past a series of predetermined checkpoints manned by men with mobile phones who were sending along news of my progress to the driver of the flatbed with the black drums on the back so he could precisely time his descent on this treacherous downhill stretch of Interstate 70.

But why? What do they have planned?

My brain was ready with the answer.

Instantaneously, the whole scenario made such perfect sense that I wasn't even surprised when the first shiny black barrel somehow slid *uphill* off the truck bed and bounced hard off the concrete ribbon of highway.

Instantly, left foot: clutch.

Right foot: brake.

Right hand: downshift. Fourth to third.

The tach needle jumped. The rpm soared close to the red zone. The 911 flexed and she readied. She knew me well, and she knew I wouldn't have done what I'd done to her unless something important was up.

The second and third barrels seemed to fly off the truck simultaneously a fraction of a second later. A pickup truck a couple of hundred yards in front of me swerved right— too hard—to avoid one of the drums. He overcompensated to the left before severely overcompensating once more back to the right. By then he was up precariously on two wheels, and a split second later the crew-cab Dodge slid left until it careened into the air, launched by the sloped Jersey barrier that separated the uphill lanes from the down. I heard and felt the resulting crash as the flying truck exploded into the vehicle of some unsuspecting driver in the uphill lanes, but I was beyond the conflagration before my eyes could make any sense of it.

I didn't dare take my eyes from the road to check the mirror and the carnage.

Left foot: clutch.

Right foot: brake.

Right hand: downshift. This time into second.

The old girl's engine screamed in protest at the back pressure I was insisting she endure. I wasn't worried about her, though; she wouldn't let me down. She never had.

And hey, there was no valve clatter at those rpm.

In front of me—and not very far in front of me—the barrels continued to tumble off the flatbed in twos and threes. The first ones off were bouncing past me on the highway just as the latest ones were tumbling from the bed of the truck.

A Lexus SUV, desperate to avoid a collision with a flying drum, sideswiped a Nissan sedan fifty yards ahead. Together they kept weaving into and away from each other, their dance completely filling the little space that remained between the three side-by-side trucks and the center highway barricade, effectively obliterating my only easy avenue to escape the tumbling drums.

The barrel that I knew was the one that was destined to hit me—the one that figuratively had my name on it—slid solo off the truck's flatbed, bouncing once, only once, before hanging back up in the air as though it were a guided missile waiting for me to drive into position beneath it.

Which, of course, I was about to do.

That is apparently what fate required of me at that moment.

And that's precisely what I was doing.

ONE

Where *to start with this guy? This shrink?*

Honesty?

Eventually, maybe. Soon, hopefully.

Not the first day, though. Certainly not the first hour.

Not with a stranger. The stakes were way too high.

The first day? The first day—it was a fine autumn day—he'd have to settle for the truth.

Not the whole truth, not nothing-but-the-truth. But the truth.

We'd both have to settle for that.

"You ever get massages?" I asked him.

Yes, that's how I started the first session with him. Un-frigging-believable.

What the hell? I thought. *Where on earth did that come from?*

"You ever get massages?" Did I really ask him that? I certainly hadn't planned to start out that way, but that's exactly what came dribbling out of my mouth, even before I'd sat down in the chair across from Dr. Alan Gregory.

His eyes narrowed a little in response to my question. Maybe he raised his right shoulder enough that I could have considered it a shrug. Maybe not. I took the combined movements to mean "sure," but they could just as easily have meant "what difference does it make?" Most likely the gestures constituted a vague editorial about the peculiar manner that I'd chosen to begin the first psychotherapy session of my life.

"I find that they help," I said. "Massages. I've been getting a couple a week." As an afterthought, I tagged the word "lately" onto the end of the sentence.

Help with what? He could have asked me, maybe should have asked me. But he didn't. He sat silently, waiting for something. Was he demonstrating patience, or indifference? Time would tell. Time, though, was something I didn't have in abundance. At that moment I was feeling neither patience nor indifference. Were our roles reversed, I know I would have asked the "help-you-with-what" question.

No doubt about it. I would have asked. Yep.

If he *had* asked I would have told him I meant help with the fact that I was dying, though I wouldn't have told him yet exactly how complicated my dying was turning out to be.

Truth, yes.

Honesty, not quite yet.

"The massage therapist I see? Her name is Cinda. She's good. Very good. Little-known fact: Some massage therapists do the bulk of their work one-handed. They do; it's not like with a baseball pitcher, or a cook, though. A painter, whatever. The dominant hand changes depending on what she's working on, where she's standing. Sometimes it's left, sometimes it's right. But what makes Cinda so good at what she does—truly special—is what she does with the other hand, the one that's not doing the heavy lifting."

I felt suddenly exhausted. The lassitude came on in an instant and floored me, like I'd been idiotic enough to turn my back to the ocean and had ended up getting flattened by a twelve-foot curl of breaking indolence. If this guy in front of me had been an analytic shrink with a cracked-leather Sigmund chaise and was sitting in front of me dripping old Viennese attitude, I might have stretched out and rolled over onto my side to be contrary. But he was a pedestrian Colorado Ph.D. in a pedestrian old Victorian in downtown Boulder and it was apparent that he'd organized the furniture in his office so that our time together was going to be face-to-face.

I asked, "Do you mind if I put my feet up?"

What was he going to do? Be a jerk, say no? He opened his hands in a be-my-guest gesture. *What is this guy*, I wondered, *a mime?* I lifted my heavy legs and rested my beat-up sneakers on the scratched wood of a table that said old, not antique. The change in posture eased my fatigue a little. Every little bit helped.

The dramatic increase in fatigue I was feeling was a new thing. The doctors couldn't explain it. I was still adjusting to it.

Other than his brief introduction in the tiny waiting room—"Hello, I'm Alan Gregory. Please come in" —he finally spoke his first words to me. He said, "The other hand?"

I'll give him credit for something: He made the short phrase sound somewhat consequential.

And he let me know he'd been paying attention.

"I actually think of it as her 'off hand,' not her other hand," I said. "The working hand is the reason we're there, of course. It's the business hand, and she knows her business. Cinda's intuitive—she finds tightness I don't even know I have. She kneads it. Traces it. Stretches it. Finds the origin of a muscle like she's an explorer looking for the headwater of a river. Then nine times out of ten, she gets the tension to release. What I'm saying is she does the job that needs doing, but she does it mostly with one strong hand at a time. Sometimes the off hand helps—does some of the same work—but most of the time . . . no, not. It's one working hand, and one off hand."

How did he reply to that little speech? His eyes invited me to go on. That was all. It was a subtle thing, but to me the invitation was as clear as if a calligrapher had penned it on good linen paper, sealed it with wax, and had it handed to me by a liveried messenger.

Thea could do that, too—talk to me in complete sentences using only her eyes.

He and I would talk about Thea later.

Why, I wondered, was I babbling on with this guy about my massage therapist's hands? I still didn't have an answer to that one, but I went with the momentum, mostly because fighting it and doing something else would have required stamina I didn't have.

"Despite how good her working hand does its job, her off hand is the reason I go back to her."

He sent me another invitation with his eyes. Or he repeated the same invitation. I wasn't totally sure which.

The rhythm of the therapy dance was becoming clear: I would appear to lead. He would appear to follow. The reality would, of course, probably turn out to be something altogether different. I reminded myself that I'd decided to be honest with him. Otherwise, what was the point?

I said, "Sometimes she'll just rest it a few inches from where she's working with her business hand. If she's doing my lower back, she might rest her off hand on my hip. If she's working my shoulder, she might rest it on my neck. No real pressure. That's not true, maybe some pressure. A light stroke, a gentle squeeze. But no real work. The other hand is doing the work. Most of the time her off hand doesn't join in—it's not there for that. It's there for . . ."

Could he think I'm talking about sex? "I'm not talking about sex. In case you're wondering. When I talk about

20

sex, I'll talk about sex. That's not one of my things—discomfort with sex. This is about something else entirely." I glanced at his left hand. He wore a ring. "You married?"

He grazed the ring with the soft pad of his thumb. Involuntary? Maybe. He didn't answer me. Or maybe he did. If he did, I missed it.

"I am," I said. "Sometimes—maybe most of the time—when my wife does things for me they're part of the deal, the marriage deal. She does *x*, I do *y*. She makes dinner; I make money. But sometimes she does something for me and I know it's meant to be a gift, something special. Something that's not part of the deal. That's what Cinda's off hand does during the massage; it's the one that says that whatever's going on at that moment isn't just a job, isn't only part of the deal, that she cares a little, that I'm not just another blob of flesh on her table, that it's not all about my muscles yielding to her fingers. That we're not only trading my money for her time."

I inhaled and exhaled before he replied. He said, "That's important to you?"

His words stopped me. *Isn't that a universal truth? Wouldn't it be important to anybody?* "Of course," I said. *Of course.*

"Her off hand provides . . . tenderness?" he said. "Is that a good word for what you're describing?"

I crossed one ankle over the other, and the change in posture offered some temporary relief. "I think about it more as a caress, but 'tenderness' is a good word for it. Yes."

"And it's the reason you go back to her?"

"Cinda's good at what she does, but plenty of people are good at what they do. Yeah, I guess the truth is that the reason I keep going back to her is because of how she manages her off hand. For the kindness, the tenderness. It's important. Essential even." I tacked on, "For me."

The shrink was silent for most of a minute. At first I thought he was waiting for me to start up again, but I saw something in his face that told me that maybe he was working on something. So I waited, too. Finally, he seemed to find whatever he'd been seeking. He said, "And . . . you're wondering whether you'll get it here? The tenderness? Whether I'm going to turn out to be all business, or whether I have an off hand, too?"

Actually, that wasn't what I'd been thinking at all.

What I'd been wondering was what it was about this bland little room, and about this unfamiliar, relatively bland man, that had somehow got me babbling about Cinda and the seductiveness of her off hand.

"Maybe," I said.

He let me digest my response. When he thought I'd had enough time, he added a coda. "You told me your massage therapist's name, but not your wife's."

It wasn't a question.

Not at all.

TWO

I hadn't told him much on the phone when I set up the appointment.

My last name, as common as dirt, revealed nothing. I'd introduced myself using the nickname my oldest friends had hung on me decades before. I'd told Alan Gregory, Ph.D., that I'd gotten the referral to him from a business associate, which was only a bit of a stretch, that I had some things going on in my life that I was eager to discuss—that part was absolutely the truth—and that on the first day I wanted to see him twice, with some time in between. One session—or appointment, or whatever the hell he called it—in the morning, one more mid-afternoon on the same day. That would be ideal.

He initially balked at my request for dual appointments, but relented when I explained that my schedule was in a "difficult phase." We worked out the times we would meet. Ten in the morning. Then again at two-thirty the same afternoon.

I didn't tell him I'd be flying into the nearby Jefferson County Airport solely for the purpose of seeing him, nor did I tell him that I'd be flying back out the same day as soon as we were done. I didn't moan that it would have been much more convenient to use the Boulder Airport, but that my plane needed just a little bit more runway than the Boulder field had to offer.

Nor did I tell him the two appointments could be considered an audition. In my mind, when you meet somebody new it's always an audition. You don't always know which one of you is auditioning, or for what. But every introduction is an audition.

If this shrink had earned even half his doctorate, I figured he already knew that.

I left his office after the first session that morning without revealing that I'd made a decision that I thought I could work with him. I was worried that if I'd told him he'd passed the test, he would have asked me what the test was.

I didn't know the answer. I only knew he'd passed.

Or he'd have asked why I needed a test.

I didn't know the answer to that, either.

Therapy was already turning out to be more complicated than I'd anticipated.

In between my two appointments with Dr. Gregory, I took a taxi across Boulder to the local Toyota dealership, asked the cabbie to wait a few minutes, and managed—as I knew I would—to get accosted by a salesman before I made it all the way to the front door.

All fake friendliness, the salesman—I pegged him as an ex-frat boy who liked beer more than he liked just about anything else—thrust out his hand and said, "I'm Chuck Richter, and you are . . ."

Not in the fucking mood.

His handshake was too firm by half, too robust by a factor of three.

I considered retracing my steps to the waiting cab, sighed, and steeled myself with a promise that this experience would soon be over.

"Chuck?" I said with my most ingratiating smile plastered across my face—the smile I used to use when, before

I had more money than I needed, I would be trying to finagle or seduce a first-class upgrade from a clerk at the check-in counter at the airport. Chuck and I made good eye contact, and he reflexively matched my smile with a grin that registered like a fingernail on a chalkboard in my soul.

"Yeah?" he said.

"I need to be out of here in fifteen minutes, thirty tops. When I leave, I want to drive away in a new Prius, any new Prius. 2006? 2007? Doesn't matter. Color? I don't care. Equipment? Whatever you got. Demo? Fine. Here's what I'd like to happen next, right now even. You go to your sales manager and get me a number. If I like the number, I pay cash for the car and I'm on my way in my new Prius in time to make my lunch appointment.

"If you're not back here with a number for me in five minutes, or if the number you bring back makes me think you and your sales manager are trying to take a lot of advantage of me, rather than just a little advantage of me, I'm going to get back into that taxi over there and go to the Honda dealership on Arapahoe and make some salesman just like you the exact same offer on one of their hybrids. You have a single chance to do this deal. No negotiating. Are we clear? You and I? A hundred percent clear?"

Chuck nodded in little narrow jerks. His eyes were wide at the challenge, as though I was a stranger in a bar who'd walked up to him and offered to buy him and his buddies beers and shooters all night long if he'd simply munch down a fresh habanero.

I thought he was wondering if he could pull it off. But maybe, just maybe, I'd misread him and he had more balls than I was giving him credit for and he was wondering how to play things to his advantage with his sales manager.

"Chuck?"

He nodded again—those same quick little jerks of his wide chin—his eyes still big as nickels.

"I'm not screwing with you. One chance to get this right."

"Yes, sir."

"Don't screw with me."

"I wouldn't do that."

"Yes, you would. But don't."

It took the various players thirty-five minutes to get the paperwork together and finally to give up trying to sell me all the extra crap—extended warranty? You've got to be kidding—that car dealers hawk to pad their profits. While I waited for this form and that form to be prepared, I strolled out and sent the taxi on its way.

When I returned, Chuck actually asked me if I had anything I wanted to trade.

I told him I had plenty of cars, but nothing I wanted to sell. I was just making conversation to keep him at bay.

"You a collector? Old cars?" he asked. It was either a lucky guess, or Chuck had the inborn Doppler radar of a born salesman.

"No. I have an old Porsche, but I still drive it. An eighty-eight 911."

"Wow. What color? Red?"

"Yeah, red." Two good guesses for Chuck.

"The coup, not the Cabriolet, right?" he said.

I nodded. Chuck was three for three. *Note to self: Don't play poker with Chuck.* "I bought it in 1993."

"Shit," Chuck said. "This Prius ain't no Carrera."

"More honest words have never been spoken by a car salesman," I replied.

To get away from Chuck I strolled over to the parts department and picked out a car cover for my new 2006

Prius—the 2007 models hadn't arrived yet. When I got back to Chuck's desk, he was ready for my money. He led me down the hall and I sat obediently in the designated mark's chair in the finance manager's prison cell of an office while I called my banker on my mobile phone and authorized a wire.

In order to pry the keys out of the clutch of Chuck's fist, I actually had to convince him that I didn't want his personal, extra-special new-car orientation any more than I wanted a colonoscopy without anesthesia.

A few minutes later I drove away in the new hybrid and found my way back across downtown Boulder to a flat that was on the second floor of a lovely old house on Pine Street just east of the Hotel Boulderado. I parked the Prius in back, and let myself inside with a key I'd begged from the friend who kept the apartment as a pied-à-terre for the rare occasions he was in Colorado. He owned a company in Boulder with which I'd done a lot of business over the years, and I could tell—when I had asked him if I could use his apartment occasionally—that he thought I had something going on the side. I let him believe it. As long as he didn't gossip about it, his suspicions were fine with me.

I collapsed onto the bed in the flat's only bedroom and fell asleep wondering if I'd live long enough to figure out what the fun graphic display meant on the little screen in the middle of my new car's dash.

THREE

I was back in Dr. Alan Gregory's office at 2:30. I'd slept for a while and showered at my buddy's apartment, and my fatigue had gone from shouting at me to pay attention to humming in the background like Muzak. I managed to tune out the dull torpor the same way I can usually tune out a corporate orchestral rendition of "Sympathy for the Devil" during a long elevator ride.

"And so we meet again," I said to the shrink. *Lame?* God, yes. But I really said it—for some reason I was discovering that I felt almost possessed in the guy's office, which of course left me wondering what the hell that was all about.

I handed him some forms he'd asked me to fill out at the end of the morning session. On the patient information form, I'd scribbled in my nickname, a post office box address belonging to my Denver lawyer, and my cellphone number. I gave him an e-mail address that went only to my BlackBerry.

Person to contact in case of emergency? *Hah! If only.* I left that one blank.

Had I offered it to him, the odds were low that he'd recognize my real name. If he were a player in the medical technology field my name would certainly ring a bell, but outside that small pond and beyond the ranks of the venture capitalists and investment managers who hung around on the sandy banks of Entrepreneurship Lake, my name wasn't a household word.

I wasn't Warren Buffett. I wasn't Bill Gates.

I was an anonymous rich white guy. One of the first epiphanies that went along with becoming an anonymous rich white guy was learning how many of us there are. How many? You'd be surprised; I was. More than enough to make it easy to blend into the crowd.

"I plan to pay cash each day that I'm here," I said, hoping that would be a sufficient explanation for the absence of any health insurance information on the forms.

"That's up to you," he said. "I'll prepare a bill and hand it to you during our last session of each month."

"Fine." Money didn't interest me. I could have told him that I'd stopped counting money the day that I decided I had enough. That day had taken place quite a few years before when a couple of the big international med-tech giants both decided that they wanted the device I'd designed and the company I'd created to build and sell it.

A bidding war ensued and I happily sold everything for two to three times what it was worth. And it had been worth a lot.

I didn't tell him any of that.

He sat back. I sat back, too, figuring he was going to wait for me to start the show again. But I was wrong.

He spoke next. His voice was as even as a mother's love. He said, "Now that I know you like massages, and that you're predisposed to a little tenderness, how do you suppose I can be of help?"

I smiled at the sardonic timbre of his words. I was pleased—doubly pleased—he had it in him. I didn't want to spend these precious hours with a slug. Now that I was dying I had little tolerance for tedious people.

Truth, right? Okay—even before I was dying I had little tolerance for tedious people.

He sensed my hesitation.

"Start anywhere," he suggested. "In the end, it won't really make any difference."

He was wrong about that, but he was speaking generally and from his experience. I knew that if I started off by hinting at the end, I might never get a chance to tell him the beginning. I had to do it right.

That's why I was there with him. In therapy. There was, literally, no one else I could talk to about what was going on, and I desperately wanted to understand the beginning better, so I could make the end different.

Maybe I was wrong, but I thought I had to be sure to start in the right place.

FOUR

Two stories must be told for this to make any sense.

A glance at my 2004 calendar would reveal that the story I tell first actually took place after the story I tell second.

The order was important. God, was it important.

Still is.

The first story:

Late summer.

I loved that boardroom.

The fog bank hovering a quarter mile from shore over the Pacific and the lush green hills of Santa Barbara spreading out below seemed to start abruptly from nothing and nowhere, as if the huge sleek table at which we were sitting was floating in an infinity pool and all of us in the room were just treading water on the edge of possibility. It was an organic space of light and air and water, a room for beginnings.

Not a room for beginners, though.

I'd only agreed to be on the board of this company because many of the other board members were visionaries. I'd long before stopped participating as a director on boards that were full of glorified rubber-stampers who collected exorbitant fees for conspiring with management to squelch creativity, to shirk shareholders, or to thwart risk.

If I wanted to waste my time watching large mammals gallop with blinders on I'd go to Santa Anita.

But this place—this company, this room—was a different animal. And the people with me on the board of directors were different jockeys. That day hundreds of millions, literally, were on the table. A radical change in direction for the company. Huge risks. Possible huge rewards. Likely, in my opinion, huge rewards. I didn't need the money that would come with the change in course we were contemplating that day—nobody in the room did—but we all needed to be involved in *making* the money that might come, should come, with the change in course.

Why? Ask five of us and you'd get six different answers. Some, just because. Some, to try to fill a dollar-sensitive hole that life's caprice had dug into their souls.

Some, to hoard.

Some, to give away.

Turning one buck into two, or three, or ten or twenty, was what we all did. As a group we didn't question it much. Individually, on days when I did pause to question it, I liked to think I did something else, too—something valuable—along the way. I also knew myself well enough to allow for the possibility that that was rationalization.

I was sitting back, letting the discussion around that table above Santa Barbara build to a crescendo, watching brilliant people spark brilliant plans and delighting as the sparks ignited the fuel of ideas like matches torching Molotov cocktails. That day, we were the revolutionaries. My role? I sat poised and ready to make my contribution, to splash the accelerants wildly, eager to stoke any fire that seemed to be damping.

Until that was needed, I was content to warm myself by the heat that came from everyone else's embers.

My colleagues around the table knew that I was an

advocate for rolling the dice. I knew they were watching me, waiting for me to buy in and demand my chance to throw the bones. It was my style in life. And in business.

The dice were truly bouncing that morning.

Sevens? Eleven?

Craps?

It was, I remember thinking, *no fun without risk.*

Life.

And then my damn cell phone started ringing.

I'd thought I'd turned the thing off. Two of my friends on the board laughed at the intrusion of the sound into the room. My ring tone for as long as I could remember was a tinny, almost comical version of "Ob-La-Di, Ob-La-Da." The merry melody was the source of some of my friends' amusement. Mostly though, my comrades were chuckling that I was the one in the group who'd forgotten to turn off his damn phone.

That I'd forgotten didn't surprise anyone in the least.

I was a big-picture guy, not a detail guy. Everybody who knew me knew that about me. Call me when you want a strategy. Call me when you need vision. Call someone else when you need to be reminded to tighten the lug nuts on your tires or to change your oil.

Turning cell phones on and off, that was a detail.

"Excuse me," I said to the room. My right wrist was still in a cast from a skiing accident in the Bugaboos a few months before, and my coordination with my damaged hand was crappy. I fumbled with the tiny phone before I managed to open it up and get it next to my ear.

I said simply, "Yeah?" My tone bore a little aggravation, as though it were the caller's fault, and not mine, that I'd forgotten to shut down the phone, and that it was the caller's fault that the Beatles ditty had intruded upon that special board meeting.

The voice I heard on the other end was a complete

surprise. Not too many people had my mobile number. I didn't think she was one of the ones who did.

I listened. She spoke nonstop for half a minute.

Shit, shit, shit.

The room darkened as though a huge cloud had blocked the sun.

But it hadn't.

Or as though the coastal fog had rolled in and enveloped the verdant hills.

But it hadn't.

"What?" I whispered, finally. I stood from the table and wandered to the corner of the room, to the wall of glass that faced west, to the place in the room where infinity started and infinity collapsed. Behind me, all of my colleagues disappeared from my awareness. All the creative fires within me stopped burning as though they'd been doused by foam.

This woman on the phone mistook my "what?" for confusion when it was actually an expression of bewilderment. *This can't be real; I barely know this woman. She can't be telling me this.* She began to repeat what she had just said. She said it more slowly the second time and dumbed it down considerably in the retelling, as though she sensed that the first rendition had been too sophisticated for me by a factor of two or three.

"You're sure?" I said after she had finished her elementary-level spiel.

She was. She began to explain in great detail all the safeguards that were in place to prevent false positives.

False positives? I didn't want to hear it. "It's okay," I said to stop her. "I believe you."

I didn't believe her. I just needed her to shut the fuck up so I could think.

"We need to consider—"

I didn't want to hear what we needed to consider.

34

I closed the phone, returned to my chair at the big table, gathered my things, and stuffed them into the battered daypack that I had schlepped around on my shoulder for more than two decades of business meetings. I think I mumbled, "I have to go," to the room. Maybe I managed to say, "Excuse me."

Maybe someone asked me what was wrong.

I don't recall any of it.

In twenty minutes I was back on my plane.

My pilot was a friend, a woman named Mary Reid whom I'd met after she'd written me a letter describing how one of my company's devices had helped save her daughter's life. I was touched by her note. We corresponded for a while—she was a single mom living in Tucson then—and talked a few times on the phone. I learned that she was ex-Navy and had been an airline pilot flying 737s out of Stapleton, Denver's old airport, but had become one of the casualties of Continental Airlines's bankruptcy in the nineties. She'd reluctantly turned her back on flying, moved in with her mom in Arizona, enrolled in the police academy, and had taken a job as a cop with the City of Tucson.

She continued to miss living in Colorado.

I thought she possessed an interesting array of skills. Three months later I hired her to fly my newly acquired plane. She packed up her mom and her daughter and the trio moved north to Denver.

Mary knew me well. She saw the numb look on my face as I climbed the narrow stairs into the cabin. The latest candidate for the copilot's chair that had been vacant for almost half a year was a handsome, competent man named Jorge who seemed to have less personality than an under-ripe eggplant. Jorge was up front, doing preflight checks.

Mary and I both knew, already, that Jorge wasn't going to be the one.

She said, "Are you okay?"

I lied. "Yeah."

"No, you're not."

I picked a seat and fell into it.

"We're leaving now?" she asked. "Destination?"

"Denver."

"Centennial?"

Mary was asking me what airport I preferred. But I didn't answer her. That was a detail.

I was definitely more consumed with the big picture.

The big picture wasn't looking too good.

FIVE

The second story preceded the first. Temporally speaking, at least. It was late March, 2004.

The timing makes a difference in understanding the nature of one man's fate.

Mine.

The second:

I'd skied the Bugaboos twice before, so I can't exactly plead ignorance or surprise over what happened that day.

I made a stupid mistake, plain and simple. Let's leave it at that. If I hadn't made the mistake, I would probably never have met the Death Angels. And if I'd never met the Death Angels, well . . .

"Death Angels?" you ask?

See, Dr. Gregory, it does make a difference where things start.

Montrose, Colorado's glam index falls somewhere around Omaha's or Bakersfield's, and it suffers in comparison with its alluring neighbors, Ouray and Telluride—but it has a consistently accessible airport close to my second home near Ridgway at the foot of the glorious Dallas Divide in the San Juan Mountains on Colorado's Western Slope. The Telluride airport is technically slightly closer as the crow flies, but its altitude and its location—the runway at Telluride is at 9,000 feet above sea level, is basically about the size of an aircraft-carrier deck, and is surrounded by the vaulting, wind-whipped, sawtooth peaks of the Uncompahgre—render it a dicey routine airfield, so I usually endorsed Mary's choice of the bland predictability of Montrose.

Originally our ski adventure was going to be a party of six, but one of my best friends—a guy who was the funniest lawyer I'd ever met, and probably the funniest trust and estates guy on the planet—got an unexpected invitation to do a deep cave dive in Belize that he'd been dying to do, and had decided that the Caribbean sun was beckoning him more than were the Canadian mountains.

The rest of my friends—five of us altogether—had convened at my house and stayed up too late the night before, playing cards and telling stories. We were in the jet before dawn as it went nose-up from the runway in Montrose. Mary had the yoke. The copilot du jour was an ex–Air Force pilot named Stephanie something. Mary seemed to like Stephanie. A good omen.

Mary brought us to a gracious stop in Calgary a little after nine in the morning. We almost filled a waiting Suburban and its twin roof racks with all our gear, and after a long drive we made it to our scheduled rendezvous with a chartered helicopter. A few minutes before one o'clock the chopper hovered just long enough to let us toss our gear outside and scramble from the cramped cabin onto a volleyball court–sized, snow-covered flat near the absolute top of the Purcells range, high above timberline in the rugged, sharp, granite and glacier, otherworldly paradise of the Canadian Rockies.

The day was glorious, perfect for skiing. Blue skies, brilliant sun, just enough of a breeze to levitate snow crystals into the air to create halos around the highest of the surrounding peaks. The majesty of the British Columbia high country stretched out below us farther than I could see. Across a valley the harsh beauty of Kootenay seemed so close that I felt that I could ski to it.

We'd heli-skied as a group before and we had a system that worked. One of us went down first on each section and picked a vantage from which to videotape the rest of us from below. We'd drawn straws in the plane; I was going to be the cameraman on the third drop, and I was guessing that my turn would come on the run that would carry us from the sparsely spotted trees just below timberline down into actual woods. Although our rationale for the video-camera procedure was safety—in case of a slide or an avalanche, the footage might provide additional clues about where, precisely, to begin a search—we all knew that the real reason for the video record was our annual Memorial Day–weekend blowout party that always prominently featured a special showing of our digitized exploits from the previous year's recreational stupidity.

The fact that I was scheduled to be third with the camera that day meant that on the first two runs, the most heavenly ones, the ones in the steepest, narrowest, granite-lined, untracked chutes above or just below timberline, I could simply enjoy what the mountain had to offer.

And I did. The first couple of runs made the entire long journey to Canada worthwhile. Fresh, virgin powder tracks—at times deep enough to tickle my nipples—squeezed between unforgiving rocks leading to almost vertical chutes, cornices, and big air. Lots and lots of thin air everywhere there wasn't forbidding rock or welcoming snow.

Once we'd crossed over timberline on the second run, we gathered together on a narrow ridge to select the next drop, the one we'd take into the forest for our first true run into the trees.

A phone rang.

Noticing a theme here?

Everybody laughed at the incongruity of the sound. If there is one place that you don't expect to hear a phone ring, it's on the side of a mountain in the Bugaboos. One by one, each of my friends looked at me.

Why? I was the designated big shot in the group. I was the guy with the plane, the one who got the calls that couldn't wait.

But the ringing phone wasn't mine. No "Ob-La-Di, Ob-La-Da."

Grant Jacobs sheepishly slid his daypack off his shoulders and pulled a bulky black receiver out of a zippered compartment on the side. "Satellite phone," he said apologetically. "Callie's been sick. I promised Ginny I'd carry it."

Groans and laughter all around. I had the camera in my hand, so I took some footage of Grant and his phone to embarrass him with at the Memorial Day–weekend party. Then I led the rest of the group a little ways ahead along the ridge to scout out a route down into the woods. Grant caught up with us a few minutes later. His dark face was the color of freshly poured concrete.

"Grant, is Callie okay?" I asked.

"Callie's fine. Her fever's down. That was Ginny. It's . . . Antonio. Marilyn just called her."

Antonio, a ridiculously handsome native-born Roman, was the lawyer friend who'd chosen scuba diving in Belize over heli-skiing in the Bugaboos. Antonio was the trusts-and-estates guy who could always make me laugh. Marilyn was Antonio's wife.

"What is it?" someone asked Grant.

I felt as though I already knew. Not the details, but the truth. A pit formed in my stomach.

40

Grant said, "He got caught in a cave. Something happened with his equipment. His BC, his regulator—something. She wasn't sure. Then he . . . banged his head on a rock, some coral. Marilyn doesn't really know the details. But it's bad. It's . . . bad."

I could tell from Grant's robotic recitation that whatever had happened was much worse than the simple facts. "Is Antonio dead?" I asked.

"He's unconscious. His EEG looks like . . . crap. They were down pretty deep, apparently—a hundred and ten feet, something like that. He hit his head, he had the equipment problem, he was so out of it they couldn't get him to take his spare air. They rushed him up to the surface. He swallowed a lot of water before they got him to the boat."

Someone—one of the divers in the group—asked, "Are you saying they did an emergency ascent? They didn't do a decompression stop? How long were they down before the accident?"

If Antonio had been down at that depth for any length of time at all, he absolutely had to do a gradual return to the surface with an interval stop to squeeze the accumulated nitrogen out of his body before he surfaced.

Grant wasn't a diver. He wouldn't know about the necessity for decompression stops. He shook his head. "Marilyn didn't say anything about that. Is that important? Is it? What does that mean?"

Without a decompression stop, along with all of his injuries, Antonio might have suffered the horrors, and dangers, of decompression sickness. The bends.

"How long was he down . . . after the accident?" I asked, dreading the answer. I left two words—*without oxygen*—unsaid.

"Five or six minutes after the accident, they think. Marilyn told Ginny she thought they were guessing. But it

41

took them another minute or two to get him on the dive boat to start CPR and finally get him breathing." Grant could barely get the details of the story out of his mouth. Finally, he added, disbelieving, "He's barely alive. Jesus Christ, Antonio almost drowned."

"No," I said with disgust. "I think you have that wrong, Grant."

The picture I had in my head was of a vegetized version of my friend. He would have been flown by a chopper—to keep him as close to sea level as possible—to a facility with a hyperbaric chamber, a tiny tubular cocoon pressurized with pure oxygen. Coarse white sheets and too many plastic tubes, the *hiss/whirr* of a ventilator. Multiple IV pumps, gurgling drains. Monitors that told too much, and way too little.

"Antonio definitely drowned," I said. "It sounds like he was almost resuscitated."

After the news about Antonio's tragedy, on another day in the mountains—a day nearer my Ridgway home with us doing chin-high bumps or floating on waist-high powder through the spindly white aspen trunks at Telluride—we would have found our way down some safe, groomed cruising runs while cutting gentle S-turns in rough formation, descending methodically to the base area, intent on rushing home to hold Marilyn's hand. But we were in the middle of the Bugaboos in the Canadian Rockies wilderness on the border between British Columbia and Alberta, only halfway to the rendezvous with the helicopter that was our only way back to civilization.

Jimmy Lee was a good friend whom I'd first met through Thea, my wife, on our wedding day. He had been attending my nuptials as the date of Thea's maid of honor. Jimmy was a law graduate of Boalt, in Berkeley, but had worked in the reinsurance business as long as I'd known him. He traveled for work almost as much as I did, and he traveled for adventure almost as much as I did.

He said, "We have to ski out of here, guys. We can't get distracted by Antonio's situation, not yet. We keep our heads on straight, we do this right, we'll be back home later tonight. For right now? The helicopter is due to meet us in thirty-five minutes. Three, five. We need to get down to it, and we need to get down to it in one piece. To do that, we need to keep some focus. Steady. Aggressive, but not rushed. The hurried-er we go, the behind-er we'll get."

Jimmy was right, of course. He usually was. If our gang were a Mafia family and not a group of successful, middle-aged businessmen/weekend athletes, Jimmy would be consigliere.

Would I be the don? Probably, but not happily.

I liked being in control more than I liked being the leader. In business I'd always seen myself emulating the young Steven Jobs, the one who founded Apple, not the older Steven Jobs, the one who came back to run it. Character-wise, I thought I had more in common with James Caan's Sonny than I did with Marlon Brando's Vito.

I was capable of leadership, but it wasn't my favorite thing. If someone else could run things well—"well" meaning in a manner that didn't interfere with my interests or my freedom—I let them.

My balance swayed and I felt the horizon jiggle side to side as I pulled my goggles down onto my eyes and cleared the pressure from my ears. I lost a moment wondering if my tears for Antonio would cause the inside of the lenses to fog before I skated down the flat ridge, pulling ahead of the group. I hoped my friends were thinking that I was scouting out the best path to take down into the trees; I knew I was creating some space to try to contain my grief.

"How does this look?" I asked Jimmy a minute later as he pulled up behind me. I'd stopped on a snow-covered outcropping of jagged Bugaboo granite. Jimmy was slightly uphill from me and he was gazing past me at a narrow chute that funneled down about a quarter of a mile into a forest that was treed to just the right density for great wilderness skiing.

The presence of two good-sized evergreens at the bottom of the chute was a reliable indication that this long narrow ribbon wasn't traditional avalanche terrain. Frequent avalanches would have prevented the trees from ever getting to that size. The snow that was exposed in the narrows appeared crusty from the sun; farther down into the woods it looked invitingly deep and completely untracked.

On a day that I hadn't just learned that one of my dear friends was near death, I would have been ecstatic about finding this spot and doing this run and being the first in our group to drop into the long ribbon of soft white down between those trees.

That day, with Antonio's situation so serious, it was just a good path across town.

"It looks fine," Jimmy said in response to my question. "Perfect. We can start over there." He pointed to a spot nearer the trees where the initial drop down onto the chute was only fifteen feet as compared to the twenty-five or so it would be if we took off from the outcropping where we were standing. "Hey, guys," he called back over his shoulder. "Over this way. Let's keep moving. Come on, we have to get going."

Just then the horizon jiggled again. But this time, I heard a sharp *cra-ack* and the shelf below my feet disappeared so fast that I felt as though I was suspended in the air like a character in a cartoon. The balcony on which I'd been standing hadn't been snow-covered Bugaboo granite at all—it had been a simple cornice of snow and ice, and faith.

Bad faith, it turned out.

The cornice had given way, as ice cornices inevitably do, its wintry debris preceding me down the chute, and suddenly I was airborne. My arms flew to the sky to grab for a handhold on what turned out to be nothing, my legs flailed to reach for the security of the snow-covered terrain far below.

I'd like to think that if you put me on that cornice ten times, and if it snapped free unexpectedly ten times, seven or eight times out of the ten I would somehow find a way to come down onto the steep slope below in some position that had some resemblance to vertical, and I would manage by luck or by skill to dig in an edge just a tiny bit, just enough to get the smidgeon of control I'd need to regain my balance and bring myself to a stop.

Later that night, I'd end up telling the story of my miraculous recovery from the treacherous fall. I'd tell it once, twice, five times as I drank red wine or cognac and my audience drank whatever it was they were drinking. The perilous drop I'd survived from the cornice to the slope would probably grow gradually from twenty-five feet to thirty to thirty-five.

That's what I'd like to think.

But that time wasn't one of the seven or eight and I didn't come down anywhere close to vertical, and when gravity completed its thing and the ground rushed up to find me, I didn't manage to get any control with the edge of a ski. What happened instead was that I was thrown too far backward as I fell and came down on the tail of my left ski. From that precarious position all hope of recovery was lost, and I began to careen and bounce down the mountain not like a freestyle skier, but like a child's jack tossed carelessly onto a playground slide.

The binding on my left ski released with the initial impact, and my right ski, too, popped off obediently as I came back down after the completion of my first full rotation in the air. My poles, tethered lightly to my wrists, flailed wildly as I bounced high off the windswept snow. My mind struggled to sort through the sparse details and the geography and the rushed geometry of my predicament. Somehow, with each rotation, and with each fresh downhill exposure, my eyes managed to lock onto those two trees that were looming large at the bottom of the chute. Right from the start, they seemed to pose the greatest danger.

Or at least the first, greatest danger.

Up above me—high above me—I could hear Jimmy Lee scream my name.

Once, twice, three times, he called me. Each sounded louder than the time before, as though if he called me loudly enough, or persistently enough, I would just stop this foolishness and roll back up that Canadian hill.

The fact that Jimmy was screaming at me meant that he hadn't fallen with me, though.

As my heels went flying back over my head, I thought, *Well, that's good.*

SIX

I tucked and tried to roll after that first spread-eagle spin but soon discovered the universal truth that bowling ball–shaped objects bounce downhill much faster than do mannequin-shaped objects. In my current predicament, speed, obviously, was not my friend.

Tumbling out of control down a mountainside didn't have the same sense of inevitability as that frozen-in-time sensation I've experienced at intervals in my life while awaiting the impact of an imminent traffic accident. Each downhill revolution was teaching me fresh lessons about my dilemma, and every few milliseconds I found myself recalculating the trajectory that was carrying me—inexorably? I wasn't quite convinced—toward those two damn trees that were standing sentry like gateposts to heaven, or hell, at the point where the woods began at the bottom of the chute.

Since I had the camera in my daypack, there would be no video to confirm for me what really happened when I reached the convergence at the end of the funnel, but Jimmy told me later that after some uncountable number of revolutions I eventually bounced high off an incline that was composed of a fallen tree topped with a thick cushion of snow. That mogul-like obstacle was about five yards in front of the trees. Flying again, I caught spectacular air—"hospital air," Jimmy always called it—and sliced through a long bough about halfway up the tree on my left. I grazed the branch first with my left hand and wrist before I felt a calf-size pipe whip hard across my abdomen. After that brief contact, which flipped me from headfirst to feetfirst and back again, my momentum carried me beyond the two deadly evergreen obstacles. I continued my rotation in space until I came to a thudding, spread-eagled, facedown plop in the waist-deep powder just beyond the two trees.

My helmeted head was resting no more than eighteen inches from the fat trunk of tree number three.

My friends, phenomenal skiers all, arrived at my side within seconds and were digging me out of my powder grave before I'd even begun to process the reality of what had just happened. I suspected I wasn't dead because I could hear Grant on his satellite phone, arguing with someone about how to get me immediate medical care. And I could hear Jimmy Lee: He was shouting at me not to move.

Not to move.

I was so bereft of air that I wasn't even able to spit out the words to tell him that I didn't think I could.

The possibility that I couldn't move terrified me. Oddly, it horrified me much more than the possibility that I was about to die, because at that moment I also seemed to be unable to find a way to suck oxygen into my lungs. The terror of paralysis was much worse than the sudden panic I'd experienced when the cornice collapsed under my feet, much worse than anything I'd felt as I'd been lolloping down the mountain totally fucking out of control.

My friends argued among themselves for what seemed like most of a month while, avalanche shovels in hand, they continued to dig frantically around me. Jimmy finally managed to forge a consensus that lifting me out of my hole was a medically risky option. They focused first on getting a wide trench open in front of my face so that I could have unfettered access to some of the Bugaboos's thin air. They were motivated and efficient; it didn't take long for them to remove enough Canadian powder that a depression had been leveled out all around me to about the same depth as my body. From my awkward vantage, they looked like a crew of arctic gravediggers feverishly trying to reverse a mistaken interment.

Jimmy dropped down into the newly dug pit, put his lips close to my helmet, and said, "Hey, buddy, you there?"

I wasn't sure I could talk, but I blew some snow away from my lips to prove I could at least do that.

"Good, good, you can hear me. That's great. Can you move? I don't want you to, but I'd like to know if you can. Try the fingers on your left hand. Just wiggle them for me, can you do that?"

He had no way to know that my left hand was the one I'd tried to use to stop the tree. And failed. The tree was still standing. I wasn't.

I felt the pressure of Jimmy's hand on my glove. Instantly, I also felt a bolt of pain shiver up my arm and down into my fingers.

That was good. I had enough of my wits about me to come to the conclusion that pain was good.

I did try to respond to his touch. I tried. Nothing happened. I tried once more. Nothing happened that time either. I wanted to tell him to check my right hand, that it hadn't just gone ten rounds with a tree.

But I still couldn't talk.

So I blew some snow again. My parents had taught me that if I ran into something in life that I couldn't do, I should always do something I could.

Well, apparently I could blow snow.

One of my other friends, not Jimmy, muttered, "Holy shit. I can't believe this. First Antonio, and now . . ."

I'm sure I wasn't supposed to hear the words that had been muttered, but I did.

My ears were fine.

That's good, I thought again. *I can hear.* I'm such a damn optimist.

"Help me up," I said, surprising everyone, including myself.

"Whoa, whoa," Jimmy replied, as though I were a spirited horse trying to break out of the corral. "Have to be careful."

"Help me up," I said. "I just had the wind knocked out of me. Get me up."

Jimmy said, "We're not going to help you. You need to stay still until we figure out what you've broken, what you've hurt. Don't make things worse for yourself, come on. Listen to me now. Don't be stubborn."

I thought about Jimmy's counsel for about the same amount of time it had taken the cornice to disappear and me to go topsy-turvy down those few hundred yards of crusty ice chute.

Then I stood up. "There," I said. "See?"

My parsimonious, yet dramatic, soliloquy would have had a much more profound impact on my friends had I not immediately collapsed back down onto the snow like a marionette after someone had snipped its strings.

SEVEN

It turned out that the collapse was a momentary setback. Though less impressive, my next move was more reasonable; I raised myself to a sitting position, elbows on my knees. My friends huddled together in a semicircle in front of me, as though they were waiting for me to draw the next play in the snow and tell them which one of them was going long.

When I didn't say anything right away, they all started chatting at me at once. I stopped them by saying, simply, "I want a promise from you. All of you."

"What?" a couple of them chimed simultaneously. Someone added, "Anything, you know that."

"Two promises, actually. Grant? Put away your satellite phone. I don't want anyone to call Thea about this. Not after what Marilyn's been through today. I'll do that myself later on. That's number one."

"Sure," he said. "Okay." Inexplicably, he lowered the phone from his ear and put it behind his back, as though if he hid it from me I'd forget he had it.

"Number two," I said. "If it had turned out that I couldn't have gotten up on my own just then—if it ever comes to the point that I can't get up when I want to—if I ever end up in a hospital bed in anything like the shape that Antonio is in right this minute . . . illness or injury, it makes no difference . . . if that ever happens to me, I want your promise, as my friends, my best friends, that one of you will find a way to kill me. Or at least help me kill myself."

Silence.

"Hey," Jimmy said finally. The tone of his voice told me that he was imploring me not to be so morbid. "You're going to be okay. Hey."

"Drugs," I said. "I prefer drugs to guns. You all know I don't like guns. Get some good advice on how to do it right, and then kill me. Got it?"

"Come on," Jimmy said.

"I'm totally serious about this," I added. "I'm not cut out to live in the condition I fear Antonio is in. Brain dead, body dead. It's not for me. This"—I spread my arms to encompass all of British Columbia and Alberta, all of the Bugaboos, all that it represented to me in terms of my personal freedom—"this is what life is for me. When I can't do this anymore, have days like this with you guys, it's time for me to leave this earth. Do you understand?"

"I feel the same way," one of my friends, I think it was Paul, said from behind me. He followed his words with nervous laughter.

"Yeah, absolutely," someone else added. "I'm in. I'd want someone to kill me, too."

I knew right then that my sincere wish had become a platitude and I almost regretted having asked.

Almost.

EIGHT

My injuries were nothing compared to what would have happened had I hit one of those two trees head-on.

If that had occurred my body would have been nothing more than a skeletal train wreck with internal organs that resembled a berry smoothie and a brain good for nothing but the amusement of trauma researchers. The glancing blow I'd suffered colliding with the evergreen bough had hurt me, but it hadn't killed me. I did a careful inventory while skiing under my own power down to the waiting chopper. I was sure I'd broken my left wrist—unsupported, it dangled at an angle that God never intended—and I was guessing that I'd fractured or bruised a couple of ribs. During one of my many tumbles down the snowy chute I'd either separated or snapped something solid in my left shoulder. My collarbone, I was thinking, but maybe something bigger. Internal injuries? Didn't feel like it to me, but up until then my reckless life experiences had magically spared me from actually knowing what serious internal injuries would feel like.

Concussion? I'd had a couple in my life, and didn't think I had one right then.

My friends had argued with me for a few futile minutes about how I should get back down to the chopper from the snowy lair where I'd finished my tumbling descent. They were unanimous in opining for the prudence of mounting an emergency evacuation with alpine rescue professionals to get me off that remote mountainside in the Purcells range. One even threatened to withold my skis, which someone had magically recovered on the way down the chute.

But I wanted no part of an organized rescue. I said it once and then shut up. Jimmy Lee was the one who convinced the others that they were wasting their breath, and wasting valuable time. He had one eye on me and the other, I knew, on Antonio.

Jimmy was a big-picture guy, too.

So I stubbornly insisted on skiing out, remembering the whole time to adhere to the sage advice of an old friend named Hawk, the guy who'd first convinced me of the seductive glories of leaving the marked trails behind and skiing through the wonders that wait in the woods. "The first rule," he'd told me years earlier, "is always keep both skis on the same side of every tree."

Hawk had been a wise man.

So that's what I did on the way to the helicopter: I kept both skis on the same side of every tree.

Worked like a damn charm.

A doctor in the emergency clinic in Banff, an amiable young woman who'd been born in Singapore and spoke English as though she'd been raised in Sussex, confirmed my injuries. She wrapped my fractured ribs, hijacked an orthopod who was just finishing up a surgery in the OR to set and cast my badly broken wrist and to hang a sling for my fortunately only-separated shoulder. The ER doc wanted to keep me overnight for observation, but I promised her I'd check myself into a hospital back home that same evening in Colorado.

She knew I was lying, but I lied with charm, and what the hell could she do, anyway?

*

The last of the daylight was disappearing behind the Rockies toward British Columbia before we finally got back on board the plane. Mary narrowed her eyes when she saw me, and immediately ordered my friends and her latest copilot wannabe off the plane after they'd helped me up the stairs.

She spent a good five minutes alone with me after I settled onto the sofa in the center of the cabin. She had to convince herself that I was a fit passenger before she would allow the boys on board. Once they were in the cabin, she handed over my care to Jimmy with a stiff warning that she wanted to know about the slightest change in my condition. Jimmy nodded.

Mary said, "I want more than a nod, Jimmy." She sounded like a cop.

Jimmy said, "I'm as concerned as you are, Mary. Don't worry."

Only then did Mary disappear into the cockpit to finish the preflight checks with Stephanie. The jet soon went wheels up from the Calgary airport, heading back home to Colorado's Western Slope.

By consensus, I was granted sole possession of the sofa in the middle of the plane, and my friends immediately delivered a cocktail—late in the evening, I was cognac and soda—and a bottle of water to my side. I used the water to wash down a couple of the Percocets that the kind doctor from Singapore had provided as part of my Western Canadian care package.

Jimmy Lee sat across from me shortly after we'd leveled off at altitude. In a low voice he said, "You're an idiot, you know."

I'd expected that Jimmy would have something to say about what happened on the mountain. Jimmy was the only one in our group whose psyche was weighted more toward superego than ego or id, so if there was a judgment to be made about my escapade, Jimmy would be the one to make it. Anticipating his criticism, I was ready to capitulate and admit to him that I should have recognized that the shelf I was on was a cornice and a not a granite ledge.

But that was as far as my planned *mea culpa* would go. I was in no mood for regret. I'd survived a legendary fall in the Bugaboos. The key word was "survived." The words "I'm sorry" weren't getting anywhere near my lips.

"We're all idiots, Jimmy. Come on, we were heli-skiing in the damn Bugaboos. Shit happens. I got lucky. Could have been worse. How about some credit for missing those two trees? That was something. Right? You think about what would have happened if I hit those trees? You guys could have brought me home in a to-go cup."

"That's not what I'm talking about. The fall? I thought that cornice we were on was rock, too. Could just as easily have been both of us going down. I'm talking about after the fall. First, you should've stayed still and let us get a rescue team in to get you out, and second, you should have stayed in the hospital in Banff tonight. You could have blown out your spleen in that fall, or ruptured your aorta. You shouldn't travel until you've been cleared."

"Doc thought I was okay to travel." That was a lie, but Jimmy didn't have any way to know that. "I'm okay, I'm fine," I argued. "Anyway, Marilyn and Antonio need us back home tonight."

"That doctor didn't clear you; she specifically told us that she wanted to observe you overnight but that you were uncooperative with her. I asked her point-blank, and she isn't a hundred percent sure you aren't going to start bleeding during the flight."

I started to shrug but shrugging hurt more than I could

have imagined. "If it happens, it happens. Hey, I walked out AMA. It's not like I'm about to sue her or anything."

Jimmy, who rarely cursed, said, "Shit." I think he thought I was making a lawyer joke at his expense.

I persisted in trying to find some humor in my decision. "Jimmy, Jimmy. You know that most women I meet want to observe me overnight. It's always been one of the burdens I bear in life."

Jimmy wasn't interested in playing along. He said, "That little speech you gave on the mountain? Where's my I'll-go-first-I'll-try-anything friend? I never saw this side of you before. Since when are you so fatalistic?"

The cabin phone chirped, the distraction permitting me a moment to construct a reply to Jimmy's question. I picked up the phone; it was Marilyn calling from Florida with the news that Antonio had arrived in Miami by helicopter and was in a hyperbaric chamber.

"Any . . . change?" I asked her.

"The doctors are not . . . optimistic." She inhaled sharply and started crying. She continued to cry while she said, "I'm begging them for hope. They're not offering any. None. He was without oxygen a long time. They think maybe he'll survive. But I don't feel as good about that as I should."

I didn't know what to say. Marilyn spoke and I tried to comfort her for another minute or so. I assured her we would all be by her side, no matter what.

I heard someone call her name. She said, "I gotta go." The line went dead.

I faced Jimmy. "Maybe since this afternoon," I said. "That's when I became so fatalistic. After what happened to Antonio in Belize I'm not sure I want to be saved by modern medicine. Dying on a mountainside in the Bugaboos looks just fine to me if I compare it to what Antonio and Marilyn are going to be dealing with after today. Antonio would give anything for the chance I had after that cornice collapsed. You know as well as I do that given the alternative he's facing, he'd gladly take that Belize cave as his final resting place."

Jimmy stared at me for a couple of seconds before he shook his head, I was guessing, at the callousness of my words. Then he stood up and walked to the galley to make himself a drink. I watched him take an inordinate amount of time stirring the ice in his vodka before he came back and sat across from me.

Jimmy usually squeezed a handful of limes into his vodka. Not that time. Cold and straight.

"That wasn't fair," I said. "I'm sorry. I'm really sorry."

What wasn't fair about what I'd said was that Jimmy was the only one of us who had been there before. He'd buried his beloved wife, El, eighteen months before, not too many months after her simple headache became a chronic headache became worrisome double vision became a terrifying tumor became inoperable brain cancer.

On my wedding day, the day I met Jimmy, El wasn't his date. She hadn't been Thea's maid of honor. El was the woman who caught Jimmy on the rebound when the woman who was Thea's maid of honor dumped Jimmy for a midfielder for the Colorado Rapids.

Yes, the Rapids.

Eloise was from Long Island and didn't know from soccer. Baseball was her game. She had been a lifelong Yankees fanatic, and found poetic justice that—once her marauding cancer had trumped the chemo and flanked the radiation and had even started sending special-forces cells out on secret missions to run covert ops on her organs— her ultimate demise would come from the bomblets left behind by those infiltrating cancer cells, which she ironically nicknamed "the New York mets."

As in metastases, not Metropolitans.

El was a funny lady while she was alive. She was a funny lady until a couple of days before she died.

Those last couple of days of El's life hadn't been pretty, though. Definitely not funny.

The falling dominoes that led to El's eventual death knocked each other over with such rapidity that when the last weeks and days came they made Jimmy's head spin. He ended up with a hole in his heart the size of his wife's smile, and every morning for months he was shocked all over again that he was waking alone to raise the two boys Eloise had given him.

I watched as he fortified himself with at least half the vodka in his glass before he said, "Listen. I probably shouldn't be telling you this, especially not right now, but I know a guy."

"Yeah?"

Although it may have sounded that way, my *yeah* wasn't simple perfunctory conversation grease. My radar had detected something monumental in Jimmy's simple pronouncement that he knew a guy.

He went back to his vodka.

"What kind of guy?" I asked.

He dropped his voice another octave or two and leaned forward toward me after stealing a glance aft to make sure our three friends were still distracted with their card game. For at least six months Grant had been trying to get us all as intrigued as he was with the medieval game of Tarot. He carried a deck everywhere. Jimmy went on with me only after he had convinced himself that Grant's latest cups-and-swords seminar was proceeding uninterrupted. "I don't actually know him. He's not like a friend of mine, but you know ... Let's say he's a contact, okay? Somebody I can ... get in touch with. If ... you know."

"Okay," I said. Jimmy was a bright guy; the sudden absence of eloquence was a sign of something important. Without trying to act too interested, I repeated, "What kind of guy?"

"This is weird," he said.

"I've noticed."

He finished the vodka and chewed on an ice cube while he stole a glance at the galley, apparently considering a refill of his cocktail. Then: "What you said before on the mountain? Everybody else thought you were joking; I'm sure you know that. None of them took you seriously. But I didn't . . . I didn't think you were joking. I know you too well."

"Yeah." I was agreeing that he knew me well.

Too well? Possibly that.

"I heard about him, you know, this guy and his . . . his business back when El was sick. Somebody I know back East knew somebody who knew about him, what he does. That kind of thing. At least three degrees of separation. Who knows, maybe more. I talked to somebody who talked to somebody who talked to somebody. Anyway, I've been thinking of telling you about him before today." He paused long enough to assess my reaction to what he'd said so far. "Because of Connie's situation. Not anything personal with you. Before what happened today, anyway."

"Connie's situation is personal."

Connie was my older brother, Conrad.

He was living in New Haven, where he'd spent more than two decades enjoying his dream life teaching ethics in the philosophy department at Yale. Just shy of three years earlier he had learned that he was suffering the inexorable ravages of ALS, Lou Gehrig's debilitating legacy illness. Connie's tribulations as the disease robbed him of control over his muscles—and his freedom—filled me with terror, even from a distance of almost two thousand miles. I didn't talk about Connie's condition much, not with anyone. Jimmy was one of those rare people that I didn't have to share much detail with; he seemed to intuitively know what I was going through with my brother.

"You said, 'business.' What kind of guy are you talking about, Jimmy?"

"A guy who'll do what you said on the mountain." He paused long enough for me to catch up, and recognized the look of mild shock that was settling on my face, before he whispered, "That's right, kill you. Arrange for your death. If you get seriously sick, like Connie. Or if there's an accident and something happens like what just happened to Antonio."

"Kill me?" I said.

"It's a business. Think of it as an insurance company." He laughed nervously. "Hey, I know my insurance, right?"

"They do this for . . . money?" For some reason the thought resonated with me at a number of profound levels. I found myself locked in a series of short exhales, totally neglecting the biological imperative to inhale in between. Part of me was shocked at the concept of what Jimmy was telling me, and part of me—not the most appealing part, I admit—was busy applauding the entrepreneurial imagination inherent in starting such an undertaking.

Grant suddenly stepped up and filled the space between Jimmy and me. Grant was a tall, light-skinned African American; he had to stoop way over to maneuver in the plane. "We can move the game down here if you guys want to play," Grant said. To me, more than to Jimmy, he added, "I think those two knuckleheads are finally starting to get the hang of it. I keep telling them to think hearts, think hearts."

I remembered to suck some air into my lungs before I

tried to speak again. I said, "It's all right, Grant. I think I'm just going to rest down here. I'm pretty sore. I don't think I'd be much fun. Anyway, I'd be at a disadvantage with all the narcotics I'm on."

Jimmy stood up. "I'll join you guys, Grant. Deal me in for the next hand. I'll be down there in a second."

Once Grant had returned to the table in the rear of the plane, I said, "Did he really say 'knuckleheads'?"

Jimmy leaned over so that he was close enough that I could smell the vodka on his breath. He lowered his voice and said, "I think I can get you an introduction. With the guy. Or the guy's guy. If that's what you'd like, of course. If you were serious before—about what you said."

I tried to act cool, cooler than I was feeling. The Percocet was helping my act. "You weren't pulling my leg? There are really people who do that? Who have a business?"

"Come on. I wouldn't joke about this."

"But it's a business?"

He lowered his voice even further. "Yes. A quiet business. Okay? Very, very hush-hush. It's not listed on NASDAQ. They don't have a Web site."

I appreciated that clarification; the web address was going to be my next question.

"I guess it would have to be a quiet business," I said. The ramifications of the enterprise were only beginning to become clear. "Sounds felonious."

"Of course it's felonious. We're talking about you hiring somebody to kill you. From a legal point of view, it's no different than hiring somebody to kill someone else. No different." He touched my good arm. "You can't tell anybody I've told you this. I'll deny it. I'm actually supposed to get permission before I . . . pass the word to a new guy."

"Tell me again, how do you know about . . . somebody like whomever you're talking about? Where did you—"

"El. Toward the end, when we learned that she was . . . terminal, an institutional liability guy I do business with in New York a sweet guy—heard about what was going on, called me and offered to put me in touch with somebody. This liability guy, both his parents have Alzheimer's. And his older sister already has early signs herself even though she's only fifty. Fifty? Can you believe it? Although he's never said, I think he's already a . . . client of these people. He's terrified of his genetic predisposition and he doesn't want to end up like the rest of his family."

Jimmy watched my face for evidence that I'd digested what he said before he added, "This is all word of mouth. Only by introduction. You have to know somebody who knows somebody to make contact with the guy. There are no business cards. No shingle, no brass plaque. No e-mail records."

"Referrals," I said, trying to find a mundane way to conceptualize what was so far from mundane.

"Yes," he said, relieved that I seemed to get it. "Only by referral. If you're interested, they'll check you out before they contact you."

"Did you . . . have you . . . ?" I asked. Despite my total lack of eloquence, he knew what I was asking.

"That's not something you're supposed to . . . talk about. You have to promise not to talk about it. Whether you decide to buy in, or not, you have to agree to keep the whole thing secret right from the start. Discretion? I'm sure you understand, right? These people can't operate with any kind of daylight." Almost in exasperation, he tagged on, "Me? I'm a single parent with young kids. My options about the future are limited. I pretty much have to catch the ball I'm thrown and run with it."

"Ah," I said, feigning that I understood what he meant

by that metaphor. But I didn't understand. Not exactly. "Jimmy, have breakfast with me tomorrow when my head's a little clearer. I'd like to hear some more about . . . the guy."

"Yeah, okay."

He took a step away. I said, "El didn't . . . ? Did she?"

"No," he said instantly. "She wouldn't have. God, El never would have." He shook his head as though he'd revisited the possibility that very instant and had reconvinced himself. "No, never."

"But you think I would?"

"If you're offended that I brought this up, please forget I said a thing, and accept my most profound apology. I heard what you were saying on that mountain. Your reaction to Antonio's . . . situation. The fall you took. You sounded sincere. I'm trying to be a friend, that's all. If I've upset you with any of this . . ."

Jimmy turned away toward the galley, and the vodka.

"Wait," I said. He stopped and faced me. I said, "It's too late for Antonio? To get an introduction?"

"With the guy?" he asked.

I nodded.

His eyes looked sad. "For Antonio, last month, or the month before, would've been better. A lot better."

NINE

Jimmy Lee and I had breakfast the next morning at Sandy's Sunshine Kitchen in Ridgway. We had stumbled out of bed without waking the others and he had driven us down the hill to town. My first act upon getting out of bed had been to grab the Percocets I'd brought home from Canada. Driving wasn't an option for me.

Ridgway, Colorado, has enough Old West charm that it has been used as the backdrop for classic Hollywood westerns. It has enough small town flavor to be a great place to live. The only people in the café at seven-oh-something that morning were Jimmy and me, some construction workers, and a table of ranchers who were taking a break from a workday that had, no doubt, started long before. A surly waitress who was usually as pleasant as the sunrise was stalking the territory behind the counter, and the typically even-tempered short-order guy at the griddle seemed to perceive every ticket she stuck on his spindle as a personal insult.

Thea had filled me in on the local gossip that the wait-ress was dating the cook's brother. Given the tension, I suspected things were in a down phase for the couple, romantically speaking.

Despite the fact that I hurt in ways and in places that were not only novel but incredibly distracting, I found myself looking at Jimmy Lee's proposal of the day before dispassionately. Before the plane landed that night I'd come to the conclusion that what Jimmy was offering for my consideration fell into the general category of risk management, and that the proposal was worthy of some deliberation.

When I was younger, and much poorer, I owned disability insurance—quite a bit of it. And when I was younger, and much poorer, I owned life insurance—a healthy chunk of it. Millions of dollars' worth at one point. My company owned an even bigger policy insuring my life. For them, I was a "key man." I remember that I liked the sound of it at the time.

Key man.

Even now that I had the personal financial resources to insulate myself and my family against the monetary consequences of serious injury, chronic illness, or death, I nevertheless took time out every few years to sit down with my posse of trust-and-estates lawyers and my financial managers to make doubly sure that the cascade of wills and trusts and tax-free or tax-deferred investment vehicles that had been set up to protect my heirs' financial solvency for the generation-skipping future were all in tip-top shape.

Responsible adults take care of unpleasant things. Ninety-eight-plus percent of my life I masqueraded as a responsible adult. The other two percent? Well, witness the Bugaboos. But I took some odd pride in the fact that I routinely jumped through almost all the distasteful hoops that were required so that I could proudly carry the membership card for the Esteemed Society of Grown-ups.

The grown-up gold standard? I was at an age where I annually allowed a relative stranger to stick a finger in my ass to palpate my prostate. Everything else I did to act grown up was measured on that simple scale.

Was whatever someone wanted to do to me worse than a prostate exam? If it wasn't, I considered it a piece of cake. If it was, I considered my cooperation serious evidence of my maturity.

A true badge of grown-up honor.

Following through on Jimmy Lee's suggestion about "the guy" he knew? Where did that stand?

It was clear that the particular brand of insurance Jimmy was suggesting that I consider was going to cost me more than a few bucks, but I had more money than I would ever need, and had already spent an inordinate amount of it with attorneys and accountants and tax planners and charitable trust advisors mapping out what was going to happen to our wealth after Thea and I died, so I knew money wasn't going to be the deciding factor.

It was also clear that further exploration of Jimmy Lee's invitation was going to cause me to think, at least momentarily, about some things—Antonio lying comatose and brain damaged was very much on my mind that morning; my brother, Connie, deteriorating in Connecticut was never far from it—that in a perfect world I'd prefer not to have to think about.

But, as I said, money wasn't an issue, and I was already thinking about Antonio and Marilyn and Connie anyway.

In the end, I decided to go forward after concluding that what Jimmy Lee was proposing wasn't any worse than a prostate exam.

Remember, I never said I was a genius.

I only said I was rich.

One of Jimmy's few flaws? He drank Coca-Cola with breakfast. Jimmy knew that it wasn't a vice that someone of his social position could get away with in polite company in many of the places that he tended to hang out, so he only risked it when he was pretty convinced he wouldn't be spotted. A weekday morning breakfast at dawn in a locals' café in Ridgway was a pretty safe bet. But Sandy's

Sunshine was no greasy spoon—think honey, not high fructose corn syrup—and his request for a dawn cola fix earned him a raised eyebrow from the waitress who was not her usual nonjudgmental self. As soon as she delivered the Coke, he poured it into a heavy ceramic coffee mug and gave the empty back to her.

To me, it looked like he'd dropped some Alka-Seltzer into a cup of Sanka.

He sipped once at his odd morning brew as though it was too hot to gulp, and said, "No one would ever know if you decided to sign up. They guarantee that. They realize that it's crucial that your family, in particular, will never know that you arranged your own death. In that sense, it's a whole lot better than suicide."

Jimmy was answering a crucial question I'd already been mulling. A deal-killing question. Could I keep Thea from ever—*ever*—knowing that I'd signed up?

"Yes, you can," Jimmy said. "That's what makes it better than suicide."

"I don't get it. What makes it better than suicide?" I asked.

He sighed. "With suicide—if you get sick, and then kill yourself—everyone, of course, knows who the victim is. Problem is that everyone also knows who the perpetrator was. People make judgments about those things. It's human nature."

Quitter. Coward, I thought. Those kinds of judgments.

Jimmy went on. "The other problem . . . is that before you know it you might be too sick, or too badly injured, to kill yourself. Like Antonio."

Yes, Antonio. "I could just buy a house someplace in Oregon," I said. "The coast is nice. Assisted suicide is legal there. Get some compassionate doc to do me in with an IV of some special good-bye cocktail."

"Sorry. Oregon's an option only if your condition is

certified terminal. Antonio, God bless him, doesn't appear to be terminal. If he lived in Eugene or Portland, he wouldn't qualify. I'm not even sure if Connie's situation would qualify if he lived in Oregon. I'd have to review the law on that. Regardless, it's a viable option only if you're willing for your family to know that you decided to check out rather than to fight. Are you willing for Thea to know that about you?"

"No." I didn't even have to think about it. Ironically, the words that jogged through my head next were *she'd kill me*. "God no."

"If El had ever found out that I was thinking of quitting early on her and the kids? I don't even want to think about it. If she were still alive . . . Even now, I bet she'd come down from heaven and . . ."

"Not to mention the message it would send to the kids," I said.

"Not to mention that," Jimmy agreed.

"So, with this guy—these guys, whatever—my demise would look . . . what, accidental?"

Jimmy said, "Exactly. They keep their end of the bargain by creating the appearance of an accidental death. The how is up to them. Your family will not suspect a thing. You won't ever know when the end is coming, or how the end is coming. They plan it. They take care of it. They promise sudden. They aim for painless."

"That's sweet."

He made an exasperated sound. I had that effect on people sometimes. "You don't have to do this," Jimmy said. "This is an all-volunteer army. Forget I brought it up. Jesus."

"Hey, I'm interested, Jimmy. It's not easy to digest all this, you know?"

"Yeah, I know. But you're not making me any happier that I clued you in."

"No one will ever know I signed up? If I do sign up. That's the deal?"

"Not unless you tell someone," he said. "Obviously they don't have any control over that part."

"You'll know, Jimmy."

"You and I will never talk about this again after today. I don't even want to know if you decide to do it. It makes me uncomfortable to talk about this."

"Insurance people always get referral fees," I joked. "You won't get a little something under the table?" I kicked him, under the table.

"That's not funny," he said. "Not about this."

"Huh," I said, lifting the Sandy's Sunshine menu with my good hand. "So what are you getting with your Coke? Eggs and fries? A banana split?"

TEN

"You're wrong," I said to Dr. Gregory. "It will make a difference what I tell you first. Maybe not to you, but to me."

My therapist said, "Okay."

I could tell he was far from convinced, but the guy apparently wasn't much of a debater. I decided to be generous, show some cards. I explained, "I don't have time for mistakes."

I said it offhandedly, like I was a busy, important guy, someone who couldn't waste time on a pedestrian faux pas. He had no way to know that the worst mistake would have been telling him too much, too soon, before I was certain I could trust him. But my nonchalance ended up sounding like arrogance and didn't exactly suck him in.

"I don't understand what that means," he said. "That you don't have time for mistakes."

"How could you understand?" I laughed a laugh that Thea affectionately called my "impish chuckle," before I added, "I mean, how could you? I know all the facts—well, I know most of them—and I don't understand what it all means. Maybe that's why I'm here."

"Maybe?"

"I have a tough decision to make. I need help, okay?"

"With?"

"You do have a certain propensity for demanding

71

clarification, don't you?" I asked, only half-joking that time.

"Therapeutically? I admit that clarity can be over-rated," he said. "But for someone like you, someone who is in some obvious physical distress"—he allowed that dust to settle for a moment before he continued—"and someone who has juggled some things to be here with me, for the time being I'm going to err on the side of caution.

"I'm also aware that you haven't quite reached a judgment about how much you're going to tell me. Or how much you're going to trust me. I think it's important to acknowledge all that."

"Well," I said, in a Jack Benny kind of way.

"Don't get me wrong; that's all fair. Your doubts about me, and about this process? Totally understandable, regardless of the other circumstances. About which, I admit ignorance."

"Thank you for that." Sarcasm seeped into my words without any conscious intent. That happened a lot with me.

Character defect. One I'll die with, I'm afraid.

"You're from out of town," he said.

Why did he say that? I wasn't quite sure, so, assuming he was fishing, I went fishing, too. "Is that a question?" I asked.

"Sure. Let's make it a question. You're from out of town?" He changed the inflection the second time he said it.

"Yes."

"Far out of town?"

"Far enough."

He tried to hide his wry smile, but failed. "You chose to come to see me rather than to see a therapist in your hometown. Why?"

"Because you're not in my hometown. The shrinks in my hometown are. By definition."

"Okay," he said. He said it in capitulation, not in agreement, certainly not to express any satisfaction at having arrived at a point of mutual understanding with me.

"It's a tautology," I said.

He digested my astonishing vocabulary for about five seconds before he said, "You're a wiseass, aren't you?"

I admit I was shocked. Not by his perspicacity—it wasn't that difficult to discern that I was a wiseass—but rather by the bluntness of his appraisal. "I beg your pardon," I said.

He added, "I bet you drive people crazy sometimes."

Coming from his mouth neither of his two assertions sounded to me like accusations, merely statements of fact. He was right with both allegations—no doubt about that—but I wasn't prepared to acknowledge that to him, yet. So I asked, "What do you mean?"

"When someone wants to slow dance with you—get a little closer, that kind of slow dance—I imagine you do with them some version of what you're doing here with me: You pull out a saber and start to fence with them instead. Your fencing is part serious, part comedy—part King Arthur and part Monty Python. Has to drive people a little crazy, especially the ones who care about you, who cherish those occasional moments close to you. Maybe even need those occasional moments close to you."

"Touché," I added, staying with the fencing analogy, and garnishing the word with my most impish grin.

"Some of the time—some of that precious time you said you don't have for mistakes—we could maybe save a bit of it by agreeing to put down the swords."

"Turns out I like to duel," I said.

"I'm sure you do. I enjoy a good joust myself. But the more immediate question is whether that is how you want to use our time together. For some self-indulgent recreation."

"My wife would be applauding you right now," I said. "People don't usually call me on my shit."

He checked his watch. "It's turning out to be expensive shit. We have half an hour left today. That's all."

"I didn't realize that this sport had a time clock." Of course I did realize that therapy was a sport ruled by a clock, but I wasn't about to put down my saber just because he'd asked me to.

He took a long, slow inhale before he responded. "Yes, psychotherapy has a time clock. Each period is forty-five minutes. What I suspect is even more germane is that sometimes the entire season is time-limited, too. But that part of the equation is totally out of my hands. Why? Because you know more about the length of the season than I do."

I felt that one. It was a clean touch. Were our sabers not tipped with rubber, it would have drawn a spot of blood.

Did he know? I wondered. I said, "I don't really. Control the length of the season, I mean."

He spent twenty seconds, maybe thirty, trying to understand what that meant. Finally, he said, "Tell me."

"Can you tell that I'm dying?" I asked.

He shook his head slowly, his eyes never leaving mine.

He hadn't known that I was dying. I was glad about that. I'm not sure why, but I was.

But he didn't say "I'm so sorry," or "That's awful." He got bonus points for not being saccharine about it. Although my motives for being in his office may not have appeared uplifting to anyone but me, I could most certainly console myself with the truth that I hadn't flown over the Continental Divide from the Western Slope only to get served a heaping dose of therapeutic pity.

After we fell into thirty seconds or so of silence, I began to think I realized what he'd known since I told him I was dying: Whatever was said next in that room was going to be of some significance, and that he'd decided that the next significant words spoken in the room should be mine.

"Well, I am dying," I said. "The engines are out, and I don't know how long this plane is going to glide."

"My impulse right now is to offer comfort, but I suspect that might be leading you in a direction you wouldn't choose to go."

"It's not that I don't have options," I said, arguing a point he hadn't made. "I can try to find updrafts and stay afloat as long as the currents will allow. I can storm the cockpit and force the damn thing into a dive. Or, I can even arrange to have somebody shoot it down."

"Your flight?"

"Yes, my flight."

He seemed surprised. "That's why you're here? The decision you have to make? Choosing exactly how to end your doomed flight?"

"That's just about it," I said.

"Just about?"

"Ah, clarification again."

"Yes, I suppose. I was thinking you may want to tell me why you are dying," he said, a slight knowing grin—but not at all an unkind one—gracing his face.

"Not really," I said, smiling right back at him, refusing to clarify everything.

Anything, really. Not yet.

He didn't respond.

I said, "Something ordinary is killing me, unless

something extraordinary kills me first. See, there are some complications."

"Why am I not surprised?" my therapist said.

I sighed. "I am a wiseass."

"Yes," he said. "You are."

ELEVEN

It turned out that New York City was the center of the Death Angel universe. That's where I had my get-acquainted meeting with Jimmy Lee's contact, his "guy." The meeting took place in the interval between my tumble in the Bugaboos and that board meeting in Santa Barbara. Late spring, early summer, 2004. My left wrist was still adorned in a cast. The rest of me had healed nicely, thank you.

Even though I'd been given a hint at what to expect that first time, the reality was disconcerting. In a quick phone call from a taciturn man two days earlier, I'd been instructed to walk slowly down the west side of Park Avenue in Midtown between 53rd and 54th over the lunch hour and to be prepared to be greeted by someone pretending to be an old friend. I should be agreeable, I was told. Jimmy must have warned somebody that I was capable of being less than agreeable.

The "old friend" who approached me on Park Avenue turned out to be a lovely, sophisticated woman a half-dozen or so years younger than me who called my name and pranced up to me on impossibly high heels. She gave me an embrace of the kind of profound exuberance that is usually reserved for airport terminals or wayward grand-children being reacquainted with bubbes and zadies.

But the woman mashed her chest into mine the way few bubbes ever do and ran her hands up and down my back and tenderly down my sides before her long fingers ended up on my cheeks. All my cheeks. First the southern cheeks, then the northern cheeks. She finally planted a not-quite chaste kiss on my lips. As she pulled away she smelled of spices and flowers and something that made me think of crisp sheets that had been dried in the sun.

I was quite aware that I had just been frisked for the second time in my life, and that I hadn't really minded it. The first time had been by a razor-burned Oklahoma state trooper on the desolate shoulder of Interstate 35 due east of Enid on a miserably hot July afternoon when I was nineteen years old. My memory's reflection was that it hadn't been anywhere nearly as enjoyable an experience as this time had been.

A black Town Car like ten thousand others in New York pulled to the curb next to us. This woman who was my newest, best, old friend opened the back door, smiled, and said, "In."

I obeyed. She followed me.

"Where are we—"

"Shhhh," she said, while she used a compact to check her lipstick and, it appeared to me, to look down the street to see if any other vehicles had pulled over to the Park Avenue curb anywhere behind us. When she was comfortable that we weren't being shadowed and that her perfectly swollen lips were perfectly edged and perfectly glossed, she scooted her perfectly shaped ass next to me on the backseat, and undid the shoulder belt that I'd reflexively fastened across my chest. In a practiced, sultry, last-call voice, she murmured, "My advice? Close your eyes and enjoy this."

If I thought that I'd been frisked on the sidewalk on Park Avenue, then what I got in the backseat of the Town

Car that was carrying us downtown was something much closer to a full-body massage. Was there a part of my anatomy that she didn't trace or palpate with her probing fingers?

Let me think.

No, there wasn't.

Not a one.

I took only part of her advice, though. I certainly did enjoy it, but I didn't close my eyes. She was much too lovely for that.

When she was done with her examination, I said, "Thank you very much. Is it my turn now?"

She laughed a laugh that not only clearly told me the answer to my question was no, but also told me that if I ever got to know her I'd probably like her a lot. The laugh told me, too, that I would never get to know her.

I don't know why, but I'd already come to the conclusion that she wasn't my Death Angel. She had a role in all this, but she wouldn't be pulling any literal triggers. Call it intuition.

Over the years I've spent a lot of time doing business in New York, and I knew the local landscape and mores pretty well, but I wasn't an honorary native by any means. Without a neighborhood map in front of me I couldn't just take a quick look outside the windows of a car speeding toward Downtown from Midtown and tell you at a quick glance whether I'd crossed a boundary line between Tribeca and SoHo, or between Chelsea and Nolita, or between the Meatpacking District and the Village. The Town Car finally pulled to a stop on a nondescript block in one of those places, though I didn't know which one. Nor, I suspected, was I supposed to know which one.

"You're here," she said, and she stepped gracefully out

of the car. I followed her out the same door, though not quite so gracefully.

Not *we're here*.

"Where is here?" I asked.

She made a disappointed face. She was playfully letting me know she had expected more from me.

"You're not joining me?" I said. "My treat. My pleasure."

She scrunched up her nose and eyes in a way that she knew was as cute as could be, took my hand, and led me into a crowded restaurant that had a sushi bar on one side. I recognized that she had succeeded in distracting me with her flirtation, which was probably her intent. Admittedly, I'd been paying more attention to the subtle curves of her butt than I had been to the identity of the place I was entering. I didn't even know what restaurant I was in.

We strolled past the front desk to a table along the wall beyond the windows. A deuce with only one empty chair. The empty chair was the one that faced away from the front door.

"Have a wonderful meal," she said, offering me one last boob-crushing embrace to remember her by. I couldn't discern any tactical advantage that she might have gained with the final hug, and I allowed myself the luxury of believing that it was, at the very least, a sincere tease on her part. Pulling back, she air-kissed me on one cheek and then the other, apparently intent on playing out her assigned ruse until the curtain dropped and the house lights came up.

To the man who had stood as we approached the table, the one who was holding a napkin in his left hand, she whispered simply, and deferentially, "Clean as a baby's conscience."

The man turned to me and said, "Please, have a seat. Thanks so much for joining me."

Before I sat, I watched my temporary consort turn at least a dozen heads—both male and female, she was that kind of gal—as she sashayed back out of the room. She'd distracted the attention of anyone who might have inadvertently noted the low-key introduction that had just occurred between my Death Angel and me.

Was this a guy who had a finger on the literal trigger? My instinct said "yes."

TWELVE

I introduced myself. He didn't. Nor did he apologize for not introducing himself.

We didn't shake hands.

"I hope you're hungry," he said pleasantly. "I find this is one of those rare places in New York that consistently live up to the hype."

I glanced down for a hint. The menu clued me in that we were at Nobu.

Cool. "I've wanted to eat here. Never got around to it."

"Yes," he said, as though he already knew that.

How would he know that?

"May I make a recommendation?" he asked. "I don't get here that often, but often enough to steer you toward a memorable meal."

"Of course." *Why not?* I closed the menu. I was thinking. *If I can't trust you with lunch, why would I put my life—or my death—in your hands?*

A waiter appeared. "We'll both have the tasting menu," my host said. He looked at me. "Any restrictions?" he asked. "Diet of any kind? Meat a problem? Shellfish?" I shook my head. He turned back to the waiter. "And please bring sparkling water, a Yebisu, and some good sake for the table. Please, you choose the sake. Room temperature, warm—whatever you think will be best. Thanks so much."

My mother would call my dining companion portly, or heavyset. My wife, Thea, might not be so genteel. On occasion I'd heard her use the word "rhino" in similar contexts, employing the word in a way that was less than flattering. When she did, she unnaturally overstressed the emphasis on the first syllable.

Her occasional lapses in decorum about people's appearances were one of Thea's few unattractive traits. In those rare moments fashion critiques rolled over her tongue like adjectives from a wine nut.

The man was about my age, give or take five years. He had a wide nose and unnaturally dark thin lips that reminded me of a matched pair of tinned anchovy filets. His hair, more blond than gray, was shaped into an old-fashioned, longish crew cut, and was thin enough that I could see a mole on his scalp an inch above his hairline. Near his right temple he had a scar that had the size and contour of a bullet hole. I assumed that it wasn't really a bullet hole—the right temple was one of those places where slugs do enough damage to bone and gray matter that the consequences tend to forever keep people from having leisurely lunches at Nobu, or from making a living as a Death Angel entrepreneur.

The overall effect of his appearance? If you saw this man on the street, you would pay him absolutely no attention.

He was just a middle-aged guy in a business suit doing business in a city chock-full of middle-aged guys in business suits.

Yebisu, it turned out, was beer. Good Japanese beer. I passed on the sake; experience told me that it rendered me sleepy during the day. My host wasn't drinking anything but Pellegrino.

"So how does this work?" I asked.

"The business?" He made a hey-who-can-complain? face. "Surprisingly, it works quite well. No complaints. Thanks for asking." He rapped on the table with the knuckles of his right hand.

"That's not what I meant."

"I know it's not what you meant." He smiled. "This is serious business we do; I was trying to lighten things up with a little humor. It's a hobby. Comedy."

Although I appreciated his attempt at levity, his humor was drier than the sake, and the truth was that, with his delivery, he was in no danger of earning a standing O at open-mic night at The Comedy Store. My experience is that if someone has to tell you he's funny, he's not.

Over the next few minutes, as we began an extended series of tiny courses of exquisitely presented Japanese food—some familiar, some almost familiar, some absolutely unfamiliar—that seemed symphonic in their careful progression and otherworldly in freshness and quality, he began to explain the nuts and bolts of the Death Angel business.

"Like any good business, we serve an unmet need," he began.

I noted the "we" and wondered what percentage of the company's employees I'd met already that day. I was assuming that it wasn't a two-person operation.

"How many times, by this stage of your life, have you learned of an unfortunate accident, or of a devastating illness that has robbed some dear soul—a friend of a friend, perhaps, or worse, a true friend, or worse yet, a loved one, someone close to your heart—of the capacity to live. When I say 'live' I'm talking 'live' with a capital *L*, of course. The ability to enjoy the bounty of the world's buffet."

He allowed the thought to settle while he sipped from his Pellegrino. I thought of Antonio.

"But say that same illness or injury has not quite robbed the person of what doctors, ethicists, and scientists currently define as life? I'm talking about the clinical definition: the proverbial beating heart, the measurable flow of sufficient electron activity in the brain."

He had stuttered, just a little, as he said "sufficient." My brother had stuttered as a child; I was sensitive to it. He sipped at his water again.

"And how many times have you heard a friend or a loved one murmur, upon hearing similar terrible news in your presence, or witnessing that same tragedy while standing by your side, 'If that ever happens to me, I hope, I pray, that I die instead.' " He watched my eyes for an extended moment before he added, "Perhaps . . . perhaps . . . you've even said words to that effect . . . yourself."

In my mind's eye I saw Antonio again—two images, vibrant at first, vegitized second—and I swallowed. There was nothing in my mouth, but I swallowed. I guessed, of course, how he knew *that*. About Antonio.

"The nature of our work, stated as simply as I can state it, is that we are in the business of answering those prayers."

Each time a server approached our table—and given the sheer number of small courses that were being delivered to us and then cleared away, the arrival of a waiter was a frequent event—my luncheon companion grew silent and made it clear that he expected me to do the same.

During the next lull in service, while I enjoyed a selection of tiny fruits that I'd never crossed paths with before in my life, he went on to explain that the structure of his business venture was akin to an insurance company that specialized in indemnifying people against an exceedingly rare, but catastrophic event. The clients of his insurance company didn't require monetary compensation if and when the rare event actually occurred—every potential client of the company had already been financially vetted and had been deemed wealthy beyond any reasonable standard. What the clients required after the catastrophe was that an action be taken.

That action?

"We like to think of it as hastening. Hastening the inevitable," he said. He was holding his chopsticks near his face in such a way that it would have been possible to convince myself he was doing an intentional impersonation of a rhino.

Had she been there, and were she reading my thoughts as she sometimes could, Thea would have kicked me below the table.

"Hastening the inevitable," I repeated, mostly because I wanted to see how the words felt in my mouth. They felt, I decided, a bit like the sliver of toro, the fatty tuna that I'd savored so slowly two or three courses before.

Rich, lush.

Just right. Almost perfect. Certainly far beyond merely palatable.

I'd be hiring someone to hasten the inevitable. And what harm, I thought, *could there be in that?*

"Yes. We set things right. We cross the uncrossed *t*. We dot the undotted *i*. Think about it. Literally, we dot the *i*. Once a client has determined that his or her health has degenerated beyond a point where, at an objective moment, that individual had already decided that he or she would choose not to continue living, and—" he paused not only for another sip of Pellegrino, but also to emphasize what would come next—"to a point where that person might reasonably be considered too impaired to make a fresh, measured, objective decision about his or her immediate future, and certainly too impaired to do anything about impacting the duration of that future, we step in."

I said, "And at that time—when you and your

colleagues 'step in'—that's when you ... hasten ... the inevitable?"

"Exactly."

"Here's the part I don't understand," I said. I made a point to use an everyday voice to try to shatter the Rod Serling echoes that seemed to have taken over our exchange. I placed my empty beer glass on the table and he immediately refilled it from the sweating bottle of Yebisu. "How, dear God, do you draw the line? How do you pretend to know your client's wishes in circumstances that are likely to be impossible to predict?"

He nodded patiently as I asked my question, like a State Farm guy waiting eagerly to get a chance to explain the difference between whole life and term to some naive newlyweds about to buy their first insurance policy. "We don't draw the line. The clients do. Positions on those parameters are totally client derived."

Positions on those parameters are totally client derived.

It had to say that someplace on the Web site, there had to be a bullet highlighting that phrase on the inside cover of the glossy brochure.

Positions on those parameters are totally client derived.

"By your own definition, the client is already too impaired to make that judgment."

"No, no, no, no," he said, his tone almost jolly. "By then, the client's decision will already have been made. Long before, at the time that the client chooses to engage our services, he or she is required to identify their wishes on what they would like us to do on a long menu of possible eventualities, not unlike the decisions responsible people make when they sign a living will. By the time the tragic time comes—the time when the client is too impaired, by either health or circumstances, to make the decision objectively—the difficult decisions have already been made. By then, no changes are possible."

That surprised me. "Why is that, exactly?"

"Should you become a client and should you become impaired—'impaired' meaning that you have unfortunately crossed the threshold you've previously identified—the contract you've entered into with us is irrevocable. Completely irrevocable. Irrevocably irrevocable. Once you have become impaired, we will consider, by contract, that you lack the capacity to change your mind."

"That is your policy?"

"No, that is our promise. We commit to our clients that the rational decision, the clearheaded decision, the forward-looking decision, the decision made with a healthy brain and a vigorous mind—unclouded by sentiment—will be the decision that guides us in implementing your wishes."

"Life is always a futures market though, isn't it?" I asked.

I could tell he wasn't sure what I'd meant. "We don't look at it that way," he said.

He never asked for a clarification, and I began leaning toward the conclusion that he was the kind of guy who would disagree with anything he didn't understand.

We ate the next small course silently before he placed his chopsticks down, dabbed his napkin on his lips, and said, "Fees."

The financial arrangements he proceeded to describe sounded odd, but then the whole damn business model was hovering somewhere north of peculiar.

Enrolling—that's what he called it—cost one million dollars. "One, six zeroes," was his precise phrasing of the amount. Next came a three-month "eligibility assessment," during which the company would do an exhaustive background check on the client to determine, among other things, the feasibility of the company being able to deliver on its ultimate commitment. If, after the background check, the client was rejected for some reason—I didn't ask for the list of reasons—$750,000 of the initial one million would be returned.

The balance was nonrefundable.

Once the client was accepted—excuse me, "enrolled"— the policy would be "quiescent" until "activated."

I asked for definitions of those final two words.

By then the next course had arrived. He placed his chopsticks down reluctantly. "Things have evolved over the years. We've discovered that during this process, loading the gun and pulling the trigger have turned out to be two very separate acts."

The metaphor had its desired effect: It reminded me that we were talking about taking lives.

Specifically, mine.

"How so?" I asked.

"When we originally conceptualized this endeavor and started providing services, we didn't employ a quiescent period, and we didn't identify a threshold event. The initial fee we charged was good for both enrollment and activation. A separate flat fee covered the costs of the eligibility assessment.

"Our clients, it turned out, especially the younger clients, the healthier ones—like yourself—occasionally needed some time to become comfortable with the idea of our service. They wanted the peace of mind that comes with having this weapon—our service—in their arsenal, but they were not quite comfortable leaving the weapon loaded and placed . . . in a complete stranger's hands. Do you understand?"

"Of course. I think I'm feeling the same way."

"Yes, that's understandable. We should have anticipated it from the beginning, but . . . Regardless, an event—usually external, something regrettable and tragic with a friend, or a loved one—would usually help these clients clearly see the peace of mind that comes with full enrollment in our program. With me?"

"Yes."

"To accommodate our clients' needs, we've adapted our service so that the contract is considered quiescent—"

"Which means revocable?"

"Inactive, actually, until the client makes the second payment. Prior to that point, the client is betting that he will not suffer an activating event."

"And an activating event is defined as . . ."

"We have a basic definition, which provides a minimum threshold for activation. The client may choose more exacting criteria, if he or she chooses."

"The basic definition includes what exactly?"

I felt as though I were pulling teeth. It was like trying to get the guy from Allstate to tell me whether I had coverage if my basement flooded after a heavy rain. *Come on, yes or no?*

The waiter approached the table. My host, who was about to answer my question, paused.

THIRTEEN

I needed a break to consider what he had said so far. Arranging my own death was a much more complicated undertaking than I had anticipated. The Yebisu had taken its inevitable toll and I excused myself at that moment to go to the bathroom. I noticed the Death Angel was watching my hands as I stood up from the table and dropped my napkin onto the chair.

When I returned a few moments later the table had been cleared. Totally cleared. Plates, chopsticks, soy, Yebisu, sake, Pellegrino. Everything except my half-filled glass of beer.

Antiseptically cleared, I thought.

"I thought we'd pass on dessert," he said. "You don't mind?"

"Not at all. I've had more than enough to eat. It was terrific."

"Tea?"

"No, thank you. You were discussing the addition of the 'quiescent' period to your company's protocol, and you were about to describe the basic criteria for an activating event."

"Yes, I was. Some clients, it turned out, fear accidents more than they fear illness. Others fear illness more than they fear accidents. The ones that have a personal experience with or a family history of debilitating illness are typically looking for a net that they can put in place when the feared diagnosis looms . . . nearer, so to speak. A man of fifty worries about heart disease more than the man of forty. Yes? You understand? Alzheimer's is typically more of a concern as we age."

"Yes."

"The addition of the quiescent option allowed everyone to have what they need. Those seeking protection against a debilitating accident could have the comfort of knowing the policy was in effect immediately after the eligibility assessment, should they choose. Those who were more concerned with the effects of serious illness could choose to extend the quiescent period until a diagnosis loomed closer."

"Gotcha," I said, as the rationale for the arcane structure became more clear. "The aforementioned second payment. An additional fee is associated with activation?"

"The initial deposit covers one decade of our services. Then we charge one million dollars for each five years of additional life expectancy, which is based on an actuarial evaluation completed at the time of the initial assessment. The total fee is paid in advance, of course. That is the second payment."

"For a young man, total premiums could approach . . . ten, six zeros," I said.

"Yes. For a very young man. Now, if our services are never required, and the client dies naturally or accidentally prior to his expected longevity, any fees unearned by us— the actuarially derived life expectancy less the actual age at the time of death—are anonymously donated to a charity identified by the client at the time the contract is entered. No moneys are ever—ever—returned to a client's estate after his or her death."

I raised my eyebrows just to see what he'd do.

"For obvious reasons," he said.

"Of course," I concurred.

"I'm sure you understand."

"I do."

"Our promise? We are prepared to act in case of an unexpected event from the moment we receive the second payment. But once the contract becomes active, the irrevocable nature of our commitment requires a nonrefundable investment on the part of the client."

Our waiter chose that moment to deliver the tab. My host took a fast glance at the total, pulled a thick clip of currency from his front trouser pocket, snapped three large bills from the wad, and left them spread on the table like a winning poker hand. He pocketed the restaurant check.

The tasting menu at Nobu was apparently pricey.

"The next step?" I asked.

"You shouldn't have any trouble getting a taxi."

More humor, I supposed.

He shrugged. It was a-guy's-gotta-try kind of shrug. I gave him points for recognizing that his humor was going over with me like a Chris Rock monologue at a Focus on the Family picnic.

"If you would like to apply for enrollment, I will provide instructions on how to make the initial deposit. At that point we will begin our evaluation. I assure you of our discretion."

"I would like to apply."

I surprised myself with the pronouncement. I hadn't been aware that I'd reached a decision.

He nodded. "Consider it done. Please open a new mobile-phone account with this carrier"—he reached into his lapel pocket and slid a small card across the table imprinted with the name of one of the national mobile-phone companies—"and give the number to no one. No one, do you understand?"

"Yes. I'm a quick study. How do I get the number to you?"

"We'll know the number within hours of activation. And we'll be in touch shortly thereafter."

"So," I said. "How many clients does your organization . . . serve?"

"I'm so sorry. I would love to be more forthcoming about details like that. Rest assured that we have sufficient resources to cover our obligations. However, we do try to be ever so discreet. For our own protection, and especially for that of our clients."

I decided to try a different tack. "You have had circumstances develop where it has become necessary for you to . . . follow through on the ultimate terms of the agreement? On . . . hastening."

He leaned forward and pursed his lips so that the unnaturally dark color momentarily disappeared. For the first time he whispered. "We call them end-of-life services." He leaned back and resumed his normal speaking voice.

"Like a hospice?"

He couldn't tell if I was joking. It was exactly what I had intended.

"Please understand our position. When you choose to enroll, we'll discuss those mechanisms, and others, in more detail, much more detail. I assure you that we do endeavor to be discreet both before and after our clients' deaths, which means we do everything possible to shield their families from the actual circumstances of the loved one's . . . end. To an outsider, either a loved one or a forensic professional, the circumstances of a client's death will never appear suspect." He smiled an undertaker's smile. "We've not yet failed to provide that shield. We don't expect to fail in the future. Is there anything else you would like to know?"

He stood to leave at that point—expecting that I would have no other questions, or at least expecting that

I would have the good sense not to ask them. I watched curiously as, holding his napkin in his right hand, he wiped the linen, seemingly absently, over the top rail of the chair.

I realized he'd just wiped away any fingerprints he might have inadvertently left behind during our meal.

The guy was dead serious about discretion.

"Please," he said, gesturing me toward the restaurant door. "I have to make a stop before I leave."

He had to pee, I guessed. He was discreet about even that.

I thanked him for the meal, and we said good-bye without shaking hands.

When I stepped outside, I walked into a day that had turned gray and was threatening the city with rain. I found myself hoping that my new, old friend was waiting for me with her chauffeured Town Car and her probing fingers.

No such luck.

I succeeded in hailing a cab right away and felt lucky to have it. I told the driver to take me out to Teterboro Airport in Jersey, where Mary would be waiting to take me home. The cabbie made a point of telling me how much the ride would cost. I was thinking about other things. I said, "Fine."

FOURTEEN

"I'd like to come back," I said to my Boulder shrink at the end of that first day's pair of sessions. "This has been fun."

"Sarcasm? Yes?" he said.

"Yes."

"Thought so," he said. "When?"

"Soon, maybe. Same arrangement. Two visits in one day. That works for me. When can you do it again?"

He picked up an old-fashioned appointment book, not a handheld computer. He spent a moment checking this and that before he said, "Thursday this week. Or Tuesday next."

"Thursday this week."

"You're feeling some urgency?" he asked.

Yeah, you could say that. "What times do you have?"

"Ten-thirty and two-fifteen."

"Can do. It's been a pleasure," I said, standing.

"If that remains the case," he said, still in his seat, "then I'm not going to be of much help to you."

"And that means . . . what?"

"My impression is that you're a guy who walks into a room and takes it over. Either by charm, or by skill, or by sheer force of will. If none of those things work, you'll do it by fiat. But you'll do it."

I didn't disagree with him. I did like to run the world,

or at least any part of it that I was currently inhabiting. I hadn't been like that my whole life—people who knew me when I was younger would've called me a free spirit—but I'd been like that since I'd decided to make some money.

But I was curious about exactly what point the psychologist was making. So I waited him out. To my surprise my wait wasn't long.

"If I permit that to happen here," he said, "I'll be conspiring with you to waste your time. And wasting your time, I'm afraid, given your circumstances and your agenda, whatever it is, would be a crime."

"How do you know so much about me?" I asked. "Or think you know so much?" He did know a lot, and then he didn't, but I wanted to see how he'd respond to being thrown a bone. I sat back down to hear his answer.

He took a quick glance at his watch deciding, I thought, whether or not he had time to answer me.

He said, "I only know what you've taught me. When you meet somebody, if you shut up and give them half a chance, in a remarkably short period of time they'll teach you almost everything you need to know about them. If it's important that you know the person, and understand him, the trick is to pay attention during the lessons and be the best student of that person you can be. That's how I know what I know about you. You are the expert on you in this room, not me. You've been teaching me things about you that you aren't even aware have been part of the lesson plan. As you teach me about you, I try to pay attention, to be the very best student I can be."

"I've told you almost nothing about me," I said. But what I was thinking was, *This guy does his work the same way I do mine. I pay attention. If there's any way at all to pull if off, I will let the guy on the other side of the table show his cards before he's ready.*

I knew my retort had been weak.

He knew that, too. He said, "Facts are crap."

FIFTEEN

I drove out to Jeffco Airport and left my new Prius in the parking lot at the FBO—Fixed Base Operator; think airplane service station, but with a clean bathroom—that had fueled the plane. Patience isn't one of my long suits, so I paid one of the line guys, a kid, twenty bucks to wrestle the car cover into place on the Toyota, a task that seemed to me like trying to force a cantaloupe into a condom.

Mary had spent the day antiquing north of Boulder and a few of her finds were strapped into seats in the back of the plane.

She came back into the cabin when I came on board, but she didn't ask what I'd been up to. She never did. Trace, the copilot, stayed up front doing preflight checks.

The flight over to Montrose was uneventful.

Little that happened those days felt uneventful, so a smooth flight over the Divide was a wonder.

Facts *are crap.*
Is that true?

SIXTEEN

I wasn't aware there was going to be an interim meeting in the enrollment process, but I was summoned back to New York three weeks to the day after I made the initial payments to Death Angel, Inc. As I had been instructed during the first call I'd received on that mobile phone I'd been told to buy, I'd dutifully sent the required funds in a shotgun pattern to multiple offshore destinations, the money going to a wide variety of charitable fronts.

My favorite was the 225K I "donated" to the ever so ironically named Youth in Asia Foundation.

It was in Singapore.

Yeah, and I was on the moon.

My assistant, LaBelle, handled the transfers for me. She handled the details and the paperwork related to everything important in my life, both business and personal. I could tell she had questions about what I was doing with all that money, even opened her mouth once to ask me about it.

I held up an open hand and said, "Don't go there, LaBelle. This one's a state secret. Okay?"

She shook her head once. That was her statement of underlying disapproval. She nodded twice. That was her assent to my caution. I knew that would be that.

LaBelle was my rock.

The "eligibility assessment" had been completely

transparent. I assumed it was ongoing, but I never noticed a thing. None of the people who typically act as the pillars that support the temples of the wealthy—my accountant, my attorney, my bankers, my financial advisors, my business partners—ever called me late at night to clue me in that someone was checking up on me or my affairs.

Jimmy Lee never pulled me aside and asked me how things were going in New York.

The Death Angels were as discreet as advertised.

The second time that my private mobile phone rang—okay, it actually vibrated—the caller was inviting me to make a return visit to New York City. The caller was a woman.

The voice sounded familiar. I asked, "With whom am I speaking?"

My question caused the woman to stumble for a split second, but not to fall. She continued to spell out the details of the "invitation." I tried small talk, and I even made an allusion to the Town Car heading downtown on Park Avenue. My flirtations were rebuffed, or more correctly, ignored. The call was all business.

Of course I wondered whether I'd been speaking with the woman with the traveling fingers, the one from the backseat of the Town Car.

Mary flew me to New York the night before the meeting. The copilot that day was a temp named Andre who'd flown with us before, but wasn't interested in our gig on a permanent basis. It was too bad; we both liked him. I asked Mary to do a couple of things for me in the city the next day. She asked if I minded if she visited her cousin in Brooklyn when she was done. I assured her I didn't.

I checked into a park-view room at the Four Seasons on 57th Street. I could have afforded an immense suite with a view of the park—hell, if I liquidated some things I could have made a respectable offer to buy the whole damn hotel—but I chose a standard room with a view of the park. I like luxurious hotel rooms but I don't like big hotel rooms. They don't feel right to me. I've never liked huge bathtubs either.

Don't know what that's all about.

If I ever got around to having the luxury of confronting my secondary demons, it's something I'd consider working out with a shrink.

A bowl of fruit, a bottle of Badoit, and an ice bucket with a tall bottle of Yebisu—nice touch, I admit—awaited me when I walked into the hotel room. I hadn't told anyone but LaBelle and Thea where I was staying in New York, so the fact that the Death Angel had tracked me to the Four Seasons was the real message. It wasn't super-spy stuff, but it was a message nonetheless.

The presence of the Badoit was the exclamation point, however. Badoit is mineral water from France—think Pellegrino, but France, not Italy.

Maybe five or six people in the world knew that Badoit was my preferred sparkling water; to my knowledge I'd never made a big deal of that predilection with anyone. If you hadn't had dinner with me in Paris or Nice, you wouldn't know I had a thing for Badoit.

But the Death Angel knew.

The note on the silver tray with the fruit and water wasn't signed. The neat, androgynous script welcomed me to New York and suggested—ha!—an eleven A.M. rendezvous in the main lobby at MOMA, the Museum of Modern Art. I hadn't been back to MOMA since Taniguchi's overhaul had begun, so I planned to walk over early and check out the progress that had been made to the building before I made my way back to the street-level lobby.

*

They're too infrequent, but New York City sometimes has days that are as crystalline as anything I get to experience four days out of five in Ridgway. What's different in the city is that the inhabitants recognize how special those days are and they all come out to celebrate. On glorious days in Manhattan the sidewalks come alive, the plazas and parks fill with people, and cafés and restaurants push tables out into the sunshine. On those days a descent into the dreary subway feels like torture, and for a few fleeting hours visitors and tourists have no trouble believing that there really are so many people squeezed onto that little island.

I woke to one of those days in Manhattan, and—like a few hundred thousand other people who decided to skip school, or work, or whatever to enjoy the weather—I gave up on my plan to spend the morning inside the usually irresistible galleries of MOMA.

She caught me on the sidewalk just outside the entrance to the museum on 53rd Street. I wondered if I was under surveillance.

Did it matter?

Nah.

She wasn't the elegant and sophisticated Park Avenue lady this time; she wore denim jeans that celebrated her ass and a supple leather jacket that was layered over a thin sweater that scooped down to reveal the swell at the top of her breasts. This was the costume of an Upper West Side wife heading out for lunch and some minor-league shopping with her girlfriends. Not Bergdorf shopping, or Henri Bendel shopping, or Jimmy Choo shopping. Not even Madison Avenue boutique shopping. Something slightly downscale and funky.

I wasn't surprised by the exuberance of her greeting this time around; I was actually looking forward to it. I'd already removed my jacket to make the initial body search easier for her, and more fun for me.

"Hi," I said into her ear as she pressed herself against me and her hands rubbed up and down my back. "If we're going to pretend to be so closely acquainted, I should probably know what to call you."

"Call me Lizzie," she whispered back. "Nobody else does. It can be our special thing."

She pulled away from me and took my jacket from my hands. For the next few moments, as she absently palpated its seams and folds without appearing to be doing anything at all, I felt an incongruous pang of envy for my sport coat.

"I was just heading inside," I said, pointing toward the museum, playing along. "Are you free to join me?"

"I wish I could, oh I do, but I don't have time. Maybe I could squeeze in a minute for coffee, though. How does that sound? Come on, let's," she said, knowing I would. Knowing almost any male would, not to mention a healthy percentage of females. She grabbed my hand and tugged me toward the distant corner. As soon as we'd started hustling to the end of the block, I recognized two important things: one, that she was walking me against traffic, and two, that she was leading me toward the familiar waiting Town Car.

"Here we are," she said. "You remember the tune?"

"I think I could hum a few bars."

In perfect pitch, she sang the first few lines of "Ob-La-Di, Ob-La-Da."

Yes, the old Beatles classic that was the ring tone on my cell phone.

I slid into the car and she followed me inside.

How did she know that?

We headed uptown this time in the direction of Central Park, which meant that there was to be no return visit to

Nobu in my immediate future. Routine midmorning congestion impeded our progress until the driver steered the car past The Plaza onto one of the roadways that weave through the park. I've never known the names of the streets in Central Park. But that was the point in the journey where Lizzie began to frisk me more thoroughly.

"What exactly are you looking for?" I asked, trying to flirt. "Can I be of some help? I know where everything is. Especially the good parts." She was busy on my left leg, tracing my Achilles tendon, squeezing a little too forcefully at the hard muscle in my calf, and using her fingernails provocatively as she skated up the vulnerable spot behind my knee. "Weapons, wires? What?"

"I'm not looking for anything," she teased. "This isn't part of my job description. I do this only because it's fun. For some reason I don't understand, people don't seem to mind."

I laughed and lifted my arms. She shifted on the seat so that her knees and my thighs were in firm contact, and began to do her thing on my upper body. She said, "I'll finish what I was doing down there later."

I relaxed and let myself appreciate her doing her thing on my upper body for the next half minute or so. True to her word, she then did indeed finish what she had started doing down there.

I was definitely one of those people who didn't seem to mind.

The driver exited the park on the Upper East Side just before we reached the reservoir. I reminded myself to pay attention to where we were. In a couple of minutes he pulled over to the curb at a bus stop just beyond the corner of 86th and Third.

I smiled as I looked outside at the storefront.

She said, "We're here."

I was still smiling. "At least I know where 'here' is this time."

"Well, it is kind of hard to miss," she admitted, glancing up at the brilliant yellow-and-tropical-fruit–colored sign.

She crossed over me on the seat, her face so close to mine that I could make a snap appraisal about the quality of her skin—a persnickety dermatologist would rate her complexion almost flawless—and stepped out of the car first. I followed her onto the sidewalk in front of Papaya King. On the way into the dog palace she stole a peek down Third checking, I assumed, for tails. I let my eyes follow hers down the block to see if I could spot any evidence we'd been followed.

I couldn't.

Cool.

Like Nobu, Papaya King is one of those restaurants in New York City that live up to their hype. At Papaya King, the hype is about hot dogs.

We joined the queue that snaked to the counter. With the weather as good as it was, the prospect of a quality al fresco lunch had apparently tempted much of the population of the Upper East Side, and it appeared that many of them were lined up in front of us waiting to eat at the legendary frankfurter emporium. With the weather as good as it was, though, nobody seemed to care about the length of the line. They get little credit for it, but in normal circumstances New Yorkers do lines well. In glorious weather, New Yorkers do lines marvelously.

"Is it just you and me today?" I asked Lizzie.

"And a pretty healthy chunk of Manhattan. Would that disappoint you? If it were just you and me."

"Hardly. So is it?"

She eyed me. She didn't just look at me; she eyed me. But she didn't answer me, exactly. "You're married," she said, at once reading my mind and mockingly dismissing me.

I decided to continue to play along. Why? I flirt for two reasons. I flirt for amusement. And I flirt for advantage. In my youth, the advantage I sought was almost always sexual. The older I get, the more complicated the advantage I'm seeking has become. The reality is that I prefer advantage. What bravado and bluster accomplished for me in repartee with men, flirting accomplished for me with women.

The amusement factor? That was more of a constant. Flirting with Lizzie was fun.

I said, "Are we discussing breaking my vows, Lizzie? What an interesting progression. I thought we were discussing lunch at one of Manhattan's fine dining establishments."

She squeezed my hand and looked away from me, up toward the big menu board. "I like you," she said. "I'm sorry about the circumstances of our meeting. I am. But . . . you know—"

I finished her thought for her. "Business is business. Don't be sorry."

She squeezed my hand again.

"I like you, too," I said.

"So what are you getting?" she asked.

Aroused? I thought, but quickly realized that her question had an alternative, more likely, connotation.

I didn't have to look up at the menu board: I knew my Papaya King preferences by heart. I said, "An Original Special with a Tropical Breeze. Or—if I feel especially adventurous when we finally get up to the counter—I may just go for a couple of Slaw Dogs and a Tropical Breeze. What about you?"

"You don't get curly fries? I love their curly fries."

"I'll steal some of yours."

"Try, and you'll leave the city without one or two of your favorite fingers."

I laughed. "You get the King Combo, then?"

"I do."

"Kraut?"

She raised then lowered her eyebrows in one quick, provocative move. "I'll do kraut if you'll do kraut," she said. We both recognized that we'd become engaged in the sort of bartering that new lovers do about garlic as they sit down at a red-sauce trattoria on a night when they know that whatever they eat is going to end up being only an appetizer.

I said, "Tell you what—I'll do one Slaw Dog and one Original with onions if you'll do kraut."

We shook on it.

Want to know what I was thinking?

I was thinking that Thea would never have kidnapped me for lunch and whisked me uptown through Central Park to the original Papaya King. She wouldn't have ordered the King Combo—no way—and she would never, ever have thought about getting kraut or onions in polite company unless she had a fresh tin of Altoids in her perfect little Kate Spade shoulder bag.

No, if I'd been with Thea instead of with Lizzie, my wife would have been leading me up Madison Avenue from the hotel on 57th, skipping from precious boutique to precious boutique like a flat stone finding its way across a still pond, telling me the whole time all the good things she'd heard about the little restaurant that just happens to be inside Barneys.

Nor was I thinking at all that Lizzie might someday be the person who would plan my death.

Funny thing.

At the time, in the simple territory of my mind, I was just out on an errand buying some insurance, having a midday meal with my new insurance agent.

I was being a grown-up.

And, sure, I was flirting with a pretty girl on a lovely day in Manhattan.

What on earth was wrong with that?

SEVENTEEN

Waiting on line at a Mickey D's drive-thru has never managed to make me hungry. I don't salivate driving past a Taco Bell. But waiting my turn at Papaya King, watching those dogs nestle together and curl and crisp on that grill, and listening to them sizzle and spit, made me ravenous. Lizzie somehow snagged us a pair of stools at the narrow counter while I waited impatiently for our food to arrive.

I was still expecting my comedically contrived host from Nobu either to join us or to replace Lizzie as my dining companion, so I was surprised, and pleased, that when I tracked her down with our food she hadn't pulled over a third stool. She saw something else in my eyes—something besides my surprise, something that I was quite aware I was feeling, but that I hadn't been intending to communicate to her, either directly or indirectly.

"You're married," she admonished me, with a superfluous "*tsk*." "Do I have to say everything twice?"

"Yeah, yeah," I replied, sitting down across from her. "This is lunch. Lunch. Married men eat, you know."

She covered an involuntary laugh with a quick exhale and a murmured, "Not all of them," but otherwise let my comment float by. She said, "Anyway, I know things about you that your wife doesn't know."

I thought about that claim for a moment, and I wondered what it was she knew and whether it attracted or repelled her. Roll of the dice. I said, "You probably know things about me that I don't know."

"That's probably true, too."

With a jab as quick as the flit of an iguana's tongue, I grabbed one of her curly fries. She gave me a look that only hinted at what I'd get if I tried to steal, say, a kiss, instead of a fry.

The look, I admit, made me tempted to try.

We sat in silence for a while. I ate slowly, savoring my food, but also savoring the opportunity to watch her eat. Why?

Figure it out.

One and a half dogs down, she dipped a final Cajun curly fry in ketchup, nibbled it slowly, and then dabbed a Papaya King napkin at a few different locations on her lovely lips. "You're not sure about us," she said. She paused just long enough at that point that I considered the possibility that the "us" was she and I. When she continued, however, and added, "About what we do," I knew that the "us" she was talking about was she and her Death Angel compatriots.

"So it's time for business," I said, stating the obvious. The clamor and bustle and informality all around us made Papaya King an almost perfect location for a confidential business meeting about insuring one's timely death. "But I have this small problem. I'm congenitally suspicious of doing business in situations where the other party knows more about me than I know about them."

"Ah," she said.

"It's a philosophy that has served me well over the years. Old dogs, new tricks, you know?"

"I'm sure it has served you well. See if this helps you with your dilemma: This business—what we do—is all about asking people like you to yield some control now, so that you can be certain to have control later."

111

"Later? When?"

"When your force of will, and your ability to move mountains, may be a little bit more compromised than you've grown accustomed to. As a general rule, we tend to serve only clients who share your control issues. Those who are indifferent about control don't gravitate our way. Think about it."

She threw her napkin on top of her remaining food, as though she needed to put a physical barrier between herself and her desire for more ... something. I made a mental note of her need for an artificial wall. This wasn't a woman to whom self-control of appetites came naturally.

I admit that I like that in a woman.

"There's something else you should know about me: I'm more of a control freak than most wealthy men," I said.

"You think so?" she teased.

"I do."

"I wasn't being completely honest with you a moment ago," she said, avoiding my eyes. "We're actually here today so that I can invite you—no, encourage you—to request a refund of your enrollment deposit."

" 'We're' here today? Who's 'we'?" I looked around. "Is that other guy here someplace? From Nobu? Or is he off practicing his set for the next open-mic night at Carolines?"

"You and me," she said. "Just you and me." She was looking at me, and she reached over and once again rested her palm on my cheek, insisting my attention be on nothing but her.

"So it's you?" I leaned closer to her. "You would like me to back out and request a refund?"

"Yes. I think that would be best."

"Are you speaking personally or for your ... company?"

"Both. I think you should withdraw. My associates agree. Your deposit will be returned."

"Less the 'eligibility assessment' fees, of course," I added, playfully. Or sarcastically.

"Of course," she concurred, much less playfully and totally without sarcasm. "Like any concern, we have bills to pay."

"Overhead."

"Overhead, exactly. Keeping our sources of information open . . . is not inexpensive. Hiring the best people isn't cheap. Anyone with your business experience knows that."

Lizzie's eyes were a deep, careless Scottish plaid, mostly dark, with streaks of kelly green and flecks of golden heather. When she lowered her voice, as she had just done, it was as husky and elusive as the wind through a thicket.

Insight moment: When a woman causes me to wax poetic, even in the silence of my thoughts, I'm in serious deep water. The nearest shore? Not even in sight.

"So what's the problem?" I asked. "With me? What did you learn during your investigation that has given you such pause? Why are you suddenly so eager to dump me?"

She was ready with an answer. "You can't cancel us, like life insurance. After the second payment is made, you're in, Once you're in, you're in. There's no backing out. No second thoughts."

"I admit I don't totally get that part of the deal. It troubles me. Life is unpredictable. One always has to adapt."

"Our experience is that clients with doubts tend to be less satisfied. And more troublesome."

"That's so subjective. And I thought this was all about the money."

"I can assure you that it's not," Lizzie said.

"That's easy to say."

She said, "Something we don't advertise: We do a healthy proportion of our work pro bono. To allow people who can't afford our fees to participate in our services, we serve ten percent of our clients for free. The thing is, they can't cancel their contracts, either. If we were in it only for the money, we'd let the pro bono clients cancel anytime, right?"

"That's something to consider," I said. "It's a compelling argument, I have to admit."

"Thank you. Thank you." She performed a cute, little, seated curtsy before she lifted the corner of the napkin with her fingertip, still, I thought, struggling with those impulses of hers. One more fry? Another bite of that dog? I couldn't be certain what the temptation was, but I liked that it wasn't easy for her.

"But then again, you could be lying about the pro bono," I said. "Marketing is marketing."

She acted offended. "Have I lied to you?"

"Your name is not Lizzie."

Her expression grew bittersweet—the face of a mother about to reluctantly admit to her child that there is no Santa Claus. "I do like you," she said, punctuating the admission with a small sigh that I couldn't interpret. "I do. Hypothetically," she continued, "let's say we allowed clients to terminate their agreements. Just walk away, whenever they wanted."

"Okay, let's say that."

"Think it through. We'd be of no help to our clients. Our services would be meaningless."

"I don't get it. Why?"

"Human nature. When the moment comes—when some doctor who knows your prostate or your colon better than he knows you, says you have six months to live, or a year—everybody will have second thoughts about living and dying. Everybody imagines an end that is

114

much worse than what will probably really happen, or much less horrific than reality will allow. Everybody, at least for that moment, forgets why they hired us, and what we promised to protect them from.

"If we allowed cancellations, we would be allowing someone facing death nose-to-nose to decide how they want to die."

"What's so wrong with that?"

"Nothing. People do it every day. Every hour of every day. But we exist to serve a more discriminating client. We're not in the business of encouraging people who are in the tumult of serious illness or horrific trauma or prospective death to delude themselves into prolonging their suffering; we're in the business of helping people who are living well decide exactly—exactly—under what difficult conditions they wish to continue to live before they are facing a life that is ending."

"Oh, yes. The capital L, that kind of living? I remember that from the seminar at Nobu."

"Yes, the capital L kind of living. Don't patronize the notion. It's . . . a special thing."

"Huh," I said, recognizing her passion about the topic, and recognizing that I was losing the debate.

"So how's Antonio?" Lizzie asked, also recognizing I was losing the debate, and eager to land a final blow.

Her casual question felt like a slap. "Don't," I said. I was confident that she knew how Antonio was: Antonio was an extension of a hospital bed, a destination for a feeding tube, source material for his waste drain. I had no doubt that she knew that the barely squiggly lines on the EEG said that Antonio had just enough brain function that debate-prone medical ethicists could argue endlessly about whether or not his current state qualified as "living."

No capital L.

And no living will.

Antonio, how could you fail to sign a living will?

She leaned toward me and took one of my hands in both of hers. "It's important work. What we do. I believe in it with all my heart." She squeezed my hand. "I'm not in this for the money. I made good money in my previous job."

I saw them lining up in front of me, so I tried to connect the dots. "I can tell that you do believe. At this moment, I no longer question that. But tell me, are you suggesting to me that Antonio canceled his contract?"

"Discretion, remember? We don't kiss and tell."

I suspected that she would reveal more if I waited. So I waited. If I hadn't been determined to wait her out, I would have said something stupid, like "I'm still waiting for the kiss."

She said, "All I can really tell you—and I shouldn't even say this—is that your friend had been made aware of the availability of our services, but at the time of his accident he was not an active client of the firm. Therefore he is . . . not a client of the firm."

Jimmy told Antonio about the Death Angels before he told me, I thought. *Huh. Why would Jimmy tell Antonio first?*

I held up my arm and pointed at my cast. "You know about the Bugaboos, don't you?" I asked, changing the subject, but not really changing the subject.

She nodded. "You make that fall ten times, you end up hitting one of those two trees at the bottom nine times out of ten."

She knew a lot about the Bugaboos. Had she talked to Jimmy? Is that how all this worked?

"Maybe. I like to think if I make that fall ten times, I get an edge down and ski to a stop eight times out of ten. One time, maybe, I graze one of those two trees. The tenth time I get lucky and thread the needle. I come up laughing."

"In your fantasies you never hit the trees? Not head-on?"

"Never."

"I'm dining with an optimist."

"Or a fool," I admitted.

"Well, there is that. But in my experience with men the two aren't mutually exclusive." She sucked hard at her straw to get at the dregs of whatever tropical concoction she'd ordered. The slurping sound definitely got my attention.

"I actually grazed one of those trees on my way down. That's how I broke my wrist."

"Yes, we know. A few more feet to the left, and . . ."

She let the thought linger like an aroma, good or bad, that hangs around a kitchen. In this case, a sour aroma. Too much vinegar for my taste.

"I'm a lucky guy, I guess."

"I guess," she said.

"Well, Lizzie, despite your best efforts, you're giving me plenty of reasons to enlist your services. Yet you want me to withdraw my application? Why?"

Her eyes grew rueful.

"Because of Adam," she said.

Dear Jesus.

Suddenly, I couldn't breathe.

EIGHTEEN

I'd flown back over the Divide for the second day's worth of therapy sessions, unwrapped my Prius at the airport, and driven northwest down the turnpike to Dr. Alan Gregory's Walnut Street office in Boulder.

He didn't know my real name, or anything about the plane or the airport, or that I'd bought a Prius so that I could drive anonymously to and from his office, or about the friend's flat I was borrowing so I wouldn't have to register at a hotel but could still get some rest between our two sessions. He didn't know much.

But I'd already decided that I was going to talk with him about Adam.

"There're probably a million things I should tell you before I tell you about Adam, but . . . there really isn't time for me to warm up to it."

"Then tell me about Adam," my therapist said.

The moment he said it—*Then tell me about Adam*—I had to swallow some fury at him. What could he know about Adam, about the feelings that go along with that word for me?

"And the rest?" I said, trying not to spit the words at him.

"What 'rest'? The million things?"

Was he taunting me? Was that possible?

"Yeah, the rest. The million things. I should just forget about all of it? Facts are crap?" I said, letting my annoyance out of its cage, and throwing his mantra from my last visit back into his face.

Why was I so snippy?

Adam did that to me.

Not Adam, exactly. Adam made me smile. What was happening with Adam. That's what did it to me.

"Tell me about Adam," Dr. Gregory said again.

What the hell else was he going to say?

"Shit," I said in protest. "Don't minimize this. How difficult this is. Don't misunderstand this."

"I'll try not to," he said, cushioning his voice with something gentle, some offhand kind of touch.

I was grateful that he didn't bite back at me, didn't reply to my annoyance in kind. I told myself to cool it. He'd replied to me warmly, as an invitation, encouraging me to set aside my reservations, my excuses, my rationalizations.

He had no way to know that I'd never been able to just talk about Adam with anyone but Thea. Some of my friends knew that Adam was out there. But I picked people to tell who I knew wouldn't ask me how I felt about it all. I'm a coward about some things.

But this guy across from me was going to ask. I could bank on it.

I helped create Adam when I was twenty-three years old, though I didn't meet him until I was thirty-eight.

In the intervening decade and a half, I had no idea that I had a son. I wasn't the kind of guy who stayed up late wondering about the ultimate destination of the billions of sperm I'd launched since the fateful day I'd enthusiastically volunteered to slaughter my virginity with a willing young saintess on the altar of adolescent hyper-arousal. I hadn't given a moment's consideration to the possibility that one of my energetic little swimmers might actually have met a wandering egg and found a warm uterine wall in which to nestle.

Does that kind of guy exist? The kind who stayed up nights wondering about those things?

I've never met him.

Never saw him in a mirror, that's for sure.

The story of actually meeting Adam sounds trite whenever I rehearse its telling in my head. Beyond trite even, all the way to clichéd. It was 2002. The strange kid on my doorstep. His own plaintive version of "I'm here to see my dad."

I could go off on an unkind riff about Adam's mother—I admit I'm still tempted; God, I hate that about me—or I could come up with a cavalcade of excuses about the muggy autumn night that Adam was conceived. Back in, I think, 1987 his mother and I met at a pre-Halloween party in an ostentatious faux manor house in Buckhead, outside Atlanta, but there is little point in either gilding those memories in shit, or in tarnishing Adam's mother's motives or character.

She wasn't a remarkable girl, and truth be told, it wasn't a remarkable night. It was at a time when AIDS was still a disease other people got, and when people like me believed that recreational sex could do nothing worse than make you the kind of sick that a vial of penicillin could cure. A carefree time. Adam's mother and I had a connection that lasted just a few short minutes longer than it took for her to raise her skirt to her waist and for me to drop my pants to my knees in a laundry room off a butler's pantry half a dozen steps from the crowded kitchen. Our coupling was illicit and it was exciting more because of its illicitness than because of any particular eroticism, and it was quick.

Satisfying?

I was twenty-three; I was never satisfied.

Same was pretty much true for me at fifteen and at thirty-three, I'm sorry to say, though by the time I was approaching my fourth decade the emblem on the scoreboard was as likely to be a dollar sign as a flashing neon profile of a shapely babe.

Adam's mother was one of two that month. Or five. Or more. Some months were better than others. Scoreboard or no scoreboard, I didn't keep score, but I kept score, if you know what I mean.

When I think of that night now, something, some memory residue, suggests that she wanted to kiss me when we were done screwing. Not during. After. I doubt if I let her. That wouldn't have been me.

By the time she wanted to kiss me I would have been done with her.

Believe me when I say that every last one of those sorry facts about my few minutes with Adam's mother say a whole lot more about who I was back then than they do about who she was back then.

I was twenty-three years old in all the wrong ways. I was twenty-three years old in none of the right ways.

Adam's mother may have been a wonderful young woman who got lost in a transient moment of hope and something that she had convinced herself resembled romance or, at least, passion. I didn't hang around long enough to give her a chance to teach me a single thing about herself, or her dreams, or the bumps and bruises she'd endured that had warped her judgment about love and life until it was so screwed up that she picked the likes of me out of that crowded room of badly costumed, drunken boys. No, I learned none of those things because I was red-eyed on the red-eye out of Hartsfield before she'd even begged a ride home from the party that night, maybe even before she'd had the first of a half-of-a-life-time of second thoughts about the charming, horny guy with the magnetic smile in the laundry room in the damn mini-mansion in Buckhead.

A promise: I wasn't a wonderful young man who got lost in a transient moment of hope or romance or passion. I was a selfish, callous kid looking to get laid before I got out of Dodge. And that night I got what I wanted.

I also got Adam.

Life plays its tricks.

"You have a son," my therapist said at that point, interrupting my story. He said it without surprise, and with some tenderness that I could appreciate deep in my gut. Maybe he had a son of his own.

I could find that out. Wouldn't be difficult. Finding things out has always been one of my specialties. One of my business mantras was "Always negotiate from a position of power."

"I have a son," I said to Gregory, without much more contemplation. "But it's not that . . . simple."

He processed my response for a moment, or two. "Perhaps I should get out of the way," he said. "You were doing fine without my help."

He was right. I was. For me, about Adam, I'd been doing remarkably well on my own.

He stayed silent; he stopped working with his strong hand and touched me with his offhand in a way that let me know he was there.

I married Thea late, in my mid-thirties. I was a mover by then, on the verge of selling the medical tech brainstorm that would turn me into a certified shaker. Thea was almost five years younger than I and I'd had to invest an inordinate amount of energy into convincing her of the sincerity of my affection. Her skepticism was a good thing for both of us. Our eventual marriage felt like a wondrous change in the direction of my life. Within a couple of years my financial ship came in, and we traded our first house, a cute but battered bungalow in Denver's Congress Park, for a big quasi-colonial thing on an expansive piece of land in the distant southern suburbs.

I liked to think that more had changed during that period than my marital status and my net worth. I liked to think that I had changed, too, and wanted to believe that I could quote evidence to support the contention that I was much less of a jerk at thirty-five than I had been at twenty-three. Still, I admit that there were days when I wondered what kind of a recommendation that was for becoming a husband.

My evidence that I had changed? I was more content. And I gave myself credit for being more mature. How was I sure of the last one? The "more mature" part? It was simple: I didn't think that my contentedness had anything to do with my wealth.

If that wasn't a sign of my maturity, I didn't know what would be.

But had I been ready for a wife when Thea and I said "I do"?

In retrospect, allowing for that generous assessment of my maturational progress, I could argue that I had been getting close to that line in the sand that was marked "ready." I could also argue that Thea had done me a great favor by making me wait before she'd made her leap of faith.

What about a family? Was I ready for one of those back then?

Again, I was getting close. Career or not, money or not, I'd done some growing up.

Dogs? Certainly, I could handle dogs.

Children? Almost. Maybe.

Problem was, unknown to me, by then my son Adam was already twelve years old.

Thea had delivered us a daughter, Berkeley, eighteen months into our marriage.

By the day that Adam showed up at the front door of our new house about a hundred-meter dash from the High Line Canal, Berkeley had developed into a high-spirited, high-speed toddler. She had Thea's eyes, Thea's long fingers, and Thea's full lower lip.

The idea for our daughter's name, too, had been my wife's. She maintained that the inspiration had been George Berkeley, the eighteenth-century British empiricist, but I had suspected all along that the true inspiration had been Thea's undying affection for her undergraduate alma mater across the bay from San Francisco in northern California.

She'd denied it, clinging tenaciously to the notion that our daughter's nominal heritage was philosophical in origin and had nothing to do with her mother's inexplicably persistent ardor for the Golden Bears. I, of course, nicknamed our daughter "Cal" and Thea pretended that it drove her crazy.

It didn't.

But Cal—we also called her "Berk"—had my speed. Thea called it my "recklessness" and seemed to rue the presence of the trait in her firstborn. But I took comfort in it, knowing that in a few years Berkeley would be the kid who'd strap on a board, or two, depending on the fashion of the day and whether she embraced that fashion or rejected it, and who'd follow her father into the almost imperceptible gaps between the trees in the hills in the dead of winter. After a couple of more decades she'd be the one who'd gladly inherit my old 911 when I could no longer find the strength to depress the German girl's heavy clutch.

I openly treasured Berkeley's natural velocity.

When the doorbell sounded late that afternoon, I had to race to beat my toddler daughter to the door.

The kid standing on the front porch had none of my speed. He was a gangly and unbalanced boy, taller and thinner than me, who moved with the unvarnished verve of a sloth.

I thought he was there to sell me something I didn't want to buy, or to try to talk me into giving money to some group I'd never heard of. I also thought that before he got to the end of the block, if he had any sense at all, he would have rightly convinced himself that he had no business being a solicitor or salesman, let alone the door-to-door variety, for anything. Ever.

As I conjured up an imaginative way to send him away from my stoop, the boy stared me up and down as though he were trying to decide whether the clothes I was wearing might fit him okay. But he didn't speak, not at first.

My impatience got the better of me before my imagination kicked in. That particular cognitive progression—impatience before imagination—was not an uncommon affliction for me.

As a general rule, I tried to keep an eye on it. History said that I did my best work when I succeeded.

I said, "Yeah, can I help you?" To be honest, relatively little of my attention was focused on the adolescent standing at the door with his hands stuffed in his pockets; most of my attention was being used to try to keep my little girl from escaping the jail bars I was forming with my legs.

The boy's first words to me?

"Is that my sister?"

Whoa.

What was my reaction to that intro?

I made the mitotic association immediately—the most important connection being the general idea that the kid at the door was implying some biological relativity between us—but not too surprisingly, I didn't make the correct mitotic association. I'm not proud of it, but my initial suspicion was something along the lines that Thea must have gotten pregnant when she was younger—much younger—and had given a kid up for adoption and that she'd never told me about it. I actually felt some pride at how nonjudgmental I was feeling about it all.

It was such an Oprah moment.

My pride changed to mild shock and embarrassing comfort with the quick conclusion I reached next: *Better Thea than me.*

But even the comfort evaporated after only a few seconds as the mirage that was providing me the transient oasis from personal responsibility vanished like vapor, as mirages tend to. Those few seconds were all it took for me to spot the color of the kid's eyes—"halogen blue," Thea called it—and the distinctive way his nostrils dilated with each breath he took.

I saw those same iridescent blue irises and that identical nasal flare every morning in the mirror.

"Go find your mom, babe," I said gently to Berkeley. "I think she's in the kitchen."

I knew she was in the kitchen, her soft feet clad in the Angelo Luzio pointes that she wore year-round to pad around the house.

I liked to think my wife went through life as though it were a pas de deux. She was, in all good ways, light on her feet.

I was her klutzy partner.

"Who is it?" Thea called from the back of the house. "Dinner will be on in a minute."

"I've got it. Take Berk, okay? I think I'm going to be a few minutes. Go ahead and start without me," I yelled back toward Thea before I stepped outside and closed the door behind me.

I was blinking at the boy, my mouth open in a pretty good approximation of a befuddled stupor. I realized that I'd stuffed my hands into my pockets and was mirroring his adolescent posture to a T. Finally, I managed to state the obvious: "You know a lot more about what's happening right this minute than I do, don't you?"

"Probably," he said. He bit his lower lip before he added, "I know who my mother is, for instance. You probably don't know that, do you?"

The words hit me like a punch in the gut. I fought an urge to double over, I exhaled once, and then I exhaled again.

This kid had some fight in him.

Paternal pride?

"Can we go for a walk?" I asked.

"Why not?" he said. "Why not?"

NINETEEN

Papaya King had grown even more crowded while we were eating. The queue snaked out of sight out onto the sidewalk. Cool as a tropical breeze, I asked Lizzie, "What does Adam have to do with any of this?"

Her warm hands were once again wrapped around one of mine—the uncasted one—on top of the grimy counter. Lost in my Adam reverie, I hadn't even been aware she was still holding on to me.

I thought, *She has two off hands*. And I wondered if maybe that was one too many.

She said, "I tend to use the word 'objective' a lot. Maybe too much. But decisions like the one a man, or a woman, needs to make to enlist our professional services require an objective appraisal about living and, more to the point, about dying. About the value one assigns to life and to death. After our evaluation of your circumstances—all your circumstances—we're no longer convinced that you are in a position to be objective about those things."

"Wow," I said. "That's a mouthful."

"We have to evaluate the appropriateness of the fit. We consider it our responsibility."

"And you have doubts because of something to do with Adam?"

"Yes, because of what's happened, what's happening, with Adam. And you."

"And you think you know those things about me and my son?" I asked. But I was thinking, *How could they? How could they know? Whom would they have asked? Thea? Never.*

Bella? Maybe. Maybe Bella. Damn.

But so what? Thea doesn't know. Bella doesn't know. Not really.

For the first time, I allowed myself to ask what should have been an obvious question, an earlier question: *Who the hell are these people? The Death Angels. Who are they?*

Lizzie squeezed my hand and nodded her reply to the question I had actually asked aloud.

I said, "Have you considered the possibility that what's going on with him . . . with him and me, that it makes me all the more objective? About life. Maybe about death. Certainly my death."

"Convince me," she said.

She sounded like a referee daring a basketball player to argue a foul. I didn't believe she wanted to be convinced; I believed she wanted me to feel that she'd given me a fair chance. But nothing in her body language told me she was prepared to change her call.

A large Hispanic woman suddenly filled the space between us and shadowed us like a cloud passing before the sun. She had a lot of food in her hands. Three dogs— she had no hesitation about kraut at lunchtime, none—two orders of curly fries, and a huge tropical beverage of some kind filled her cardboard tray to overflowing. "You two done? This ain't no Sta'bucks. People eat here, they leave. They let other people eat," she said.

"Want to walk?" I said to Lizzie.

She glanced up at the woman who was so eager to poach our spot. "We'll be gone in a minute. Or two."

"Hon, your two minutes 'sup a while ago. My feet are burnin'. My legs ache. I'm so hungry my stomach's playin' drums. And I need to get back to my goddamn job in fi' minutes."

"We're all done," I said, lifting Lizzie's hand. With my casted hand I gathered our trash together. I noticed that Lizzie was watching me carefully as I crumbled up the detritus of our meal and that she was watching me carefully as I dumped it into a nearby trash can. I led her outside onto the sidewalk and explained, "That woman looks like she's had a rough morning."

"I don't like to be pushed around," she said.

I noted a little gesture she made with her left hand as she spoke, a little sweeping arc that instructed the driver of the Town Car to follow us on our impromptu stroll up Third.

Is he just a driver, I wondered, *or a bodyguard, too?*

"I'll remember that about you," I said.

I would.

Did she glare at me? Hard to say.

TWENTY

The shower at my friend's flat in between the sessions with Dr. Gregory helped a lot. The nap not so much.

"Thea was terrific," I said. "With Adam."

"Yes," my therapist said. "What year was that? That he showed up?"

"A few years ago. 2002."

"Go on," he said.

It was like hiking up a steep hill with some guy a half a step behind you who kept poking his finger into your ribs.

Looking out the windows of his office, I was transfixed by so many leaves falling from the trees in one concentrated flurry. Autumn.

Without even an emotional hiccup at the confounding circumstances, Thea welcomed Adam into our home that first night as though he'd always been her favorite nephew. When she sensed that I didn't know what to do next, she steered me gently to my son's side. When my tongue couldn't find my lips and my lips couldn't form a word, she hugged me and whispered to me to "try honesty."

As Berkeley's bedtime approached, Thea plopped our daughter onto her half-brother's lap and handed him a well-worn copy of *The Snowy Day*. I thought that Adam read to my daughter as though he'd done it before, and I found myself wondering whether he had other siblings. Other than my daughter.

What I wondered, Thea voiced. "So do you have any other brothers and sisters, Adam? Besides Berk?"

"Not really," he replied.

Thea waited a moment for him to go on before she sighed at the cryptic nature of his response. It was something she did with me when she found my natural parsimony irritating. I could tell she wanted more from Adam, but she found a patient place. "Keep reading," she said. "You read beautifully."

He told us precious little that night about his life, his terse replies to our questions a clear indication that he wasn't eager to be quizzed. Instinctively, both Thea and I gave him room. He'd made the first move by coming to our door.

We figured that we'd make the second by making him welcome.

I kissed Berk good night and she gave her half-brother a big hug before she crawled under her covers into bed. Thea stayed behind with her to deal with her inevitable curiosity about Adam.

As he and I settled downstairs at the kitchen table, Adam said, "You're way too trusting."

"Yeah? I've been accused of a lot of things in my life. That's never been one of them."

"I could be a con, a sociopath. I could be anybody. Somebody who's done his homework about you. A serial killer, even. What proof do you have I am who I say I am?"

The melodrama of it all amused me. I could have told him about the halogen sparkle of his irises and the distinctive way his nostrils flared, but I didn't. I could have told him that I already felt a connection to him as solid as the one that anchored the roots of the big old oak to the soil in the backyard, but I didn't.

I simply shrugged. I was enjoying the novelty of being accused of being too trusting by my very own son.

"You like old movies?" he asked.

"Some. I'm no Roger Ebert."

"*Citizen Kane?*"

"Heard of that one."

"Remember the sled?"

I recognized the reference. I was relieved. "Rosebud," I said.

"My mom said if I ever met you, I should say a single word."

"Rosebud?" Was this some kind of odd memory quiz? "I took your mother to a movie?"

He laughed. It was, to be generous, an ironic laugh.

He said, "The word is 'Buckhead.' You didn't take my mother to a movie." He looked away from me for a long moment and when he finally turned his attention back toward me, his voice was much more somber. "You took her to a laundry room."

TWENTY-ONE

I didn't know then whether or not Adam had any idea what to expect when he arrived at our house, but by the end of that evening his heart, if it was open to us at all, must have registered the reality that Thea at least had made it clear to him that he'd found a family, if indeed he wanted another one.

Did he want another one?

I wasn't convinced. Part of me—the part of the iceberg below the surface, the cynical part, the skeptical part, the biggest part—was convinced that he'd come to the Rocky Mountain West on some quest that was nothing more than a psychologically twisted version of tourism, eager to see, finally, his personal family-tree version of Pike's Peak or Mesa Verde or the Royal Gorge, or whatever real-life natural attraction I represented in his curious mind. I was guessing that his visit would last just long enough to take a few snapshots—digital or figurative—and then he'd head back to wherever it was that he lived.

A more cynical part of my brain considered the possibility that he was preparing to lay claim to some of my wealth.

But mostly I believed that Adam would eventually leave the way he'd come, surreptitiously and without fanfare, and I would end up being nothing more than a four-by-six glossy on the bulletin board in his brain, or on the refrigerator door in his kitchen. The medical technology big shot. The distant father in the Rocky Mountain West. The Rosebud/Buckhead guy. I saw my smiling mug hanging at a cockeyed angle just below an uninspired shot of the Sears Tower or the big arch in St. Louis.

A magnet shaped like a pineapple would be obscuring most of my head.

"Did I say Thea was terrific?" I said to my therapist.

"You did."

"Well, Thea was terrific. She could have made that day hell. She could have pinned me to a figurative rack and stretched me in all kinds of uncomfortable directions. But she didn't. She was a dream."

Once it became clear that he was staying the night, and that staying the night had been his plan all along, we settled Adam into the guest room on the first floor. Adam maintained that his mother knew where he was, and since I was quite aware, and he was quite aware, that I didn't know his last name, let alone his mother's first name, he also knew that I was in no position to question his contention that he had parental permission for this sleepover. I thought I'd try to act just the slightest bit fatherly, and I handed him the remote control and helped him find the channel that would allow him to watch the late edition of *SportsCenter* on ESPN.

He asked me if we got the History Channel.

I was being tested.

I said we did, but that I didn't know the channel number.

The smirk on his face was my grade. I hadn't passed.

"I'll find it," he said. The undertone of his words said *"lame attempt, Dad"* but I got the distinct impression that he appreciated the fact that I'd given it a try. Maybe I'd get a B plus for effort.

"I'm sure you will. Good night, Adam. This day has been . . . something else."

I reached for the knob to pull the door closed behind me.

He said, "Bella."

"Excuse me?"

"Don't know if you care, really. But my mother's name is Roberta. Everyone who likes her calls her Bella. I guess you qualify, or you did once." He paused. "At least for a few minutes you qualified. That night in Buckhead? She probably told you that her name was Bella. She's friendly, outgoing. People like her. She would have told you that her name was Bella before . . ."

He didn't want to have to finish the sentence.

And I didn't want to finish it for him.

I put some dedicated effort into ignoring the knife he'd just slipped into the narrow space between my ribs. "Thank you," I said. "I didn't remember her name. I'm sorry."

"She knows yours," he said, his eyes on the TV screen. "Knew exactly where you lived, where I could find you. Showed me an article about you in *Business Week*. Taped an appearance you did on one of those stupid business channels on cable."

I nodded. I had a desirable combination of live TV talents—I could think on my feet and could make interviewers look smart—so I did a lot of cable interviews. I had no way of knowing which one Adam had seen, but the *Business Week* piece was a one-and-only. It wasn't a bad piece; they'd accurately portrayed the meteoric nature of my early success, and fairly concluded with the fact that the promise I'd displayed in the first act of my entrepreneurial life was still awaiting an encore.

In wunderkind terms I was a one-hit wonder. I

considered the possibility that my son was reminding me of that while I comforted myself with the fact that at least it had been a hell of a solo hit.

Adam wasn't done with whatever he wanted to say. His eagerness betrayed him. From the quick way he tied the words together, I could tell he'd been waiting quite a while to ask me the next questions, had maybe even rehearsed them. "Did you know back then? That night at the party? What her name was?"

Bella? Roberta?

Rang no bells. Not even the faintest little *ding-dong*.

Admitting the truth wasn't as difficult as I might have imagined. I shook my head to indicate that I hadn't known the girl's name that night, but Thea's earlier counsel about trying honesty continued to resonate, and I knew that although my headshake may have been truthful, it hadn't been either sufficient, or honest.

"No, Adam. I don't think I knew her name that night. I wish I could say I did."

"Yeah."

His "yeah" was dismissive. Nothing more than a polite version of "get the hell out of here."

I said, "I'm not proud of who I was back then, Adam. It was . . . It's hard to explain . . . Growing up is, I mean."

"Yeah?"

"What happened when I was younger. It's—"

He exhaled loudly through his nose to interrupt me. "I'm what happened when you were younger. I'm what happened."

Ouch. "I never knew. That's not an excuse. It's not right that I didn't know. But it's who I was. I never gave a moment's thought back then to anything about . . ."

I lost momentum as I struggled to figure out how to relate to a fourteen-year-old boy some context about being twenty-three, about being the center of the universe, or about the night I'd had anonymous sex with his mother in Georgia.

Bored with my nakedly self-serving act, waiting for me to crawl away with my tail between my legs, he started flicking through channels on the remote control. Whatever channel I was on as I fumbled for a way to finish my sentence and to rationalize away my behavior was the very first casualty of Adam's attention.

Not too surprisingly, he'd had all of his dad that he could tolerate that night.

I watched Thea undress. First her pale pink pointes, then her satin pants. Finally she twisted the long-sleeve cotton top over her head in that one patented corkscrew motion I never tired of seeing. She curled next to me in our bed around midnight. Her flesh felt hot and lush with just a hint of sweat sticking her skin to mine. The draperies hung open, as they did most nights, and in the distance the purple-black outline of the craggy-topped Rockies made a shadowy silhouette against the midnight blue of the western sky. She kissed my shoulder once and then again, and right at the moment when I was steeling myself for the reality that she was about to press me for details about that fateful tryst with Adam's mother—had Adam said something to her about the laundry room? I hoped not, *Jesus*—she said, "So why do you think Adam came today, babe?"

Adam hadn't told either of us much—he was parsing out the details of his personal history as though they came from a ration that needed to last a long, long time—but since he'd reminded me about the washing machine in Buckhead I had managed to narrow down my recall enough to be pretty sure when the encounter had occurred. In my early twenties I'd only been to Georgia once—a trip that lasted a couple of days, total. I'd been visiting an old college friend who was in graduate school at Emory back in '87. With some effort, prompted by the clues Adam had provided, I had also recalled a few foggy details about the pre-Halloween party at the Buckhead McMansion, and I'd pieced together some even foggier reminiscences about the young woman with whom I'd coupled—and whom I'd apparently impregnated—in the laundry room off the butler's pantry during the height of the premature celebration of All Hallow's Eve.

Bella had been tall and skinny. Back then she had short, blond hair and bright eyes. The washing machine had been a top loader. She and I had joked about getting it agitating without even starting it up.

Okay, I'd joked about getting it agitating without even starting it up.

Thea was surprised but not shocked by any of the day's developments; she knew who I'd been when I was a twenty-three-year-old kid. It wasn't a secret between us what kind of life I'd lived before we met. During our courtship, while I'd been busy trying to convince her of the sincerity of my affections, she'd made it clear that she'd pushed away plenty of guys like me during her single days. Guys who never, ever put a girl and a responsibility in the same sentence. And she'd told me about it in such a way that I was confident that despite her caution she had been ambushed by a few guys like me. The scars from those encounters were faint—Thea had made sure they healed well—but they were there. No doubt.

Despite that, all she was seeking from me at that moment together in our marital bed were my thoughts about why my apparent undiscovered progeny had arrived that day—that day—at our door in Colorado. The question perplexed me, too, once I got past how grateful I was that Thea was able to postpone the more prurient aspects of her curiosity. I was also insightful enough to know that

I wasn't ready to provide complicated answers to any inquiries that had to do with the teenage boy who was watching the History Channel in the guest room downstairs.

I said, "To see who his father is, I guess. That has to be a strong pull for a kid his age."

"You think it's that simple?" she said. Obviously she didn't think it was that simple. Not even close to that simple. She threaded her long fingers through the sparse hair between the nipples on my chest. There was no seduction in her touch, just connection. Her voice was as understanding as could be, but I knew she was prodding me to dig a little deeper.

Okay, a lot deeper.

I said, "His mother's told him all about the . . . time he was conceived. The details, I mean. Where we . . . you know. A kid his age? Don't you think that's odd for a parent to . . . I find that . . ."

"Inconceivable?" Thea said with a tiny laugh.

Although the humor was spot on, the joke was on me, and the word hurt a little bit as she said it. Recognizing that I'd just started a conversation I didn't want to finish, I said, "Adam's watching some history something on TV." I knew at some level that I was trying to race through the channels with Thea as my son had done with me earlier.

She found the fact that my son was watching history ironic, of course. "Well, then," she said.

"He'll tell me why he's here when he's ready," I said, trying to persuade her of my thoughtfulness, my tone swollen with pretense that I was drawing on a wealth of knowledge about the motivations of teenage boys. The reality was that I remembered only one particular adolescent motivation with any clarity. And that was the one that had endured far beyond my adolescence and had gotten me into trouble with Bella.

"Or when he senses that you are," Thea replied.

Many honest words were spoken in our house that day, but perhaps none any more truthful than those.

Thea's last thought that astonishing night? They were a mother's words, nurturing words, all-inclusive words. Mostly, though, they were hopeful, surprising words. She said, "We have a son."

Her breathing revealed that, within heartbeats, she was asleep.

Me? I wasn't.

My new therapist's reaction to my narrative? In a tone that had no inflection whatsoever, he said, "You had a daughter. Before that you had a son."

I thought it was his way of letting me know that he knew there was much more to this story.

He was right, of course.

But he didn't know the half of it.

TWENTY-TWO

I made sure my therapist was paying attention—truly paying attention—before I continued.

"While I was on the phone the next day and Thea was in the shower, Adam left. Just walked out the door, no note, no good-bye—nothing. I drove around the neighborhood looking for him for a while, but he was gone. His mother, Roberta—Bella—called our house a couple of hours later. Thea answered. Bella was concerned, but not frantic, and wondered if we'd seen Adam."

"You're saying his mother hadn't known that he was visiting you?" Alan Gregory said.

"You're quick," I said to the shrink. My unkindness was reflexive. I didn't give it a thought.

He did. "This makes you uncomfortable, talking about your son with me. When you're uncomfortable you seem to get a little—what's a good word—unpleasant? Testy?"

I was surprised to recognize the fact that his words didn't add up to an accusation, just a question. I wasn't accustomed to being confronted without being accused. In my family growing up they were Siamese twins.

"Yeah, I get unpleasant." Left unsaid: *That's a problem?*

"I wanted to be certain we both recognized the tendency. It may prove relevant, that's all. Go on."

"They were living outside Cincinnati. Bella was

separated from her second husband. Thea said Bella sounded nice; she liked her. Friendly, unassuming, just like Adam had said. They talked about Adam's time with us. They talked about Berk."

I thought my psychologist would say something then—maybe hoped he would—but he didn't.

I started talking about Berkeley, what a character she was, when I noticed my therapist's eyes start to squint. "What?" I asked.

"Tangent?" he asked.

"Probably," I admitted. "His mother said Adam had run before. A few times. She called them his 'adventures' and made them sound kind of romantic. But he'd always called and let her know where he was. This time he'd been gone for almost three days and she hadn't heard from him. She was getting concerned."

I paused to give my therapist a chance to impart some wisdom, or maybe to take a gratuitous shot at Roberta's laissez-faire parenting philosophy, but he either didn't have any wisdom for me, or any spare criticism for Bella, or maybe he was just one constipated son of a bitch.

"You got nothing?" I said.

He had a little something. "Bella thought of calling you. Despite the fact that she had no reason to think you even knew that Adam existed—literally—she must have sensed something to suspect you might know where he was. Why else would she call your house looking for him?"

I shrugged. "Doesn't matter."

"No?"

"No." I could have stopped there, but I knew I was already appearing petulant to him. I wanted to be petulant—I felt like being petulant—but I wanted to appear reasonable.

"Adam showed up in Ohio the next day. Bella called us back and said he was fine. I spoke with her that time. She asked me to let her know if he ever showed up again. She was curt. But her voice brought back memories from Buckhead. You ever notice that Southern girls sing when they talk?"

"Yeah?" my therapist said in reply, answering me without telling me a damn thing about his impression of the melody in Southern girls' voices.

"Back then?" I said. "She was a nice girl. I was an asshole."

Again, nothing. *Why am I paying this guy?*

I went on. "That day on the phone? Even though she wasn't in the best mood, she was still a nice girl. I wasn't as much of an asshole. I took some pride in that. I did."

I didn't know that's where I was going with the conversation.

Did he?

I'm thinking he did.

Maybe that's why he'd been so taciturn.

Maybe that's why I was paying the guy.

TWENTY-THREE

Lizzie recovered quickly from the run-in with the woman in Papaya King.

"You have unfinished business. I don't say that to be critical, but rather to acknowledge how difficult the situation is. I have a lot of empathy for your situation. Any parent would want to feel that his connection with his child was . . . secure before – –"

"With Adam? You're talking about Adam?"

"With Adam," she confirmed.

"I go back to the question of relevance. Why is that important to you, your . . . organization?"

Her mood had darkened; the captivating brilliance was gone from her eyes, replaced by something brooding. "We've learned—sometimes the hard way—that this arrangement works best when our clients are at peace with the world. When we've run into resistance from clients in the past about carrying out end-of-life arrangements, the culprit is often unfinished business— occasionally a pending deal involving significant money or major work issues, but mostly it's unfinished emotional business. Family business, usually. Doubts about living inevitably create doubts about dying. My experience is that the doubts about living that haunt us most are the ones about our children. Experience has taught our organization that for our service to be maximally effective, we must do everything in our power to ensure that our prospective clients are secure financially, secure emotionally, and secure . . . psychologically. Being in a settled place with your children is an important part of that."

I wanted the sparkle back in her eyes. I gave her a sly grin and asked, "Financially, emotionally, psychologically." I ticked off the three criteria on my fingers. "So what's my score? One out of three? Two out of three?"

She brightened suddenly, poked me in the ribs, and skipped ahead of me. For a moment, I congratulated myself on flirting her back into a good mood, and then I stepped back and realized I'd done it without learning what monster had darkened her soul in the first place.

I thought I *shouldn't have let that go.*

"I take it that's a one," I said. "So I get an F minus."

She pirouetted and began walking backward, facing me. Doesn't take a genius to know that it's not a wise form of ambulation in Manhattan. "You have money," she said. "We both know that. So you get a one, at least. Rich boys always get a one."

"So do pretty girls," I said.

"True. And pretty boys get a half."

"So I'm a pretty boy?" I asked, too desperately wanting her to say "yes."

She didn't answer me.

"I'm up to one and a half, then. Trash can," I said.

She swerved around it as though she had radar.

"Old lady, shopping cart."

That time she turned and looked. The sidewalk behind her was clear.

"Liar."

"Sometimes, yes. Trick is knowing when I'm lying, and figuring out why. Back at Papaya King you told me you don't like to be pushed around. Well, I don't like to be told no," I said. "I'm not accustomed. My money's good. And I'm a big boy; I know what I'm buying into."

Once again, as though she had inborn, back-scanning radar, Lizzie stopped just before she would have smacked into a stack of flimsy wooden crates jammed with fresh fruits and vegetables that were on their way into the cellar chute of a restaurant kitchen. I closed the gap on the sidewalk between us so that I was close enough to lean over and kiss her.

She hadn't refreshed her lipstick since Papaya King and I could still smell the tartness of kraut on her breath.

"I read your profile," she said. "I know about your penchant for . . ."

I found it sweet that she was trying to find an uncritical way to complete her thought.

"You know about my penchants? I've been told that they're, you know, larger than . . . most men's . . . penchants."

"You're making this difficult," she cooed.

"My penchants have always gotten me into trouble. But you probably know that, too. If you know about Adam."

"We do thorough background . . . investigations."

I decided to let her off the hook. "Then you must know everything about Antonio. You know about my brother, too? I bet you do." But I didn't give her any more space physically. I was still inches from her.

"Conrad?"

"Connie."

"Connie then. MS, Princeton."

"ALS, Yale."

"What . . . ever."

I realized from her tone that she'd known all along that Connie was ALS, Yale.

"Then you know that I have reasons—great

reasons—for signing up with your company. *Objective* reasons." I'd intentionally emphasized her word. "I know what dying slowly is like. I know the price of not planning for the unexpected. More than most men, I know the value . . . of living. The capital *L* kind. To the fullest."

She seemed to be considering my argument.

"Your brother would detest what we do."

She was right.

I detested that she knew that about him. *How the hell,* I wondered, *does she know that about Connie?*

"What makes you so sure?" I said.

"You disagree?"

"No. I'm wondering whether you spoke with him."

She shrugged.

She flitted her gaze down to my mouth. "Are you planning to kiss me?" she asked.

"I'm thinking about it," I said. I hadn't been, but I started.

"Don't."

Don't think about it, I wondered, *or don't kiss you?*

"You got sad before, when we were talking about Adam. What was that? Let me in a little, Lizzie."

I hadn't intended the double entendre that was inbred in my choice of words, and as soon as I recognized it, its presence unsettled me.

She either didn't see the dual meanings, or she didn't care. She didn't yield an inch of space, either corporally or rhetorically. "We sell peace of mind. The fulfillment rate on our policies? It's not that large. The percentage of our clientele that end up in situations requiring us to provide end-of-life services would surprise you."

"Because it's small?"

"Yes. Young people, like yourself, tend to die suddenly. Accidents, heart attacks, strokes. Some chronic health tragedies—cancers, cardiac illness—do linger long enough for us to intervene. But we don't sell death. And, although we are prepared to provide end-of-life services in the case of a prolonged condition, we're not in the euthanasia business. Don't misunderstand that. We're in the quality of life business. What we sell, and what we do very, very well, is we sell assurance that if the worst occurs, your last days will be on your own terms. That . . . is true peace of mind."

"Yes?" I'd covered the rational parts of her argument already on my own. Despite her eloquence I wasn't that impressed with her soliloquy.

I still wanted to kiss her, though.

"Then I'm in?" I said.

"We don't believe in selling voice lessons to a mute. We don't believe in selling a Monet to a blind man."

"That's me? I'm dumb and blind?"

"Where peace of mind is concerned, maybe," she said. "Remember what I said about unfinished business?"

"Everyone has unfinished business."

"No," she said, the word sharp as a crack of gunfire. "Everyone has unlived days. Children they won't see graduate from college. A daughter's wedding they won't attend. Holidays to the Mediterranean they won't take. A retirement palace they won't enjoy. A mountain they won't climb. But not everyone has unfinished business like you have unfinished business with Adam. Every inhale but the last requires an exhale. With Adam, you haven't exhaled."

"How do you—"

The Town Car rolled into place beside us and pulled to a stop. *Had she just signaled for it?*

My final question hung in the air. She slithered away from me and stepped off the curb. As she pulled the door of the car open, she said, "We'll be in touch with a final determination. I have to go." She climbed in and closed the door.

"Thanks for lunch," I said.

The dark rear window rolled halfway down. "You paid," she said.

"And I got my money's worth."

TWENTY-FOUR

That evening in New York City, I walked over to 55th and Sixth and picked up a couple of cellophane-wrapped sandwiches at Pret for dinner and ate them in my room at the hotel while I drank half of the Yebisu. Some kind housekeeping ghost had placed the big bottle of beer in a silver champagne bucket and kept the cubes refreshed all day long.

Nice touch.

I allowed myself to get lost watching Central Park turn black as the day's light seeped into . . . where? Where did it go?

A knock at my door.

Housekeeping yet again? *More towels to add to my stash, just in case I have a sudden urge to pat down a wet elephant? Perhaps another chocolate for my pillow?*

No, a guy in a suit, a young guy, a black guy, a nice suit. Accented English. African, maybe. Not South African. Kenya? Perhaps.

He wasn't with the hotel; that much was clear. No name tag.

He handed me an envelope. I noted he was wearing gloves. White gloves. The gloves were not intended to denote the elegance of his service.

No.

The white gloves were to avoid leaving fingerprints on the envelope.

"Good evening, sir," he said.

Once he'd placed the envelope in my hand, he cocked his head just the slightest bit, and said, "Thank you, sir."

I stood in the doorway and watched him march down the hall until he entered the distant elevator. When I returned to my room I threw the envelope on the bed. It was a thin envelope and I was assuming that college admission rules were in effect. A thin envelope meant rejection. A fat envelope meant: Fill out all these forms, send us a check, and you're in.

The real message was, of course, the messenger. They were telling me that they could insert themselves into places—like the Four Seasons—that it shouldn't be easy to insert themselves into.

I figured I could read the rejection letter later. The euphemisms that the Death Angels employed to refer to the services they were denying me would undoubtedly give me a chuckle.

My heart wasn't broken.

Frankly, I was suffering slightly more regret that I wouldn't be seeing Lizzie again than I was feeling regret that I hadn't been judged a suitable candidate for the Death Angels. If I had to choose between having Adam in my life and being one of the Death Angels' minions, it would have been an easy choice. I'd already begun rationalizing their rejection: What were the odds I'd ever need their services, anyway?

Most people died predictably, or suddenly.

Lizzie had said so herself.

I would be one of those. My 911 and I wrapped around a tree. Off a cliff. Head-on into a semi.

A bolt of lightning from the blue.

Or taking a breather on a winter afternoon on a rock shelf that was really a cornice . . .

Or, maybe, the one and only time I didn't quite get both skis on the same side of every tree.

Thea called and put Cal on the phone so I could talk with her before she got totally distracted by other things. Cal was old enough by then that talking to her father when he was on one of his all-too-frequent road trips felt quaint to her, but she was a great kid with a soft, playful heart and she put up with most of her parents' peculiarities.

Thea got back on the line. "How did your meeting go today?" She thought I was in negotiation on an offer to consult with GE on the development and marketing of their new line of portable scanners. Why did she think that? Because that was the lie I'd told her for going to New York.

GE didn't need my help.

"Fine. I just need to decide if I want the aggravation."

"Do you?"

"I haven't decided."

"Want to know what I think?"

"You think I should pass."

"I married a brilliant man. You still going up to see Connie tomorrow?"

"Yeah, I think I'll take the train to New Haven in the morning, spend the day with him."

"I can't tell you how much admiration I have for your brother. He inspires me every day."

"I know."

"When I find myself growing impatient over nothing, or feeling sorry for myself because I have a cold, or cramps from my period, I think of Connie. Please say hi to him for me. Tell him I'll try to get to Connecticut soon."

"I will."

"You sound down, babe."

"Tired, that's all. I'm afraid of what I'm going to find tomorrow when I see Connie. You know. He doesn't get better. That's hard to watch."

"I know."

"I love you."

"Me, too," she said.

When the drivel on the television bored me, I opened the envelope that I'd tossed on the bed. The note inside was written in the same unremarkable script as the one I'd received after checking in to my room. This one said, "I will be in the lounge until ten o'clock."

That was all.

My watch said I had twenty minutes to get downstairs.

Lizzie, I thought, and my heart jumped just a little. Okay, my heart jumped a lot. I went from not knowing I had a pulse to knowing I had a pulse.

Did I think about Thea in the next few moments?

No.

But it wasn't Lizzie waiting for me downstairs in the lounge. It was the would-be comedian from the lunch at Nobu.

The joke was on me.

TWENTY-FIVE

He'd been sitting at a table near the entrance to the lounge while he waited for me. He was nursing a snifter of something amber. When I arrived he stood up to say hello and then I followed him to a distant table that fronted 57th from a mezzanine above the sidewalk. I waved off the cocktail waitress.

"Once you're sick or hurt, you're in. If Adam suddenly decides he's your best pal, or if he doesn't, it won't change anything," he said in lieu of a greeting.

Maybe not for you, I thought. But for me? I knew that if Adam suddenly showed any interest in moving to Colorado or letting me further into his life it would change everything for me. Everything. But I said, "I understand that."

"What I'm saying is that once the second payment is made and you have an activating event, you can't change your mind."

"I understand the commitment. Your associate has made the policy's lack of flexibility crystal clear." I almost said her name—Lizzie—before I remembered that it probably wasn't really her name.

"Don't be glib about this. We aren't." He tried to catch my eyes. I eluded him for a moment, just to show him I could. When I relented and locked onto his gaze he said, "Don't light this fuse unless you're absolutely willing to have the bomb go off. At some point, there will be no way to defuse it."

"I said I understood."

"Good." He swirled his cognac or Armagnac or Drambuie or whatever it was. But he didn't drink any.

"I'm curious about something, though," I said. "What if I simply chicken out? I mean before I get sick or injured. What if I just tell you to keep all the money I paid and leave me alone. Let you off the hook."

"It has never happened. Theoretically, it's possible, but realistically? You won't be able to find us to give us the instructions. We'll have no further contact with you after your final fees are received and the client-derived parameters are specified. Discretion serves our clients well, and it serves us well. To protect our promises we need to protect ourselves. Invisibility at all stages. All stages. Always."

"How will you know if I'm—"

"All monitoring of your health status will be done remotely, and invisibly. It's part of the comprehensive nature of our service."

I shrugged. "I have resources," I said.

And attitude.

"We work only for people with resources. Believe me when I say you won't be able to find us, so don't bother to try. If you don't like the rules, don't play the game. There are nursing homes filled with people who ultimately chose not to play. You can be one of them if you would like. Unless, and until, you are a client, it makes no difference to me."

"Jimmy reached you to let you know I was interested."

"If you complete your enrollment, and you're so inclined, we'll provide you with a way to make referrals. That will be up to you."

"Jimmy's enrolled?" *He said he wasn't.*

"I didn't say that."

"But enrollees can make referrals."

"If they wish."

"So then I can reach you. See?"

"We use a series of intermediaries. Always. Your friend Jimmy became aware of our organization during his wife's . . . decline. When you expressed interest in controlling the circumstances at the end of your own life, Jimmy Lee reached an intermediary. Each intermediary is under instructions not to forward any information but the contact information for the referral. Don't be childish about this. If you need a way to beat our system, our services aren't designed for you. No one's coercing you to enroll."

"I don't like to be told what to do. I'm spending a lot of money."

He sat back. His voice turned dismissive. "When you buy a Bentley, you can't tell them you want one that drives on three wheels. When you choose your next Gulfstream, you won't be given the option of insisting that it fly with one wing. Money has its limits. Get real."

Did this guy just tell me to "get real"? Was he trying to provoke me?

"This is a service, not a thing. Your analogy is flawed."

As are your manners.

"A specific service. Bentley-type service. Gulfstream-like service. Four wheels. Two wings."

"I like to do things my way."

"We know. It's why we've ultimately decided to accept you, and it's what will ultimately make you a good client. Our services are designed for people who don't like to be dictated to by fate. Sign on with your eyes wide open and you'll ensure that your life will end your way. Or walk away now and leave yourself vulnerable to fate. The choice is yours."

He had a point. He knew he had a point.

More important, I knew he had a point.

"We don't need the work," he said. "Go to one of our competitors."

"I don't know your competitors."

"We don't have any," he said.

It was his first joke of the evening. I hoped it would be his last.

It also marked the moment that I realized that he and I had moved, figuratively, into the little room at the car dealership. The bland room where the real negotiations take place. The room where the sales games are played.

He was trying to convince me that he could walk away from the deal we were negotiating. He was wondering if I could.

I didn't like my bargaining position.

He reached into his coat pocket and dropped a photograph on the table. A man, or a reasonable facsimile, in a bed hooked up to enough tubes and monitors to fill a ward at the Mayo Clinic.

"Recognize him?"

Antonio? I thought. *Is that Antonio?*

"Of course you don't. How could you? His mother wouldn't recognize him. That's Toby Bonds one month after—after—his limo was broadsided by that cement truck in Miami. You heard about that, I assume. The cement truck? Toby's side airbag didn't inflate for some reason. But Toby's head did." He paused for a moment. "You know Toby, right?"

Was the "But Toby's head did" one of this guy's jokes?

"Yes," I said. "I know him." Prior to his accident, Toby was a bigwig in the venture-capital world. We'd crossed paths a number of times in our professional lives. I'd indeed heard about his tragedy. It was one of those things that was *tsk-tsked* about at cocktail parties.

I'd always thought Toby was a pompous prick.

"Thought so. Then you probably know the story about the cement truck. Toby was ambivalent about us, not unlike you. He never made the second payment. He was still thinking about it when fate dealt him the low card." He touched the photo. "Not making the second payment? It's kind of like drawing on an inside straight. Risky. You lose sometimes."

"Some people take risks."

Like me.

"Antonio?" he asked. The way he said my friend's name made it sound like a profanity.

I said a silent prayer that the funny man didn't have a photo of Antonio. I watched his hands.

He went on. "He took a risk in that cave in Belize, didn't he? You've been known to take a few yourself. Is the outcome that Antonio suffered a consequence of risk that you're willing to endure?"

"I get your point."

He threw down another horrifying picture and I began to wonder how thick his deck of disaster was. "Margo Johannsen."

I knew about Margo. She was a colleague. She'd been COO of one of the big players in biotech, and she had suffered a stroke at age forty-seven. We usually saw each other a few times a year, and I enjoyed her company when we ran into each other at industry meetings. The photograph on the table was of her in a rehab facility. She was being supported by two physical therapists. She didn't look much like a COO. She looked like a train wreck.

"Okay, okay," I said. "I've seen enough. I don't need to be told most things twice."

His dark lips flattened out as though he were putting some effort into hiding a smile. "Do you know that 'gork,' that terrible word that's so full of meaning, is actually an acronym?"

"No, I didn't know that." I was going to add "For what?" but I already knew he was planning to tell me.

"God . . . only . . . really . . . knows. Before it became part of the vernacular, it was originally medical slang. A description for conditions that are unfathomable to medical caregivers." He lifted his eyebrows and gestured toward the photo of Margo. She was the current GORK in question.

I sighed.

I was the future GORK in question.

He flipped another picture onto the table. I recognized this hospitalized zombie right away and I swallowed and fought a swell of pressure behind my eyes. I said, "Oh my God. That's Will Durrell, isn't it? What the hell—"

"Aortic aneurysm. Three days ago. An astonishing surgical achievement saved his life, but . . . he had bled a lot, and the doctors didn't quite save enough of his brain. You know him, too, don't you? You know Will?"

He knew that I knew Will. I could tell.

The photo of Will had not been chosen at random. I wondered how the funny man had gotten hold of it.

"Yes. I consider him a friend." The picture of Will Durrell hit me harder than the others. I hadn't even known he was sick. The previous summer Will had invited me to be his guest in a small camp at the annual Bohemian Grove gathering on the Russian River in California. I'd learned a lot about him, and from him, during our week together. He played an alto sax that could make the redwoods weep and he could sketch a dead-on caricature of anyone he wanted in about three minutes flat.

I said, "Let me guess. Will never made the second payment?"

"Mr. Durrell withdrew his application prior to acceptance. But I'm so glad we're beginning to understand each other. It makes the final negotiation so much more straightforward."

I spent some more time lost in the photograph of Will. The last time I'd seen him he'd been smoking a fat Monte Cristo and drinking an '82 La Lagune while trying to get a group together to form an impromptu marching jazz band through the Russian River redwoods. He had already recruited one of the Marsalis brothers—I don't recall which one—and he was pretty sure Eric Clapton was going to join in, too.

I'd offered to carry spare instruments just to be in the vicinity when they started to play.

It had been ten o'clock in the morning and the sun was just finding its way through the majestic trees to the camp. The marching band never materialized. Will got distracted by an opportunity to do a canopy tour with Richard Branson.

"I don't get it," I said to the dull man across from me. "Your associate spends the day trying to convince me to back out of our arrangement. Yet, you come to my hotel to try to convince me to ante in. What gives?"

"Our paying clients are in the top one–one hundredth of one percent of the population in wealth. We don't market our services, yet we reject two potential clients for every one we accept. If we had a door, people would be beating it down. If we had a Web site, our servers would be jammed. We've identified a true need. Consider yourself one of the fortunate few."

Was he congratulating me, or himself? Time would tell, I decided.

"What distinguishes the rejects from the enrollees?" I asked.

"That's . . . proprietary."

I expected no less. I reminded myself I didn't have to like the guy. Any antipathy I had for him was more than compensated for by my affection—if you want to call it that—for Lizzie.

"My associates and I have reached a determination that you're an acceptable risk. My role this evening is merely to ascertain that you understand the irrevocable nature of our agreement. Irrevocable, regardless of what happens between you and your son. Since we're unable to put anything in writing we go to great lengths to be certain we've covered all bases. All bases."

I'm in? Hurray.

I didn't feel all that excited. I was still trying to get over my disappointment that I wasn't having this drink with Lizzie.

"I understand," I said. "How do we proceed?"

He mentioned the name of one of the big national mobile-phone carriers, a different one than the one I'd used the time before. "Get a new line when you get home. We'll be in touch."

His tongue caught on the roof of his mouth as he formed the *t* in "touch." The childhood stutterer briefly revealed, once more.

"That's it?" I said.

"Be frugal. Get a basic phone. It will be used only once. Shortly thereafter, you'll get directions on how to make the second round of contributions, and we'll review the client-derived parameters. After that, you won't hear from us again. We function in the background, like any good security system."

He drained the contents of his snifter in one long swallow, shivered at the shock to the back of his throat, and stood up.

"I have one more question," I said.

"Yes?"

"I wasn't frisked this time. Why?"

"Review our conversation. I didn't say anything this

time. That's why. We could have been talking about irrevocable life insurance, couldn't we? Or disability insurance, even. A new kind. A special kind. The kind that says you never, ever, have to worry about being permanently disabled."

Although flirting is a form of recreation for me, infatuation is a force of nature. I flirt a lot. Thea does, too. She's great at it. Deadly, actually, better than me.

It's harmless. It is.

Infatuation is something else. If flirting is a tease, the first sip of an icy beer, champagne bubbles on the tip of your nose, or the kiss of a cool breeze on a hot summer day, infatuation is a more profound phenomenon—a hurricane, a tornado, a wildfire.

An avalanche.

Something dangerous and kinetic. Something too big to hide from. Something too big to trifle with.

If I'd bothered to look around I would have realized I was already engulfed.

After the man left the table in the Four Seasons lounge, I waited a few minutes and walked out into the sedate evening choreography of 57th Street. Hands in my pockets, I strolled aimlessly a few blocks until I found myself back in front of the entrance to MOMA on 53rd, and I realized that my ambling had been anything but aimless. Although I'd just made a monumental decision about my health and my future, my thoughts were about Lizzie.

I wasn't going to see her again.

I continued on toward Times Square and allowed the energy of the crowd to swallow me up. I heard words from a dozen languages and saw a thousand faces of a hundred colors on every block.

But none of them belonged to the woman with the plaid eyes who smelled like fresh laundry.

If they had?

I don't know.

It's better that way, I told myself.

I love Thea. I do.

TWENTY-SIX

The next day I took the Acela from Penn Station to New Haven to visit my brother. Connie's deterioration had accelerated in the six or so months since I'd last seen him, and his body was so wasted that it took my breath away. I suspected that it might be the last time I would see him alive, but I'd suspected that before and I'd been wrong before.

Connie was a survivor.

His ALS had progressed to the point that a wheelchair was a necessity and talking had become a chore for him. To inquire about Thea and the kids, he would raise his chin—he could still do that—and say simply, "Family?" The enunciation of a five-word sentence took him most of a minute. Although he'd always been the rare academic who was stingy with adjectives and adverbs, as his disease robbed him of verve he'd begun speaking with Raymond Chandler–like parsimony—almost all modifiers were tossed overboard as needless ballast. For Connie, total inability to speak seemed to be lurking right around the corner.

Complete social isolation couldn't be much further away.

For the previous couple of years, Connie's care assistant had been a Guatemalan Mayan named Felix. Felix was a short man with a face like a well-tanned moon, and he was patient and kind with my brother. Felix covered his mouth, and his rotting teeth, with his open hand when he smiled, something he did often. In return for Felix's generosity, Connie was Connie. He spent most of an hour one afternoon telling me about the mistreatment and horror that Felix and his family had endured during the Guatemalan civil war. He described the harrowing escape he'd made from the turmoil and poverty around his home in rural Chocola in the early 1990s.

Connie paid Felix well, and always included a healthy monthly bonus that Felix sent straight to Guatemala for conversion to quetzals to help his impoverished relatives.

Connie's message to me? It wasn't hard to discern. He was telling me that some things are worse than *this*.

Than ALS.

We talked about the latest travesty in the Sudan, the tsunami orphans in Asia, and the triad of ravages in sub-Saharan Africa—AIDS, poverty, and lack of access to education. We talked about the fate of women with fistulas in Ethiopia, the child sex trade in Asia, and the futility of searching for a solution to the dilemma of the Jews and the Palestinians. Things that were to Connie ever-so-much worse than a privileged guy who had lived a dream life in New Haven who was now burdened with ALS.

Much, much worse.

Connie never complained to me about his circumstances. Not once since his diagnosis. During my visit, I considered the possibility of confiding in him about the meeting I'd had the day before in the city, but I didn't. Why? Guilt was part of it, of course.

Shame was a larger part.

Although I'd suffered no qualms about the decision I'd made to throw in my lot with the Death Angels, I nonetheless felt a smidgeon of shame that I was tacitly admitting to myself that I couldn't handle, or would choose not to handle, the challenges that Connie and a million others like him faced every day. I was confident that one of the "client-derived parameters" I'd have to respond to would ask me whether I would choose to continue to live if routine daily activities required a full-time assistant.

When my day came to endure the cut of one of life's sharper arrows, I didn't want to be one of those who complain, but I knew myself reasonably well. And one of the things I knew was that I wasn't blessed with Connie's perspective or his equanimity about fate.

So, instead, on the train up from New York that day I had reached a decision to go ahead and buy my deluxe do-not-complain insurance policy from the Death Angels. And one of the things I would tell my death brokers was that if I ever got to the point that I was as physically impaired as my brother, yes, I would choose dying over compromised living.

I had asked Mary to do a few more things for me in New York. When I was done visiting with Connie, she flew to the Tweed New Haven airport, picked me up, and flew me home.

Somewhere over Ohio she left the controls in the hands of her latest copilot ingenue and joined me in the cabin. I asked her how things had gone in the city.

"No problem at all. You want a report?"

"Not now. I'll tell you when. Keep it to yourself, okay?"

"Cool." She made a zip-it motion across her lips and gestured forward. "You want to fly for a while? I'll give Trace a break, and you can take the yoke." Mary was—still—auditioning copilots. This was Trace's second trip with us; he was the first applicant to get a call-back in some time.

I was a licensed pilot, but not rated to fly the jet on my own. Some days I loved to fly her. That wasn't one of them. "No, don't think so. Thanks."

"How were your meetings?"

"Fine, you know."

"Yeah," she said, humming along with me. As much affection as I had for Mary, I didn't feel like chatting. She could tell, and began to leave the cabin for the cockpit.

"Mary?"

"Yeah, boss."

"I appreciate your help. Everything."

She rested a closed fist over her heart. "It's nothing," she said. "I have a great job."

I nodded. "Is Trace a keeper?"

She smiled. "Maybe. He's a great kid."

"Let me know when you want me to talk to him." Mary would choose her own copilot. When she sent the guy or girl for a sit-down with me, it would be only a formality.

Three days after my visit to the East Coast I was back in the Colorado high country. I sat facing the huge windows in my study—they framed a spectacular chunk of the angular Sneffels Range—while I arranged for the second round of payments to be transferred to the Death Angel overseas charitable fronts.

Across the Rockies in my Denver office, LaBelle made it perfectly clear how she felt about whatever it was I was doing with my money, but she nonetheless sent every dollar on its merry way overseas.

The day after the last transfer was confirmed, I was driving the Porsche down the hill from my Ridgway home toward the hardware store in town when I spotted a pickup truck parked, hood in the air, on the shoulder of the two-lane road. The driver was dressed in pressed corduroys and hiking boots that had never, ever seen a trail—he looked like a typical Ralph Lauren wannabe to me—and he waved at me to stop. I pulled over.

I was thinking the guy had suffered a double-dose of misfortune. In addition to having car trouble, he was lost. The road from my ranch to the picturesque town of Ridgway was far from the well-worn tourist route that looped up the Dallas Divide past Designer Ralph's sprawling Double RL spread and then toward Telluride.

"Trouble?" I said after I lowered my window. "Need a lift into town? Can I call someone for you?"

"No trouble," he said pleasantly. Then he said my name.

In a small town like Ridgway almost everybody knows almost everybody's name. Thing is, when a guy on the road knows my name, I tend to know his, too. But I was sure I'd never seen this young man before in my life.

For a split second, for some reason, I thought *Kidnap!* Why? I don't know, maybe I'd just been going to too many bad movies. He must have seen the alarm in my eyes, because he raised both hands—they were empty— and said, "Nothing to worry about, sir. I'm —"

Too late. I'd already ignited the volatile rocket fuel mixture of paranoia and adrenaline. I didn't wait for him to finish his sentence. I pounded the clutch down and reached to force the gearshift into first.

"A friend of Lizzie's," he said. Calmly.

I dropped the shift lever back into neutral and slowly eased the pressure off the clutch.

"You scared the shit out of me."

"It wasn't my intention. I apologize. Everything we learned about you said you'd stop for someone needing help on the road if we were out in the country. I didn't think you would . . ."

Totally freak out?

"What do you want?"

"I'm here to finish your application, more specifically to ascertain your positions on the client-derived parameters of your policy. That will allow us to complete your file and initiate your coverage. That's all, sir."

He invited me to join him in the front seat of his rented Ford pickup. After chewing for a moment on the question of whether or not I believed him, I pulled off the roadway onto the shoulder in front of his truck, got out of my car, and climbed onto his passenger seat and asked, "Are you going to frisk me?"

"No," he said. "It's quite obvious I surprised you with my visit. What possible reason would you have to be wearing a wire?"

Decent logic.

He placed a digital recording device between us on the truck's center console, and pressed the button marked "record." A tiny red light next to the switch brightened to the color of fresh blood.

He said, "I have a series of questions to ask you."

"Shoot."

"Most of the questions are either to be answered 'yes' or answered 'no.' A few will require you to choose among multiple choices. Your answers will be recorded. Is that clear?"

"Yes."

"The recording will serve as the agreement between you and us. There will be no written record. No signatures, other than your verbal assent. Understood?"

"Yes."

"I am authorized to tell you that the guidelines that you communicate to me today will be honored as faithfully as we are able. The policy you have purchased will be in effect from this day forward, until your death, whether that occurs naturally or if it occurs after you receive end-of-life assistance."

I swallowed.

He asked, "Do you understand?"

"I do," I said.

I thought that there was some irony that it was the second time in my life that I'd used that particular two-word phrase in the context of "till death do us part."

Setting the client-derived parameters involved responding to a long series of questions, only a few of which were more complex than the ones that had been included in the recent review I'd done of my Healthcare Power of Attorney. The man doing the quizzing was, I guessed, in his early thirties. He was physically strong, and intellectually sharp, and not at all rattled by my status, or his own. He was a man unaccustomed to being messed with at any level. He posed the questions to me from memory in an uninspired monotone, the series of queries patiently and methodically elucidating my preferences about the threshold of disability or illness I would be willing to tolerate before my Death Angel benefits kicked in.

And, the threshold at which the policy became irrevocable.

As I answered his questions I realized I was setting the bar quite close to the ground. But I'd already acknowledged that my tolerance for disability was low, and felt confident that when the time came, I would be more content leaving this earth a few days too early than a few days too late.

The entire process took about twenty-five minutes.

When he said we were done, I waited for him to click off the recorder. He didn't. He said my name once again, spoke the location, and the date, and the time, and then asked me a series of final questions: "Do the questions I have just asked and the answers that you have just provided accurately and honestly portray your wishes in regard to the services of our company?"

"They do," I said.

"Have you been under any duress or coercion during the course of this interview?"

"I have not."

"Is there anything you wish to modify before we terminate this interview?"

I thought about it for a moment. I pointed at the recorder and I said, "I'd like a copy of that recording."

He smiled warmly, as though he thought I was kidding.

I said, "I wasn't kidding."

He said, "We don't permit any outstanding records of any arrangements with our organization. I'm sure you understand the rationale for our policy. We are protecting our clients as well as ourselves."

I did understand. My behavior as a young man had convinced me, however, of a universal truth: If you don't ask her, you rarely get laid. Until I was dead, I was likely to continue to ask.

"Please state your name, the date, the location, and the time," he said.

I did.

He said, "You forgot the year."

I said, "Two thousand and . . . four."

He flicked off the recorder.

"What happens now?" I asked.

"Within the hour, I'll encrypt this recording and enter it into our central storage system via a secure Internet connection. I will then physically destroy the flash memory. Your policy will be in effect by lunchtime. Congratulations."

"Will I be surprised again by any more visits on the side of some road?"

"No. You won't be disturbed again after today. I apologize if I startled you earlier. Privacy is paramount. Surprise helps us ensure it."

"Wait," I said.

"Yes?"

"Is her name really Lizzie?"

"No," he said, without hesitation. "But she told me she thought using it would get your attention, should the need arise."

TWENTY-SEVEN

As strange as it sounds to me now, within days I was able to forget that I'd actually hired the Death Angels to shadow my guardian angel, and I was able to forget that my new, highly paid, lethal angel was prepared to slay my dirt-cheap protective angel the moment that my health deteriorated enough that I had crossed the line of one of my client-derived parameters.

But nothing really changed about the way I lived my life. I worked when I worked. I tried to be the husband I'd promised Thea I'd be and the father Berkeley deserved. Most nights I rested my head on my pillow content with my efforts. I was a better husband than I'd ever imagined, and a much better father than I'd long feared I was capable of being.

I also played. I assumed my injuries from the fall in the Bugaboos would heal, so I was still planning to do the Ride the Rockies bike ride that summer with Jimmy, and I made arrangements to give hang gliding a shot while Thea and Cal and I were in Sun Valley that fall. I hadn't surfed since I was in my early twenties, but the use of Wave Runners had changed everything in big-wave surfing and Thea and I were talking about getting a house north of Kapalua over the Christmas holidays so I could try to catch a really big one. I was still hoping to finagle a way to get invited back to the annual gathering in

Bohemian Grove and hang out with the creative and powerful guys who gathered each summer on California's Russian River.

I had every intention of returning to the Bugaboos the following spring. And the divers among the boys and I were talking about making a pilgrimage to the grotto that had claimed Antonio's vitality in the deep water near Belize.

I'd stopped by to visit Antonio weekly for a few months after his accident, but the long sojourns by his bed soon seemed pointless and the chronic-care facility where he was existing in Denver—I still considered "living" a way-too-generous description of his lingering state—was too depressing for me to tolerate. I started making my visits to Marilyn, instead.

After a period of intense grief and some paralyzing confusion, she seemed to be moving on. Her beloved husband wasn't going to be getting any better. She knew it in her heart.

His spirit died long before his body would.

Not too long after I'd completed my business with the Death Angels, I got a call from a mutual friend that Will Durrell had succumbed to his illness, or from complications of the surgery that had temporarily extended his life, or some combination. Thea and I flew out to Chicago for his funeral. I spent much of the service and virtually all of the wake wondering how many of the mourners—many of whom were Will's peers, and mine—were clients of the Death Angels.

Was I the last one to hear about their peculiar service, or had I been one of the first?

TWENTY-EIGHT

The clock was running out on my second psychotherapy session of the day with Dr. Gregory and my tank was dry. Despite my midday nap and my post-nap shower I was suffering the consequences of all the activity. What had been nothing but fumes in my tank earlier in the day were now mere rumors of fumes. I considered using my few remaining watts of power to stand up and say a definitive good-bye to my therapist, but decided it would take even less of my waning energy to allow the remaining time to simply evaporate into the ether.

If this were football, I'd be the guy taking a knee.

Dr. Gregory, I'd already learned, tended to treat silence like fine wine—he consumed it slowly and didn't jostle it unnecessarily—so I didn't expect any complaints from him as I allowed the seconds to fritter away.

He surprised me. After less than a minute of silence and one power yawn—mine, not his—he asked, "There's another visit to come? Yes?"

"With you?" I said, surprised that he'd asked. Was I witnessing signs of therapeutic insecurity?

"With Adam," he said. "And you. Another story you need to tell."

Ah, of course.

It was clear he had an eye on the clock, too, and that he wasn't content just to allow the time to expire.

"Why do you think that?" I said. I admit that I was curious how he'd reached his conclusion, but I also thought it would be easier for me if he was the one who was talking. That way I could continue to practice energy conservation, and I could keep the clock ticking.

He didn't answer me. We both knew he didn't have to.

I said, "I thought facts were crap."

By then we were both aware that I'd adopted his line as a mantra—I did like it—and I expected it to function for me the way it had functioned for him, as an all-purpose conversational trump card.

He'd been playing this game longer than I had, though, and he had other ideas about my facts-are-crap ploy. "I'm not interested in how long you were in line for the Matterhorn when you took Adam to Disneyland. I don't care if he snagged a foul ball at the Rockies game, or how many trout he caught when you guys were fly-fishing the South Platte. I'm interested in what Adam's visit, or visits, meant to you. Or better, mean to you."

"Why?"

"Because you'd like me to be interested, or perhaps more to the point, because you need me to be interested. Because I suspect that it's a big piece of why you've come to see me." Maybe I looked unconvinced. He added, "And because planes don't glide forever with their engines out."

That got my attention.

"Okay," I said. "Maybe next time we'll talk about Adam's next visit to our house."

"You get tired," he said. "Really tired."

I didn't want to admit it. I considered lying before I said, "Yes. It's part of what I'm dealing with."

"Your . . . condition?"

"Yes."

"What else?"

"Nausea. My balance isn't what it was. The nausea and the balance problems aren't unexpected. The doctors are puzzled by the fatigue."

He nodded a nod of acceptance. He knew I hadn't provided all the pieces to the puzzle and he wasn't planning to waste any effort on solving it until I did.

"Something else, I think," he said. "I'll hazard a guess that you're not accustomed to this. To talking about things that are . . . important."

He'd selected that last word carefully. His choice got an instant rise from me. "Oh, intimacy? Is that what you're talking about? Shit, now that's different, that's fresh. Are you suggesting I have *issues*?" I said, parroting a criticism I'd heard flung my way a hundred times by a dozen women over a span of at least a score of years.

I was kind of sensitive about it.

"Don't kid yourself," he said. His voice had adopted none of my intensity. "This isn't intimacy, what's happening in this room between you and me. Openness, maybe. I underline 'maybe' because I don't know you well enough to know that for sure. But I do know that for this to become intimate, it has to include something else, too. At a bare minimum."

"What the hell are you talking about?" My protest was lame; I was a punch-drunk boxer defending myself against a superior opponent's agile right cross. But I had to try to mount some kind of protection—if spilling my guts to this guy about Adam wasn't intimacy, I didn't have any in me.

"You could walk a block over to the West End Tavern"—he recognized from my face that I didn't know what the hell the West End Tavern was—"it's a good saloon over on Pearl Street—and pick out a seat at the bar and tell some stranger doing tequila shots everything you've told me. About Adam, his mom, about dying. Everything. Doesn't make you intimate with the guy."

Point. "Okay. What would? Would I have to wait until last call and invite him home with me?"

I thought it was a pretty good line. He didn't seem so impressed. I glanced at the clock and tried to will the seconds to tick away faster. The big, sweeping hand seemed to slow down, of course.

Choosing to ignore my juvenile sarcasm, he said, "What's missing is something that Adam had within moments of meeting you that day."

By then I was lost. A blind man bombarded by white noise. I forced patience into my voice. "And what is that exactly?"

"The capacity to hurt you."

I wasn't following him. "Two questions," I said. "Why would I want someone to have that power? And why is it important?"

"One answer. It's a necessary, but not a sufficient, criterion for intimacy."

Gregory waited for me to catch up. When it was apparent that I wasn't able to follow his tracks, he went on. "You were vulnerable to Adam. From his first words to you on your front porch. 'Is that my sister?' I think is what he said. From that moment on you've been vulnerable to that kid."

"I still am," I said, without any reflection.

None was necessary. I was vulnerable to that kid. No argument.

"Yes," my therapist said.

"Okay." My "okay" was a conversational "so what?"

"Without vulnerability," Gregory said, "there is no intimacy."

I recognized the repetition, and could identify the progression in his thinking. I guessed, too, at the next move he wanted me to make. "And you're thinking I should become vulnerable to you? That's your point?"

"Over fifty years ago, a neo-Freudian named Karen Horney warned against the 'tyranny of the shoulds.' It's good counsel, I think. Anyway, I didn't say that you should become vulnerable to me, and I didn't mean to imply it. But I have noticed that when you tell me something that might leave you a step closer to feeling vulnerable with me, you tend to go quickly on the attack."

"Then what's your point? I'm exhausted. I'm ready to go home."

He didn't reply.

He was telling me something. I was too tired or too thick to know what. I was almost—almost—as curious as I was aggravated. "What do you say we do this again?" I said.

"Sounds like a good idea," Dr. Gregory deadpanned.

I pulled myself to my feet. In my most sardonic tone, I said, "This is helpful? Right? It's good for me?"

"You get to decide," he said.

"I decide? What's your job?"

"That's a good question. I'm still at a loss as to exactly what our goals are. I don't know why you're coming to see me. Because you're sick? Because you're dying? Something else entirely? Something to do with Adam? That's where I'd put my money—on Adam—but I don't know, and I readily admit that it's hard for me to hit a target that I'm not allowed to see."

"Yeah, well," I said. "Welcome to the club."

He tapped his watch. "I have more time, if you would like to continue."

"Right now?"

"Right now."

"I thought that was against the rules. I'd always heard you guys were big on 'Your time is up. Get out.' "

"There are lots of common misconceptions about therapists and therapy. But that's not one. As a general rule we are a little time-conscious. To a fault, I admit. I do make exceptions sometimes."

"I'm exhausted." I yawned to prove it.

"I know," he said. "I'm sorry."

"I don't want your pity."

"I wasn't offering you any. From my point of view, your fatigue is a good thing. Your defenses won't be so flexible or so resilient. I was offering some empathy, however. I'm not asking anything of you right now that you haven't asked of yourself at other times."

My face revealed that I still wasn't following him.

"I'm thinking about the story you told me, and the courage—or stubbornness—it took to ski out of the Bugaboos with broken ribs, a separated shoulder, and a fractured wrist. Compared to that, staying with me for another twenty minutes is nothing, right?"

I sighed. I considered explaining the prostate-exam standard to him but decided against it.

Jesus.

"Okay," I said. "Adam's next visit."

Vulnerability, I was thinking. *How the hell does he know this is all about vulnerability?*

TWENTY-NINE

Adam had come back to Colorado seven months after his first visit. By then, it was 2003 and he was fifteen. He somehow knew he'd find us in our Denver home, not up in Ridgway.

I'd told myself it was a guess on his part.

Bella called Thea and warned us that she thought her son was on his way. She couldn't predict how long he would choose to stay. The mothers of my children mutually decided that we should be surprised about Adam's imminent arrival at my home, which meant that we had to keep the secret from Berkeley, whose ability to sustain a ruse was questionable at best.

I wasn't offered a vote about the plan. The women had already computed, correctly, that their united maternal voting bloc could render superfluous any bias I might possess against the plan.

This time Adam didn't get to our house until well after dark. Thea was giving Berk a bath, so I answered the door.

"Hi, Dad," he said.

The words caused me to break into a wide smile, not because they were spoken in any fashion that was particularly heartwarming, but rather because the delivery was so spot-on ironic.

"Hey," I said. "Good to see you, Adam. Come on in."

Adam carried his daypack over both shoulders. He wasn't really dressed warmly enough. He followed me inside.

"Can you stay a while?" I asked.

"We'll see," he said. He studied my face for a few seconds before he added, "Bella called, didn't she?"

At times he called his mother by her first name. Other times he didn't.

"Yeah. But I'm supposed to pretend she didn't."

"You're a terrible actor."

"Actually, that depends on the role I'm playing. This isn't one of my best. Come on in." He joined me inside the house. I said, "I take it missing school's not a problem for you?"

"Hardly. I don't go." His tone turned puckish before he added, "The world is my campus. Is Broadway asleep already?"

"Broadway?"

"My sister. The little drama queen. I want to see her."

I laughed and said, "She is a little drama queen, isn't she?" Adam had Cal pegged accurately; Berkeley was a kid who was born to hit her marks and nail her lines. If the world was my son's campus, the same world was my daughter's stage. "Thea's giving her a bath right now. She'll be excited to see you. You can read to her before she goes to sleep; she loves it when you do that. Are you hungry?"

"Starving." He lowered his daypack off his shoulders, dropped it onto the floor, and preceded me down the hall toward the kitchen. "Don't worry, I'll play along with whatever Bella and Thea worked out. You can go ahead and be shocked that I'm here."

"You're so sure I wasn't part of it?"

"I know you," he said.

You know me?

I made my son some food. A couple of chicken quesadillas and a big bowl of tortilla chips. I pounded an avocado, a tomato, and a serrano chile into a passable guacamole, and I popped the cap off an icy bottle of blackberry Izze. It felt damn good to watch him wolf it all down.

We learned over the course of his visit that Adam had been homeschooled since the sixth grade. Bella had recognized his unusual intellectual gifts much earlier than that and had tried to keep him stimulated at various gifted and talented programs near their home until she tracked one down at Johns Hopkins that allowed him to take the SAT when he was twelve. He got a 1460 combined that year and she immediately gave up on the public schools and started homeschooling him. He aced a repeat administration of the test—a perfect 1600—one year later.

I knew Adam wasn't a typical teenager, which meant nothing more than that he wasn't anything like I had been as a teenager. I was no expert on adolescence, but I could make the claim with confidence that my son and I inhabited different teenage galaxies. I couldn't be sure what was chicken and what was egg—whether Adam's unusual adolescent demeanor was a factor of his intellectual gifts or whether his social idiosyncrasies were the result of the inevitable differences in influences that come from homeschooling.

During that second visit to our house he was reading Aeschylus as part of a self-directed adherence to the St. John's College great-books curriculum. When he tried to engage me in a discussion of *The Choephoroe* in the context of Aeschylus's influence on the development of tragedy, he seemed disappointed that I hadn't read it.

He would have been even more disappointed had I admitted to him that I'd never even heard of it.

I didn't admit it.

Yeah, that vulnerability thing.

Adam kept a Rubik's Cube in his daypack. He pulled it out one morning while we were sitting at the breakfast table and bet me ten bucks he could solve the puzzle in less than a minute. I scrambled it and handed it back to him; he took my ten dollars fifty-five seconds later. "Double or nothing, thirty seconds this time," he offered, after returning the cube to me so that I could once again scramble it. I twisted it up good. Twenty-eight seconds later we exchanged his ten for my twenty. He immediately offered me back my money. "That wasn't nice," he said. "Of me."

"What's your record with that thing?"

"That was my record. Twenty-eight seconds. But I can almost always get near thirty if I'm not distracted."

"Congratulations."

"It's not exactly a cure for cancer," he said dismissively.

He was right, but I told him to keep the twenty.

In response to my question about how he usually got hold of spending money, he explained that he made good money ridding his mom's friends' personal computers of viruses and worms and spyware. He also played poker online. With the limited stakes his mother would let him wager, he averaged about twenty bucks an hour. Bella had set up the account for him. His cyber-poker buddies knew him as "belladonna" and thought he was a thirty-eight-year-old depressed single mother in Cincinnati.

"How did you get here from Ohio?" I asked.

"Took the train to Denver. I met somebody at Union Station who gave me a ride down this way. Then I walked."

"That's kind of risky, isn't it?" I asked, obviously paternal.

"I'm a good judge of people," he said. He sounded

perfectly confident that he could sniff out a bad guy at twenty paces. Juvenile bravado? With this kid I couldn't be sure.

I said, "My dad, your grandfather, was a smart guy. Not as bright as you seem to be, but smart. But I don't think you got any of those genes from me. Or if you did, they're recessive. I suspect they're part of your mom's contribution to your genetic bounty."

"Never," he said, "underestimate the power of mutation."

I swallowed a laugh. Was my son that funny, and that dry, or was the comment a dig at his mother? I couldn't quite decide.

THIRTY

"**What** are you working on?" he asked me early on in the visit. "At work. Anything I can look at?"

I caught myself before I muttered "Oh, nothing much," which is how I would answer the question ninety-nine times out of a hundred with nine people out of ten. "Work" for me was a couple dozen smart people doing research and development on a few —we hoped—revolutionary medical technology concepts. A couple of the ideas were mine, but the most promising weren't. The R&D was technical and dry; the concepts that were most interesting were also proprietary. But I told Adam the truth. "We're exploring the development of small implantable nerve stimulators that might help people regulate their appetite. To fight obesity."

"Yeah?"

"It's early, but it's promising."

"Big market," he said. "Literally, and . . . well, literally. What nerve are you focusing on? Vagus?"

"Yes." *How would he know that?* When I was his age I couldn't have identified the vagus nerve unless possessing that knowledge would somehow help me get into some girl's underwear.

"Do you have a prototype?" Adam asked.

I nodded. "Not implantable, but the technology's mocked up."

"Doing any animal studies?"

I couldn't believe I was having this conversation with a fifteen-year-old. I routinely dealt with investment bankers with Wharton MBAs who needed the paint-by-numbers version.

"Yes, sheep."

"Sheep. Huh. Sheep are a good model?"

"Turns out they are."

"Who knew?" he said.

Holy shit, I thought. *Holy shit.*

He came to work with me the next day, and every day after that until he left town again. When what I did at work bored him—basically when I went to meetings—he read one of the classics he kept stuffed in his daypack, or he played the latest computer games on our company network, or he followed our IT girl from machine to machine as she made her rounds. I guessed—I even hoped—that he was tailing her because she was gorgeous, but she pulled me aside and told me that Adam was a natural with Java and that she'd learned a few things from him about hardware firewalls and open-port vulnerability.

By then, I wasn't surprised.

Everybody in the office seemed to like having Adam around. Although far from gregarious socially, he had an endearing way with people and usually left smiles in his wake.

When he was asked, he told my colleagues that his mother and I had once been close, and that he was doing an internship with me for school. He said he was "shadowing" me.

The third day at the office he took over an unused workstation and began playing with an idea for an implantable device that would irritate the common duct every time a person's stomach reached a certain degree of fullness. He began to familiarize himself with our CAD software and he peppered our engineers with questions about precisely what fraction of a volt would be sufficiently irritating without being debilitating, and challenged them about the reliability of available mechanisms for objectively measuring gastric fullness.

Adam's mother suffered from recurrent gallstones and he knew from observing her agony that the pain of having a stone in her common bile duct was a stunningly successful appetite suppressant. I suggested to him that there might be some ethical considerations he would have to contend with in regard to the commercial applications of his proposed device.

Torturing people in order to get them to avoid Burger King and Krispy Kremes might be looked down upon by the FDA.

I also grabbed the opportunity to reveal that he had an uncle at Yale with whom he might want to discuss his ideas. An ethicist.

"Yeah? I have an uncle at Yale? A teacher?"

"Professor. Yeah."

"Does he know about me?"

Try honesty. "No."

Without any obvious bitterness, he asked, "You're embarrassed about me, aren't you? How come you haven't told him I exist?" The questions were half-tease. Only half.

"Anybody ever tell you you're kind of blunt?"

He tried not to smile, but he smiled.

Inadvertently, I'd just complimented him.

I said, "I'm no more embarrassed about you than you are about me, Adam. What are you telling people here? That I was 'close' to your mother? That you're an intern? My shadow? Please. Who's embarrassed about whom?"

"Consider it an act of generosity on my part. I'm

sparing you having to deal with the whole bastard question among your employees. That can't be a good topic for the lunchroom or the water cooler." He watched me open and close my mouth before he went on. "You were explaining your rationale for hiding my existence from your Bulldog brother. Go on, I'm waiting."

He was better at sarcasm and irony than I was, which simultaneously troubled me and filled me with pride. His skill had an additional side effect, one I was certain he intended—half the time I couldn't tell whether or not to take him seriously.

"I didn't tell him about all of . . . " *Try honesty.* "My brother—your uncle—has ALS."

He exhaled in a solitary *poof.* "Well then, there you go. Now—now—it makes perfect sense. Everybody knows that suddenly finding out you have an illegitimate nephew is like a death sentence for people with ALS. Say no more."

"Adam," I said. I said only his name because I didn't have any idea how to rationalize my secrecy any better than I already had. His focused mockery had left me without ammunition.

"How sick is my uncle?" he asked.

I didn't want to tell him he had an uncle, and in the next breath tell him that his uncle was dying. That's why I hadn't told him he had an uncle.

"You know about ALS? Lou Gehrig's disease?"

"Football, right?" He waited a moment for me to stick my foot in my mouth by going into a paternal rap about the maudlin legend of the baseball Hall of Famer. When I didn't bite right away, he said, "I'm more of a fan of Stephen Hawking, actually. If you'd been paying attention, you might have been able to guess that."

Okay, Adam knew about ALS. "Your Uncle Connie is pretty sick."

He looked at me sideways. "I have an uncle named Connie?"

After Adam had been with us a few days Thea came to the not-too-surprising conclusion that his visit was an audition. "He's thinking of moving here, into our house. He is," she insisted that night in bed. "Isn't that exciting? That he might come live with us?"

Thea's enthusiasm for my son was heartwarming and felt supremely generous. His relationship with Cal—he did indeed call her "Broadway"—was a joy to watch. And although it was my nature to focus on the inevitable bumps that would certainly be found on that road, the prospect of having him come to live under our roof was exciting to me. The possibility also left me struggling with echoes of feelings that I probably should have been struggling with that night in Buckhead with Bella when I was twenty-three years old: *What would be the consequences of this for her?*

I wondered out loud to Thea whether she thought Bella was aware that Adam was testing the waters in Colorado. Thea assured me that such a thing wasn't possible. I tended to agree. I'd only known him for six months, had spent fewer than ten days with him, and I was admitting to myself that I loved the boy in some essential way that I couldn't explain by anything I'd ever experienced before in my life except the birth of my daughter. Bella had known Adam since before his birth and had been an active, caring parent to him for fifteen years. Could she really tolerate sharing him with a man who, for that entire time, hadn't known either of them had even existed?

No, I couldn't believe she could.

Adam left before dawn the morning after he'd spent nine nights in our home.

Thea stared for a long moment at his empty bed in the guest room before she pulled her bathrobe tight around her, set her lips into a flat line, and nodded as though she'd expected his exit to come in the dark. She marched into the kitchen and phoned Bella and told her that Adam was once again on the road.

I'd purchased him a mobile phone while he was with us, and I tried the number repeatedly in the first few hours after we discovered that he'd left. I wanted him to turn around. Accepting that his immediate return wasn't in the cards, I wanted to say good-bye to him and I wanted to offer him transportation wherever it was he wanted to go next. Each time I called I was routed to his voice mailbox. I suspected that he didn't even have his phone's power turned on. His voice-mail message was "Hey, this is Adam. Odds are I won't ever pick up your message, but if you feel better leaving one, please go right ahead. Hello."

I felt better leaving a message. I said, "It's your dad. Have a safe trip. We love you. I love you. Come back anytime. If you need some money, check the zippered pocket on the side of your daypack. If you need anything else, I'm here."

THIRTY-ONE

"**We** getting anywhere yet?" I asked my therapist as the session wrapped up.

Dr. Gregory said, "Somewhere. Yes, I think. But it's a big country, a lot of ground to cover. Mostly though, that's going to be your call."

I ignored the qualifier. "Good," I said. "I'm beat. Next time."

He responded without looking at his calendar. "I can do the same two times on Monday."

"I was thinking later in the week."

"Monday," he said.

"Okay," I said. I was tempted to argue just for appearances. But I didn't. Monday was fine. God I was tired.

"That's when you'll talk about how Adam has hurt you?" he asked. He was scribbling in his appointment book.

I kept expecting things to wind down so I could get out the door with some sense of peace. Instead he kept raising the volume. "You're that sure that he did? That Adam hurt me?"

"It doesn't matter how sure I am. I'm wrong a lot."

I laughed. "Ah, I see. That's why I pay you so well? Because you're wrong a lot?"

"You pay me so well because my persistence—some do call it stubbornness—is a decent match for your resistance. The surprise about all this? About psychotherapy? I don't always have to be right to be helpful. I just need to be able to help you be right."

"I'm too tired to make any sense of what you just said."

"No, you're not. But if you want to leave under that illusion, there's not much I can do about it."

I felt like flipping him off.

But mostly I felt like getting the hell out of his office. I made it almost to the door before he spoke again.

"I think you know why you're here, why you've come to see me for psychotherapy. I don't."

I was using the doorknob for support. He was absolutely right. I did know why I was in psychotherapy, and if I wasn't going to trust him with knowing, I was wasting my time.

"Let me think about that," I said. I didn't wait for him to reply. I closed the door behind me as I left.

Once my extra-innings psychotherapy session was over, I found the Prius where I'd left it at a meter on Ninth Street across from the St. Julien Hotel. The meter, of course, had expired. A parking ticket under the windshield wiper reflected the efficiency of downtown Boulder's parking patrol officers. I grabbed the citation, threw it onto the floor of the backseat, and promptly forgot it existed.

Parking tickets are one of the many things in life that become less consequential for people who are dying.

The kid who worked at the FBO at the airport seemed to be waiting for me. He told me the plane was ready. Fuel tanks were full. I gave him another twenty bucks and asked him to keep an eye on the car for me.

"Your pilots are inside the office. You want me to get them?"

"Please."

"Want the car covered up again?"

"You bet. Trunk's open. Cover's in there."

"Back soon?"

"Couple of days. Tell me something: How old are you?"

"Sixteen."

Adam's age.

"You fly?"

"I have my license. This is how I get money for flight time. I like being around planes."

I nodded and gestured toward the airplane that was ready to take me back over the Divide. "You want to fly it sometime?"

"You serious?"

"Right seat, but yeah, I'm serious. I'll talk to Mary—she's the pilot—see what I can do."

THIRTY-TWO

I could argue that I ran out of time that day in therapy. Or I could argue that I ran out of energy. Both statements are true. But what is also true is that I left Gregory's office that afternoon with some things left unsaid.

Important things. Crucial things. Next time, I told myself. Next time I see him, I'll tell him.

He'd known I was holding back, which truly pissed me off.

Next time.

Here's the prologue to some of what had gone unsaid:

The phone rang late the night that Adam had left our house after his second visit. After a bumbling response to her series of questions about why her brother was gone and why he wasn't doing that night's bedtime routine with her, I'd read that evening's stories to Berk and tucked her into bed. Thea was in the master bath enjoying a soak in the tub.

The caller ID lit up on the tiny screen on the portable phone. It read "Wireless Caller." Could have been anybody, but I knew it was him.

"Thanks for the money," Adam said after I answered. "It helps."

The money's easy, I thought but didn't say. *I have all you need. Ever.*

"My pleasure," I said, forcing calm into my voice. "You okay? You make it home?"

"Tomorrow, I think. Yeah, I'm fine."

Where are you tonight? Right now. Are you safe?

I didn't ask. I played it fatherly cool. "It was great seeing you, Adam. Terrific. I hope you come back soon."

Silence, hollow and cold, filled the territory between us for five seconds or so before he said, "I told you my stepfather was killed by a drunk driver."

The sudden change in direction jolted me like unexpected turbulence during a flight. I checked the tautness of my seat belt and fumbled a reply that I hoped would keep him talking. "When you were seven, yeah."

"Well, he was. Killed by a drunk driver, I mean."

I'm quick on my feet when skis are attached to them and I'm being forced to read a fall line on a hillside dotted with moguls. In relationships, I'm not quite so nimble when I'm forced to read subtle lines of communication. All I could manage for my son right then was, "I'm sorry, Adam. It had to have been . . . awful for you to lose him. It's a tough age."

I could hear him breathing into the cell phone that I'd given him. The signal was strong and consistent; I suspected he was stationary someplace while he was talking with me. Where? Down the block? Across the country? In the parking lot of a bus station in Omaha? I didn't know.

"He was the drunk driver," Adam said.

I didn't get it at first. My son's words were a simple declarative, but I couldn't make sense of the sentence. "What?" I said in confusion.

"My stepfather was the drunk driver. He killed himself. Ran into a tree."

Oh shit. I got it. "Adam, I—"

He terminated the connection.

I held the dead phone to my ear for most of a minute,

hoping that some magic would allow the conversation with my son to resume.

I was feeling that I'd done something terribly wrong, but I wasn't wise enough to know what.

For the rest of the evening I felt the resonance of Adam's revelation about the circumstances of his stepfather's death deep inside me, but I couldn't put what I was feeling into words.

Thea could.

An hour later, she and I were in bed. She was lying prone between my legs propped on a couple of small pillows. Her head was resting on my lap so that I could rub some knots out of the firm muscles on her upper back. Her flesh was still warm and supple from her bath. She was moaning—nothing sexual—she was just letting me know I'd found the right place. I was finishing describing the short, poignant phone conversation I'd had with Adam.

"He was telling you what a huge risk he's taking with you," she said, almost immediately.

"How so?" I asked, simultaneously wondering how some people—specifically my wife—could come to confident conclusions about other people's motives so easily. I didn't get it.

"He's vulnerable," she said.

There was that word again.

"To us? We've been great. Terrific, stupendous. Given the circumstances, I give us an A. Or I give me an A. You get an A plus."

I felt her body quake with the force of a short, ironic laugh. The laugh said, "You don't get it." She said, "We have been great—you've been great—but that's not the point. Adam's vulnerable to you. You're the important one here. He just told you that the only father he has ever known left him suddenly. Carelessly. Selfishly. The women in his life have proven to be a little bit more reliable."

Was she including herself? Of course she was.

"What's his message, though? I don't know what he was saying. Why did he hang up? When he decided to come here and reach out to us, it was risky for everybody. You, me. Adam, Bella. Even Cal. Everyone's affected by it. Everyone will be affected by what happens next."

Thea sat back on her knees and pulled the comforter around her waist. Her breasts were at my eye level and her nipples seemed especially pink.

The bath. Right.

She placed her left hand on top of mine and squeezed. "Last night, late, when I got up to see why Berk was awake? Remember? Adam was up, too. I sat with him for a bit. He was watching all your old Memorial Day–weekend DVDs. All the crazy stuff you've done with your friends. He asked me if you still did . . . things like that. I told him about the trip you've been planning to the Bugaboos next spring."

"That's fine. So what?"

"Don't you see? Adam told you that his stepfather was reckless. Driving drunk? Remember? And he's letting you know what an impact that had on him. Think about his loss. Go ahead."

I thought about it for a moment and shrugged. "It must have been awful for him," I said.

My wife sighed at me. "Extrapolate, babe. He sees what . . . you do. With your life. That call? He's telling you how frightened he is. He's asking you not to be reckless."

"Reckless? What kind of reckless? I know what I'm doing."

She sighed. "You take lots of risks, babe. He probably suspected that about you. Now he knows that about you.

And the truth is that it scares him. That's what he's saying."

"I don't drive drunk."

"Not drunk, but you drive sometimes after you've had something to drink. But that's not what worries him, that's not his big fear. Look at your life, babe. You race cars on Friday nights with your buddies. You dive wrecks. You take your mountain bike places no sane person would go. You're about to heli-ski the damn Bugaboos— again. You fly into weather you should fly around. He knows all that about you. He's seen the pictures all over the house of you and your friends and all your macho adventures. Adam's idea of the great outdoors is taking a walk on the High Line or fly-fishing in the South Platte. He doesn't understand all the X Games crap you guys do. He's not a kid with any spare testosterone. Risk for Adam was walking up to our front door that first time and knocking. He took that risk and now—now—he's vulnerable to you and he wants some assurance that it's safe to put his heart in your hands. He's scared to death that he's going to lose you the same way he lost his stepfather. Think about it; it makes perfect sense."

To her, maybe. "His stepfather killed himself by drinking and driving. That's all he was saying—that he doesn't want me to do that. He's a kid. He's concrete. That's how they think."

Thea's eyes told me that she was trying hard to be patient with me.

I could read people if the question was about power. I was great at poker, decent at chess. Put me in a business negotiation and I could identify my adversary's bottom line before she recognized she had one.

Seduction? I was practiced and reliable.

But nuance and love? Sadly, until I met Thea, I was almost illiterate.

Thea took a deep breath and exhaled slowly before she said, "You think Adam is a concrete thinker? No, don't answer that. Don't. I don't even want to hear that rationalization. Because he's not, not even close. From where Adam stands, risk is . . . risk. It's a simple thing, but monumental for him. I think you should step back and try to see all this from his point of view."

I saw the vague outlines of a plot developing, and shot from the hip to defend my lifestyle. "I should just give it all up? All the things I love to do?" I was a little ambushed by the fact that my words sounded so petulant and so immature. Even to me. "I'm sorry," I said immediately. "That didn't come out right."

Thea, I think, suspected the words came out exactly right and that I wasn't as sorry as I would like to appear to be.

She said, "What's more important to you? Those crazy things you love to do? Or the people who love you? Is that really such a tough call?"

"Thea . . ." Belatedly, I realized that we were no longer talking only about Adam's feelings about all of my "X Games crap." Thea had some deep feelings of her own.

"You want me to back off, too, Thea? You've never said anything. I thought you—"

She stopped me with a quick shake of her head. "He only has one father now. When he came here the first time, he didn't know what he was going to find when he knocked on our door. Me? I knew what I was getting into with you when I said 'I do.' My eyes were wide open. But . . . earning Adam's love—long-term love—may be trickier for you than it was to earn mine."

Her tone wasn't self-congratulatory; it was self-mocking. The self-mocking tone made it all quite disconcerting to me.

"What does that mean, Thea? What are you saying?"

She pulled her hand away from mine, climbed over me, and rolled onto her side of the bed. She pulled the covers up under her armpits and was staring at the ceiling when she said, "I hope you get another chance to ask your son what he thinks you should do. I bet he has some thoughts. Some perspective on all this. You know, about responsibility, and . . . and recklessness and . . . loss. Something that might help you understand what he told you tonight on the phone."

"Thea."

"I'll raise our daughter by myself if I have to. Adam, too, if I get the chance. Happily. I will. I love you, and I knew what I was getting into when I fell in love with you. But if the time comes that I have to bury you, and it turns out that you bailed out on all of us—all of us—for some stupid, selfish, macho thrill, I'll . . ." She left the thought unfinished, except for a throaty growl.

I suspected the omitted part had something to do with defecating on my grave.

THIRTY-THREE

Things were not the same with Adam.

After his dramatic disclosure about the true circumstances of his stepfather's death, and my obviously inadequate response, Adam never expressed any interest in moving in with us in Colorado. He'd stayed with Bella in Cincinnati and continued his homeschooling adventure.

Thea stubbornly maintained that my even more stubborn adherence to a lifestyle that was chock-full of risk had short-circuited Adam's desire to move west. I wasn't convinced. I placated myself by rationalizing that it was my son's risk-avoidance, and not my risk-approaching, that was the real issue. He was looking for an excuse to stay within the odd cocoon he enjoyed with his mom, and my X Games lifestyle provided him with a convenient reason to do it.

My wife and I disagreed about Adam's retreat from our home and our lives, and chose not to argue about it. We didn't exactly agree to disagree. We merely agreed not to bicker.

Although Bella had previously been unwilling to cash the checks that Thea and I had been sending to Cincinnati to help support my son, she finally relented and began to allow us to contribute financially to Adam's care. Bella, whose employer had recently stopped providing his staff with health-care coverage, was especially grateful that I put Adam on our family health insurance policy.

I was thrilled to provide the support. But I recognized the irony, too: Now that Adam was excluding me from his life, I was becoming a caricature of an absentee father. To cushion my hurt, I focused my paternal energy where it was always accepted with a wide smile: Berkeley.

Thea and Adam and I settled into what for me was an unsatisfying routine. Thea and I phoned him frequently. He didn't answer. We left messages. He rarely returned our calls. When he did call, the conversations were brief and awkward. He'd ask about his sister. They'd talk and laugh.

We frequently invited him to join us at our home in the mountains in Ridgway. He would say he'd think about it. We'd never get an actual reply. He never showed up on that doorstep.

He didn't totally avoid seeing us. We managed to lay eyes on him occasionally. But the visits were in Ohio, not in Colorado; they lasted for a night or two, not a week or two. We took him out to dinner at neighborhood places he liked near his home in Cincinnati. He gave us good-natured lessons on how to eat a three-way without getting covered in chili and cheese. He laughed and giggled with his sister and was cordial and friendly with Thea. But when he was alone with me he acted like he had someplace else to be.

The biggest change in my life? The connection—the one that had been growing between us since that first day he'd asked me if Cal was his sister—disappeared. My son treated me like a distant uncle.

Each time I saw him, each time we spoke, though, I fell more and more in love with him.

Each time I yearned to get a little closer.

Each time he eluded me.

*

I did manage to finagle one more extended visit with Adam. It took my best bait.

At my invitation, Adam agreed to accompany me on a visit to see Connie before his uncle's health declined any further. The father-and-son trip to visit the brother and uncle took place in 2004 shortly before I broke my wrist in the Bugaboos—and therefore before I knew anything about the Death Angels—but not before Connie's illness had robbed him of his ability to maneuver around his own house in his chair.

Adam refused to let me pick him up in Cincinnati in my plane on the way east, so we took separate commercial flights to New York City. My first chance to hug him didn't happen until he strolled up to me on the platform at Penn Station only five minutes before the Acela was scheduled to head north toward New Haven.

Our embrace was awkward. I hugged him, forcing myself to temper the exuberance I felt. He didn't hug me back.

Morosely, I thought that the physical act was a lot like hugging my disabled brother. Emotionally, it was more like hugging a statue.

Connie and Adam connected during the visit like two flat surfaces painted with contact cement. Connie was wheelchair-bound and both his energy and his mobility were gone by then, but despite his limitations he and Adam were inseparable for the few days my son and I were in New Haven. When Connie slept or rested Adam didn't hang out with me, he hung out with Felix. Adam peppered Felix with questions in fluent Spanish about his uncle, or about Guatemala. He was fascinated by Felix's stories about the history of hostilities and the local politics in Chocola. He had a particular curiosity about the plight of the local coffee economy. I was hurt at being excluded, and actually considered the possibility that Adam was using his relationship with Connie as retaliation for whatever it was that had fractured between him and me.

On another level, I was touched by Adam's connection with my brother. I saw evidence of what was missing between my son and me, and I felt an unfamiliar emotion, too.

Envy.

Adam made long solo walks to campus to spend time in Yale's libraries and to visit the philosophy department where Connie had taught for so long. He read every word that his uncle had written since he'd arrived at Yale as an assistant professor. He somehow tracked down videotapes and DVDs of lectures Connie had given and even got hold of a copy of the old dissertation his uncle had written at Penn more than two decades before on the ethical considerations of post–World War II foreign policy in Europe.

Connie gave Adam gifts of books from his personal library—dozens of volumes of texts that were full of his penciled annotations. To ensure that the tomes wouldn't be bruised or battered on their journey from Connecticut to Ohio, my son and I packed the books up as though they were Fabergé eggs. I took pleasure in the mundane tasks of wrapping and shipping because the chores gave me time with my son.

For Adam? I could've been the guy behind the counter at the local pack 'n' ship store.

That trip to New Haven was all about nephew and uncle, not about father and son.

THIRTY-FOUR

Remember the phone call that interrupted the board meeting I was attending in that wonderful conference room that floats above infinity on the hillside above Santa Barbara?

The phone call that caused me to gather my things, interrupt the meeting, and stumble from the room?

That telephone call?

No? How about the riff of my ring tone?

Ob-la-di, ob-la-da, life goes on, bra/La la how the life goes on.

Not mine. Not my life. My life seemed to stop right then and there.

With that phone call.

The bones in my wrist—the one I'd busted in the Bugaboos in the spring of 2004—hadn't healed properly. My arm was still casted more than five months after I followed Newton's Law and the crumbled cornice down that icy chute in Canada. Every time my local orthopod did a final X-ray to check how my two fractured bones were fusing, he would shake his head and say, "You're really a slow healer. You know that?"

I didn't know that. I'd always thought that I'd bounced back from injuries like a kid.

I remember being puzzled for a minute or two. But that was all.

The woman on the phone that day, the one who'd surprised me with the call on my cell during the board meeting, was an orthopedic surgeon at the Health Sciences Center in Denver. She was also the Rocky Mountains' designated wrist goddess—"the best wrist guy in the state"—my local doc had called her. By any measure, she was brilliant; she was an Israeli who had trained at Brown and Harvard, and had ended up in Denver to be close to the mountains. I'd heard from friends who had seen her in the back bowls at Vail that watching her attack the bumps was a physics lessons and a dance recital all at once. But her bedside manner? Think about the attitude an Israeli soldier might adopt at a border checkpoint in the West Bank: That was the atmosphere in her clinic.

Cuddly, she wasn't. But she was the doc that I'd been referred to after my wrist bones seemed immured from the prospect of healing.

My wrist, and its bones' prolonged reluctance to fuse, had caused my Israeli genius some head-scratching angst. After making a not-too-subtle insinuation that the root cause of the medical mystery was probably my fault—it certainly wasn't hers—she'd questioned me at great length about my diet, my current health, and my exercise habits. I'm sure my aggravation at her digression showed as she'd focused particular attention on three things that to me seemed immaterial to understanding the genesis of my recalcitrant scaphoid: I'd had a recent pattern of headaches, some intermittent mild nausea, and I'd had a cartoonish episode on the treadmill during which I'd lost my balance and almost broken my other wrist.

After hearing my litany of woes, she'd mumbled something in a language I didn't speak and ordered—yes, ordered—me to submit to a slew of additional tests, including a bone scan and two MRIs, one of my wrist, the other of my head.

I squeezed the inconvenient scans into my schedule early in the morning of the day of the board meeting I had to attend in California. The second the technicians were done with me, I raced from the clinic to the airport where Mary was waiting for me with a warm jet and hot coffee.

The phone call to my cell phone in Santa Barbara was my Israeli wrist guru's way of passing along the results of that morning's workup.

"You have an aneurysm," she'd said. "In your brain. It's not good." No warm-up. No "Is this a good time to talk?" No "I have some bad news."

Simply "You have an aneurysm. In your brain. It's not good."

Just like that.

My first thought upon hearing the news? *How the hell would you know? You're a wrist guy.*

La la how the life goes on.

I'm an *n* of only one, but days later, when I was finally able to take a deep breath and reflect on what had happened, the post-diagnostic blur struck me as something like waking up and suddenly finding myself being escorted into the front car of a particularly sinister roller coaster.

The events of those days flashed by rapidly, way too fast for my senses to experience them as any more than momentary blurs. Landing at Centennial, driving to Denver, checking in at the wrist doc's clinic, her hushed but perfunctory "I'm so sorry," the raw images from the MRI, the elevator ride to see another doctor, this time a neurosurgeon—a frigging neurosurgeon, Jesus—his take on my bulging artery, and his use of the words "natural history" to describe the life cycle of aneurysms like the one I had sitting in such an inconvenient location in my brain. The guy actually wasn't a bad artist and drew a cartoonish depiction of my brain and its aneurysm so I would have a concrete representation of my condition to share with friends and loved ones.

Appointments were made for me at clinics for more tests, prescriptions filled. Instructions given. I passed by person after person whose faces were saying "I'm sorry about your news."

The greatest irony? The guru still didn't know why my wrist wasn't healing.

Ha.

I drove home that first day and tried to be even-keeled as I told Thea the news. How bad was the timing? It could hardly have been worse. Thea was in the beginning of the third trimester of her pregnancy with our second child.

She nodded a lot and held my hand. Underneath, I was a wreck. I was counting on her to be my rock. She was, undoubtedly, counting on me to be around to help her parent our children.

I gave her all the good parts of the bad news first.

"It may have been there my whole life," I said.

"The doctors say it could be stable," I said.

"Nothing may have to change at all," I said.

By nature, Thea wasn't as optimistic as me. Or her denial was worse. Sometimes I can't tell those two things apart. "Can they operate?" she asked.

"He said it's not in a good location for surgery. They can't get to it easily. It would be risky to go in."

"How risky?" she asked.

"There would almost certainly be some damage."

"Damage?" She swallowed. "To your brain?"

"Yes."

"How much damage?"

I pondered the question. I'd pondered it plenty already, but I wanted to be clear as I presented the dilemma to Thea. The truth was this: Where damage to my brain was concerned I'd already concluded that there was no such thing as an acceptable amount. Finally I said, "Much more than if they leave it alone and it doesn't rupture. A lot less than if they leave it alone and it does."

My wife recognized the conundrum immediately. "Dear God," she said. "Now what?"

"More tests. More opinions. We take it slow. No rush to judgment."

Overnight I'd become a medical cliché machine.

I'd also decided to let my optimism, or my denial—whichever is the part of me that lets me believe I can survive anything—do the talking. "Hey? Maybe it doesn't change," I said. "Ever. It could've been there my whole life, right? That's what they said. It could be stable. They said that, too. They did. It could just . . . stay there. But I'll get all the new tests. I'll listen to the doctors. For now, though . . . for now we just sit tight and we watch it."

Thea's inclination was to fix broken things, not to watch them. "Then why are you having headaches? And why the nausea? If the bulge is stable, why did you fall off that treadmill? Why all that? Why now?"

I could tell that maintaining my denial around Thea was going to be a chore. I said, "I don't know."

"After the tests, if the doctors say it isn't stable, then what?"

"What do you mean?"

"If it blows?" she asked, dabbing away tears. "Ruptures, I mean. What then?"

Blows? I had a sudden image of my head exploding like Krakatoa. I shook it off. "It could kill me. Or it could end up being . . . like a terrible stroke. I could be . . ." I decided to use the word from the conversation with the comic in Nobu. "Gorked."

I didn't reveal the derivation of the acronym.

She didn't ask. "Oh God," she whispered.

"Yeah." I reached out and held her.

"What do we do?" she wanted to know.

"We go on," I said. "We just go on. We watch it."

"We do," she agreed after a few seconds of indecision, but her inflection was unclear, and I could easily have attached a question mark to the end of her two-word declaration.

I realized something then that provided me with no solace: If she and I were running toward a finish line, and the most terrified would have been judged the winner, we would have broken the tape together, tied for that dubious prize.

Was the aneurysm going to kill me?

Depended on whom I asked.

I was being treated by some fine doctors, but I didn't trust anybody's opinion much. I had spent enough time in academia that I was a subscriber to the belief that experts are actually people from out of town, and since I was fortunate to be in a financial position to be skeptical, I took a few side trips with Mary and Trace, flying around the country getting second opinions from the nationally recognized aneurysm gurus. And then I got second opinions to the second opinions.

Presbyterian in New York.

Mayo.

The Cleveland Clinic.

Mass General.

UCLA.

Multiple strategies were discussed. Some of the wizards preferred to clip the thing, others felt a surgical bypass was the way to go. A minority felt I was a perfect candidate for endovascular embolization, or coiling.

The whole time, I was checking the professional literature myself to translate everyone's advice into English and to learn what I could about my bulging artery.

The best data I could find showed that the five-year survival rate of people approximately my age with aneurysms like mine wasn't great. The percentage of people with similar arterial bulges who didn't suffer a leakage or rupture during that period was low. Too low for comfort.

I didn't love those numbers. Any of them.

Not too surprisingly, Thea and I interpreted the risks differently.

She had asked me this: If I were standing on my skis on the top of an impossibly tough cliff in known avalanche country, and God himself told me that my odds of making it down alive were twenty percent, or thirty percent, would I go? Would I point those two boards down that hill and push off?

Thea's question was born of her point of view: She believed that with that aneurysm, fate had dealt me a bad hand. The odds I faced weren't good. And I had no choice but to rue that hand.

Fight like hell, yes. But rue that hand.

I had begun to look at my dilemma slightly differently. In the weeks since my diagnosis I had begun to see the whole game, the big picture. With that long lens, I actually liked my hand. I'd lived forty-something interesting and satisfying years, had managed—against odds—to mature during those years, had a great family, a terrific wife, and more money than anybody had the right to ask for.

I'd had a career that was mostly a joy, one that had made a difference in a few lives. I had some terrific friends.

And now I had an aneurysm, sure. That part of the hand was certainly a clunker. With that turn card flipped up on the table, I granted Thea that it wasn't a *perfect* hand I held. But play it I would. After all, the river card could still change everything.

In my game, life always has a river card.

I thought about the question she had posed for a long time before I answered.

I finally explained my perspective like this: "If I were standing on my skis on top of that same impossibly tough cliff in known avalanche country, and God himself told me that my odds of staying alive and healthy were piss-poor *unless* I skied down, would I go? Would you want me to point those two boards down that hill and push off? Would you?"

Thea's mouth opened about a centimeter. Her eyes opened a little wider than that. "Is that your version of optimism?" she asked finally, just the slightest cushion of affection in her tone.

"It is."

"You believe you can beat this, don't you? Defy those odds?" she said. "Don't you?" Her eyes were tearing up when she asked me, her voice cracking from the pressure of my peculiar strain of optimism.

She was querying me about hope. She was praying that she had enough for me, and that I had enough for her.

I said, "I have three reasons to believe I can beat this." I pointed to her belly. "Make that four. How much motivation does a guy need?"

I never told her, of course, that my risks were limited. If the aneurysm ruptured but didn't kill me, I had already hired some professionals who would complete the job.

Death Angels or no Death Angels, I planned on beating the aneurysm. It was that simple. Although some people lost their fights against the same foe, I knew that a few other people had lived long productive lives with conditions like mine. The neurosurgeons I consulted early on didn't talk much about odds. One of them, a particularly cold prick in Rochester, told me in response to my question about probabilities that the outcome for me would be binary. He explained that if I chose to avoid surgery, I'd either survive the aneurysm, or I wouldn't. "Odds are for Vegas," he went on. "I went to Harvard Med. I didn't go to Caesars Palace."

The surgeons all preferred to talk about minimizing risk. After listening to their opinions, I decided that there were three possible outcomes for me. The preferred outcome? Easy, the thing doesn't blow; it stays stable. The second best outcome? Intervention. Successful surgery. But even the most optimistic surgeons warned that because of the unfortunate location of my aneurysm I would suffer some, hopefully tolerable, amount of brain damage during the procedure. The third option had two parts: (a) The thing blows on its own and I suffer a massive stroke. Or (b) the thing blows during surgery and I suffer a massive stroke.

Not surprisingly, I never developed any real fondness for 3a or 3b.

The minimizing-risk argument screamed at me to go for the surgical option. But I wasn't like other patients; I'd never been inclined to settle for a life without risk. I was less risk-averse than most people and tougher than most people, and therefore, I was going to find a way to live life my way whether or not I had a flimsy artery in my brain. To do that I would be a better patient, a more diligent patient, a more optimistic patient.

I would wait and watch and I would beat the fucker.

Since I was going to beat it—and also because I couldn't stand the thought of people treating me as though I was as fragile as a Ming vase—Thea and I both agreed we would keep the news about the aneurysm to ourselves. What was the point of announcing a silent battle against an enemy that would ultimately be vanquished? After some period of time, some period long enough to prove that I could indeed be victorious over some silly bulging blood vessel in my brain, she and I would throw a kick-ass party for all of our family and friends to announce to the world what we'd been able to overcome.

It would be a hell of a bash.

Yeah.

That was the plan.

Right from the beginning, I did my part. Fighting many instincts to the contrary, I became a patient par excellence. Positive attitude? I was Mr. Optimistic. Good patient? If they gave one out, I would have gotten the Golden Gown award. Healthy lifestyle? Exercise and fiber, vitamins and essential oils. I gave up red meat. Yes, I even did meditation and . . . yoga.

And massage, of course. Massage.

Off-hand massage.

My wrist bones eventually healed. The cast came off. But I kept the secret of my illness from everyone. I made up excuses for the absences I took from work; I explained away my continuing symptoms—the headaches and the nausea—as this stress or that virus.

In the meantime, I was convinced that we could convince everybody I was still healthy.

To complete the ruse, I continued to live my life the way that I'd always lived it.

I called it "fully."

Thea still called it "recklessly."

Didn't matter.

I was going to beat this thing silly.

That was the plan.

THIRTY-FIVE

Ironically, or not, I didn't give much thought to the Death Angels during the days and weeks after I was diagnosed with the aneurysm. Dying was on my mind, most definitely, but still as an abstract, eventual thing, not as an impending danger. The previous year, at the time I'd completed my enrollment on the side of the road outside Ridgway, I'd been assuming that the arrangements I'd made would never prove necessary, and if they did, that I'd be in my seventies or eighties before I was debilitated enough to need them.

The presence of the aneurysm didn't change anything, not acutely. I didn't wake each morning thinking that the day had come that the vessel in my brain was going to blow. That just wasn't my mindset about life.

The Death Angel insurance I'd purchased wasn't a policy I'd ever deluded myself into thinking was going to protect me against dying. And no one—not one of the many doctors I spoke with in those months after my diagnosis—had any confidence that he or she could predict when I would suffer a life-ending event or any near-term disabling impairment from the bulging artery they'd found. There was the a-hole in L.A. who thought I'd be dead before Christmas. I'd asked which Christmas. He'd said, "This Christmas." And a neurosurgeon in Boston who said he'd be surprised if the weak-walled vessel lasted three years. Another one guessed five. One sweetheart in New York said she'd probably die before I did.

Every last doctor, though, reminded me that the thing could blow in the next five minutes.

I used the inconsistency as evidence to convince myself that they didn't really know what was going to happen with me and my aneurysm. And then I convinced myself that was a good thing.

The one facet of the whole Death Angel enrollment that I did consider during those days—but only briefly—was the fact that I had crossed the threshold that rendered my policy noncancelable.

The rule that Lizzie had stressed that day at Papaya King was that once an enrollee had received a diagnosis of a potentially fatal or disabling illness, or had suffered an event—the Death Angel euphemism for a stroke or a heart attack, I think—or received injuries that were likely to result in serious disability or death, the agreement with the Death Angels became irrevocable. My memory was that we'd discussed it a little, maybe even argued about it a little, and that I'd ultimately agreed without too much thought, and without any determined protest.

In the natural course of aneurysms like mine, a significant proportion of people die from rupture. Another significant proportion become severely debilitated from rupture. The ones who choose surgery on aneurysms in awkward locations, like mine, inevitably suffer deficits. Those simple facts meant that I had probably crossed the line into the domain of the irrevocables. I had no choice but to accept that reality.

But it wasn't a big thing to me. As a Death Angel client, I had always thought that I was in for life.

Or death.

I just never expected the issue to become real so soon.

I knew the only line left to cross was the one that would put the target on my chest.

And that was a line that I had drawn myself during that impromptu meeting on the side of the road outside Ridgway: the line that marked the client-derived parameters and initiated the provision of end-of-life services.

When, oh when, would I exceed those parameters?

Something else I had never thought about much was exactly how the Death Angels would complete their end-of-life activities. The specifics, I mean.

The mechanics.

How—exactly—would they kill me once I'd suffered a threshold event?

Think about it. How would someone make a stranger's death appear accidental, not too unexpected, without raising suspicion from the victim's family, or the police, or . . . ?

I guessed that back when I enlisted them, and I figuratively signed on the figurative dotted line, I was assuming that the logistics of causing my life to cease were their problem, not mine.

But soon enough, it seemed, it might be mine.

How the hell were they planning to kill me?

Damn good question.

What was most surprising to me, however, during those post-diagnosis weeks and months was that the presence of a Death Angel on my shoulder didn't provide much comfort. I didn't find myself with any inclination to drop to my knees and thank some deity for my prescience in signing up for the quick-exit plan.

THIRTY-SIX

Once the shock of the news had worn off, Thea and I were both glad that we had a reason to focus our energy on the bulge in her belly, and not the one in my brain.

Amniocentesis had revealed that we would soon have two daughters, not just one.

Cal was almost five then.

Her older half-brother, Adam, was seventeen.

Death wasn't done begging for my attention, though. Connie's death came suddenly late in 2004, interrupting my cross-country quest for second opinions. Adam took the train north from Cincinnati to join Thea—who had just entered the final trimester of a difficult pregnancy and shouldn't have been traveling—and his sister, Berkeley, and me for his uncle's funeral in New Haven.

Connie had been a converted Quaker, and the funeral was a traditional Friends send-off that consisted of a zillion people jamming into a New Haven meeting hall sharing reflections and stories about Connie's remarkably generous life.

The service was much more spiritual than it was religious. I found it comforting.

Adam, I thought, seemed stoic.

Felix spoke in Spanish when he chose to stand and

reflect on Connie's life. While Felix talked, my son leaned over and placed his lips near my ears and translated every word for me. Adam's warm breath on my flesh felt like a caress. It was so distracting and so comforting that I remembered almost nothing that Felix had said.

Late in the service I spoke, too.

My brother's nephew waited to speak until the end, until the room had been quiet for a few minutes. Adam's eloquence about his uncle, and the depth of his understanding of the meaning of his uncle's life, gave me chills. He was the last to stand and consider Connie's life that day; no one in the room would have dared to follow his lovely soliloquy with one of their own.

My son never cried during the service. Not once.

I never really stopped.

In the succeeding weeks, as the birth of his new half-sibling grew closer, Adam mounted a spirited long-distance lobbying crusade from Ohio to continue the nascent philosopher-inspired naming trend that we'd started in our little family. He was advocating that we call the new kid "Wittgenstein."

" 'Witt' for short," he'd said in a call to Thea, pronouncing the *W* like a *V*. "How cool would that be?"

I'd had to go online and Google the name to learn something about Ludwig Wittgenstein—early twentieth century, Austrian, logician—the particular philosopher who'd inspired Adam's naming campaign. I spent about five minutes trying to understand anything at all about Wittgenstein's contributions to the grand oeuvres of anti-metaphysics and the logic of language before I got a splitting headache.

Although I was half-sure that Adam was only half-serious about the name he was espousing for our baby, I had thought I might find a clue why Adam had gravitated

221

toward Wittgenstein in particular, but ended up just being grateful that he wasn't lobbying to call my new kid "Schopenhauer."

"Schop" for short.

Thea put an end to what morphed into a rather extended naming negotiation by belatedly admitting that Berkeley had indeed been named after her mother's alma mater on the gentle rise above San Francisco Bay and not after the late British empiricist. Adam accepted Thea's change in position graciously; he immediately embraced the idea of college-inspired baby names, and started lobbying to have us call his new sibling "Yale" in honor of his recently deceased uncle Connie.

It wasn't lost on either Thea or me that Adam had chosen to honor yet another philosopher. And an ethicist, at that.

Thea had begun crying when Adam made his "Yale" suggestion to her over the phone. I heard her say, "That's so sweet. I'll think about that, Adam. I'll think about it seriously. I will." Then she handed me the phone. Her free hand was on her swollen belly.

"He wants to call her 'Yale,' " she said to me, the phone's microphone palmed in her hand. "He wants to name her for Connie. You talk to him. I can't." After she'd handed me the phone, she wiped away a tear.

I did talk with him. Adam didn't offer to talk with me too often then. But I loved talking to him.

He was dead serious about naming his new sister Yale.

The holidays came and went. The New Year started. When she was born a week early, we ended up calling our second daughter, our *new* daughter, Haven.

Nothing for short.

Adam thought the name was great.

So did we.

Cal's two cents? She thought we were all spelling "Heaven" wrong.

Later that year, as summer ripened into fall, Thea and I felt the time had come to tell Bella that it would be our privilege to pay for Adam to go to college. Bella, who struggled to connect one payday with the next, was thrilled with our offer.

Adam wasn't as grateful. He was even more skeptical about my money than he was about me, and he was supremely skeptical about going anywhere for a formal education.

"You'll meet people like your uncle Connie. Inspiring people," I told him. "And make friends for life."

"Yeah?" he'd said, unconvinced.

"Yeah."

He said he'd think about it.

A while later Bella called Thea and said that Adam had decided to give college a try.

I was ecstatic. I volunteered to coordinate the logistics of his college search. I was shocked, and relieved, when he accepted.

For a wondrous few months during what, had he ever attended high school, would have been the winter and spring of Adam's senior year—he was, he pointed out with mock pride, valedictorian of the Class of 2006 at Bella High School in Cincinnati, Ohio—I was at a strange intersection in my life. I had a daughter starting kindergarten and a son searching to find the right college. In the course of the same week, Thea and I would sit in the small chairs in some kindergarten classroom assessing the fit of a local school for our daughter, and then I would board a plane—an airline plane; Adam still wanted nothing to do with my jet—and meet Adam in some region of the country for a frantic three- or four-day tour of the local elite colleges.

I considered myself a young man. But because I'd spent most of my adult life living under the illusion that I had become a father late, I had always imagined I'd be a much older man before I had the responsibility and joy of helping a child of mine choose a college. When Adam and I headed out to visit schools, I found the time with him on the college-campus road show to be a rich terrarium of discovery. We both learned about colleges. We sat through mind-numbing admission presentations at schools from Pomona to Penn; we took unbelievably unrevealing campus tours in college towns from Palo Alto to Princeton.

We learned how Swarthmore was different from Williams, and why Duke was no Washington University, and vice versa.

We also, I think, learned about each other.

We didn't grow closer during that time. Adam made it clear that wasn't an option. I was left to accept the role of financier and observer of my son's life and to his process. But what seemed initially to me like a cursory, shallow, impatient—read: adolescent in all its pejorative connotations—process was actually a winnowing procedure for my son that was as personal and thoughtful and as idiosyncratic to him as would be picking out the right hat. The day we said good-bye after the last of the college visits was over, he was still treating me like I was a father he hadn't met until he was fourteen, a father who had spent a chunk of a lifetime not knowing that his son existed.

Adam didn't do things my way at any stage of the journey, but I was able to recognize, and even momentarily accept, that he was doing things the way he needed to do them.

*

The following August, and the actual beginning of college, arrived quickly.

Adam had been accepted to six of the seven schools to which he had applied. He'd only been turned down by what anxious parents like me called his "safety" school, his backup. The one he was almost certain to get into. Adam considered the rejection a badge of honor. He decided to attend Brown—if you had asked me to rank his favorites, I wouldn't have put it in the top three—and was scheduled to start classes just up Interstate 95 from New Haven in Providence. Adam had asked Thea and me not to go to Rhode Island to drop him off, so Bella had driven him to Providence from Cincinnati a few days before school began and had helped him settle into his dorm. His new roommate was a lacrosse star from Virginia whose father had been a lacrosse player at Brown.

When I told Thea about Adam's first Ivy roomie, I bet her that the first thing Adam would learn at college was which end of a lacrosse stick to hold. He confirmed my suspicion in an e-mail he sent that evening marveling that there was actually a sport played with a "jock strap at the end of a stick."

Despite the fact that I was aching to talk with him, I didn't call him right away. The long interlude of relative stability I'd been enjoying with my aneurysm was over. I'd begun experiencing serious fatigue on a daily basis, and the headaches and nausea were growing more and more persistent. I wasn't confident I could keep the fact of my illness out of my voice, and I remained determined that Adam not learn about my condition.

The neurosurgeon in Denver I was seeing—I'd chosen him because he was the one who creeped me out less than the others—had my head re-scanned, and told me matter-of-factly that the bulge was bigger. "It's not stable," he said. "We'd like it to be stable."

Yes, we would, I thought.

"Bigger?" I asked. I had an image of a water balloon in my head.

"Not much. Fractions of millimeters." He paused. "But you have to know it could rupture at any time. You could have a bleed on your way home tonight. Or tomorrow."

I didn't like the fact that I was a patient for whom "bleed" had been transformed from a verb into a noun. The thin-walled excuse for an artery in my brain wasn't holding up its end of the bargain I'd made with my denial.

To make a complicated medical situation simple, an unstable aneurysm wasn't a good sign.

After my appointment, I reiterated to Thea that I didn't want Adam to know about the aneurysm.

Thea was, as always, a step ahead of me. "He can't blame you for this. This isn't reckless."

I feared she was wrong. Adam could blame me for this. And it was a little reckless. But she didn't know about the reckless part. The Death Angels part.

"You have to reconsider surgery, babe," Thea said.

"Yes," I said. The neurosurgeons were saying the same thing. I'd consider it and reconsider it until rocket ships were making daily flights to Mars. But I knew it wasn't going to happen.

My circumstances—and my Death Angels—made that choice impossible.

The next day I got a call on my *Ob-la-di* phone as I was sitting in my Denver office pondering my fate.

No greeting. The voice in my ear was female and familiar.

Tender, too.

"You're right on the line now. With any more new symptoms, the threshold will be crossed," she said.

I thought, *God, you people are good.* "Lizzie," I whispered.

"I bet they're pushing surgery harder, aren't they? Your docs?"

"Yes."

"Well, consider this, Yossarian: It's a classic catch-22," she said. "If you choose not to have surgery, the aneurysm will soon bulge a little more, and you'll get increasingly symptomatic. And if that happens we will, of course, kill you.

"Or the aneurysm will rupture. Sooner rather than later. Given its location in your brain, you'll likely die if that happens. If you don't die, you'll be severely impaired. And if that happens we will, of course, kill you."

She paused to let the weight of that scenario sink in, or to steel herself for what she would say next. "If you do choose to have surgery, assuming it goes well, you will undoubtedly suffer some deficits from the procedure. And those deficits will almost certainly exceed the parameters you've set to trigger your insurance to kick in. And if that happens we will, of course, kill you."

"Lizzie," I said again.

"If you have some business to take care of, I suggest you take care of it."

She hung up.

I thought she'd sounded sad.

THIRTY-SEVEN

True to my word, I did finally disclose to Dr. Gregory the ways that Adam had hurt me.

After I decided I would go there with him it took me a while to cover the necessary ground. First I had to tell him about Adam's relationship with his uncle, then about me getting diagnosed, and about Connie's death. Only then could I tell him about what had started all the hurt. I filled in that blank with a session-long tale about Adam's momentous second visit to our home, and the revelation that he'd shared with me about his stepfather's death.

I concluded with an admission to my therapist that he had been exactly right, that Adam had made me vulnerable.

I shared stories with him about the joy I felt during the college trips with Adam, and about the remarkable process of getting to know my son over that time period. I acknowledged the heartache of being forced to stay out of his reach.

My therapist listened patiently, but I could tell that he recognized that I was dealing with prelude, and he was waiting for the crucial part of my story. The part when Adam twisted the knife.

So here goes with that part.

Brown University in Rhode Island is as close to the academic environment a brilliant, homeschooled, self-directed, eclectically minded kid is accustomed to as any new college student is likely to find. Brown's undergraduate college is without curricular requirements, a place that actually encourages its students to taste freely from the academic bounty the university makes available. Brown allows a student to choose from a menu of majors, or to cobble one together on his or her own from bits and pieces of academic passion. My son had chosen his college well. If Adam was going to thrive in any organized academic setting, I'd come to concur with his decision that it would be the one provided at Brown.

Given his idiosyncratic and prodigious intellectual gifts and his unorthodox approach to learning, however, I wasn't certain that Adam was really going to thrive in any organized academic setting. Thea, Bella, and I each had our fingers crossed that the experiment in formal higher education would work out.

Adam, too, had his doubts. His final words to Bella before she drove away from his dorm?

"Don't be disappointed if this doesn't go too well."

She promised she wouldn't be.

Five minutes later, when Bella told us about it on her cell phone, Thea and I promised we wouldn't be disappointed, either.

We were all lying.

The first month of school seemed to fly by. Thea and I had taken advantage of Berkeley's late birthday and decided to postpone the onset of her kindergarten adventure for another year, so we—Thea, Cal, Haven, and I—were all together as that autumn began. A long Indian summer interlude dominated Colorado's weather as we split our time between Denver and Ridgway.

Although my contact with my son continued to be more sporadic than I would have liked during those weeks, I communicated with him just enough—mostly by e-mail—to satisfy myself that his adjustment to being in college fell someplace on the scale between "okay" and "fine."

But all hell broke loose sometime in October.

When exactly? That was hard to pinpoint because Bella had kept the early signs of the developing crisis to herself. The first time Thea and I heard that something might be up was after Adam had been absent from his scheduled classes for four days. And by that time, his roommate was also reporting that Adam hadn't slept in his dorm room for six nights.

The roommate actually thought it was six, but since he'd been gone on a road trip with the lacrosse team for some off-season something at the front end of the time period in question, he admitted that it could actually have been as long as seven or eight nights that Adam had been AWOL from Brown.

Shit.

"He's on one of his adventures," Bella explained on the phone during her we-may-have-a-situation-but-I'm-not-really-that-worried-but-I-thought-you-should-know call. "He's always done this. Always."

It was clear that Bella, bless her heart, was far from exasperated about the situation, and hadn't actually crossed the line that distinguished "concerned" from "worried." She labeled her state of mind as "puzzled."

"He's already away from home, Bella. Why does he have to run at all?" I asked her.

"He's not running—he didn't run. Adam's exploring. Something out there caught his eye, maybe something he was studying at school. He decided to take a closer look at it himself. It's what he does; it's how he learns. When he was thirteen he was reading about how salmon spawn, so he took off for a river in Washington State to see it for himself. That's who our son is. He's an experiential learner."

The kid had been out of contact with anyone for more than a week. "Experiential learner" wasn't enough of an explanation for me.

God help us.

But Bella had also said "our son," and hearing those words made it hard for me to recover any traction for my frustration with her.

Thea was oddly quiet about the whole affair as it developed. At first I applauded the prudence reflected by her silence, and I admired her ability to keep some distance from the battle that I feared was about to be joined between Bella and me over what to do next about Adam's absence.

Then I had an epiphany about what was really going on with Thea. I thought about my conclusion for most of a day, trying to reject it, trying to convince myself I was wrong. But the more I thought about it the more right it felt.

It also felt terrible.

I'd taken Haven from Thea's breast, changed her, and returned her to her crib before I'd read Cal her nighttime stories and tucked her into bed. After the girls were settled, I sat down next to my wife on the love seat beneath the window in our Denver bedroom. Thea was stretched out reading a book, and had to make room for me. Her accommodation was reluctant.

"Hey," I said.

She put her finger on a spot near the bottom of the left page, turned to me, and smiled. The smile was halfhearted at best. It said "I love you" but it also said "This had better be good. I'm enjoying the silence, and my book."

I smiled back. I wanted the smile to shout "I love you,

too." In a calm tone, a conversational, nonconfrontational tone, I said, "You told Bella, didn't you?"

She made the mistake of responding too quickly.

"Told her what? What on earth do you mean?" she said, turning her attention back to the book as though she couldn't bear to be parted any longer from the story she was reading.

My wife was a terrible liar. When she tried to prevaricate she almost always ended up forcing false assurance into her words like a woman who hadn't seen single-digit sizing for a while squeezing herself into a size eight.

"About the aneurysm."

I never called it "my aneurysm," always "the aneurysm." As part of the campaign to maintain my own optimistic charade, I needed to treat the damn weakness as an interloper, not a resident.

As parasite, not partner. I had to regard it as nothing integral to me. If it were integral, it couldn't be vanquished. I wouldn't allow it to become integral.

Thea made a dismissive face that was almost comical. From her expression it appeared that she thought that I'd begun speaking in tongues and she wanted to make it clear to me that it wasn't her fault that she couldn't decipher my babble.

I pretended not to notice her feigned disbelief. It was easier that way. "When?" I asked. "When did you tell her?"

She closed her book and placed it on her lap. She'd lost her place. She took a quick look at me—I think she wanted to judge whether or not I was angry—then she turned away from me and nodded two or three times into the darkness beyond the western windows. "End of September, maybe. She was in Ohio. I was up in Ridgway. It was a pretty day. We were talking on the phone. And we were both cooking. She was making bread. I was making cupcakes for Berk and her friends."

"Damn it," I said, without any passion, and without any real anger. I already knew in my heart that Thea had talked with Bella about the aneurysm, and long before I confronted her I'd already spilled all the passion I could muster about it. The "damn it" was a simple recognition on my part about how complicated things were going to be with my son from that moment forward.

Thea said my name then. She said it as a plea.

I sighed. "Bella told Adam," I said. "That's why he split." It all seemed so obvious to me.

"Why would she tell him?" Thea asked.

Thea wasn't being curious; she was being defensive. It was obvious to her, too, how these dominos had tumbled.

"Because Bella is Bella," I said.

"Maybe not," Thea said. It wasn't an argument; it was another layer of defense. She knew it and I knew it. "Maybe you're . . . wrong about her. You've always been hard on Bella. She said she wouldn't tell him. She promised me that she wouldn't."

"Thea? We're talking Bella. She can't keep things from Adam. She can't tolerate any boundaries between them. We both know that. Come on."

Thea didn't want it to be true. "Why would she tell him?"

"It's her way of being a good parent. It always has been. She uses license as a substitute for responsibility, and she uses honesty as a substitute for judgment. That's Bella. It's who she is."

Thea thought about my words for a while before she decided not to argue with my conclusion. Instead, she decided to throw herself on the mercy of the court. It was a wise decision; the court was feeling merciful.

"No," Thea said protectively. "It's me. I screwed up. Bella's so nice. She is. After we got the news about the aneurysm bulging more, I needed to talk. It's been so hard to keep everything quiet. She's so far away . . . I thought it would be safe to . . ."

So it's my fault? I almost said. *This all happened because I wanted to keep my illness a secret?* I didn't, but I came close. Instead I said, "Where Adam is concerned Bella is like the mother without borders. Her judgment sucks. That's why we weren't going to tell her, remember? We talked about Bella specifically."

I realized at that moment that the entire I-don't-have-an-aneurysm ruse had been concocted to protect Adam. Or, more to the point, had been concocted to protect me from Adam's feelings.

"I screwed up. I'm sorry," Thea said.

I kissed her. "It's not your fault. I shouldn't have put you in this position."

She touched me on the face. I was grateful for the caress.

"Adam thinks I'm going to die. That I'm going to leave him. It's his greatest fear about me. The aneurysm will be a huge thing between us. A mountain range. An ocean. I don't know how to mitigate this, the fact that he knows about it. I don't know how to erase it. I need to try to figure out what to do next."

"Why would he run, though?"

"To sort things out? I don't know. I don't know my own son well enough to answer that question."

That admission took the breath away from her. From me, too.

"Well, he's wrong about you. You won't die. We'll just have to find him and tell him that," Thea said when she recovered, endeavoring to sound defiant. "We'll show him the numbers, the odds, explain all that you're doing to maximize your chances, let him talk to the doctors—whatever he wants. He's smart; he'll see."

"It's growing, baby. It could blow. We both know that."

"But it might not. Right? Right? Hope. Determination. Right? And there's always surgery."

Denial, I thought. It's contagious.

"We don't even know where he is, Thea. Makes it kind of hard to convince him of anything, right?"

"We'll find him."

"Of course we will," I said. "Of course we will."

THIRTY-EIGHT

I'd hired three detectives to look for my son. I didn't tell Bella I was doing it.

I didn't even tell Thea.

I didn't ask for anyone's permission.

I had to connect with him. Even if it was only to say good-bye.

In early November I phoned one of the detectives. My call found him in Wisconsin; he was following a soft lead that had taken him to Milwaukee from Illinois. A girl in Chicago thought a photo of Adam resembled a guy she'd met at a party at a frat at Northwestern who said he was going to Milwaukee.

"Milwaukee?" I asked. "You hopeful?"

"Honestly? No. People tell me things, I check them out. Most of the time they're unreliable. I still don't have any data records—credit card, nothing—that tell me where your son is. He's not using the phone you gave him. It's not even turned on. Until I get lucky or I get a hard clue, I'm following rumors. You want me to stop, I'll stop. You want me to keep going, I'll keep going. It's your money. I got nothing but time and good intentions."

I wasn't sure how competent the guy was, but he was honest, and I liked him for that.

"Keep going," I said.

THIRTY-NINE

I wouldn't have gone East on pretend business if Adam hadn't stayed missing.

But he did stay missing, and I did go East.

Thea had begged me not to go on the trip. She'd had to rush me to St. Mary's Hospital in Grand Junction earlier that week after I'd suffered worsening symptoms. The doctors had hospitalized me overnight to rehydrate me after some prolonged vomiting. They ultimately decided that the bulge in my brain wasn't bleeding, yet. It was just getting fatter.

I'd only been back in Ridgway from the hospital for an hour before Lizzie called again on my *Ob la-di* phone.

She said, "We've just had a teleconference. With your new symptoms, the client-derived parameters have been exceeded."

I tried to swallow. Failed. My throat was so dry that I couldn't talk.

She hung up.

The target was officially on my chest.

A bull's-eye.

I was fair game.

Adam had been gone from Brown for almost a month.

I'd scheduled some meetings in New York to maintain

appearances. To my dismay, the meetings—in lower Manhattan, in the absent shadows of the void of the World Trade Center—took up most of the afternoon. It was the kind of mindless financial foreplay that Adam would have walked out of, the kind of meeting that if I had any guts I would have walked out of. The suits ran out of ideas long before they ran out of words, so I was ready for them to shut their mouths long before they finally shut their briefcases. I hustled out of the building and slunk down into the subway with about a million other people and stuffed myself into a crowded car on the Lexington Avenue line heading to Midtown. I could have taken a cab or arranged for a Town Car or limo to go uptown, but despite my whining I liked the crush of life in the tunnels below the city, especially during rush hour.

When I made it back to the hotel on 57th it was just before six and Mary was waiting for me in the second-floor lounge, the same one where I'd met the funny man for my final tutorial on Death Angel rules and regs. Mary was drinking sparkling water; she never touched alcohol when she was on call to fly.

"Good day?" I asked, happy to see her round face.

"Pretty good," she said. From her vantage, any day she spent away from her family wasn't eligible for a more exalted status. She never sugarcoated that fact. She loved to fly; she didn't love the fact that flying often meant spending the night somewhere away from her daughter.

"You rescued me from being a cop before I ever got to be a detective. Now sometimes I get to play one on TV. It's kind of fun." She reached into her purse and pushed some handwritten notes across the table. "You shouldn't have too much trouble with any of this. The woman is a true creature of habit."

"Thanks. You don't think she knew you were there? On her?"

"In this city? I don't see how." She paused and gave me a querulous look. "She's not a pro, is she?"

"What? God, no. No. Just a business . . . associate. She's too secretive for my taste, that's all. She knows plenty about me, and I prefer a level playing field." I sat back on the chair. "Who am I kidding? I don't like a level playing field. I like home-field advantage."

"That's true, you do," Mary said. I could tell that she didn't believe the story I was telling her.

"You going to see your cousin tonight?" I asked.

Mary nodded. Her cousin was a FedEx delivery driver who lived in Brooklyn but worked out of a big facility in Greenwich Village near Hudson Street. "She's window shopping and drooling—simultaneously, I'm sure—over on Fifth Avenue right now. We're meeting up for dinner a little later at a Chinese place she likes by the bridge. Just need to give her a call."

I reached into my jacket pocket and held out a pair of theater tickets. "On me. For the two of you. Enjoy."

She looked at the precious tickets—fourth row, center— then back at me. There was wonder in her eyes. "How'd you get these? This has been sold out for like . . . ever."

"It's not important." I didn't want to admit that LaBelle had cashed in a favor with one of the investment bankers who had assisted with the sale of my company years before, and he'd gotten the seats for me. "There's a seafood place not far from here, on 54th. It's called Oceana. I think you'll like it." One of Mary's few apparent weaknesses in life was good seafood. Especially shellfish. "You and your cousin have reservations for a nice pretheater dinner. They have terrific oysters. Get whatever you want; it's all taken care of."

She smiled. "Thanks, boss."

"Thank you, Mary. Go on—you don't have any time to waste on me—find your cousin, you have a curtain to

239

make. I'll try to give you a few hours' notice before I'm ready to head home."

"You don't have any time to waste, either."

Hearing those words, I'm sure I looked shocked. Did she know?

She gestured at the folded papers on the table. "Your lady's due home soon. Trust me." She stood and gathered her things. "You all right, boss?" she asked.

"Fine."

Mary called "Good-bye" as she hustled from the hotel. I picked up the notes she'd left and started reading.

She'd never asked me why I really wanted her to follow Lizzie. She never even acted like she was curious.

I wondered, again, if she already knew.

If I had the time I might have walked uptown through the latest incarnation of Columbus Circle. But I didn't have the time, so I had the hotel doorman whistle for a taxi. I finished reading Mary's notes from the smooth plastic backseat of a New York cab.

I hadn't spent a lot of time in Lizzie's neighborhood over the years, but I'd been there before. An occasional symphony concert at Lincoln Center. A friend's daughter's violin recital at Juilliard. A restaurant visit or two with colleagues. Was I surprised that Lizzie lived nearby? No, not particularly. After our first encounter, but before the Papaya King lunch, I would have guessed she was an Upper East Side girl. But I assumed she would never have taken me to lunch near her home—too much risk of being recognized in her own neighborhood—so I'd ruled out the possibility she lived on the Upper East Side anywhere near the hot dog palace. The Upper West Side would have been among my top two or three alternative choices. I couldn't visualize Lizzie as a loft-rat in Chelsea or the West Village or the Meatpacking District.

Mary's notes provided me with Lizzie's address and an apartment number she'd marked "likely, not definite." Lizzie seemed like the type of woman to live in a quality building with a doorman. To get in to see her, I would be forced to either charm or bribe my way past the liveried gatekeeper, some street-smart guy who was immune to charm, and resistant to all but the most exorbitant of bribes. But I wasn't planning to stop by her apartment, not during this visit. I wanted our first encounter, at least, to appear serendipitous.

"She has this thing for magazines," Mary wrote. *"I've now followed her home three times. All three times she's stopped at a newsstand near the corner and picked up some magazines. Two or three each visit."*

I'd been curious whether she lived alone. Reading a pile of magazines every night, I was guessing she either lived by herself, or was feeling disaffected from whomever it was she was living with.

"There's a deli right behind the newsstand. Two nights out of three, she went in and picked up something at the deli. I think fresh fruit, but I'm not sure."

I checked my watch. It was 6:50.

"Times home: 6:55, 7:05, 7:25."

Traffic around the park was no worse than usual for the hour, which meant it was awful.

I knew I might miss my chance to run into Lizzie outside her home.

I stuffed Mary's notes into my pocket and sat back. I needed a moment to decide how to play this.

At my request, Mary had been waiting outside the Museum of Modern Art the day that I'd had the rendezvous with Lizzie that had ended with our business lunch at Papaya King. The only hint I'd been able to give Mary that would make it any easier for her to follow us that day was that I thought that there'd be a black Town Car with tinted windows parked at a curb nearby. In New York City, unfortunately, that was about as useful a clue for her as a suggestion to keep her eyes peeled for pigeon droppings.

But Mary had arrived early, reconnoitered the area, and had picked the right Town Car, guessing correctly that it would be one that was parked illegally around the corner at the end of the block where traffic entered the one-way, not parked around the corner where traffic exited the street. To follow Lizzie's car, any vehicle already on 54th would be forced to backtrack all the way around the block.

In New York City, that kind of delay would mean a failed surveillance.

Mary's cousin from Jersey drove an old, lovingly restored BMW motorcycle that had belonged to her brother, who had been killed by an IED outside of Fallujah fourteen months after the end of major combat operations in Iraq. With Mary perched on the back of the bike, the two cousins had had no trouble sticking to the Town Car while Lizzie was frisking me as we were making our way through Central Park in the direction of Papaya King.

The cousins had hung out at a window table in a deli down the block while Lizzie and I enjoyed our dogs and fries. Later, Mary followed us on foot for our brief post-meal stroll, and then she and her cousin had remounted the two-wheeled Beemer and stayed close to Lizzie for the rest of that day, eventually tailing the Town Car to an office building in the four hundred block of Park Avenue, where Lizzie had spent the rest of that afternoon. Later on they trailed her to her apparent home on the Upper West Side near Lincoln Center.

That was the first time that Mary had noted the stops

Lizzie had made for magazines and for something at the Korean deli.

The taxi dropped me at 67th and Broadway. My watch said it was a few minutes after seven. I realized I may have already missed Lizzie's return home.

I quickly spotted the sidewalk news kiosk Mary had mentioned, and not far behind it, the Korean deli. Lizzie's building, a Depression-era high-rise of dirty blond brick, filled the middle of the block. What the building lacked in architectural character—sadly, it paled beside its neighbors—it made up for in glass. Some of the large windows in the upper units undoubtedly afforded great views of the Hudson, and of the sunset.

I hoped she had one of those apartments and one of those views.

A waist-high wall of mini-crates of first of-the-season Moroccan clementines marked the leading edge of an abundant fruit and veg-gie display that stretched from outside the door of the deli toward a decent-looking buffet of cooked food inside. I bought a *Newsday* from the newsstand guy—from our brief encounter, I thought it was likely he was deaf—and picked up a small bottle of Poland Spring from the young Korean woman manning the cash register in the deli before I strolled back out to the sidewalk. Assuming Lizzie might arrive by cab, as I had, I found a spot near a bus stop down the block beyond the entrance to her building. I held the tabloid at an awkward angle so that it obscured most of my face while I waited for taxis to pull to the curb delivering passengers.

Lizzie would have no reason to pay attention to me. I was a guy reading the paper, waiting for a bus. One of a hundred thousand people doing the same thing that evening in New York City.

I should have considered the likelihood that she'd arrive by subway, but I didn't, so I was almost totally ambushed when she walked right toward me from the general direction of the Lincoln Center station at 66th and Broadway.

Her hair was shorter than it had been at Papaya King and she'd added some alluring highlights. Even in the fading light she wore tinted lenses over her eyes. But she was firmly in Manhattan pedestrian mode; she had someplace to be, she wasn't browsing, and she wasn't making eye contact with strangers.

When a New Yorker has a destination in mind, she doesn't walk as much as she marches.

When Lizzie made it to the stretch of sidewalk behind the newsstand and then past the deli, her motion seemed to still for a split second with her eyes pointed in my direction. I feared for a moment that she had made me. I felt a stunning sense of relief when she pirouetted and retraced her steps to return to the newsstand. It took her less than a minute to pick out and pay for a couple of magazines. She stuck them into her shoulder bag and stepped immediately toward the deli.

I made my move.

I followed her in the door, walked directly to the front counter, picked up a package of M&Ms and got in line to pay. Lizzie was behind me—her back to mine—standing at the display of fresh fruit on the other side of the narrow store, no more than ten feet away.

The line in front of me moved too quickly. My hasty plan called for Lizzie to fall in behind me in line while I paid and spoke my line. When my turn came at the register, I went to plan B, said, "Forgot something, sorry," and stepped away from the counter. I pretended to be confused about my choice of breath mints while I waited for

Lizzie to finish selecting her fruit—she was either picky or indecisive—and get into the line. When, in my peripheral vision, I saw her turn to join the queue, I quickly stepped to the end of the line. A moment later she fell in behind me, so close that I could smell her.

My turn came. I placed the candy and the mints on the counter. The clerk hit some keys on the register and said, "Twotwoseven."

In a voice a few decibels louder than I would normally use, I asked, "I'm looking for a restaurant called Picholine. Do you know where it is? I think it's somewhere close by."

The clerk looked up at me as though I'd spoken to her in a foreign language. I shouldn't have been as surprised as I was: I had spoken to her in a foreign language. Before I'd recovered my composure she barked something short and, I thought, impolite in Korean and then something else that sounded like "no angish."

I handed her five dollars, and turned to the person behind me in line: Lizzie. I said, "Excuse me, would you happen to know where Picholine is?"

Lizzie's eyes widened in recognition and, well, dismay.

I said, "Oh, my God. I can't believe—I have a business dinner at Picholine. Am I close by?"

She smiled then, more with her eyes than with her mouth. The smile seemed sincere at first, quickly became awkward, and then devolved into artificial. She whispered, "Just a second." She lifted a small basket of raspberries. "I need to pay for these."

She held up the fruit for my inspection. Organic. I wasn't surprised.

I grabbed my change from the counter and stepped outside onto the sidewalk to wait for her.

When she joined me the tinted lenses were gone from her face, and her plaid eyes were suspicious. Lovely, yes, but suspicious. "It's on 64th, between here and the park. You'll enjoy it, I promise."

"I bet I don't enjoy it as much as I enjoyed Papaya King."

She looked away for a second, then back. I found the gesture coquettish. A good sign.

I made my play. "Hello, Lizzie. It's . . . great to see you."

She saw something in my eyes, too, I could tell. I hoped what she was sensing was mischief and I prayed she misinterpreted exactly what kind of mischief. She shook her head. "Go," she said. "Go to your meeting. You know better. You know you know better."

"I know nothing. I'm an idiot."

"If you did this on purpose, you're more than an idiot."

"What are you—"

She held up her index finger. She wasn't just interrupting me; she was dismissing my protest. "We can't see each other. Period. Not in a deli. Not on a sidewalk. Not in a coffee house in Prague."

A coffee house in Prague? "Oh, come on. Just have a drink with me. I have some time before I have to be at the restaurant. What harm can it do? A drink? We'll have fun. You know we will. We always do."

Her tone became insistent. "This"—she waved her arm between us—"can't happen. Go to your dinner. I'll forget about this encounter. I suggest you do the same." She turned away from me and took two quick steps.

"I'll happily blow off my meeting if you let me take you somewhere. My treat."

She snapped back in my direction like a soldier obeying a marching order. "That is not possible. No." Her jaw stiffened and her glare sharpened. "This has never happened before. It *cannot* happen. The consequences are . . . severe. Do you understand what I'm saying? Do you?"

I pretended she wasn't shoving me away. What choice

did I have? I needed time to find Adam. "You work around here? Live around here, what? On your way to the symphony or something? Is it ballet season?"

"Leave. Now, please."

She was begging.

Thing is, I've stood at a lot of doorways in my life, stealing kisses, weaseling my way inside for one-last-drinks. I know when a woman means it when she tells me to leave. I know when a woman doesn't.

Lizzie didn't really want me to leave.

"A drink, Lizzie. A drink. Harmless." She didn't respond right away, so I pushed. "Come on, do I have to say everything twice?"

That brought back a memory for her, and with the memory, a smile. A tiny smile, sure, but her veneer was cracking.

"I can't. You have to go."

"Our business is over. The contracts are signed, so to speak. What's the harm in a friendly drink?"

"Over? Over?" She made a sound from her throat that conveyed supreme exasperation. With me. "You know exactly . . ." She stumbled as she realized she couldn't quite put her finger on what it was I was supposed to know, exactly. "This can't be happening. This can't . . . oh, Lord. Just go! Think! Think! Please, please, remember what business we're in."

I wasn't going to follow her there. If I followed her there, I knew I'd lose my resolve. "Really, though," I said. "What do you think the odds are of us running into each other? A city this size? A neighborhood I never visit? Fate is talking. We can't ignore that, can we?"

"Yes," she said, suddenly regaining her composure, and her perspective. And suddenly finding her suspicion. "What are the odds?"

I certainly didn't want her to go there. I wanted her

off-balance, not suspicious. "I'll do kraut," I said, moving suddenly closer to her, close enough to kiss her, "if you'll do kraut."

She glanced in the direction of my lips, sighed a deep sigh that sounded swollen with both possibility and regret, spun away from me, and began marching back toward the entrance to the Lincoln Center station, her plastic bag with the raspberries swinging back and forth at her side. When a cab pulled over to drop a well-dressed couple off at the curb, she quickly changed course and hopped into the empty backseat. I couldn't hear the instructions she gave to the driver.

Lizzie didn't wave to me as she pulled away.

After losing sight of the taxi as it headed uptown on Broadway, I followed the general path that she had taken, first strolling down the sidewalk toward the subway, then after a change of heart, over to the curb to hail a cab of my own. As I passed by the newsstand, the deaf guy selling magazines said, in a baritone as deep as the Grand Canyon, "That didn't go too good, did it?"

Okay, so he wasn't deaf.

I stepped over and stood in front of a tall stack of *Maxim*, reached down into my pocket, and played a hunch. I silently placed a hundred-dollar bill on his tiny scratched counter. "You know her?"

The bill disappeared in a flash.

He wasn't blind either.

"She's a reg'lar. One of my bes' customers. Course I do." He used his head to gesture toward her apartment.

"You wouldn't happen to know the doorman in her building?"

He hesitated as though he were calculating whether that kind of question should be included in my initial hundred-dollar investment. Then he said, "Sure. Been working this stand 'leven years. Know a lot."

"Reasonable man? The doorman?"

"Depends who approaches him. Has his moments. Sometimes he sees things . . . sometimes, hey."

"Turns out I can be generous."

" 'At's one of the many things I already know 'bout you. Turns out I can be persuasive. 'At's somethin' you should know 'bout me. With the right incentive I could 'proach him for you. Come to an agreement. A . . . rapprochement, so to speak."

A rapprochement? "Then you may be able to help me out."

"Who knows 'bout that? Anything's possible in this world. That's what my momma used to say."

"Good. I think I'll be in touch. You here every day?"

"Every day's a lot of days."

"Tomorrow?"

He shrugged. I put another hundred dollars on his tray.

"Bright and early. If she be working, she be out the door a little bit before nine. Never before eight-thirty."

"Subway or cab?"

"Seventy one, thirty the other. Nice day? Ninety-ten. Doesn't work every day, though. No reg'lar schedule. She travels some, too. Gone overnight. Gone a week. Never know."

I began to walk away. Stopped. "Did your momma really used to say that? That anything's possible in this world?"

"I never even knew my momma."

As I climbed into a taxi I was thinking of Connie. *There are worse things,* he'd tell me. *Worse things.*

FORTY

One of the pleasures of fine hotels is room service.

A half-dozen perfect, fresh strawberries in a silver bowl? Eighteen dollars. Why so much? Why not? Add the six-dollar "service fee." Why the service fee? It's nothing more than a way for the hotel to avoid the embarrassing reality that what they really want to charge for that simple bowl of strawberries is twenty-four dollars, not eighteen dollars. The price they wish to collect is not an exorbitant three bucks a berry, but instead a ridiculously exorbitant four bucks a berry. And that doesn't include the seventeen percent tip that's necessary to compensate some poor waiter for the dual traumas of not only having to endure an elevator ride but also then being forced to look at some rich guy in a bathrobe.

Or maybe a rich guy wearing less than a bathrobe, much less.

Hey, why not?

Room service isn't about dining; it's about indulgence. Six dollars on top of indulgence is still indulgence. Seventeen percent more than indulgence is still just indulgence, isn't it?

I needed some indulgence.

I'd convinced myself—blindly, arrogantly, perhaps, yes, even optimistically—that my faux-surprise encounter with

Lizzie would conclude with us sitting side by side in some New York City saloon sharing small plates of better-than-average food and drinking from the same bottle of good wine. A nice Auslese is what I'd been thinking. I'd believed that she'd set aside her misgivings and accept the ruse that my ambush was serendipity and that she would listen with compassion to my tale of woe and would generously agree to intervene with her Death Angel compatriots to bend the rules just the slightest bit to accommodate the peculiar circumstances I was facing regarding my son.

My son, Adam.

I had to find him. Soothe him. Convince him.

Love him.

A few months' delay, maybe, in the threshold. Six months, tops. That's all I needed.

I'd charmed enough women out of their underwear in my youth that I was supremely confident I could charm Lizzie out of a few months' delay in carrying out the Death Angel mandate.

Obviously, I'd been a little wrong.

To partially compensate for my disappointment on the Upper West Side, I ordered too much food from too many categories on the room-service menu. The young woman who took my phone order greeted me by name as though we'd been acquainted for years—or more accurately, as though I'd known her parents for years—and informed me that my meal would be delivered in about thirty-five minutes. She never sounded even the slightest bit perplexed that I'd ordered well over a hundred dollars' worth of food and had asked for only one place setting.

She sounded, I thought, French. Southern French, pleasant. Not Parisian French, unpleasant. I thanked her. She told me it was her pleasure.

We both knew it wasn't. Her pleasure, that is. But the illusion of a good hotel accomplishes the same magic for me as does a good book, or a compelling movie: I gladly suspend disbelief in order to be coddled in the experience of other, of elsewhere.

While I waited for the food to arrive, I took a quick shower and selected from the pay-per-view menu a movie that Thea had refused to see with me in the theater. The knock on the door came about five minutes early.

A fine hotel always strives to exceed expectations.

I opened the door. A black man in his twenties stood behind a husky stainless steel cart topped with linen. He asked permission to enter. I asked him to leave the food on the cart, said I'd pick at it at my leisure. I moved to the other side of the room and gazed past the tower of the Pierre at the dark shadows of the park while he fumbled with the trays.

"Sir?" he said a moment later.

I turned, ready to sign his chit, prepared to add a few bucks to the seventeen percent he was getting already.

More indulgence.

He was wearing white gloves. Had the guy who delivered my breakfast that morning been wearing white gloves? I didn't think so.

But the guy who had delivered the note to join the comic in the lounge had. I remembered him.

This was that guy. I glanced at his lapel. No name tag.

The man with the gloves was between me and the door. The room-service cart sat between us like a stainless steel fort.

He said, "I've been instructed to order you not to make any further contact with anyone in the organization."

My heart was pounding. I was thinking, *These guys are good. And nimble? My God.*

Then, *Did he say "order"?*

"I don't know what you're talking about. If you're done here, please leave before I call security."

"I would suggest, respectfully, that you not trifle with us. Our resources will surprise you."

"Please leave my room." With forced nonchalance, I lifted the phone off the nearby desk.

No dial tone.

"It's been temporarily disconnected, sir. Service will resume shortly, after I exit with your assurances in this matter."

"What are you going to do if I don't offer my assurances? Kill me?"

He seemed to be gazing at me with some pity.

That really pissed me off.

He said, "I'm here in good faith, sir. Everything we do, we do in good faith. We ask the same of our clients. Is that so unreasonable?"

He'd chosen patronizing. Wrong strategy with me. They should have known that.

"I need a few months," I said.

"Perhaps fate will make those months available to you. We don't control fate. We never pretend to. But we keep our commitments once fate has shown her cards. That's all—nothing more, nothing less."

"Well, I'm freeing you of your commitments. I'll sign whatever you want. Keep my money. I don't care."

"As you well know, sir, once the threshold event has occurred, canceling the contract is not permitted. Now that you've been diagnosed with a life-threatening illness, and the threshold event has come, the line cannot be redrawn."

"Can't you see what I'm saying? I don't want out. I need a few fucking months. Then you can go ahead and kill me, goddamn it."

In response to my profanity, his face became a mask.

He retreated to his opening line: "I've been asked to instruct you not to make any further contact with anyone in our organization."

"Last time you said 'ordered.' "

"Ordered, then, sir. Ordered."

"Get out of here. Get the fuck out of here."

He didn't budge. "Consider this, sir: How would you feel if we suddenly decided to abrogate a portion of the contract. For instance, the part about keeping your wishes secret from your loved ones. We understand, for instance, that your wife—Thea? Is that her name? What if—"

"Enough," I said.

"Or your daughter, the older one? Berkeley. I suspect she is old enough to understand that—"

"Enough," I said again, but without the same fervor. I sat down on an upholstered chair and stared out at the park. My back was to the well-spoken man wearing the white gloves. I was in a perfect position for a well-executed maneuver with a garrote, were he so inclined.

"Sir, I wish you would reconsider—"

"Enough," I said again. "I heard you the first time. I heard you the second time. Go."

A few seconds later I heard the door open and then close.

He'd come to deliver a threat. He was a competent man; he'd certainly delivered it clearly. If I continued to break the rules the Death Angels would inform Thea—or worse, Cal, or, Jesus Christ, Adam—about all the money I'd spent to ensure that I would be provided with a quick exit if things got tough for me.

The room-service tray was still hogging the passageway at the end of the bed. After a while I stood up and checked the cart, not because my hunger had returned, but rather out of curiosity. I was beyond surprise when I discovered that beneath the silver warming lids on top of the cart was no food. Nothing.

In the warming oven below? Nothing.

So much for my indulgence.

I sat on the bed and picked up the phone. The dial tone had returned. I touched the button to connect with room service. The woman who answered the phone wasn't French, neither pleasant French nor unpleasant French. I thought Nebraska perhaps.

Pleasant Nebraska. The only kind. She addressed me by name. I wished her a good evening and asked her where my order was.

She said she had no record of an order from my room since breakfast. If I would like to order something, though, she would be delighted to assist me.

FORTY-ONE

I waited until almost midnight so that Mary and her cousin would have time to grab coffee or dessert and get back to Brooklyn after the final curtain of the play they were attending.

Mary answered her mobile phone after half a ring.

"Yes," she said. She knew who it was.

"That errand you've been doing for me? It turns out that I need some more of the same stuff that you picked up at that place on Park Avenue. You know the one? Can you do that?"

Mary didn't need a road map. "Of course," she said. "What I picked up already wasn't ... enough? Satisfactory? What?"

"No, no, it was great. But it turns out I didn't use it well. It may have spoiled. My fault, entirely. I'm hoping that I'll do better with another batch."

"Tomorrow?"

"Yes, first thing. The people at the store will probably have guessed that you'll be stopping by."

"Okay. Shouldn't be a problem, as long as I know."

I sighed. "How was the play?"

"We had a lovely time. It was even funnier than I expected, if that's possible. Can't thank you enough. I'll take care of the errands tomorrow and be back in touch."

We said good-bye and I closed the phone. I reopened it and speed-dialed Thea in Colorado.

"Hey," I said. "Miss you."

She was sleepy. We talked kids and dogs and my health for a while. She hadn't heard from Adam. I told her I had at least another day of meetings. She took it in her stride. I told her I loved her and asked her to kiss the girls for me. She told me to take care of myself.

It all seemed so normal.

FORTY-TWO

The next morning I ordered room service again—this time for real—and ate eggs and bacon and rye toast with the curtains wide open to the park, and with Matt and Katie telling me their version of the news. Dessert was that elusive silver bowl of fresh strawberries.

I thought I'd end up regretting my indulgence. My stomach hadn't successfully processed that much food in weeks. I had to distract myself from imagining the vomit I'd produce with bacon and strawberries.

One news story caught my eye. A story from home. A man had been shot on Interstate 70 on the west side of the Denver metropolitan area the previous night shortly before eleven o'clock. Given evidence at the scene, the authorities were investigating the possibility that he was the victim of a sniper. *The Today Show* was using a local feed of a familiar Denver reporter standing high on a stepped mesa that rose above another bluff that was roped off with crime-scene tape. Far over the reporter's shoulder I could see the wide ribbon of highway that led from the rising plains into the mountains.

It was one of the highways that led from my Denver home to my Ridgway home.

The victim was a forty-two-year-old father of three. He'd been driving a white Honda Odyssey in the slow lane heading westbound just beyond Ward Road.

I sometimes drove that route on my way from Ridgway to Denver's suburbs, or back.

Huh. I adjusted the time of the crime to account for the Eastern time zone and realized that the sniper had killed his victim about an hour after I'd sent the faux room-service waiter on his way without the promise he'd demanded.

On my way out of the hotel one of the front-desk clerks replenished my supply of pocket cash. I suspected I was going to need a good-sized wad.

I took a taxi back to the Upper West Side and had the cabbie drop me off a block before we got to Lizzie's building. I bought a cup of coffee at a Starbucks, snuck a look to confirm that the newsstand was open for business, and found a deserted stoop with a good vantage of the canopied door to her building.

I parked my butt on the stoop, sipped coffee, and read the *Times,* one eye on the sidewalk.

It was eight-thirty. I wanted to be early in case she was early.

My caution hadn't been necessary. Eight forty-five came and went. So did nine o'clock. No Lizzie.

Nine-fifteen, nine-thirty. Ditto.

My coffee was gone and I had to pee. I stood up to try to see if that would relieve the pressure on my bladder. If not, I was looking at a quick jaunt to Starbucks for a toilet break.

"Boss? She be gone."

I looked behind me and saw the man from the newsstand, the one whom I'd originally thought was deaf. His presence surprised me, spooked me even. So did the fact that he was about five foot four.

He noticed my eyes take in his height. "I stand on a Coke crate when I'm working," he said. "It's an antique."

An antique? I nodded. "Good morning. What do you mean, she's gone?"

His hands were in his pockets. His dark eyes danced. They were as convivial as could be.

Oh.

I pulled the roll of cash from my front pants pocket and peeled off three one-hundred-dollar bills. After fanning them open for his appraisal, I asked, "Is what you know worth this?"

"My personal opinion is that no woman is worth that. Least I never met her. But it ain't my money, and it ain't my dick."

"This isn't about my dick."

He shrugged. "First rule: It's always about your dick. Second rule: If you don't think it's about your dick, go back and study the first rule."

I handed him the money. He slid it casually into his shirt pocket as though he had three big bills in extra cash on him every morning of his life.

I liked the guy.

"She packed up a bunch of shit, couple rolling suitcases' worth, and was gone before midnight. Little later on two guys popped over and loaded even more of her stuff into an unmarked panel truck. A half-dozen cardboard boxes, a' least." He handed me a piece of paper. "This is the license number from the truck. Jersey. It's pro'ly bogus." He poked at the scrap. "And 'at's 'at other number. On the side, by the cab. Bogus too."

"The guys?"

"Young and buff. Don't-fuck-with-'em types. One was carryin'. Big piece of blue steel."

"You were here all night?"

He made a "you crazy?" face. "Need my sleep. Gotta get eight. I'm a mess if I don't get eight. Night doorman was 'round, though. I gave him some of what you gave me last night, axed him to keep an eye out."

"What you give him?"

He smiled. "Twenty."

"I'm overpaying you, aren't I?"

"You can afford it, boss. Say we jus' call it reparation. Your people and my people? What came down? Ya know?"

I was tempted to hear his version of history, the one about my people and his people and what came down, but it wasn't the time.

"I'd like to see her place," I said. "Inside." I'm not sure why I said it or what I hoped to find if I made it into Lizzie's flat, but the moment I said it, I knew that I really meant it.

He shifted his weight from one foot to the other. "Give me half an hour to set that up. Come back by the stand."

"Thanks." I turned to leave.

"No need to thank me. It'll cost you," he said.

"Everything does, one way or another."

"I don't take checks. You need it, there's an ATM in the Korean deli." He pointed over his shoulder. "Careful of the old lady. She be a witch."

I walked back to Starbucks and waited in line to use the toilet. Mary called when I was in the middle of everything. I answered one-handed. The signal on my cell was fractured and inconsistent, accurately reflecting my circumstances.

"Yeah?"

"Turns out that the store on Park Avenue is closed. Just like that. Totally shut down. Furniture is still there, but the desks are cleared, everything is gone. Laptops, phones. Weirdest thing."

I was surprised but I wasn't surprised. Know that feeling? "See what you can find out about other locations where they might do business. See if their neighbors in the building noticed anything."

"Will do." She hesitated and then she asked me, "Are we in some kind of trouble?"

I liked the "we" part. Mary saw herself as part of the team, even if she wasn't sure of the nature of the game. I tried to sound blasé. "We have a bit of a puzzle to solve, Mary."

"It's important, though? It's about more than money?"

"Yeah."

"More than a girl?"

I reminded myself that Mary might have seen Lizzie hold my hands at Papaya King. She might have seen how close I came to kissing her.

"It's not about a girl, Mary. Not that way."

Mary wouldn't be pleased to play a part in encouraging any infidelities on my part. She liked Thea.

"Okay."

The "okay" was acceptance on her part, not belief. She was waiting to be convinced.

"It's about family, Mary. Family. And it's complicated."

For Mary, that was better than me swearing on a Bible.

"Gotcha," she said.

I waited until ten o'clock came before I stepped down the street to my rendezvous with newsstand man. The guy in front of me in line was buying a flesh mag—something about rockets and boobs; don't ask, I don't know—the *Financial Times,* and a Snickers.

"See, I tell ya, it's always about the guy's dick," the man on the Coke crate said in greeting when I edged up to the counter. He was reflecting on the previous customer. "You got my job, you get to know things. You do."

I smiled. "Maybe he's embarrassed that he's a broker or

an investment banker and he's only buying the porn to hide his pink sheet."

" 'At's good. Like 'at one. Got you a discount, by the by. My man inside is Gaston and he'll be needin' another hunderd from you. That's a bargain for what you be askin'. Other 'partments on her floor are empty till lunchtime, at least. People on her side are in Bo-ca Rattone, the folks on the back side are all at work. Gaston says one of them owns a titty bar on Eighth that's open for lunch. He won't be home; likes to keep an eye on his girls. My man Gaston's big on rules, so here's the deal: You got five minutes inside her place, that's it. Not a second more. If the lady's phone rings, you lock up, walk out the door, and take the fire stairs. No bullshit. You wait there fi' minutes before you go back to the lobby."

"Alarm?"

"Nope."

"Sure?"

"Yep. One more thing: You take nothin' out. I mean nothin'. No panties even. Nothin'."

I opened my mouth to protest the insinuation—*"This isn't about my dick"*—but realized, *why bother?*

"Deal." I peeled off another hundred and rested it on his tray. I wanted him grateful and had a feeling I would require his services again. "Thanks for all you help," I said and turned to walk away.

"You want a magazine?" he said. "On the house."

"What?"

When I looked back up he was holding the *Robb Report* up for me and he was smiling.

"Service door'll be open in back. You go in that way. You come back out that way. See how you like it."

At least he was still smiling.

*

Gaston was a skinny guy about my age, a man of indeterminate racial heritage with short nappy hair and buggy eyes. His dark skin had fat freckles and he had a red aura around his nose and ears as though he suffered from some chronic inflammation. Despite his distinctive features he had wise eyes above a jaw that seemed set in concrete. He wasn't into banter or negotiation. He knew who I was the moment I walked into the lobby from the rear and he assumed that I knew the rules.

I shook his hand and said, "Hello." The greeting started with one hundred dollars in my palm and ended with one hundred dollars in Gaston's.

"Sixteen oh-two," he said. He held out his hand to shake mine again. One quick pump and I had a pair of keys—one an old brass, one a modern security type—glued to my sweaty palm.

In my solo elevator ride up to sixteen, it crossed my mind that it was all a setup, that Lizzie had offered Gaston and the newsstand man a much bigger chunk of change than I was shelling out to deliver me right back into her hands.

I wondered what would happen were that true. In my head, I saw a very interesting scene with Lizzie and the comic from Nobu, and the black man with the white gloves, and maybe the young MBA type who faked being lost on the side of the road near my house in Ridgway before he'd taken my instructions regarding the client-derived parameters.

So be it.

There was no turning back. I'd already pointed the boards downhill. The slope below me was steep—calling it a double black diamond wouldn't do it justice—and I was aiming at a tight grove of aspen. There was no time to think about when to turn; I had to rely on instinct to fly between the knobby white tree trunks.

To stay alive all I had to do was follow the advice of my old friend and keep both skis on the same side of every tree.

How hard was that?

I firmly believe that, like the path to any woman's heart, every lock in every old door has its own set of tricks. It's one of those rare universal truths about the world. To master quick entry you need to know when to push the key an extra millimeter and when to tug, when to be gentle and when to be forceful, whether to put your weight into it, how to hold the key, and what it all feels like just before it goes *click*.

For me, the experience of trying to break into Lizzie's flat was like being with a woman for the first time; I didn't yet know the intimate tricks, I didn't have the touch. With a woman, I usually loved the process of discovery, everything involved in the liberation of the secrets. But that time, alone in that corridor, I didn't. I felt like a clumsy dime-crook shoplifting candy bars in a corner store, waiting to be caught with my hand down my pants.

Standing there alone in the hallway of the sixteenth floor, I fumbled to finesse the locks on Lizzie's door for way too many seconds before I was finally able to ease both sets of tumblers to release at once.

I forced myself to turn and relock the locks behind me. Just in case.

Then, only then, did I turn and look into Lizzie's flat.

I hadn't allowed myself to have expectations about what I would find once I was inside the door of 1602. Not having expectations means I shouldn't have been surprised.

But I was. Oh, I was.

FORTY-THREE

I was going to Boulder to see Dr. Gregory whenever I could fit in a trip. I accepted the need to see him. Time was limited. I had to get where I was going.

Where was I going?

It all had to do with Adam, of course, and with dying. My daughters would have Thea and all her gifts and strengths to help them cope with the loss of their father. Adam would have Bella and her big heart and her bad judgment. But Adam also had a malignant history to overcome. I understood that much, but not much more. I wanted Gregory to help me do the best that I could with these last few weeks. Adam's disappearance, his vulnerability, and the possibility of my imminent death made the visits with my shrink more urgent to me. I understood the urgency, but I wasn't comfortable with it.

I never felt urgency with a man before. Only with women.

"Today's topic is suicide," I said a moment after I'd settled onto my seat across from him. It had been the last visit with my shrink before my trip east to find Adam. To find Lizzie.

We'd covered the ways that Adam could hurt me—the vulnerability thing—and now it was time to take my disclosures to the next level.

My gut told me that this was the reason I was in Dr. Gregory's office—the real reason—and I'd decided that the time had come for him and me to take at least one step nearer to that truth. We'd been edging ever closer to an answer to that question he'd asked the first day: *How can I be of help?*

"Okay" is how he replied to my statement about the topic of the day. He said it without surprise, without even blinking. I wondered whether my overture about suicide was really that banal or whether his years of listening to people like me had caused him to develop calluses to the monumental.

I knew I'd said it the way I said it—without preamble—to try to get some visible reaction from him, but my ploy hadn't worked. I could just as well have said that the day's topic was hemorrhoids or jock itch for all the excitement and concern he showed.

At least he didn't yawn.

"If, hypothetically, I told you I was thinking of killing myself, what would you do?"

"Depends," he said.

The guy had been there before.

I pressed my index fingertips into the corners of my eyes. *God.* "That's not particularly helpful," I said. Understatement time.

"I'm not trying to be unresponsive. Nor unsympathetic. I just don't know enough about your hypothetical situation."

Fair. "Let's say I wanted to end this—my life—before nature takes its course. While I still have some control over how things end. What would you do if I told you that? How would you handle it? With me? Here today."

"I'd ask you to talk about it."

I faked a smile for him. I was getting exasperated, but blowing up at him would waste time I didn't have. "No. I mean, what would be your responsibility? Do you try to talk me out of it? Do you try to stop me? Do you have legal or ethical responsibilities that dictate your response? What? I'm trying to understand the rules. You seem like a rules kind of guy."

"Yes, I would have obligations. Ethical obligations and legal obligations. If I determine that you're a danger to yourself, I'm required to take some actions based on my assessment of the situation."

I noted that he hadn't bitten on my rules-kind-of-guy dig. Probably wise. But I could tell he'd been tempted. "Inform somebody, for instance? That might be one of your obligations?"

"Possibly. More likely I'd evaluate you, and hospitalize you if I thought the risk was real."

"Hospitalize?"

"In a psychiatric facility."

"If I didn't cooperate? Cooperation isn't one of my characterological predilections."

He smiled at that. I felt a small sense of triumph.

He said, "Again, based on my assessment, I might try to enlist some outside assistance to get you to a safe place."

"The police?"

"Yes."

"A 'safe place' being a euphemism for the aforementioned psychiatric hospital?"

"Yes."

I counted to five, silently. "Don't patronize me, please. It's insulting. More to the point it isn't necessary. And I only have time for the necessary."

He said nothing. He could have reminded me that I wasted much more of our time than he did. Were our roles reversed, I probably would have.

I hadn't realized I was leaning forward toward him, but I was. I sat back and in a low, calm voice, I said, "That's kind of ironic, don't you think? Putting me in a hospital against my will because I don't want this illness to develop to the point that I end up confined . . . in a hospital, against my will."

"You asked about my responsibilities. I'm thinking you would like me to reply honestly. In that spirit, I'm acknowledging that my responsibility would be to intervene. The circumstances would determine how I intervene. Obviously, I'm not going to be much help to you if you succeed in killing yourself."

"You don't think so? What if I disagree with that premise? What if I've reached a determination that—because of events that have spun out of my control—the only way you will have ended up being of much help to me is if I prove ultimately successful in ending my life on my own terms."

"If that's the case, then I don't understand my role. Why you're here. In therapy, I mean."

"Why is that so perplexing to you? It seems to me that the only reason a psychologist might be confused by my situation is if he insisted on assuming that the sole reason a man might have to tell a shrink he's thinking of killing himself would be so that the shrink would save him from the impulse."

He didn't reply right away, but I could tell from his eyes that he had indeed been thinking exactly that.

"Go on," he said.

The sign of an open mind?

"Suicide is not always irrational; it's not always pathological."

"Yes," he said. We both knew he wasn't agreeing with my thesis. "I assume what you're alluding to is the metaphorical airplane, the one you talked about the first day, the one with the engines out? That's the helplessness you're feeling? One option you mentioned was taking over the controls and pointing the nose into the ground."

"I don't ever want to be the guy who can't perceive any options."

"Euthanasia?" he asked, though initially my mind's ear heard *Youth in Asia*.

His question seemed sincere. Naive—oh so naive—but sincere. Without any awareness of their existence, he was trying to understand the Death Angels and their little business.

"Not exactly. In this hypothetical situation I'm wondering about, I'm not talking about looking for a compassionate way to end my . . . suffering. Euthanasia is choosing death in order to interrupt useless torment prior to an inevitable, near end. This isn't a Dr. Kevorkian thing. And it's not a Terri Schiavo thing. I'm talking about something else, about ending my life on my own terms while I'm still well enough to do so, so that I die before I become disabled mentally, or disabled physically, or before I become debilitated by pain. I'm talking about acting before euthanasia becomes necessary. Long before pulling a feeding tube even becomes a consideration."

"A lifestyle choice?"

He made it sound like a nose job or breast enhancement. "In a way," I said.

"I've never been confronted with this question before."

I sighed. It wasn't a sigh of frustration. It was a sigh of relief that Dr. Gregory was finally realizing the novelty of my situation.

"Neither have I," I admitted. "But I feel a very strong need to get it right the first time. That's why I'm here."

He smiled. I can't tell you how much pride I felt that I'd gotten the guy to smile at that moment.

"So, are you?" he asked.

"Am I what?"

"Considering suicide?"

"If your professional responsibilities require you to try to thwart plans like the ones I'm curious about, I don't think it would be wise to reveal to you whether or not I'm considering them."

He sat silently for a moment.

Over our relatively few hours together I'd come to recognize at least two different forms of silence from him. One, the more common one, was the silence of entreaty. It was invitation via patience. It was the silence that said I'm willing to wait a long, long time for you to take us wherever it is we need to go next.

The other was the silence of cogitation. Although he was blessed with a quick mind, I had occasionally been able to pose an issue or a dilemma that caused him to pause and think.

What I was observing right then, I thought, was typetwo silence, the silence of reflection.

The pause in our conversation grew from seconds to a minute, and then more. Finally, he said, "I misspoke earlier. I said that if I thought you were a danger to yourself, I would be compelled to take some action, based on the circumstances."

"Yes? But that's not completely accurate?"

"I omitted a word. The word I omitted is 'imminent.' I am only required to take certain actions if I judge that you are an *imminent* danger to yourself. Or to someone else."

"That allows for some leeway," I said, seeing his invitation for what it was. "Wiggle room."

He didn't exactly nod, but he certainly didn't shake his head, either. He was agreeing with my assessment.

My doctor had some wiggle room.

"So we can talk?" I said, thinking I was accurately reading the invisible-ink message he'd inserted between the lines of our conversation.

"I think we can talk," he said. "When we reach unsteady ground—if we reach unsteady ground—I'll let you know. If I see unsteady ground looming up ahead, I'll let you know that, too. When I do, you can decide if you would like to proceed any further with me. How is that?"

"You're asking me to trust you?"

He pondered the question. "I'm . . . inviting you to trust me. Without it, there's not much point for you to talk with me any longer."

"There's some risk here for me," I said. "Serious risk. If my trust turns out to be misplaced."

"For me, as well," he said.

I saw that was true, too.

He grew silent again, but that time it was most certainly type-one silence, the entreaty silence. I used the void to try to recognize what it was he expected I should be seeing.

I couldn't see it, whatever it was. *Nada.*

"We've been talking about vulnerability," he said, offering me a hint.

Generous of him. "Yes. Yes, yes, yes. That cocktail of self-disclosure and vulnerability I've been learning about," I said. "What is necessary, but is not sufficient? We're about to get intimate, huh? You and me?"

"Looks like it," he said. "Looks like it."

"My first time with a man," I said. I couldn't resist the joke. Character flaw, no doubt.

He could.

"Actually, I think the first time was with Adam. But I'm honored to be the second."

"You may be reluctant to believe what I'm about to tell you," I began. "But it's all true."

"Go on," he said.

"I'll deny this if it's ever repeated to me outside this room."

"Tell me," he said.

"There are these people that I call . . . the Death Angels."

I felt an electric shock of pain travel from someplace deep inside my skull, into my brain stem and then down my spinal cord, where the agony dissipated into my tissue as though my backbone was a lightning rod buried in loamy soil. I took a deep breath to recover from the shock before I said, "You really can't tell anybody any of this."

"I understand. I can feel your vulnerability all the way across the room."

"That's kind of you to say, but you can't understand. Not really. I haven't told you anything yet. But this is where you're going to have to trust me."

"Okay," he said. "Probably vice versa, too."

"Yes," I said.

I was determined to tell him everything but it took me another minute to begin. I tried a number of transition lines in my head. Some cute. Some not. I finally said, "At great expense, I've hired them—these people I call the Death Angels—to kill me if I ever get sick or injured in a way that will leave me incapacitated."

I studied him as I spoke, but could see no reaction from him save an involuntary change in the size of his pupils.

"Recently, I learned that my illness has advanced to the point that a previously agreed-upon threshold has been reached. I'm now fair game for the Death Angels. They are obligated to end my life. There is no mechanism for me to reverse that process."

"You're serious?"

"Dead serious," I said.

"Go on," he said.

I did. I told him everything.

273

FORTY-FOUR

I reminded myself that the newsstand man had insisted that I had only five minutes inside Lizzie's place.

I wasted too much of one of those minutes in a zombied, open-mouthed amble through the flat's spacious front rooms—the living room, dining room, study, and kitchen—thinking this stupid thought: Thea could have been the person who'd decorated Lizzie's apartment. That's how familiar it all felt to me.

The decor was a mix of contemporary and antique styles dotted with a few quirky pieces that fit neither category, along with enough of an Asian influence to make a noticeable difference. Designwise, the place looked like small versions of similar rooms in our Ridgway home.

How weird was that?

The focus and flow of the living room were both directed toward a series of three big windows that faced the Hudson. Later that day the windows would frame the sun as it set to the west, toward Colorado. A lovely chenille chaise—an upholstered altar to solitude and comfort— rested in front of the windows, flanked by a delicate Chinese tea table that supported a reading lamp and a foot-high pile of books.

The books were all novels, mostly genre titles written by popular writers who showed up on weekend morning shows. The whole scene felt quite poignant.

I felt illicit being there, seeing it.

What was I hoping to find inside Lizzie's place? I didn't know. I'd decided that I wanted to be able to guess what had been in the boxes that had been carted off overnight by the Death Angel Moving Company. And I wanted to find an indication of where Lizzie might have gone next— a note on the refrigerator with a forwarding address would have been a particularly welcome touch.

I wanted to know what was missing from her home.

I wanted to see photographs of her with her family, or her lover.

I wanted to learn her real name.

I wanted to know what magazines she bought every evening from the newsstand man.

Mostly, I wanted to find something that might give me leverage that would buy me the time I needed to wrap things up with Adam before the Death Angels implemented their end-of-life services plan.

I checked the refrigerator door for that note with her forwarding address. Alas, no luck.

Although it was far from full, the refrigerator hadn't been cleaned out. Lizzie liked plain yogurt, and the labels on disposable containers revealed that she was disposed to buy takeout from the Whole Foods in Columbus Circle. She drank Sancerre, and had a dozen itty-bitty cans of Sapporo beer on the top shelf next to a four-pack of Starbucks Double Shots and a six-pack of stubby cans of Diet Coke.

Lizzie liked her caffeine.

On the second shelf of the refrigerator sat the clear plastic clamshell of organic raspberries that Lizzie had bought from the Korean grocer downstairs.

She hadn't eaten any of the berries.

She had indeed been home, though. The newsstand guy wasn't lying.

Lizzie's study was oddly masculine. It was a small room, maybe seven or eight feet by ten, with frosted-glass pocket doors that faced toward the living room and the distant George Washington Bridge. The back wall of the study was lined with a long built-in credenza and floor-to-ceiling shelves of a solid dark wood—walnut, I thought, or mahogany. A simple desk—nothing more than a huge piece of lovely old teak on a couple of cast-iron trestles—sat in the center of the room.

Other than one more reading lamp the desktop was a void, but I thought a vague rectangular outline of dust showed where a laptop computer had rested directly in front of the chair. The bookshelves on the opposite wall were packed spine to spine; I figured it was safe to assume that Lizzie's library hadn't been disturbed during the impromptu move the night before. The credenzas below the shelves appeared to have solid fronts. I pressed on the wooden panels in a few places, expecting a hidden door to pop open.

Nothing. What a waste of space.

Damn. Who has an office without yesterday's mail, without files, without unpaid bills?

Who has an office without photographs?

My watch said I'd killed two minutes by then.

Where are all the magazines she buys?

What had I learned? Nothing.

Shit.

A narrow, wainscoted hallway with parquet floors led from the entryway toward a powder room and two bedrooms. I skipped the powder room and turned in to the door of the first bedroom. It was an afterthought room, not a guest room. Lizzie didn't have frequent guests, or if she did, the guests slept in her bed. The only furniture in the spare room was a pair of matched Queen Anne chairs that I imagined had once been sitting where the chaise currently rested in front of the Hudson River windows.

The closet? Off-season clothes, nothing else. No shoe boxes of canceled checks. No old love letters tied with ribbon secreted on the top shelf.

Her scent, yes. Plenty of that. On those hanging clothes. Spices and flowers and that alluring aroma of fresh laundry that had been dried in the sun.

Three minutes gone.

Off to the master.

I took one step inside her bedroom and the phone rang. The ring was muted, but still distinct enough to cause my heart to jump in my chest.

Fuck.

What was it I had agreed to with the newsstand man? If the phone rings, I was supposed to exit immediately, make my way to the fire stairs, wait five minutes, and then head back down to the lobby.

I stopped dead in my tracks and looked around for the phone, thinking, *Caller ID, have to see the caller ID.*

There was no phone next to Lizzie's bed.

Had there been one on her desk in the study?

No.

Had there been one in the kitchen?

I didn't think so.

Huh?

Where were the phones? Had the middle-of-the-night movers packed them up? If they did pack them, why?

Most important, where was the phone that was ringing?

I decided that the ringing noise was in front of me, not behind me. I stepped farther into Lizzie's bedroom.

I'd entered girl land.

Dream time for Lizzie was a whimsical palace in the French country. Not subtle French country, but biting-into-a-lemon French country, or being-buried-in-lavender French country. There was enough Provençal fabric and toile in front of me to upholster a fleet of Citroëns.

Thea hadn't decorated that room. Not at all. No way. *Don't get distracted,* I told myself. *Don't get distracted.* The phone was still ringing.

Where is it? Where?

I followed the sound to a small walk-in closet. One side of the space was hung with clothes. Plenty of gaps, which told me that Lizzie had packed enough of her things to last her for a while. When she decided to leave, she knew she might not be making only a brief exit. The other side of the closet was lined with two floor-to-ceiling built-in storage units, one that was all adjustable shelves, and another that was a tall stack of drawers topped by more shelves.

Is the phone in one of the drawers?

It sounded that way.

The first drawer I tried was the one that held her panties. It wasn't luck or happenstance that I opened that one first; it was simply my nature to make that kind of discovery. My peculiar radar. There, right on top of a perfectly folded, tantalizingly delicate pair of pink and purple lace—

Focus!

The caller ID on the mobile phone in Lizzie's underwear drawer read, "Pay Phone."

Before I could make the necessary mental and motor connections to reach for it, the phone stopped ringing.

I said, "Whew."

Perhaps for the first time in my life, I actually said the word "Whew."

Instantly, I convinced myself that the fact that the phone had stopped ringing meant that I didn't really have to immediately leave Lizzie's flat, that I could use my last—what?—minute to finish looking around.

One minute? Shit, shit, shit. I only have one more minute in here. I haven't found a thing.

I left the phone where I spotted it and opened and shut the other closet drawers quickly. Nothing. I patted down the folded and hanging clothes and opened a couple of purses.

Nothing.

Then I heard some scratching. Or clicking. Some metal-on-metal sound from the other side of the apartment.

I stepped out of the closet, padded across the bedroom, and stood at the entrance to the hall.

Where are her magazines? I wondered again.

Huh? What's that noise?

It took me about three seconds to recognize the sound that was so compelling to me: Someone was fiddling with the locks on the front door to Lizzie's apartment. Someone who didn't have experience, someone who didn't know the secrets, someone who didn't have the touch. Someone who didn't even know which key went in which lock.

Someone who wasn't Lizzie.

Behind me, the damn phone started ringing again.

Shit.

FORTY-FIVE

I was on the sixteenth floor. If I rejected the option of taking a flying leap off the balcony that faced the Hudson, the apartment had one exit.

Given those limitations, I couldn't see any margin in advancing.

So I retreated.

Back into the master bedroom, back to the closet, back to the phone. Why? I had to quiet the damn thing before whoever was on the other side of the door finally finessed Lizzie's locks, made it inside, and heard the phone ringing.

I allowed myself the luxury of believing that the intruder was Gaston, the doorman, coming to warn me. The thought calmed me just a little, until I realized that if Gaston had hustled up to the sixteenth floor to warn me, the situation had already seriously deteriorated.

I opened the phone to kill the call and was about to shut it again when I heard my name from the tiny speaker. Twice.

I moved the open phone to my ear.

"Are they there yet?" she asked.

Lizzie.

They?

At worst, I'd been hoping for a "he."

Shit.

"Yes," I whispered. "At the front door. Someone's trying to get in."

"The locks stick. It'll take them a minute to figure it out. You're in the closet? My bedroom?"

"Yes."

"You're not good at listening, but I need you to listen to me now. Do you understand?"

Was I tempted to argue? Of course. Instead, I said, "Yes." I was all ears.

"Reach behind the stack of drawers that's directly in front of you with your right hand. Feel for a small hand-hold toward the back. A slot where you can stick your fingers."

I switched the phone to my left hand and felt behind the drawer unit with my right.

Nothing.

"Got it?" she said.

"Not yet."

"Go lower. Pretend you're my height. Five-seven."

Five-seven? *I thought you were taller.*

Focus!

I slid my hand lower.

"Now?"

"Yes. I have it."

"Pull. Hard! Jerk it."

I heard the distant clunk of the dead bolt releasing in the front door.

"They're almost in," I whispered.

"Pull," she said. "Do it."

I yanked. The entire shelving unit rolled forward about ten inches. It was on some kind of track system.

"It moved."

"Squeeze in behind it. There's room back there, I promise; you'll fit. Go! Don't trip, there's something on the floor inside."

I felt for the opening and squeezed in, my shoes banging hard into whatever it was that was on the floor.

"Stand facing toward the closet. Now grab in front of you—straight in front of you. Get a grip on one of the shelves and pull—gently this time—the whole unit toward you. It will slide."

I did. It did; the drawer unit clicked back into its original position.

"There's room for you to step behind you a couple of feet or so. Back up slowly until you feel the wall. Got it?"

"Yes."

"Good. Then feel to the side with your right hand, waist high. My waist, remember? You'll find a light switch. Flip it. Yes? Now you can see where you are. Don't worry, no light will escape."

I followed her direction, found the back wall, and the light switch, and flicked it.

I saw where I was.

I didn't process what I was seeing right away. At first, I managed nothing more than a stammered "Oh my God." Then further recognition descended and the pieces began falling into place. I stammered, "Are you— Do you—"

She said, "Shhhh. Later. It's not soundproof. Put on the headphones you see on the shelf."

"Is all this for—"

"Shhhh," she said. "Don't let them find you. You won't like what happens."

She hung up.

I whispered, "Lizzie?"

One of three small color monitors right in front of my eyes showed the front door of her apartment opening and two men that I'd never seen before entering Lizzie's apartment. *Young and buff. Don't-fuck-with-'em types.* That's how the newsstand man had described them from the night before.

I quickly decided that I didn't disagree with his assessment.

I added them to the roster of Death Angels in my head and thought, *And then there were six.*

As directed, I pulled on the headphones that were resting on the shelf in front of me at eye level. Instantly, I was listening to the array of sounds emanating from the rest of the apartment.

The two men separated in the living room. The huskier of the two started marching through the apartment and began doing a quick but thorough surveillance of the space. He was looking for someone.

For me, I worried.

The other man—he was tall and thin and had wireless glasses and a prominent square jaw—stood by the window looking out at the river. His feet were roughly shoulder-width apart. He held his right wrist with his left hand behind his back.

He struck me as a guy who wanted to be seen as a serene, patient man with an edge. But I suspected that his demeanor was covering a nascent explosiveness. The legs-apart stance told me he was maybe ex-military or ex–law enforcement.

He also gave off a vibe that he wasn't expecting the other guy to find anything during his search.

I spent most of the next minute watching the first man make his rounds through the apartment as he paced down the hallway, and into the guest bedroom, master bedroom, master bath, and closet.

One of the three monitors in front of me carried a fixed shot of the living room, and one carried a fixed shot of the master bedroom. The third, however, presented the output of a more sophisticated setup; the image automatically followed the man walking through the apartment and changed its view as he moved from place to place. I guessed that motion detectors were sensing his progress through Lizzie's flat and signaling specific cameras to pick up his progress. After a quick search of the apartment he marched back into the living room, stopping a half dozen feet from the other man, who continued to gaze out toward the river.

The man who had been searching said, "Not here."

"Go back out and check the fire stairs," the boss man said, confirming my suspicion that he was in charge. "First go all the way up to the roof, then all the way back down to the basement. I want to hear from you every three minutes. And make sure none of the fire doors leading to any floor are blocked open."

"How could—"

"I don't know. That's one of the things we need to figure out, right? But first? We need to complete our search. Go."

After the other man was out the door of the apartment, the boss man went to the kitchen and poked around in Lizzie's refrigerator. Unfolded some white deli paper. Wasn't pleased with what he found sliced inside.

Looked like cheese to me. Muenster or jack. But the camera resolution wasn't great. It could have been smoked turkey.

My eyes followed him as he reached in and grabbed the organic raspberries Lizzie had bought the night before. He flicked open the box and scanned the contents carefully. Apparently convinced of the berries' freshness, he pulled a sheet off a roll of paper towels, stepped back out of the kitchen, and resumed his position at the windows in the living room. He began popping the berries into his mouth one by one, as though he was eating popcorn at the movies.

FORTY-SIX

The man ate about half the raspberries before he set the box on the tea table by the chaise and wiped his fingertips with the paper towel. He folded the towel into thirds as though he was preparing a letter to slide into an envelope, and began a casual stroll through Lizzie's flat. Unlike his compatriot, this guy wasn't searching for anything specific.

He was merely intent on seeing whatever was there to see.

Using the folded paper towel as insulation, he pulled a few titles—I thought at random, but there was no way to be certain—off the bookshelves behind Lizzie's desk, flipped them open, allowing the pages to fan from end to beginning, and then left the books in a haphazard pile on top of the lower cabinets. Those credenzas interested him, as they had me, and he felt around in obvious places for a release that would prove that the flat panels were indeed doors.

He couldn't get them to open, either.

I kept waiting for him to lift something heavy to use as a hammer to obliterate the panels and reveal their secrets. He didn't.

The cabinets, if they were cabinets, retained their mysteries.

The spare bedroom interested him more than I thought

it should have. He stood dead center in the room and slowly rotated three hundred and sixty degrees, almost as though he couldn't believe that the room held nothing more than some out-of-season clothes and a couple of discarded chairs.

Lizzie's bedroom received even more of his attention. He sat on the edge of her bed as he rifled through the single drawer on the bedside chest. He examined a box of condoms with surprising curiosity, almost as though he'd never seen one before. He read the label on an amber bottle of prescription drugs, and took off the top to examine the contents. He dropped one of the tablets into the pocket of his shirt before he shut the drawer.

He lifted one of her bed pillows to his face and inhaled its scent. There was nothing at all sensual or prurient in the act; he seemed more like a bloodhound filing the aroma for future reference.

He wasn't wasting any time; his entire perusal of the master bathroom took less than a minute.

Next he came into the closet.

I held my breath. He'd stopped in front of the tall drawer unit deliberately, as though it had been his destination all along. I thought he seemed to be staring right into the lens of the camera, which was obviously built somewhere into the drawer unit behind which I was hiding. It felt as though he was looking right into my eyes.

Does he know about this space? Does he know about the cameras? Does he know I'm back here? Did Lizzie—

A squeal filled my headphones, and I almost yelped.

The man grabbed at his hip and then flipped open his phone in a smooth, practiced motion. He held it in front of his face like a walkie-talkie. He hissed, "I said every three minutes."

"Sorry, I lost track of—"

"I don't care. When I say three, I don't mean five. Did you find anything? Where are you?"

"Nothing on the way up to the roof. I'm on my way back down, passing the doors on five. I'll be in the basement soon."

"Call me when you get there." He closed the phone and stuck it back into its holster.

He began to rifle through the drawers. The angle of the lens prevented me from seeing where his attention was focused. After he was done with the drawers, he turned and began to touch Lizzie's hanging clothes, patting them, squeezing them. I thought he was exceedingly gentle with the garments, as though he was a lover lamenting the loss of something he feared he would never see again.

Was he her lover? I wondered. I tried to imagine them together, but I couldn't see it.

I told myself it didn't matter.

Occasionally, he would pull a sleeve of a shirt or sweater toward his face, adding some new variation of Lizzie's scent to that olfactory library in some primitive part of his memory.

The squeal from his phone shocked my ears all over again.

He grabbed the phone from his hip, stepped from the closet, and said, "Yeah." With the phone in front of his face, he marched across the bedroom and down the parquet hall.

"Nothing. You want me to come back up and start to knock on doors on her floor? See if the neighbors saw anything?"

"No point in going that route. There're too many units in the building. Wait for me in the lobby. I'll be down in a minute."

I exhaled. *Thank God, he's leaving.*

He stepped toward the door, but instead of exiting the apartment, he spun and retraced his steps down the hall, across the master bedroom, and back into the adjacent bathroom. He stared for a few seconds before he opened the medicine cabinet—even though the camera had him in profile, I could tell that he was frowning at the contents—and then he pulled open the fluted-glass doors of a tall narrow cupboard. Linens. Toilet paper. Tissues. A filigreed silver tray of bottles and lotions and creams. Nothing remarkable that I could recognize. He closed the doors gently, poked his head into the shower stall, and then he backed out of the room.

Immediately, he came back into the closet.

This time he was looking for something specific.

Something that he thought should have been someplace in the bathroom, but wasn't. Something he'd expected to find in the apartment that he hadn't found.

What?

He reopened the closet drawers. Every one of them. I couldn't see him feel around inside the drawers but I could *feel* him feeling around inside the drawers. He slammed the last one shut.

He kicked it with his foot.

I'd been right. The guy was tightly wound. Only a small frustration away from explosion.

It was clear that he still hadn't found what he'd thought he should find.

He marched back to the kitchen and methodically began to open all the cabinets and drawers. He stared into each space for a few seconds before he shut the door or drawer and moved on to the next.

Once again, it didn't appear that he discovered what he was looking for.

He left the folded paper towel on the kitchen counter.

Within seconds he was gone from the apartment. He

didn't bother to relock the dead bolt, which meant he didn't care if Lizzie knew that someone had been there.

Given the unique way he'd folded the paper towel, I considered the possibility that the tri-fold was a personal signature, and that he was leaving Lizzie an unmistakable message that he had been there.

My knees were weak. Would he come back?

I didn't know.

But I didn't dare move.

What I suspected he'd been looking for in the master bathroom and the closet and the kitchen was surrounding me in my cubby.

The tiny space where I was hiding—the open area was no more than three feet square—was lined with narrow shelves on two sides. Melamine, I thought. Antiseptically white and unadorned.

The closet within a closet was a hidden pantry, really.

A tiny refrigerator, smaller even than a dorm fridge, was built in below the shelves on the right side.

The shelves—all of them except for the one that supported the surveillance monitors and related electronics—were lined with medical supplies, medical journals, medical textbooks, and vertical files of medical records.

An IV pole took up half the floor space. Its heavy rolling base was what I'd kicked as I squeezed into the space. The attached pumps and infusers intruded into the hiding place's volume, forcing me to stand back against the wall.

On the shelves were vials of drugs, bottles of pills. Racks of files. Dozens of texts. A stack of journals.

Sealed packages of syringes, needles, tubing, connectors, gauze, alcohol pads, bandages.

On the bottom shelf opposite the refrigerator was a

monitor for pulse, respiration, oxygen saturation. Other things, too. An automated blood pressure cuff sat beside the monitor.

The smells were familiar. The sights were familiar. Even the labels on some of the drugs were familiar.

I lifted the top file from the stack of the medical records—there were maybe five files total—and I began to read.

The names of the patients on the file tabs were all different.

None of the first names were Lizzie, or any of its obvious variations.

But each of the patients was a thirty-seven-year-old unmarried female.

With breast cancer.

I came to the reluctant conclusion that Lizzie had directed me to hide from the Death Angels in her tiny, secret, nursing station in her own very private cancer treatment clinic.

I suspected that the only patient being treated in the clinic was Lizzie.

I also suspected that she was the clinic's only physician.

Why was it all so secret?

I had a guess.

FORTY-SEVEN

While I was waiting to see if the two guys would return, the phone rang. Not my phone. No *Ob-la-di*.

Her phone. I pulled it out of my pocket as fast as I could. This time the caller ID didn't read "Pay Phone." It read "Out of Area." I flipped the phone open and lifted it to my ear. "Lizzie?"

"Don't say my name."

I almost replied *It's not your name*. Didn't. I said, "What do they want? Do these guys want to talk to me? Do they want to kill me? What?"

She didn't answer me.

"What?" I demanded.

She said, "They're gone for now; but they'll be back. Look at your watch. What time do you have? Exactly. Be precise."

"One-twelve."

"Take the stairs down to the first floor. Wait there, in the fire staircase, and time your entrance into the lobby for exactly one-twenty. Go immediately out the service door, not the front door. Head away from Broadway, which means turn right. Do you have all that?"

"Sure. This stuff? Here in the closet? What the hell is—"

She hung up on me.

Again.

Damn.

FORTY-EIGHT

My exit, timed according to Lizzie's instructions, was anti-climactic.

At the appointed minute I entered an empty lobby—I could see Gaston outside on the sidewalk arguing with a homeless man who seemed to be protecting a shopping cart full of rusted rebar. The reason someone would be so possessive of a shopping cart of used rebar escaped me. Figuring it was part of some ruse Lizzie had arranged on the fly, I hustled out the service entrance. Within a minute I was in the backseat of a yellow New York taxicab that was pointed uptown.

"Where?" the driver said. He was a gruff, burly guy with about three days' growth of whiskers and three decades' growth of ear hair. His voice was accented with the weight of a few generations of eastern European history.

"Just keep going for now, thanks."

Right after we passed the near corner at 89th Street I told him I'd made up my mind and I wanted to go to Midtown. He responded by making an instantaneous hard right turn from the center lane in the middle of the intersection, cutting a perpendicular swath onto 90th toward Central Park West. During the maneuver, a bus bumper passed about eighteen inches from my nose.

Didn't even raise my pulse.

"Where we go in Midtown?" he said.

I hadn't decided where. I said, "I'm thinking."

He looked at me in the rearview mirror and tapped the meter, letting me know that my cogitation was going to cost me money.

"It's okay," I said.

After we'd covered a few blocks, I'd begun feeling the familiar rumblings that told me that the consequences of the pressure from my bulging artery on some nerve were once again taking a toll on my upper GI tract. I asked him if he would please pull over to the curb for a moment.

"Here? Now? Central Park West? No! No stop," he said, once again finding my face in the mirror, the whole time gesticulating with his right hand. I stared right back at him—he was a man whose face had seen many years in the sun, had endured the ravages of the poisons from tens of thousands of cigarettes, and clearly showed the capillary corrosion of having consumed enough vodka to fill a Jacuzzi. The picture on his taxi license made him look at least ten years older than he appeared in person. And he didn't appear to be any fountain of youth in person.

The taxi license revealed that his name was Dmitri. His last name was consonant-rich, vowel-light and, to my tongue, unpronounceable.

In as level a tone as I could muster in the circumstances, I said, "Then I'm afraid I will puke in your cab."

"What 'puke'? What?" he replied.

I think he thought I was threatening him.

"Vomit," I said. This time, when I caught his gaze in the rearview mirror, I pantomimed sticking my index finger down my throat. "I think . . . I am about to . . . throw up."

Simply saying it, of course, almost precipitated it.

Dmitri hit the brakes, yanked the wheel to the left, and

began to pull over to the curb that was directly opposite the whimsical planetarium on the west side of Central Park. As I swallowed down vomit and waited for the car to come to a stop I found myself staring out the side window at a big sign that read THE FREDERICK PHINEAS AND SANDRA PRIEST ROSE CENTER FOR EARTH AND SPACE.

Even before the cab had come to a complete halt, I threw open the back door, leaned my head out into that space, above that earth, and emptied the entire contents of my stomach into a foul Upper West Side gutter. Behind us a symphony of honking horns and shouted profanities accompanied my energetic retching.

Two teenage girls wearing the white blouses and pleated skirts of some private school were walking past the cab on the sidewalk. Between fierce spasms, I watched their faces as they took a hasty, scornful look at me. One of them said, "That is too gross! Yuck. Look at him. No! Don't!"

Dmitri leaned out of the window and flipped them off with both hands. He yelled at them, "He puke," as though that alone should have been enough for the girls to excuse me.

My cabdriver was defending my honor. The act felt kind and generous.

"Okay? We go now?" he said once I was again upright in the backseat. "No more puke?"

"Yes, we go now. Thank you for stopping. I really appreciate it. Thanks. I hope no more puke." I wasn't a hundred percent sure about the no-more-puke part, but I would have placed a sizeable bet that anything that came out of my mouth next would come from some organ farther down the alimentary canal than my stomach.

I could feel the disconcerting presence of something grainy lining the inside of my mouth. The textural sensation was of old coffee grounds; the taste was as though I'd just gargled a cocktail of vinegar, puppy pee, gin, and Taster's Choice.

"Where we go?" Dmitri asked, his voice tinged with compassion for my condition, whatever it was.

"Four Seasons."

"Restaurant? You eat? You sure? I don't think good idea." His tone actually conveyed the reality that he thought it was a psychotic idea.

"No, not the restaurant. The hotel. On 57th. Or 58th. Whatever."

"You sleep. I think better idea," Dmitri said.

I sat back against the seat and took a slow deep breath. *What the hell*, I wondered, *is going on?*

"You from Russia?" I asked.

"Ukraine," he said. "Kiev." He smiled with pride. At being from Kiev, or not being from Russia, I couldn't tell.

Dmitri picked up Broadway at Columbus Circle in order to head over to the hotel near Park Avenue.

That's where I realized that I was being rash with my destination decision.

"Pull over again, please, Dmitri."

"Puke?"

"No. But please, pull over."

He did, again tapping the meter with his index finger. This tap was a caution for me, not a warning.

I pulled the roll of bills from my pocket and peeled off a fifty that I lofted into the window in the Plexiglas panel between us. The meter read ten dollars and change. "For you," I said. His thick eyebrows jumped up an inch—the international nonverbal symbol for "No shit?" I assured him, "Yes, for all your kindness."

Dmitri smiled at me then, and bared his teeth. As he did, I realized he needed a month locked in a room with a talented dentist.

Once the cab was at a full stop in a no-parking zone on the uptown side of 58th Street, I used my cell phone to call the hotel and had the operator connect me with the concierge, a young woman who identified herself as Jennifer Morgan.

"How may I help you?" she asked.

I gave her my name and room number and said that I had a strange request and was hoping she could, indeed, help me.

"I'm happy to do everything within my power to assist you."

"Could you arrange to have someone pack up my things? Everything in my room?"

"Of course. You'll be checking out today?"

"Actually, no. I'd like to keep the room for two more nights, just as I had originally planned. I will continue to need access to the room."

"But you would like us to pack up your things?"

"I said it was a strange request."

"You did. I should have taken you at your word." Her tone was pleasant, almost playful. On another day, in another time, I would have been sure to take her temperature to check to see if she was also being flirtatious. "Then you'll be collecting your luggage at a later date?"

"No. I would like to arrange to have someone come by to pick it up in . . . ten minutes, if that's possible. I'll be sending a taxi to the 58th Street entrance, the driver's name is Dmitri, the cab number is"—I opened the back door and got out so I could read the number on top of the cab—"2-K-1-7."

The second I was back on the seat I saw that the same identifier was plastered all over the inside of the cab, too.

"Ten minutes?" Jennifer Morgan said, obviously, and appropriately, dubious about my deadline. "Will we be needing to do much packing? That doesn't allow a lot of time."

"No, I travel light and I don't mind wrinkles. I apologize for the short notice."

"I will be happy to arrange for your request, but . . . in order to protect your security, I will need to confirm your identity. I'm sure you understand."

In response to the questions that followed, I rattled off my home address, the date of check-in, my phone number, and the last four digits of the credit card I'd used to guarantee payment. "Is that sufficient?" I asked.

"Actually," she said, "do you mind confirming what you had for breakfast this morning?"

From a security point of view it was a very good question. I told her about my room-service meal, emphasizing the silver dish of strawberries. "Did I pass? Do you think you can help me out?" I voluntarily added that I'd asked for two newspapers to be delivered that morning instead of one.

"Indeed. It will be my pleasure. Your things will be at the 58th Street entrance in ten minutes," she said.

"Ms. Morgan?"

"Sir?"

"Put a fifty-dollar gratuity for yourself on my bill. And twenty each for the bellman and the doorman."

"Thank you, sir."

"I would like this request to remain our secret, Ms. Morgan. I assume no one else needs to know."

"I can't see why that would be a problem," she said.

"I do appreciate your assistance."

"It is my pleasure," she said.

I closed the phone and faced Dmitri, who was waiting with great interest to find out what would happen next. I slid another bill, this one a hundred dollars, into the gap in the Plexiglas. "Would you mind running an errand for me?"

He narrowed his eyes and glanced at the advancing total on the meter. We were north of fifteen dollars by then. "The company," he said.

"Of course. Absolutely," I said. "The meter is separate. Keep it running. Keep it running."

He said something in his native language that had the cadence of a blessing.

I sat in a deli on 58th and sipped at a bottle of sparkling water while Dmitri made his round-trip to the hotel, which was only a couple of blocks down the street. I was tempted to try to eat something bland. Some applesauce. Maybe some crackers. But my upper digestive tract felt raw, and I feared it was again going to erupt like Kilauea if I tried to send any more food its way.

Before I sat down in the deli, I had stepped into the shop next door and bought a cheap, packaged mobile phone with prepaid service. The Death Angels had proven that they were good, they were resourceful, and that they were obviously connected at the hip to the mobile-phone networks. I didn't want to tempt fate by discovering too late that they were somehow tracking my movements from cell tower to cell tower via my "Ob-la-di" phone.

I pulled Lizzie's phone from my pocket and placed it on the table in front of me, willing it to ring.

It didn't.

Dmitri pulled up outside the deli after he'd been gone about fifteen minutes. He honked the horn and waved at me. When he caught my eye, he gave a big thumbs-up.

I left a five on the table, walked outside, and crawled into the backseat. Whatever adrenaline I'd been using for fuel was spent. I was dragging. On the far side of the seat I spotted my carry-on bag and the familiar small, black, beat-up suitcase that had accompanied me around the world a few times.

"Where to now, boss?" Dmitri asked me.

"Brooklyn."

"Brooklyn?"

He shook his head and showed me his rotten teeth again.

He hadn't been expecting Brooklyn.

Me? I didn't think that the Death Angels were going to be as easy to surprise as Dmitri was.

While we were stuck in Midtown traffic, I used my I-hoped-still-anonymous new phone to call Mary.

"It's me," I said. "I'd like to meet up with you. Near your cousin's place. That okay with you?"

"Of course."

"Cross streets?"

She told me, then added, "You don't want the address?"

"No. I'm not sure that things are as private as I might like. Is there a market or a deli, or somewhere close by her place where we could meet?"

"Place called Julio's. You can see it from that corner. Red awning. When?"

"Good, I'll be there within half an hour."

"Me, too," she said.

"Wait." I didn't like my own plan. "Mary, I just changed my mind. I want you with the plane. Go keep an eye on it—do a real good check. Call your cousin. See if she can meet me at Julio's. I'll make it worth her time. Then she can take me to . . . meet up with you."

"This is serious, isn't it? Are you in trouble?"

"Serious? Yes. Trouble? It's all relative."

I could tell that Dmitri was sorry to see me go when he finally dropped me off in Brooklyn.

In addition to having learned the meaning of the word "puke," he probably hadn't had a more interesting couple of hours or a more lucrative shift since he started driving cabs in New York.

I shook his hand, said my good-bye, and thanked him with another hundred-dollar bill.

I'd actually had him leave me two blocks from the intersection that Mary had indicated was near where her cousin lived, and I'd walked the final distance over to find Julio's, which turned out to be a bodega with a few old rusty steel tables out front where locals drank coffee and argued and gossiped.

I went inside and bought a bottle of Gatorade to sip to try to restore some electrolyte balance in my brain so my neurotransmitters had a prayer of firing when I needed them to. I carried the unnaturally blue potion outside and planted my butt at one of the battered tables where I listened to a spirited discussion about how the cops had handled a hit-and-run at the corner the night before.

Not well, was the consensus.

I heard the old BMW motorcycle long before I saw it coming. The percussion of the Bavarian motor rumbled in gorgeous bass echoes off the brick and stone buildings. Mary's cousin rolled to the curb, spotted me—I'm certain I was the only stranger at Julio's—and held a helmet out in my direction. The fact that she'd shown up on the bike was a surprise, even though it shouldn't have been, and I knew I had a decision to make. My old, reliable suitcase wasn't going to be making this trip to the airport; there was no room. I made my decision, smiled at Mary's cousin, and climbed onto the back of the bike with my carry-on slung over my shoulder.

My old suitcase, full of all the clothes I wasn't wearing, stood upright where I'd left it beside the table at Julio's. Somebody in the neighborhood, I was sure, would put the stuff to good use.

I pulled the proffered helmet onto my head. The thing

fit me like I was doing a modeling session for a designer of bobblehead dolls.

Mary's cousin watched me, bemused, as I tried to tighten the chin strap. She said, "My brother had a big head."

She'd said it affectionately. "Mary says he was a special guy," I said.

"You know how he died? A friggin' waste."

Before I could think of something to say that would honor his sacrifice, she kicked the bike into gear, pulled out into traffic, and we were off, zooming down the streets of Brooklyn, doubling back the way I'd just come with Dmitri toward Teterboro in New Jersey. Despite the events of the day, I felt the familiar rush that comes along with the dawn of a new adventure. I had a big smile on my face and was more than prepared to end up with a few bugs crushed on my teeth.

FORTY-NINE

Once we were back in the skies over Colorado, I stepped up into the cockpit and asked Mary to wait until the last possible moment and then modify our flight plan to land at the Jefferson County Airport, across the metro area from our usual home field at Centennial.

Just a precaution.

At my request, she agreed to arrange for a private hangar and twenty-four-hour armed guards for the plane. I asked her if the plane was due for any work. She assured me that it had just undergone a major overhaul and that we were almost a hundred flight hours away from any required scheduled maintenance. If anything came up unexpectedly, she promised to monitor the repairs herself.

Thea and the girls were up in the mountains at our home in Ridgway, which was just as well. I was desperate to be with them every moment I could, but I recognized that prudence demanded I keep my distance. I didn't know what the Death Angels would do next. I did know that I didn't want Thea or Cal or Haven to be any part of it.

Giving in to my paranoia, I left the Prius where it was and called a taxi to take me down the turnpike to my friend's flat in Boulder. On the way, I phoned the detectives I had spread out around the country looking for any sign of Adam. I wasn't surprised that they had nothing new to report.

I climbed into bed in Boulder between seven and eight, rationalizing my premature fatigue by reminding myself that it was after nine back East. I was sound asleep when the phone rang. Not just asleep, but I was already deep into that REM fog that accompanies the most convoluted of dreams, and at first the sound of the ringing phone became just another stimulus for my brain to insert into the extremely flexible confines of my nocturnal musings. Soon enough, though, I stumbled reluctantly from dreamland to a vague state that left me quasi-awake, at best. I recognized that a phone was ringing, and that the phone was not in my dreams but was in the physical space where I had been—*what?*—sleeping.

I admit that I failed to recognize exactly where I was at that moment. My first guess was that I was in a hotel, and I grabbed for the ubiquitous bedside phone.

There wasn't one.

My mind allowed me to consider the alternatives.

Cell phone?

I fumbled to find a switch and flicked on the bedside light. Three phones, not one, littered the surface of the bedside table.

I mumbled, "Shit," and grabbed one, punched a key, and held it to my ear. "Hello," I mumbled.

Nothing. I tried a second phone. The screen on that one was lit—a good sign. It read, "Out of area."

"Yeah?" I said.

"I'm tired," she said. "But I can't sleep. Did I wake you?"

Lizzie.

My eyes found the digits on the alarm clock by the bed.

I decided I was in Boulder. Eight forty-seven in Colorado meant 10:47 on the East Coast.

"No," I said. "I had to get up to answer the phone anyway."

"You're cute," she said. "Sometimes."

I rolled over onto one side and propped myself on an elbow. "I don't feel too cute. Quite a day we've had. Or a couple of days."

"You could say that. You all right?"

"I'm confused, troubled, too, but . . . yeah, okay. You?" I said. I was trying to force myself to be alert, to put some defining parameters on the circumstances I was in, but I was still recovering from the depth of my slumber and the edges of my reality were more than a little blurry.

"Things have become more complicated than I'd like," she said. "But . . . life is like that sometimes."

"Tell me about it." I laughed.

Her voice turned serious. "I have some advice for you."

"I'm all ears."

"No, you're not. You like to think you are, but you're not all ears at all. From what I've seen, you're mostly brain and penis, but since I'm an eternal optimist, I'm going to give you the advice anyway."

I laughed. "Should I be insulted by what you just suggested?"

"Hardly," she said. "And I didn't really suggest anything. I just describe what I see. Truth be told, I suspect that the ratio between brain and penis is much more favorable for you than it is for most men." Her voice had turned husky and I let it soothe me like an open palm rubbing lightly on the flesh of my back.

"Is that necessarily good? Are we talking big brain, small penis? Or vice versa?"

She laughed that time. Then she grew quiet.

I wanted her to keep talking. Her voice was like music

to me. "Tell me," I said, using yet another line that I'd co-opted from my shrink.

"Tell you what?" she asked, obviously inexperienced with the open-ended nature of the psychotherapy "tell me" prompt.

"Your advice."

"You're not at home, are you?" she asked.

"No, given the events of the last couple of days, it didn't feel particularly prudent."

"Hotel?"

"It's not important."

"You don't want to tell me? That's fine. But you're right; it doesn't matter. Something you should know about us: We wouldn't fulfill our obligations to you in your house. That's off-limits. You're safe at home. Your family is safe there, too."

"Yeah?"

"Unless you become homebound, of course. Then . . ."

"Of course. You promise?"

"I promise."

I fought an urge—the instinct of an eight-year-old—to add, "Cross your heart and hope to die?" But it was the wrong thing to ask in so many ways. Instead, I tried something more mature, more rational. "Why?"

"Why what? Why are you safe there?" she said. "Or why should you trust me?'

"Both."

"I'm not supposed to tell you any of this, but think about it. Initially, clients routinely express their desires that their homes not be violated to fulfill contracts. It's understandable. We put a tremendous amount of care into developing the end-of-life strategies that we employ. Based on client queries during enrollment, we've developed guidelines. Limits to what we'll do to accomplish our goals. We don't skimp on our resources there. Homes are inviolate."

"Okay. Then *why* should I trust you?"

"I think I've proven myself to you."

"That's *if* I should trust you. Not why."

"Nice," she said.

It was a compliment. I said, "Thank you. Now please tell me why."

"Why?" she mused, more to herself than me. "Maybe you touch something deep inside me. Maybe you're a note in the melody to my favorite song. Maybe . . . because it's the right thing to do."

"Maybe?"

"Best I can do on short notice. I'll get back to you when I have a better answer."

"Thanks, I think."

"Something else. What you did today with your plane? Changing airports, moving it around? New hangar? All that security you're paying for?"

"Yeah?"

"Not necessary. And even if it was necessary, it wouldn't be sufficient. You couldn't hide a Gulfstream from the group, not in a million years. The company is way too resourceful for that. Fact is, nobody in the organization is going to bring your plane down. The group tends not to sacrifice any assets that are more valuable than a car. Your plane is safe."

"Client relations, once again?"

"Partially. Client satisfaction is the heart of our business. But bringing down a multimillion-dollar plane isn't necessary to do our work, and would inevitably involve investigative agencies like the NTSB, or the FAA—these days, maybe even the clowns at Homeland Security—that no one is eager to have curious about our endeavors. Our clients would rightfully balk at the waste and the unnecessary risk that might be posed to their families and colleagues if we started bringing down aircraft. The bottom line is that people don't sign up with us in order to have their most valuable assets plundered. They sign up for peace of mind that they won't have to spend the end of their lives with physical or mental limitations that they are unwilling to tolerate."

I thought she sounded like a spokesperson on an infomercial.

"What if I drove a Maybach, or a Ferrari?" I said, trying to be funny. "Those are expensive cars. Trashing something like that would be a travesty."

She wasn't amused. "Maybe my assessment of the ratio of penis to brains in your case needs some adjusting."

"I like you, Lizzie."

"I know you do."

"Why are you helping me?"

"Now there's a question," she said.

I waited fifteen seconds for a better answer than I'd gotten the last time. She wasn't about to provide one.

"You like me, too, don't you?" I said.

"Maybe."

I waited some more. She didn't bite. I don't know how my therapist did it. How he always waited for the silence to end.

"Are you with them right now?" I asked her, suspecting something.

"With whom?"

"With their team? Are you still with them? Or have you gone out on your own? Have you quit?"

She ignored my questions. "That little space in the closet in my apartment? Where you hid? Funny story. It was originally built as a combination jewelry vault/safe room for a woman from Paris who owned my apartment in the early nineties. She had a vision of America as a very dangerous place, and wanted a nook where she could hide if someone invaded her home. When she sold the place

307

and moved back to France, a couple moved in and the man had all the cameras installed. He was a Venezuelan diplomat at the UN, and he was a dedicated voyeur who was into watching his wife with other men. He'd go back into that little room and watch his wife with men that she'd picked up and brought home. They didn't last too long as a couple, apparently. She got the apartment in the divorce and told me all about it after she sold it to me. I invited her back to the apartment with me and she showed me the room, all the electronic toys. She'd left all the equipment in place. I've updated some of it."

The story Lizzie was telling was interesting—I had to give her that—but I wasn't about to be distracted by it. "Do they know you're sick?"

She wasn't knocked off balance at all by my change of focus. "My colleagues? Yes, of course."

"Do they know you've reached a threshold event?"

I counted to ten before she answered me.

"No."

"And you don't want them to?"

"I didn't call to talk about me."

"Do they know where you are right now?"

"I'm not required to check in with them. It's not that kind of an organization. I have responsibilities. I'm expected to fulfill them, that's all. My free time is my free time."

She didn't know that I knew about the midnight movers who'd carried boxes and suitcases from her flat. Or maybe she did. The newsstand man had probably told her.

"I assume that you're not permitted to make social calls to clients," I said. "There have to be rules."

"Of course there are rules. But you may assume what you would like."

"Is this a social call?" I asked.

"Next," she said. "Move on."

"You're a physician. That's your job with . . . them?"

"Yes. Among other things, I analyze end-of-life thresholds. It takes someone with a medical background, obviously. We deal with lots of technical information. Labs. Scans. Pathology reports. Doctor-speak."

"Do you provide end-of-life services, too?"

"Next question."

"I'll take that as a 'yes.' Your specialty?"

"*What?*"

She was wary that I was asking what form of life-taking was her specialty.

"Your medical specialty?" I said, clarifying.

"Oncology at first. But it wasn't right for me. I burnt out after a few years, did another residency, became a neurologist."

"Lot of irony there. Hippocratic irony. And burning-out-on-oncology-and-then-getting-breast-cancer irony."

"Hippocratic irony? You think I'm doing harm by what I do? That's an interesting perspective from one of our . . . clients."

She had me there. "Maybe," I mumbled. "But considering your life now? Yeah, I see irony."

"Life is full of irony."

"You don't practice anymore?"

"No. In a strange way, I feel like I do more good now. This seems like a better job for me. A better fit."

I softened my voice. I wanted her closer so I did what came naturally for me. I started flirting. "But you're not just a doc; you also frisk people in Town Cars."

"Only the cute ones."

"And you take clients out for fine lunches at Papaya King."

"Only the really cute ones."

I did like her. God, I liked her.

"Tell me something. Do they know where you are right now? Did those two guys show up at your place looking for you, or looking for me?"

"Two different questions."

"Answer either one."

"I do my job."

"That's not an answer to either of them."

"Don't be so picky," she said.

"Okay, tell me this: Would they hurt Adam? Or my girls?" I said.

"What? No! Absolutely not."

She sounded shocked at the question. I felt a wave of relief that she sounded shocked.

"You're sure? Not for leverage? Not to be punitive? I crossed some line by tracking you down. You made that pretty clear when we were talking on the sidewalk outside of your building."

"Someday you'll have to tell me how you did it. Found my home. I'm pretty careful."

"I'm pretty resourceful. Tell me again: They wouldn't do anything to my family?"

"Hurting clients' families? We'd be out of business in a heartbeat. You're much too savvy not to see that. That's not how it works."

"I can't tell you how glad I am to hear that."

"I do find it interesting that you didn't mention Thea on your list of family concerns."

I had. Thea was one of "the girls." But I didn't want to go there. "I'll settle for the 'no.' Thank you."

Lizzie pushed me. "Thea? Your wife? Remember her?"

I still didn't want to go there with her. Thea and the kids were mine. All mine. They had changed my life. I changed the subject. "How does it work? At the end?"

Without a moment's deliberation, she said, "Once the end is in sight, you shouldn't be buying any green bananas."

310

She'd made me laugh. I didn't think it was possible right then.

"That's not what I meant. When the time comes, how do they—or you—do it?"

She grew quiet for a long moment. I could sense the pounding in my heart as I waited for her reply.

She said, "They'll hurt you. They'll hurt you once. They'll hurt you well. One moment you'll be sick, and alive. The next moment you'll be dead. Any problems you have will go away. Any problems you've caused us will go away."

The words weren't surprising but hearing them spoken aloud was stunning.

"Why are you helping me?" I asked again. "Today? Why?"

"Who says I'm helping you?"

"You helped me earlier. I want to know why."

"I helped you?"

What? "Are you saying you weren't helping me when I was in your apartment? In that closet?"

She didn't reply.

The doorbell rang in my friend's flat.

FIFTY

I'd never heard the sound before. I thought it was the doorbell; it was definitely a doorbell-like sound—an intrusive, electronic, metallic *ding-ding-dong*. My pulse jumped. I felt the raw horsepower that comes from a sharp spasm pumping adrenaline into my blood.

"Someone's at the door," I said. I doubt I managed to keep the panic out of my voice.

"You expecting someone?" I initially thought she was buying into my alarm. When she added, "Room service, perhaps?" I knew she wasn't. In addition to the subtle mockery, there was a message in her tone: She was telling me that she knew about the white-gloved guy at the Four Seasons.

And that she did think I was in a hotel.

"No," I said. "I'm not expecting anyone."

"I'll hold on. Go check and see who it is. Get rid of them."

"This isn't a setup? It's not those two boys from your apartment?" I asked.

"Not that I know of. I certainly didn't send them." She paused and pondered. "No, I'm sure it's not them. They wouldn't use the bell. They'd pick the lock, or knock down the door, depending on their mood."

That made perfect sense. The realization that those two wouldn't use the bell calmed me. If they were in Boulder

to pay me a visit, they wouldn't knock. If they were looking for me, odds were that I would never hear them
coming. I'd awaken to find one of them pinning my arms
to the bed, the other one pressing a gloved hand over my
mouth.

"Go see who it is. Tell them to go away," Lizzie said.
"You and I aren't done talking."

Phone still at my ear, I walked from the bedroom to the
front door and gazed out the peephole into the hallway. A
girl, maybe ten years old, maybe twelve, stood staring at
the door with an odd smile on her face. I looked left and
right as far as the peephole would allow; the hallway
around her was empty.

*Girl Scout cookies? What time of year do they do that?
Isn't nine o'clock a little late for cookie sales?*

I cracked the door about six inches and leaned my head
toward the opening so I could camouflage my nakedness.
The phone was still at my ear. I opened my mouth to say,
"Can I help you?" but before I'd uttered a sound, the
little girl took one quick glance up at my face, giggled, and
skipped toward the stairs twenty feet away. I watched her
turn the corner and disappear down the staircase.

"That's exactly how it will happen," Lizzie said into
my ear, her voice suddenly alive with the provocative
timbre of a storyteller. "Just like that. You'll open the
door—literally or figuratively—just a tiny bit. Your guard
will be down, just a smidge, and then . . ."

She appeared at the top of the stairs where the girl had
vanished seconds before. Without pausing, she turned
down the hall toward me. She was winded—from exer-
tion or anticipation, I didn't know—her chest visibly
rising with each breath. I could hear the crackle of each
exhale through the telephone speaker at my ear.

A soft, deep-purple skirt, made of something like
Ultrasuede, hugged her hips and followed the contours of

the firm muscles on the front of her thighs. A pale gray turtleneck—I was guessing cashmere—fit her upper body like a second skin. Her nipples were erect and stood out, at least to me, like beacons in an ocean mist.

She was pale. Oh so pale, the pallor of her skin only a bare hue away from the tint of her sweater.

". . . Something you don't expect. Someone you don't expect," she went on, continuing to walk slowly toward me, one hand by her side, empty. The other hand held a phone to her ear. "Someone who doesn't threaten, who raises no alarm, or maybe—maybe—just a little . . . alarm."

I allowed my left hand, the one cradling the phone, to descend from its perch by my face.

She mirrored me, dropping her phone to her side, too.

"But the alarm will arrive too late, or you won't recognize it until it is too late," she said, staring directly into my eyes. Freezing me. "Too late. The awareness of your imminent passing will be a fleeting thought, though. You won't suffer the torment of any prolonged fear. You won't anticipate your near death for long enough to inspire any despair. That part is a gift. That . . . is our parting gift."

Parting gift? She made my murder sound like the consolation prize on a game show.

"Are you here to kill me?" I asked her. The words tasted funny—odd funny, not humorous—as I spit them from my lips.

She laughed. "Hardly." She was standing in front of me by then. She leaned her head into the gap in the doorway, and she raised herself on her toes, and kissed me on my lips. She lingered there for a second, long enough for me to know that the kiss wasn't a mere greeting. Once our lips were separated by a centimeter or so, she said, "If I was here to kill you, you would already be dead."

She placed a boot against the door and pushed it open.

I watched as her eyes tracked a line from my knees back up to my face. She grinned. "I now have a more accurate way to calculate that ratio."

The ratio?

"Penis to brain?" I said.

"That one," she admitted. "You going to invite me inside, or what?"

FIFTY-ONE

Lizzie was sitting on the sofa in the front room of the apartment. I was a foot away from her. In order to disguise my ratio from further view, I was wearing a robe I'd found in the closet. We both had our feet up on my friend's coffee table.

Lizzie obviously knew all about my Boulder subterfuge.

"So you know about Dr. Gregory, too?" I asked her.

The corners of her mouth turned up in response to my question. "Of course. The guy keeps crappy notes, by the way. Hardly anything in them. If I'd done that when I was practicing . . ." She rolled her eyes dramatically. "Hope you're not paying him too much."

I wondered if she was teasing me. I thought she was. Something told me she knew exactly how much I was paying my shrink. "Have you spoken with him? Has anyone from your . . . firm?"

She found that question amusing, too. She shook her head. "When the time comes, maybe. But no, not yet."

"He's a funny guy. Ethical, maybe to a fault. I don't think he'll talk to you. He's been in some strange legal situations before." I knew all that because I'd Googled him before I made the first call to Boulder to set up that initial session. For a small-town shrink he'd crossed paths with a lot of odd characters, and found himself in some precarious places that had left his name in the public record.

One thing I liked about him? He'd absorbed some significant penalties for doing what he thought was right.

She shrugged. "He's a father, right? He has a little girl?"

"I don't know about that. He's never said anything about his family. I haven't looked into that part of his background."

She was surprised to hear me admit that. "Well, we have, and he is," she said. "A father. He's married to a prosecutor. His wife is chronically ill? Did you know that?"

"No. What does she have?"

"MS. Given their personal circumstances, he might not have a whole lot of compassion about your decision to enlist our help."

"Then again, he might."

"You never know," she said.

"I'll be surprised if it's the case with him."

"Whatever. He and his wife have a girl who's just a little bit younger than Berkeley. Her name is Grace."

Why would that kind of detail be important to the Death Angels? I felt a chill, and didn't allow the thought to go any further. "So?"

"Jeffrey always says that—"

"Who's Jeffrey?"

"The man you had lunch with at Nobu. It's not really his name, of course. We use code names for each other like we're the Secret Service or something. I find it all kind of silly. But I'm a lone voice. A lone female voice, I might add. The boys in the band do like their intrigue."

"Jeffrey's the comic?"

"He can be funny sometimes. Don't underestimate him. It would be a mistake on your part."

I made a dubious face.

"In *any* way," she said.

I sighed involuntarily. "What's your code name? Is it Lizzie?"

She shook her head. She wasn't going to tell me.

"Before? You were telling me something that Jeffrey always says."

"Yes, I was. Jeffrey always says that if a person has kids, and that person is unwilling to tell you something you really want to know, then you're not asking the right way."

I felt like I'd been punched in the gut. "Jesus Christ," I said. "How callous is that?"

"Pretty callous," she admitted. She touched my knee. She didn't squeeze it, though. It was just a slice of comfort. A lover's idle caress. I recalled the texture of the touch from her hand on mine on the plastic tabletop at Papaya King.

She said, "Something to remember about us? Something always to remember about us?"

I wasn't sure I wanted to know. But I said, "Yes?"

"We kill people," she said.

I must have looked at her as though I didn't want to believe her, because she said it again. "We do. Not too often. But when we have to, we kill people. It's not a good line of work for the squeamish or the faint of heart. Rest assured, our operations staff is neither squeamish nor faint of heart."

At that pronouncement, I stood and stepped away from the couch toward the windows. There was a small break in the trees that allowed me to see the tops of Boulder's Flatirons and enough moonlight to see shadowed places on the faces of the vaulting rocks.

"You warned me," I said. "You told me I'd reached the threshold."

She shrugged.

"I suspect you weren't supposed to do that."

She shrugged again.

"Are you on the operations staff, Lizzie?"

"Don't . . . go there."

"Okay. Then how about this: You saved me today, in your apartment. I have two questions about that. How did you know I was there?"

"That's one."

"The second depends on your answer to the first."

"Lewis, and Gaston," she said.

"I know who Gaston is. The doorman. Lewis, I'm guessing, is the newsstand guy?"

"Yes. In New York City, you don't buy as much loyalty for a few hundred dollars as you might think you do. Gaston gets more than that from me in tips every month. Lewis keeps the change every time I buy magazines. If the total comes to twelve dollars; I give him twenty, or even thirty. It adds up."

"Especially from someone who buys magazines every day."

"Lewis talks too much."

"Maybe. But I bet it buys you a lot of loyalty."

"I don't know about 'a lot.' But it buys me more than you were able to rent for a few hundred dollars. Gaston was seriously offended that you didn't sweeten his pot, by the way. I rent Gaston. I suspect someone else could outbid me for his services if they were so inclined. That was a serious judgment error on your part, not finding out what the price was to outbid me. When you really want to succeed at an auction, you have to be prepared to bid your passion."

"Not that it would have made any difference, right?"

"In this case, who knows? Loyalty counts, too. But I think for the right price, Gaston could have been yours."

"What a fool I am," I said.

She didn't argue with me.

"Okay, then why? That's the second question. Why did you help me?"

"That's none of your business. You get to decide whether or not to accept my help. You don't get to demand to know why I offered it."

"You're kidding."

"I'm not. Jesus," she said, suddenly exasperated. "Think! I didn't call you when you were up in my apartment alone. Right? You were wandering around to your heart's content before the phone rang."

I tried to remember.

She didn't give me any time to organize the memories. She repeated, "Right? Right?"

She was right. "No, you didn't. You didn't call me until things started to get crazy."

"I called you when Gaston called me to let me know that the boys were on their way up."

"Okay."

"I didn't care that you were there. You could spend all day in there and not find anything significant about me. That's the way I live. I called to warn you. That was all."

"Kindness?"

"Call it what you want."

"Why?"

"I'm not sure."

I actually believed her, believed that she wasn't sure.

"Then I get a third question," I said playfully. "Where are all the magazines you buy? I didn't see one in your apartment. Not one."

She laughed, but to me the laugh sounded sad. Then she distracted me. "You saw my panties. My nice ones."

"I did."

"Don't complain. They're much more interesting than last month's *Vogue*."

I had no advantage to exploit. None. I wasn't accustomed to that state of affairs, and I didn't like it. Then I remembered that I had one.

Maybe.

"The boss of the two men who came in? Military bearing. Wireless glasses. Cryptic. Seems like he could be explosive if you pressed the right buttons."

"Ted," she said.

"Code name?"

"Of course."

"He was looking for something specific. The other one was looking for you. But Ted was looking for something he expected to find in your apartment that he couldn't find."

That seemed to concern her. "Where was he looking?"

"Your bedside table. The bathroom cupboards. The closet. The kitchen."

She frowned.

"What was he looking for, Lizzie?"

"I don't know," she said.

She knew.

I made a decision not to press her. Not then. I said, "In my head? When I think about all this? The introduction, the negotiations, the buy-in? The mess I'm in? I call you guys the Death Angels. Since I don't know any real name for your organization, that's what I use. You're the Death Angels."

I looked back at Lizzie to gauge her reaction. The age lines at the corners of her eyes had softened. "We've been called worse, believe me. I like that, though. 'Death Angels.' Most of the time, it fits what we do. Most of the time, our clients are so grateful that there's someone around who does what we do. We answer prayers. If disability is the devil, then we are their angels of death."

"But other times?"

"Other times—and thankfully they are rare—there are people like you, people who end up wanting to bend the rules, or break them. People who wish they'd never met us, never signed up. When that happens people end up seeing us as more satanic than angelic."

"It's too much to ask for some compassion at the end of one's life?"

"Our compassion is infinite, but it's also totally inflexible. It has to be; it's the nature of the beast. Our compassion takes only one form, the form that we describe at the beginning of the enlistment process. We make a delicate but profound commitment to our clients that is unwavering. The client may waver. We expect the client to waver. But even if the client stumbles, we are determined to finish what we've promised to finish. We keep our commitments."

"You guys are that ruthless? Everyone on your . . . team?" My questions were an awkward way of wondering aloud whether Lizzie was as ruthless as the rest of them. As Jeffrey, or the white-gloves guy, or the guy in the pickup in Ridgway, or the duo who busted into her apartment that afternoon. Ted and . . . whomever.

" 'Ruthless'?" she said. "Ruthless. That's a very a harsh word. Let's compare it to, say, 'reckless.' Who's to say which, ultimately, is the more damaging trait for a human being?"

It was an intentional thrust with a sharpened saber and she'd hit her mark dead-on. She'd left me wounded. After I allowed myself a few seconds to absorb the blow, I discovered that, for the ensuing moments, I couldn't breathe. I felt, too, as though drains had suddenly been opened wide in the arches of my feet and that all the blood was pouring from my body, emptying me of all that was essential.

Lizzie was telling me she already knew all about what was going on with Adam.

The most intimate things about Adam. And me.

And Thea.

I wasn't so much surprised as I was realizing how desperately I didn't want it to be true.

"How?" I said.

I didn't have to say more. I didn't have to ask her in a complete sentence. She knew what I meant.

For a split second, I thought she was going to tell me. But her eyes grew rueful and I knew that she wasn't.

"You want to find your son before the end-of-life services are provided, right? I'm offering to help you."

"Why?"

" 'How?' 'Why?' You certainly ask a lot of useless questions for a big-shot entrepreneur. We don't have much time."

"How much do we have?" I asked.

"I don't know. Not a lot," she said. "But first, tell me something. Why just Adam? Why not your daughters? Your wife?"

I didn't have to think about how to reply. "Since I learned about the aneurysm, I've been with them constantly, every minute I could, and I've given them . . . more than I ever thought I was able. They've given me even more, of course." I swallowed back tears. "If I die right now, I'm at peace with them. With Adam, I'm not."

Her eyes closed. Her shoulders slumped. "Well, we have work to do. But I'm dead tired. Which way is the bedroom?"

I didn't know what she meant by any of it. By the work part of it.

By the bed part of it.

*

I was realizing I didn't know much.

She was already asleep when I whispered into the dark room the question I'd been wondering about since I'd scooped her cell phone from its silk cradle in the underwear drawer in her Upper West Side closet.

"Are you on my side, Lizzie?"

FIFTY-TWO

She was still asleep just before eight the next morning.

I'd been awake for almost an hour and had already walked over to Pearl Street where I picked up some take-out food for breakfast, a few newspapers, and most important, some organic berries, and a large quantity of coffee.

The tiny kitchen in my friend's flat faced east and the morning light was brash and brilliant. In some soft, ironic homage to my aneurysm and to hyper-spiritual Boulder, I made a conscious effort to try to let the morning rays invigorate me and heal me in ways that had nothing to do with an infusion of vitamin D. Just in case that didn't work, I guzzled coffee and forced myself to eat spoonfuls of yogurt that I didn't really want. I also took a handful of pills that my various doctors had prescribed.

Headaches had become a constant companion, but my nausea was under control for the moment. That was good. I knew I couldn't count on the respite for long, but I was grateful for it while it lasted.

I had arranged my growing collection of mobile phones—by then numbering three; Lizzie hadn't asked for hers back—into a triangle on the counter in front of me after I'd methodically set them all to vibrate.

The headlines of the local papers, along with a good proportion of their front pages, were focused on another apparent attack by the sniper who authorities feared was targeting travelers on Colorado's main route into the mountains. This second shooting appeared to have been as random as the first. A twenty-eight-year-old woman, the mother of two, had been standing, or crouching, outside her car examining a flat tire on her Chrysler minivan at dusk on the eastbound shoulder of I-70 just west of Genesee.

The location was familiar to anyone who made the drive from the urban communities along the Front Range into the Rocky Mountains. I-70 was the primary pathway to skiing, to hiking, to fishing. The section of the highway near Genesee was bordered on both sides of the interstate by woods. The steep, tree-lined slopes offered a hundred places for a resourceful sniper to set up a secret blind.

The story in the paper was full of details. The slug had caught the victim in the neck, just under the chin. She'd died instantly. Although a few local residents reported to the investigators that they'd heard the retort of the shot echoing off the cliffs, no witnesses had come forward to point the authorities to any particular location in the narrow valley.

At press time, the cops still hadn't determined where the shot had originated, though they were focusing their efforts on the south side of the road.

I made a mental note to talk with Thea about her plans for driving between Ridgway and Denver.

As I dug into the sports section of *The Denver Post*, one of the cell phones, the "Ob-la-di," began to dance around on the granite counter, announcing, "It's me, it's me!" Next to it, I noticed the red light on my BlackBerry was flashing. I had an e-mail.

The caller ID screen identified the caller on the *"Ob-la-di"* phone: Mary. That was good. I wasn't prepared to talk with Thea right then.

"Hi, boss," Mary said.

Her voice was cool and unenthusiastic. Something else, too. The "something else" made me wary. "What's up?" I asked. While I spoke, I thumbed the trackwheel to bring up the e-mail on the BlackBerry. The message was nothing but a Web link. I clicked on it. Something from Google News.

Slowly, the page started to load.

Mary said, "I just got a strange call from . . . you know, that . . . person we know with the old BMW bike. You with me?"

What? Why is she talking like this about her cousin? Something had to be wrong. Seriously wrong.

"Yes, I'm with you."

"Well, that person was just watching the local news thing on cable in the city. You've seen it?"

"I know what it is."

TAXI DRIVER EXECUTED read the headline that was emerging on my BlackBerry.

My eyes were riveted on the device in my left hand. Mary continued to speak into my ear. "Turns out that a cabdriver was murdered last night near the Hudson River up around 151st Street. It's in West Harlem, an industrial area, the place Columbia's considering for its second campus."

The details she provided about the neighborhood were Mary's police background talking. I said, "Okay." While I was listening to her I was simultaneously reading the same story on my BlackBerry, so I was prepared to hear what she said next.

"The cops are calling his killing an execution, not a robbery. Single shot to the head, and they found a fat wad of bills still in his pocket. No attempt to hide his body. You had told me yesterday about that cabbie who was so nice to you, and I . . ."

The fat wad of bills probably included two hundreds and a fifty with my fingerprints on them. The news Mary was imparting was monumental, of course, but I felt calm. *Maybe too calm,* I thought.

"Did they give a name for the man who was killed?" The moment I asked Mary the question, the screen on the BlackBerry revealed Dmitri's long Ukrainian last name. *God.*

"The vic's first name is the same first name as the name of the driver in the story you told me on the plane."

I tried to digest Dmitri's tragedy for a moment and tried to understand what might have happened to him.

The concierge at the Four Seasons—Jennifer, so-eager-to-assist-me, Morgan—knew the cabbie's name and his cab number. How did she know? I'd told her. The doorman who handled the luggage exchange at the curb undoubtedly knew all about Dmitri, too. Anybody who had been watching my things being loaded into his cab from the sidewalk on 58th Street would have been able to see the cab number displayed so boldly on the ornament on top of his taxi.

Dmitri could have been followed from that point on. Easily. First, back to the deli where I was waiting for him. Then over the bridge to Brooklyn to see where he'd dropped me off.

From there, if they'd wanted to, they could have followed me on foot over to Julio's bodega.

But why would they kill him if they'd followed him and knew precisely where he'd gone?

Why kill him if they did indeed trail me all the way to the bodega?

There was only one conclusion: *They must not have followed Dmitri from the hotel.*

No, they must have found Dmitri by backtracking. They'd used the information I'd provided to the concierge to track Dmitri down later so they could find out exactly where he'd taken the luggage, whether he'd reconnected with me, and if he had, where precisely he'd taken me next.

Why?

The night before, even before Lizzie's arrival, the Death Angels knew I was back in Colorado. The only conclusion that made any sense was that they had decided to talk to Dmitri because they were trying to discover the identity of anyone who might be part of my support network in New York.

I had to assume that Dmitri would have told them everything. In his shoes, I certainly would have.

Then, to cover their tracks, the Death Angels had killed him. They'd made certain his body would be discovered. They had then sent me the e-mail announcing their work. Why?

They wanted me to know what they had done.

I said, "You know what you have to do next, Mary?"

"Yes."

"Spare no expenses. None. Security comes first, for everyone you think might need it. Everyone. Err on the side of caution. All expenses will be reimbursed, but given the circumstances I don't think you should use . . ."

"Whose security comes first?" Lizzie asked from behind me.

I covered the microphone. "It's a business thing. Can you give me a second?" I faked a smile.

She said, "Of course." But she looked offended.

She also looked sexy as hell. Her hair was flying every which way, her eyes were much brighter and clearer than they'd been the night before, and she was wrapped in the duvet that we'd slept under.

Yes, slept. We'd just slept.

She was holding three of the four corners of the duvet

together under her chin. The skin on her exposed arms and shoulders was the shade of pale pink that illuminates the lowest clouds on the eastern horizon during those special sunrises that happen only one morning in a thousand.

I waited until she'd retreated back into the bedroom and had closed the door behind her.

"I understand," Mary said, either ignoring the interruption or assuming I wouldn't tell her anything about it. "Will you need it yourself?"

She meant the plane. "Maybe, if I get word about Adam. But there's no . . . no news yet. I'll let you know. Take care of the other thing first. That's your priority, okay? Family."

"Yeah. Family."

Was there sarcasm in her "Yeah"? Or irony? I couldn't tell.

She killed the call.

FIFTY-THREE

I stepped into the bedroom and leaned against the wall near the bathroom door. The drapes were still drawn from the night before and the room was dark and chilly. Lizzie was curled up on the bed, facing away from me, the duvet wrapping her as though she were the sliced apples inside a crepe. She didn't look toward me when she said, "If you want this to turn out for the best—for you, for Adam—you're going to have to trust me. I know that's not easy for you, but I'm not sure you have a choice."

I'd already decided to tell her what had happened to Dmitri. I'd start the trust thing there. "A cabdriver helped me get out of the city yesterday. He was a good guy. Last night, he was murdered up in West Harlem. Your friends sent me the news in an e-mail. A fucking e-mail."

My words tasted bitter from the guilt and anger I was feeling. My tone, I'm sure, conveyed any bitterness that my words lacked.

After a long pause she sighed deeply, as though the air in her lungs was toxic and she had to expel every last molecule before she could continue. There was no surprise, no dismay, in her manner when she spoke.

"Look, I'm sorry. I am. But you need to get some distance. Step back. It's a message," she said. "That's all."

I raised my voice, and the intensity I forced into it shocked me. "That's all? A message? Jesus Christ. He was a nice man, a generous man. He helped me. He trusted me. He was kind to me when I puked in the goddamn gutter. He was an immigrant trying to make a life for his family. A fucking message? The poor guy was brutally murdered."

She didn't buy into my intensity. In a voice that a teacher might have used to explain long division to an arithmetically challenged pupil, she said, "He wasn't murdered. He was executed. The difference is significant. They're telling you not to seek any help. Not to spread suspicion or alarm. They're announcing the consequences if you do."

"What?" I was shocked. I should have been beyond shock, but I wasn't.

I was shocked.

"They're making it clear that the end is coming. For you. They're asking you not to hinder their work. Not to interfere. Not to risk others. Not to force them to risk others."

"They killed an innocent man to make a point?"

"They tried to make the point in a more civil manner. You ignored them."

"So they killed an innocent man?"

"His innocence was gone the moment you asked for his help." She rolled over in my direction. Her eyes were colder than I'd ever seen them. "I told you last night: We . . . kill . . . people. You—*you*—hired an organization that kills people. Yes?" I didn't respond. Couldn't. "Well, you did. Killing is one of the things we do. It's our business. Don't act so surprised when we do exactly—exactly— what we advertised that we're going to do. Don't act so surprised when we do exactly—exactly—what you hired us to do. That kind of naïveté is a luxury you absolutely can't afford right now."

"Innocent people, too?"

"Innocent people die every day."

"Not on my dime."

"Really? Tell that to the people in Baghdad, or Kabul, or Fallujah, or Gaza. Abu Ghraib ring a bell? What about Darfur, or Rwanda? I can go on. Should I include Central and South America? Or Asia?"

Her list gave me pause. "That's different, and you know it. This isn't the same thing."

"No? Ask the families of the victims if they agree. You're okay splitting hairs about whose dime is whose if the dead strangers lived in another country?"

I put my hands flat against the wall behind me. In my mind I saw Dmitri's sun-and-alcohol carved face reflected in the rearview mirror of his cab. In the next frame I saw him dead, his sallow skin sagging. "I'm complicit," I said, my voice no longer loud. Instead, it was hollow. I was finally recognizing the consequences of what I'd gotten myself into.

What I'd done.

"You bet you are," she said. There was no compassion in her voice. No offhand in her manner.

I was appalled, but not quite ready to accept responsibility for what had happened. "None of you ever said that anyone would be at risk except for me."

"You didn't ask." The words flew out of her mouth without any hesitation.

She was right. I didn't ask.

"If I just give up? Right now? Today?"

"No one else gets hurt."

"If I don't?"

"To reduce suspicion they may take you out in a crowd. You never know. I never know. The number of ancillary casualties isn't . . . consequential to Jeffrey. It's not always true, but sometimes numbers help disguise intent."

I felt nauseous.

"Human nature," she said, looking at me, unblinking. "It's a funny thing. Clients ask us if their deaths will hurt. They ask about their families' safety. About their homes. Their yachts and planes. But they never ask about strangers. How many will die. It's a funny thing."

She let the words settle.

"Problem is if I give up before I find him, Adam will get hurt, too," I said.

I expected to hear scorn from her in response. But I didn't. She said, "Yes, Adam gets hurt."

Lizzie slid her feet to the floor and stood up. For two languid steps across the room she allowed the duvet to begin to drift behind her like some down-filled wedding veil. Then she let the hem slip away from her right hand and she continued walking in my direction.

One more step and she was completely naked.

She was turning the page. I felt forced to follow along. That, of course, was her plan.

Given what had just transpired between us, given that her intent was so obvious, I'm embarrassed to admit that I was distracted by her nakedness.

The first thing I noticed?

Regardless of the circumstances, I've learned, and accepted, that I'm incorrigible about some things. Instinct is instinct: The first thing I noticed was that she had shaved her pubic hair.

Interesting.

I was standing against the far wall. She stopped a few feet before she got to me, and waited until my eyes moved up and found hers. Then, using her left hand, she reached up and with a swift motion curled her fingers up under her hairline and stripped her tousled hair off her head from front to back.

She held the wig out in front of her as though she were

a Sioux warrior who, having met and overpowered a bitter enemy, was presenting his scalp in honor to her chief.

Although I didn't know how much she was feeling like a triumphant warrior, I knew that I wasn't feeling much like a chief.

Lizzie's head was as bald as a kneecap.

I didn't take the proffered hair from her hand, but I made an instant reconsideration of my earlier, more prurient, assessment: Lizzie had *not* shaved her pubic hair.

No.

Lizzie had sacrificed her pubic hair—and her head hair, and her underarm hair, and probably all the other hair on her body—to the noxious consequences of chemotherapy.

The next thing I noticed? No, surprisingly enough for me, it wasn't the shape of her breasts. The next thing I noticed was that Lizzie still had eyebrows.

It was a stupid thing to notice, but there it was.

How the hell could she have eyebrows?

I opened my mouth to speak.

She could somehow tell what part of her body I was staring at, and she could tell precisely what I was confused about. "Brow implants," she said, shaking her head. Was the headshake an expression of dismay at herself, at her vanity, or at me? I couldn't tell. "And the eyelashes, too. I have appearances to maintain. I'm sure you know all about that."

She walked past me into the bathroom and closed the door behind her.

I was so stunned that I didn't even bother to steal a peek at her departing ass.

"Lizzie," I said, through the door.

"What?"

"What work is it we have to do?"

She didn't answer me for about ten seconds. I'd almost

accepted that she wasn't going to answer me at all when she said, finally, "We have to find Adam. Isn't that what this is all about?"

The white noise of shower water splashing on limestone tiles ended our conversation.

Or so I thought. As I stepped away from the door I heard her call out, "You don't know everything. Not even close. Don't think you do."

"That's not one of my current delusions," I said. I mumbled the words under my breath, not anticipating that she really gave a shit.

A moment later, the door swung open. Steam was filling the bathroom behind her. She looked like she was emerging from the depths of some dark, cloudy place.

She was still naked.

Some women are uncomfortable being naked. Caught suddenly without a stitch of clothing, those women can't seem to find a pose that feels natural. They don't know what to do with their hands, or the best way to balance their weight. On one leg? Both? Hip thrust out? Not?

Cover this? Cover that?

Lizzie wasn't one of those women. As uncomfortable as I was being out of control? That's how comfortable she was being naked.

"What did you say?" she said.

"Who are you?" I asked.

"Don't you get it? It's not important."

It was to me. And seconds after she returned to the bathroom, I thought I might have just discovered a way to find out the answer to my question.

I used the newest of my mobile phones to call LaBelle at my office.

"It's me," I said.

"Caller ID doesn't say you. Caller ID says 'Out of Area.' Where's your phone? Are you out of area?"

"I'm close enough. Good morning, LaBelle."

"So that's how it's going to be?"

"Yes, LaBelle. That's how it's going to be."

"Good morning. *Now,*" she said. Used in the manner she had just used it, the "now" was an entire sentence for LaBelle. From experience, I knew that with the particular inflection she'd employed the word constituted a prelude to an admonition that I should take seriously. "Don't want to hear you been driving any of those cars of yours on I-70. You understand what I'm saying? You going up to Ridgway, there are other ways to get into those mountains. You use one of them, you hear?"

"I know," I said. "It's awful what's happening."

"285? That'd work, except for that storm that might be coming up from the south. Coal Creek Canyon up to the Peak to Peak? That new road out of Central City to I-70—I hear it's very nice. You want more alternatives, I can get those for you."

"I do understand, LaBelle. How are you?"

"Mmm, mmm, mmmm," she said. "A young woman like that? Two kids? Who would do something like that? Just pick a woman off on the side of the road. Those poor kids. What is wrong with this world?"

The water in the shower was still splashing loudly against the tiles, but I knew that it wouldn't provide me cover for long.

"I know, I know. I need a favor."

"What can I do?" she said, sensing my urgency. If I were standing beside her desk, I knew that I would have just watched her pull a pencil out of the nest of hair above her right ear. She would have the pencil tip poised a centimeter or two above the steno pad on her desk.

"I need for you to cross-reference two databases. One

337

is of physicians who are board-certified in oncology. Limit it to the U.S. I don't know who does the certification, but it shouldn't be hard to find out. Define the certification as generally as you can—use all the oncological subspecialties, too, if there are any. The other list is of physicians who are board-certified in neurology. If there are subspecialties there, include those as well. Specifically, I want all the names, if any, that show up on both lists. Addresses and phone numbers if you can get them."

She made a dismissive sound. "Those folks you're looking for? They would be the ones who spent way too long in school, you know that? Need to spend more time in the world. On the streets. With the people."

I laughed. "I hear you. As soon as you can, okay?"

"No problem. Assuming I can get hold of the data in digital form, I should be able to cross-reference them and get you the information before lunch. E-mail the names to you?"

"No, send me a general e-mail of some kind. If you do end up having names for me, say that the data I've been looking for is in. I'll call you for the details. If not, tell me you're still waiting."

"Why all the drama?"

"I'll explain later. One more thing?"

"Shoot." She caught herself. "Ba-ad choice. Go on, now."

"Do a search for me. LexisNexis, Google, whatever. There was a murder last night in New York City. A cabdriver. First name Dmitri. Up near 150th Street in West Harlem. Manhattan. Got all that?"

"Uh-huh, I got that. I'm getting older, but I'm not getting any slower. You can talk as fast as you want."

LaBelle made me smile. "Next step is complicated. Find out what you can about his family. Who he's been

338

supporting. People he's responsible for, that kind of thing. We're going to be setting up a trust to help out."

"We are?"

"Yeah, we are."

"I'll do the other thing first. Then I'll get you the low-down on Dmitri, so we can set up that trust."

"You're a doll."

"I am that. Lord knows I am that," she said. "The man who gets to crawl into bed after I warm the sheets . . . now that is one fortunate, fortunate man. Mmm, mmm, mmm."

The bathroom door opened. Lizzie stood in the doorway. This time she had a caramel-colored towel wrapped around her body. Her exposed flesh glowed slightly pink and glistened softly, as though she were illuminated from within by the light of a dying candle.

"Who's a doll?"

"Thea," I said, without even a hint of hesitation. I killed the call.

"Oh yes," she said. "The wife. I remember her."

FIFTY-FOUR

I used the microwave to reheat some of the coffee that I'd bought earlier that morning and gave Lizzie a cup. She sat beside me in the kitchen and cradled it in both hands, but didn't bring the mug near her face.

I remembered from my intrusion into her flat that she drank tea, not coffee. "You prefer tea," I said. "Sorry."

She said, "This is fine." But she still didn't drink from the mug.

I decided to share the suspicions that had been growing since I'd cowered in her safe room the previous afternoon, seen the medical supplies, and read the files. "Those two guys in your apartment? They weren't looking for me, were they? They were looking for you."

"Yes, they were looking for me," she said. It was a simple declaration on her part, but I could tell she wasn't planning to go any further with the disclosure.

I mimicked my shrink. "Go on."

To my surprise, she complied. She said, "They'd been trying to reach me . . . to discuss some things. My loyalty, I think. I wasn't responding to their messages. I'm sure that they didn't know you were in there. If they thought you were . . ."

I waited for her to finish that thought. She didn't. I asked, "Were they there to . . . kill you?"

"Maybe. Could have been that, but probably not.

Unless all other remedies have failed, home ground is sacred, remember? Maybe they wanted to protect me—insulate me—because you'd managed to penetrate my security. But the odds are they wanted to take me elsewhere, probably to stage something convincing. I didn't especially want to find out exactly what they wanted, which is why I left after I reported the contact with you."

"Why did you report the contact?"

"I had to assume they were tailing you, that they saw us talking. If I wanted some time, I had no choice."

"Your breast cancer has relapsed, I take it? Those files in the closet? Those are all your aliases?"

"Yes."

"I'm sorry."

She shrugged. I didn't know what the shrug meant.

"You're treating yourself?"

"I have some outside help, consultants, but yes. For now."

"The other Death Angels? They don't know about it?"

"They know about the diagnosis, of course, and they know all about the first round of treatment I went through. I found the lump over three years ago. The initial treatment—lumpectomy, chemo, radiation—was successful and the disease had been in remission for almost two years. Until yesterday, I was thinking they didn't know about the relapse or about how far the disease had spread. Now? I'm not so sure. I've been careful. I know how they collect medical data about clients. Information about the progress of my disease is not available through any of those channels."

"You're a . . . client?"

"All of the employees are clients. It's . . . required."

"The man in your apartment. The one who thought something was missing? He was looking for meds, wasn't he? He was surprised that there weren't pill bottles, or . . . what?"

"Probably," Lizzie said.

"What if they know about your aliases?" I was thinking about the medical files I'd read while hiding in the safe room in her closet.

"They don't."

I didn't think she sounded totally confident.

"Do they know you're here?" I asked. "With me? Right now?"

She inhaled some of the steam that was rising from her mug and shook her head. "I don't think so. They lost track of me the night before when I left the apartment after you'd showed up outside. I can't think of a single reason for them to suspect I'm with you."

"I hope you're right," I said.

She raised those implanted eyebrows. "Me, too."

I went to the refrigerator and returned with a carton of plain yogurt and some washed raspberries. The yogurt wasn't part of my morning grocery run; it belonged to my host. I checked the expiration date before I set it in front of her, along with a spoon. "The berries are organic," I said. "How many of you are there? I've met six, altogether."

"Thank you." She dropped a few berries into the yogurt. "That's unusual. A typical client will meet only three or four at the most. Six is a lot."

"I suspect that I'm more annoying than the typical client. That probably accounts for the higher number."

"That's true, you are."

"You haven't answered my question."

"You've met less than a third of the group." She paused. "I think I've only ever met half. We compartmentalize."

"Wow. That's a lot more manpower than I thought

there would be. Much more than I expected. I thought you guys would be lean."

"Most of the time the numbers are unnecessary. During peak times? We need everybody. But there's no natural flow to this work. Nothing's predictable. There's no Christmas rush we can count on. No Augusts off. And, let's face it—we can't just recruit temps to help us through the inevitable rush. The business is lucrative, but the expenses, especially the staff expenses, and the intelligence costs, are high. Collegial trust takes on a whole different meaning when the work you do every day constitutes a capital offense."

I stood up and turned my back so she couldn't see my face. "Your offices on Park Avenue were cleared out."

She waited until I turned toward her before she responded. "You knew about those? We suspected you might—I thought you might. You *are* good. Bravo." She feigned some applause and blew me a kiss before she ate a few spoonfuls. Each spoon was graced with a solitary raspberry. "It means nothing that we moved out. And it means little that you know we were there. At the first whisper of any indication that our cover has been blown, we're able to vacate a location in twenty minutes. Less even. As long as it's large enough, we can use space in just about any configuration. Uptown, Downtown—doesn't matter. We either rent furnished or rent the furniture through a shell. We don't keep any paper records. None. Not an address, not an appointment. Our phones are all cellular. Our computers are all notebooks that run on wireless networks or Wi-Fi. The password protection is state-of-the-art. Our financial records are offshore and are indecipherable without access codes. Client medical records are deleted when they're no longer needed. If anybody tampers with anything in one of our machines, all the data gets bleached beyond NSA standards. Backup files are encrypted and completely hidden."

"I don't know what that means. Bleached." I thought, *Adam would know. Adam could tell me.*

"It means we're good. And we're careful."

I wasn't surprised.

She went on. "The entire company fits in the trunk of a Town Car with room to spare."

"If you don't count the employees."

"Yeah, cramming all of us in, that would be tight."

I nodded at the yogurt. "Want something else to eat?"

"You went out this morning, didn't you, to get this food?"

"I went out, yes. Coffee and raspberries. The yogurt? It spent the night."

"Don't do that again; don't go out alone, without me. If it turns out that they do know where we are, and if they do know we're together, they'll hesitate before they kill us in the same place at the same time."

"Why is that?"

"Appearances. The company philosophy is to arrange deaths that draw no suspicions about foul play, that cast no aspersions on the reputation of our clients, and that leave no recognizable connections back to the firm. If they were to kill us together, they would run the risk of embarrassing your memory with your family by killing you in the company of a strange woman who is not your wife, and they would run the risk that someone could tie me—and thus you—back to them. I guarantee that they would prefer not to kill us when we're . . ."

The last word seemed to be difficult for her to say. "We have to stay together? Really?" I said. I wondered why I bailed her out.

"Yes."

"Thea might have some objections. I need this time with her. And with the girls."

"Noted."

"Noted?"

She reached across the table and touched me the same way she'd touched me that day in Papaya King. "Thea's about to be a widow. She's preparing herself for that. She knows how much you want to find your son. You'll have to convince her that's the most important thing right now. I suspect she'll have some feelings, but she'll understand. You picked a tough, resilient woman. It's one of the most attractive things about you."

I did marry a strong woman. I said, "Okay," feeling dutiful, and not liking feeling dutiful.

"She doesn't have to know we're . . . working on something. I'm not going to tell her," Lizzie said.

"I'd like to talk to Dr. Gregory once more," I said. "Is that risky?"

"You never know. That's the whole point. Can you call him? Talk to him on the phone? We'll get a fresh cell."

"I don't know."

"Does he know about us? The pact you've entered?"

"I've alluded to it. But no." The first sentence was the truth. The second? Almost the truth.

"He knows about Adam?"

"Everything."

She pulled the robe tight and covered the triangle of flesh on her chest below her neck. "Why do you want to find him so badly? Adam?"

"To tell him I love him, I guess. To tell him that if there was any way I could extend my life to be with him, I would. I can't let you guys kill me before I get a chance to let him know that."

"He doesn't want to hear it?"

"I think he does want to hear it. I'm not sure he's able to believe it. He's been wounded. He needs to hear it from me."

"Where is he? Right now?" she asked.

"I wish I knew. I have detectives out looking. They can't find him. He's left no trace since his last night at Brown."

She narrowed her eyes, then looked away. Almost casually, she asked, "What does your gut tell you? Where do you think he is?"

"He may be here. Colorado. Watching me from a distance. He may be someplace close to his mother. She's in Cincinnati. He's a brilliant kid. Street smart, too. Resourceful."

"He could be anywhere?"

"Yes."

"You don't sound convinced that he's here or in Ohio."

"I guess I'm not."

"Where else then?"

Without any hesitation, I said, "Maybe New Haven."

I could hardly have been more surprised by my answer.

"New Haven?" she said. I could tell she wasn't as surprised as I was.

"Adam got really attached to his uncle Connie before he died. That's where Connie lived. That's where they got tight. He felt comfortable there."

"Connie's the brother with ALS? Why would Adam go back?" Lizzie asked.

"I don't know that he would. I don't know why I said it, why I thought it. It just came out. You asked for a gut reaction. That was it."

"We'll go with it," she said, leaning forward toward me. "What else are you thinking? Right now."

"I'm thinking maybe I should find Felix," I said. "My brother's caretaker when he was ill, before he died. Felix. He's from Guatemala. A Mayan. He's a sweetheart of a guy. If Adam's in New Haven, he'd be in touch with Felix."

"You're sure Felix is still in New Haven?"

"Just a guess."

"New Haven's not far from Brown, is it?" she asked.

"Right down I-95." I allowed a moment for reality to settle. "I'm probably wrong about all this, you know."

"Yes, you are probably wrong about all this. But right or wrong, you're about to die. Today, probably not. Tomorrow, possibly. Within a few weeks, undoubtedly. Most likely you're wrong about New Haven, but maybe you're right. You know you'll die more contented if you find out. There's nothing to be gained by dying wondering."

Our eyes locked. No challenge passed between us; the moment was more like the intimate connection that happens at special moments between lovers. I asked her, "What about you, Lizzie? What do you want to do before you die? What will leave you more contented?"

"This may come as a great surprise to you. But I've always wanted to see New Haven."

FIFTY-FIVE

Alan Gregory told me on the phone that he could only fit me in for one session, not two. I didn't have an appointment, so I felt fortunate to get even that amount of time from him.

Lizzie and I walked together up the Pearl Street Mall toward the mountains. I took her to The Kitchen, near Eleventh, told her I'd heard great things about the french toast, and that it would be a comfortable place to hang out. I'd be about forty-five minutes.

She chose, instead, to linger in my therapist's waiting room.

I said, "You really think they would—"

She touched a finger to my lips. "It's not what I think. It's what I . . . know. Trust me when I talk about dying. I know about dying—capital *D*—like you know about living."

The thought gave me a chill.

I didn't want to waste time on pleasantries with Gregory. "Did you put anything about what I talked about last time into your notes? Anything? Anything at all? Tell me you didn't."

He could sense my tension. Okay, call it fear. He could sense my fear.

"Obtusely," he said. He considered it for a moment

before he added, "Probably something like 'Patient discussed D.A. Expressed concerns.'"

D.A. *District Attorney.*

Or Death Angels.

Lizzie knew that I called them the Death Angels. Did anyone else?

Probably.

"That's it?" I said.

"Yes. I'm intentionally vague in my notes. I put just enough in them to trigger my memory. Facts, remember—"

"Are crap. I know. I'm concerned that you may not have been vague enough. Are the notes here in your office? Right now?"

He hesitated before he said, "Yes."

"For your safety, I'd like you to destroy them. Right now."

"For my safety?" he said. He swallowed visibly before he added, "Is that a threat?"

"Not from me," I said, laughing uncomfortably at the irony. "From . . . some determined people with lots of resources who already seem to have pretty easy access to your records."

He swallowed again. I expected him to argue with me. He didn't. He stood up, walked over to an oak file cabinet behind his desk, unlocked the bottom drawer, removed some yellow legal sheets from a red file folder, and fed the sheets two or three at a time into a confetti shredder. Task complete, he sat back down across from me.

"Thanks," I said.

"Thank you," he said. "We're both kind of vulnerable, I guess."

He was much cooler than I thought he'd be. I manufactured a smile for him and said, "It's part of intimacy, you know. Vulnerability."

"That's what I hear."

I felt a surge of nausea and it took me most of a minute to swallow down the eruption of stomach contents that was oozing up into my throat. "I need to find Adam before they . . ."

I stumbled, I think because "Kill me" seemed like such an awkward way to end a sentence.

"Kill you?" my therapist said. Awkward was his forte.

"Yes. I'm going to be taking some risks to do what I want to do next. If you don't hear from me again, keep your eyes on the obituaries."

"What can I do to help?" he asked.

I smiled. "That's how you started with me. You asked a question just like that the first day. How can you be of help."

"Probably."

"You have been. Helpful. I came in here feeling I needed to connect with my son before I died, but not clear if that was just another selfish thing I was doing." I paused. "Thank you for helping me shed some light on that."

"You're welcome."

"There is something you can do. Can I sign a release of some kind, something that allows you to talk to Adam? If he wants, I mean. After I'm gone."

"About therapy?"

"About how I feel about him. About what I've done. Why I did it? The selfish parts."

"The generous parts?"

"That, too."

"Who you are?" he asked.

"I think he knows that already."

"Maybe. Maybe not. Yes, I can do that kind of release," Gregory said. He stood and went to his desk, pulled a preprinted form from the file drawer, and scribbled on it for half a minute or so. "Adam's last name?"

I told him. He filled out the form, brought it over to me, and handed me a pen.

"This releases you to do it, right?" I asked.

"Yes," he said.

"I want to go a step further. I want you to do it. Not just if he asks. I want you to find him if you have to. Offer to talk to him. You need to tell him everything."

He hesitated.

"I'll pay in advance."

He looked insulted. "That's not necessary." He took the form back and scrawled a fresh couple of lines on the release. "That should do it," he said, handing the form back to me. "Initial there, by my handwriting. Then just one signature at the bottom will do it. Don't worry; I'll take this home with me. I won't leave it here."

"No, not your home. Put it in the mail today as soon as I leave. Carry it to the post office. Send it to your lawyer, or something like that. Be safe, okay?"

"That's really necessary?"

I thought about Dmitri in West Harlem. "These people? They know you have a daughter. And that your wife is ill."

He blanched. "Holy shit."

"I'm so sorry. I didn't tell them. I didn't even know. And I didn't know they'd . . . I didn't know a lot. I never would have . . ."

He nodded.

"One of them is out in the waiting room, right now. I told you about her. Lizzie? She's either helping me, or she's setting me up for something. I'm not at all sure which. But when I leave, I'm going to go out your back door and leave her waiting where she is. I need to get away from her so I can say good-bye to Thea and the girls. Lizzie can't be part of that. I wouldn't be surprised if she comes back here looking for me."

"What would you like me to do if she does?"

"Tell her I just left."

"Is she dangerous?"

"I wish I knew." I stood to leave. "I don't think she'll hurt you," I said.

He swallowed and glanced at the clock. "We still have twenty minutes," he said.

"I know. In the running-for-your-life business, that's called a head start," I said. "Thanks for everything."

He came forward and gave me a tight hug. He had tears in his eyes.

I did, too, as I walked out the french door that led from his office into the small yard behind the house.

I doubled back a block to the St. Julien Hotel at Ninth and Walnut and used a pay phone inside to call Mary. She didn't answer, so I tried LaBelle to find out where the plane was. LaBelle sensed my impatience and skipped the usual banter. She told me that the plane and its pilots were at an airport at some city she'd never heard of in South Carolina.

"Good. Don't tell me where," I said. "If you hear from her, and she feels things are under control with her family, have her meet me in Telluride. Let me know if that's a problem."

"When?"

I didn't know. I thought about all that I had to do first. Finally I said, "Tomorrow night."

"And how are you getting to the mountains?"

"Back roads, LaBelle. Back roads. Not to worry. No sniper is going to get me. I drive too fast. You know me, faster than a speeding bullet."

"You're such a damn liar," she said.

"About some things."

Her voice told me she didn't like the fact that she didn't

know what the hell was going on. She didn't have to tell me.

I was relieved that Mary had managed to whisk her cousin out of harm's way. That part was perfect.

I moved on to plan B. I walked to the front of the hotel and caught a cab to take me up the turnpike to the Jeffco airport. I retrieved the Prius from the parking lot of the FBO and headed toward Denver instead of toward Golden, which would have been my most direct route into the mountains. The side trip to get to my home in the southern metro area would cost me some time at the front end of my journey, but I knew that there would be significant advantage to trading the Prius for my old Porsche for the long ride over the Divide to Ridgway.

I left the keys inside the Prius in my garage, signed the title over to LaBelle, and stuck the square piece of paper in the glove compartment. When I died, LaBelle would discover that I'd set up an educational trust to take care of her three sons. She'd appreciate that much more than the Prius. The Prius was just the ribbon on the package.

But the Prius would make her smile. She's such an environmental sap.

FIFTY-SIX

If a blizzard hadn't been threatening the southern Rockies, I would have gone out 285 and gone over Monarch Pass to Ridgway. Instead, I took 470 to Golden along the hogbacks of the Front Range where I picked up Interstate 70 for the steep climb into the heart of the Rockies. To avoid the sniper's territory completely, I could have headed farther south on I-25 and taken unfamiliar back roads into the mountains, but I decided that the sniper risk was relatively small and that time was more important. Much more important.

The old Porsche felt terrific in my hands. Ignoring speed limits, the drive to the Western Slope of the mountains would take me over five hours and I was determined to enjoy every minute of the journey.

I knew it might be the last time I drove the Porsche.

Or crossed the Rockies.

Or felt the trance of the Uncompahgre.

Or saw my girls.

I set those thoughts aside the same way, and for the same reason, that I'd set aside my efforts to comprehend string theory—my brain was too limited to imagine it—and allowed my attention to drift to the car and to the road.

As we started to climb into the foothills, I heard the telltale ping that told me the German girl had a little valve clatter.

She'd been prone to it since she and I had first fallen in love.

I noticed a man was standing near the Morrison exit talking on a cell phone. His presence made my heart jump until I got close enough to be sure he wasn't holding a sniper's rifle.

He wasn't.

He was holding only a cell phone.

I was near Red Rocks. The climb was about to get steeper. More fun.

The valve clatter increased in volume; the girl was begging me for higher rpm.

I usually gave her what she wanted.

I was about to downshift.

FIFTY-SEVEN

Two more guys. Two more cell phones.

Three big trucks blocking the lanes in front of me on the steep downhill below El Rancho.

Shit.

I should have seen it coming sooner.

Still, the conclusion reached, when it came, was a complete surprise.

I can be such an idiot.

At first, it felt like I was participating in a disaster drill.

Engine out in an airplane.

Failed regulator at ninety feet below the surface of the Pacific on the back side of Molokini.

Collapsed cornice in the Bugaboos.

I'd been there. I'd done that. I knew the rules.

Assess. Decide. Act.

But most of all—react.

No time to waste.

The variables this time?

The Porsche's speed. High—eighty-five, ninety.

The flatbed truck's speed. The one with the black barrels flying off the bed? Not so high—thirty-five, forty.

In front of me, a Dodge truck swerved to avoid a barrel, overcorrected, and flew over a Jersey barrier into the oncoming traffic. My attention was locked onto a different black metal drum—one that was heading right at me. There was no time to do the calculus, but the black barrel with my name on it was at the apogee of an orbit that would bring it down to earth perilously close to me and the Porche.

How close?

Too close.

I braked hard before I downshifted.

Will *the drum hit just in front of the car? Right on top? On the sloping back deck that covers the engine?*

I could only guess.

The other cars and trucks on that steep downhill stretch of I-70? It was impossible to calculate what they would do.

Should I brake more? Accelerate? Swerve?

The swerve option was especially dicey: On my left, a hard-braking Chrysler minivan packed full of people had squeezed onto the narrow ribbon of pavement between my car and the Jersey barrier that separated the downhill lanes from the uphill lanes. On my right, a ridiculously large SUV blocked any escape fantasy I might have that would take me in that direction.

The barrel with my name on it seemed to hang in the air, waiting for me to make my move.

Acceleration was an especially tempting option. I was on a steep downhill grade; gravity would provide a welcome boost. One quick upshift, followed by a sharp thrust at the accelerator pedal and the Porsche would gleefully do the rest, jumping at my command to gallop. She would love it. Love it.

But I didn't goose the gas. I braked. Why?

Because I'd gone into automatic. I was no longer driving. I was skiing, and every instinct told me I had to feather an edge and control my speed if I was going to have a prayer of keeping both boards on the same side of every tree.

Instantly, as I braked, the minivan and the SUV jumped ahead of me. I felt that I had only a split second to maneuver away from the descending arc of the falling drum's trajectory. I had just started to turn the wheel right to start my escape when I felt a firm impact on the right-rear quarter of the car.

The barrel? Have I just been hit?

No, the black drum was still airborne.

As my tires yielded to the unexpected force on the rear end by relinquishing their grip on the pavement, the Porsche began to ease into a spin. I realized that I'd just been clipped by a car that I hadn't even seen coming up behind me.

Careless. Shit.

Watching the barrel with my name on it bounce harmlessly past my car, I wondered if the German girl could endure a spin at those speeds and still keep her four rubber pads on the road.

The barrel passing by was the good news.

The bad news? I was watching the tumbling drum buffet past me out of my windshield—and not in my mirrors—which meant that for that instant, at least, my German chariot was pointed back uphill, which wasn't the direction I'd been driving a split second before.

I could feel the g-force from the continued sideways pull of the spin. The Porsche's paws weren't finding traction. I knew if she didn't find some connection with the planet soon, I was going to crash into something, or the German girl and I were going to roll.

Or both.

I thought, *Thea would consider this reckless.*

No doubt about it.

FIFTY-EIGHT

Saying good-bye to Thea and the girls up in Ridgway was like draining the life out of my soul with a high-capacity sump. The extended farewell sucked at my spirit until the density of what was left inside me made every step I took heavy and clumsy. I was an elephant trying to climb a tree.

I did the au revoirs bit by bit over the course of about twenty-four hours. The whole time, of course, I had to pretend that I wasn't doing it at all.

Not surprisingly Thea saw something in my manner that raised red flags for her. "Did you get some bad news about your health? Something new you're not telling me?" she asked me gently. When I said no, she grabbed me—grabbed me—her strong hands squeezing into the muscles of my biceps, and she demanded, "Are you sure? Tell me."

Tell me? Her eyes pierced my facade. I could feel the intensity of their power cutting like lasers into the dura lining the back side of my skull.

"I'm sure," I said.

Sure of nothing, I thought.

"Why are you so . . . ?" she asked.

"Why am I so . . . what?" I replied.

"Something is going on," she said. "You're not . . . You're too . . . cuddly. Is it Adam?"

"I haven't found him. I need to find him, babe."

She softened her voice as she said, "I know. You seem . . . sad, I think."

Does she know? How could she? I wondered.

I'd convinced myself that I was hiding all the pathos I was feeling. It disarmed me that she saw it. "Maybe," I said. "One of these days will be the last day I see you. And Cal and Haven."

"You've been a great father," she said. Thea knew my self-doubts, or at least most of them.

"A better father than we worried I would be," I said with a little whimsy in my voice. "The girls have made it easy, but Adam's been a challenge. I need to find him before—"

"I know," she said again.

Does she know?

I decided that she couldn't know, and that she was interpreting my sadness as some form of self-pity about my health, or about my missing son, and I let her think it. Because even if it wasn't honest, it was true.

"It's hard," I tried, aware it was a deflection.

"When you're gone," she said. "If that's how it ends—"

Does she know? "I'm not—"

"Shhhh," she said. "Listen. When you're gone, when the time comes, promise me you'll visit me in my dreams. That you'll hold me while I sleep. That you'll make me strong enough to be everything for the girls."

"And Adam," I said.

"And Adam," she said.

I wanted to tell her she was the strongest person I knew. Instead, I said, "I promise."

"I'm sorry," she said. "I know you're not going to die tomorrow, but . . ." Tears were welling in the corners of her eyes. "I'm going to need an angel. I will. I'm so, so sorry to be selfish right now, but"—she sobbed so hard she shook—"I'm not as strong as you are, I guess."

If she only knew how much stronger than me she was.

I left all the misperceptions floating in the air between us. I felt like the fraud I was.

FIFTY-NINE

What I'd thought I was buying from the Death Angels was peace of mind. It had seemed like a reasonable bargain at the time. I was agreeing to trade a few sick-but-ambulatory days for a promise that I wouldn't have to endure endless days when illness or injury had robbed me of the vitality that I was convinced was so essential to my well-being. My rationalization was a simple one—that I'd rather die a few days too soon than months or years too late.

What I didn't realize at the time was that I was blindly giving up a few other important things in the deal.

Hope, for instance. I was giving up hope.

Not hope in any infinite lifesaving sense, not hope that science would prevail, or hope that prayer would yield a miracle and that the inexorable flow of my illness would have its path to the final sea altered by intervention from fate, or from one of the idols we include on the roster of deities that we call God.

What I was giving up instead was hope in its purest, most basic form. Hope that I might have one more good day, or one more good hour, or one more intimate meal, or even one last shared smile with Cal and Haven, one more night where I was still strong enough to lie under a layer of down and hold my wife, and comfort her, and be comforted by her.

One embrace with my distant son.

I was giving up hope that the next night I would still be able to see the stars or the next morning I would still be able to gaze upon the sunrise. Hope that I could have one more day surrounded by family photos that yanked me through time to memories that made me laugh and made me cry and made me grateful for every hour I'd spent on the planet.

Instead of buying peace of mind, it turned out that I'd paid the Death Angels millions of dollars for a dose of fear that shook molecules I didn't even know were part of me.

Fear of death, yes. Ironically, the thought of dying had never before been one of my paralyzing fears.

But even worse, I had begun to fear dying before I had to. Had to.

For years—how many? I don't even know—I'd been allowing myself to subscribe to the absurd, preposterous notion that the value of my life was defined by what I did with it. I had somehow convinced myself that to be truly alive I had to be always stretching a rubber band to its breaking point.

I'd somehow mixed up recreation with living.

God, the absurdity. The irony.

I wasn't totally naive about the choices I'd made as a young man, but in recent years I'd been living under the delusion that although I'd grown up late—sometime in my mid to late thirties—I had grown up.

That day of good-byes in Ridgway with Thea and Berk and Haven, and with a clear view of the future with them I'd never know, I realized I hadn't really begun to grow up until I knew that dying was inevitable and until I accepted the consequences of hiring someone to kill me.

Not once while I was silently saying good-bye to the girls that I loved, my death certainly imminent, did I feel the slightest remorse about the grand adventures I would miss by dying young. All my regrets were about missing Thea and Berkeley and Haven—and yes, Adam—and about not being part of their futures.

What a fucking shame.

What a fucking idiot I am.

The Porsche was parked on the far left side of the big garage in Ridgway. The damage to the driver's side wasn't visible unless someone had a reason to be on the left side of the car. Thea didn't. She wasn't fond of the old sports car and her big SUV was on the opposite side of the garage in the spot closest to the mudroom door. My old German mistress was drivable, but she looked like she had endured a very bad day at Talladega.

I never told Thea about the drama with the flatbed truck on I-70.

After I'd been clipped from behind while trying to avoid that flying black drum—the one I was sure had my name on it—and I was spinning on that steep hill on I-70, I could feel, just *feel*, the German girl struggling to keep her four feet on the ground. We endured another hundred fifty degrees of rotation—I was almost pointed back downhill by then—before I knew that the two tires on the passenger side had started to laugh at gravity and float above the concrete. Not by much. They were maybe a few millimeters above the pavement, maybe a centimeter.

But they were floating—I could feel it—and whatever illusion of control I had was disappearing along with the rubber's contact with the earth.

Not much, I kept telling myself. *Only some silly millimeters, okay, maybe a centimeter, or two. She'll fall back down. She will.*

But she didn't.

And I didn't see the Jersey barrier coming up fast on my

left until I hit it. My attention was turned to the right toward those levitating tires, and toward another barrel that was bouncing off the back of the damn flatbed. The Porsche smacked into that sloped concrete divider hard, cinching me against my shoulder belt, showering the air with sparks, and filling my ears with the sounds of scraping and crunching metal.

The lucky part, in retrospect, was that I didn't hit the barrier at an angle. The impact with the low concrete wall came just at the precise point that the Porsche was aimed straight back downhill, and she absorbed the blow evenly along the sheet metal on the length of her left side. The sudden concussion with an immovable barrier stopped the car from spinning any farther.

The unlucky part? The impact with the angled cement wall caused the German girl's right tires to lift even higher off the pavement. Almost before my brain could make sense of what was happening, those bare centimeters of levitation became a foot, and the foot became two. My mind jumped ahead and I actually pictured what would happen next as those wheels continued to lift and the Porsche and I rolled over the top of the barrier into the oncoming uphill traffic. Instantly, I saw myself upside down, looking out the spider-web glass of the broken windshield, examining for a millisecond the undercarriage of whatever vehicle fate had selected to be the one that was going to kill me.

Instantly.

But the Porsche didn't roll any farther. The feet of elevation of those right wheels became twenty inches, not thirty. Ever so slowly, the twenty inches became ten. With a deep thud and a jarring bounce, the ten inches suddenly became none.

We were back on the ground, and I felt a sudden assurance, an innate confidence that I knew this terrain: All I had to do to survive this hellacious conflagration was to ski through the remaining trees in front of me, and keep both boards on the same side of every trunk.

Instinct took over and I found third gear, steered away from the Jersey barrier, adroitly dodged a bouncing barrel, did a graceful slalom through a trio of demolished cars, squealed the tires in a desperate maneuver to squeeze between one of the two eighteen-wheelers and a spinning Subaru, and in seconds the German girl and I were in the clear, braking hard just in time to finesse the nearly ninety-degree left turn at the bottom of the hill.

While I was doing that desperate, instinctive slalom I was trying to keep an eye peeled for the flatbed truck that had been carrying the black drums. But by the time I'd weaved through the narrow canyon and made it to the outskirts of Idaho Springs, I'd concluded that the driver had probably exited, as he had planned all along, at Highway 6 at the bottom of the hill. I was certain, too, that he had already ditched the truck.

The flatbed was undoubtedly stolen, anyway.

The Death Angels would disappear.

Until the next time.

No one, but me, would know what they'd done.

The valve clatter resumed as I urged the battered Porsche on the long climb from Georgetown up the insanely steep hill that leads to the twin bores that pierce the Continental Divide. I downshifted and forced the rpm higher to keep the tinny patter under control.

The rest of the way up to the Eisenhower Tunnel I didn't see a single soul standing by the side of the road with a cell phone.

Nor anyone with a high-powered rifle.

"*We kill people.*" That's what Lizzie had said.

Earlier, as I'd driven away from the mayhem that had

ensued after the tumbling black drums, I hadn't looked back to see the carnage on the highway behind me. I hadn't wanted to count the lifeless bodies or the fractured, bleeding ones. I didn't want to know the final number of mangled vehicles. I admit that I felt some exhilaration that my own corpse wasn't among the ones being counted, but the relief lasted only as long as a bolus of adrenaline could carry it.

The exhilaration was replaced by selfishness, and then by guilt.

Shame wasn't far behind.

"We kill people," Lizzie had said.

Yes, we do.

Damn, we do.

SIXTY

I turned off Lizzie's cell phone—the one I'd originally found in her lingerie drawer—while I was up in the mountains with Thea and the kids. If she was still on the roster of the Death Angel varsity, she would know that I'd survived the mass murder that they'd arranged for my benefit on I-70, and she would know that I was up in Ridgway with my family. She would probably even be able to guess why I was there. She would certainly be able to guess why I didn't want to be talking with her.

I took her at her word that I was safe in my home.

More crucial to me, of course, was that I took her at her word that all my girls were secure there, too.

LaBelle e-mailed me, as promised, with the results of the search I'd asked her to do. The gist? She needed more time to track down the names of physicians who were board-certified in both neurology and oncology.

"It's not as straightforward as you thought," she wrote. "I'll stay on it until I get it right."

FedEx delivered a package for me shortly after eight o'clock the next morning. I knew the FedEx guy almost as well as I knew the mailman; that's how frequently he came to our house. His arrival caused absolutely no suspicion from Thea.

Inside the flat FedEx envelope was a single piece of stationery from the St. Julien Hotel in Boulder, the new hotel that was only a block away from my shrink's office.

On it Lizzie had scribbled, "Found him. You were right. He is in New Haven. We don't have much time."

Adam?

Why, I wondered, *don't we have much time? Her health? My health? The Death Angels' plans?*

Or is it a trap? Has she found Adam at all?

I phoned LaBelle. "Any word from Mary?"

"Good morning to you, too. And yes, dear Mary did call. She stays in touch." LaBelle put the emphasis firmly on the *she*. "She phoned to say there's a problem with the backup generator on the plane. A part's being shipped to Centennial and she is flying there this afternoon from her current location to have it installed. She doesn't want to get the plane repaired by anybody other than the people we usually use at Centennial. You may know why, but she's not telling me."

LaBelle waited for me to tell her. She expected me to tell her. I didn't tell her.

"O-kay. She thinks the plane will to be ready tonight, late. She said you can count on her meeting you in Telluride, as you asked, but it will have to be in the morning, after sunrise."

"Please tell her to rush the repairs if she can, and I'll count on getting to Centennial tonight. She should be prepared for a red-eye."

"You bet," LaBelle said. I could almost hear her heels clicking together; she'd resorted to her good-soldier voice. LaBelle didn't like being out of the loop and she wasn't trying to pretend otherwise.

"That other thing, LaBelle? The search you were doing for me? Any progress since yesterday?"

"Progress, yes. Answers, no. Soon, I hope. By lunchtime maybe. End of the day for sure. It's turned out to be more difficult to get those databases than I expected it would be."

"It's okay to spend money. As soon as you have something, okay?"

"You got it. You still want the word through e-mail?"

"Or text, but yes. Just notify me that you have what I want. I'll call you."

"Anything else?"

"No, I don't think so."

"Well, I have something else. I don't know if you know; don't even know if you care, but the sniper hit again last night. A sixty-two-year-old man driving a gorgeous '62 Chevy pickup. See the symmetry in that? It's some kind of message, I tell you. He was an African-American man. A church-goin' man. His hair was the color of an old nickel and he kept it in a gorgeous ol' 'fro I swear was the size of a basketball. Now he's dead. Bullet damn near blew the back of his skull off. The pickup he was driving? It just rolled to a stop on the shoulder as it was heading up that hill to El Rancho. Like it was running out of gas, you know? Nice and gentle? Other than the broken glass—just a neat little hole in the driver's window—there's not a scratch on it. That's what they said on the news."

"God help us," I said.

"If you're coming down by car, you be careful."

"El Rancho?" I said. I added an inflection between the two words to turn the repetition into a query, but I wasn't really asking her anything. El Rancho was the exit on Interstate 70 at the top of the hill where I'd seen the third of the three men with cell phones just before my run-in with the flatbed truck full of barrels.

I was wondering if I still believed in coincidence.

I wondered if the sixty-two-year-old church-going

black man with the silver afro had been murdered to send me a message.

Like Dmitri.

"That's what I said. El Rancho. Bad wreck up there yesterday, too. Dozen cars or something. People died."

"I haven't seen the news. I didn't know about the sniper . . . that he'd hit again last night," I said. I didn't tell LaBelle that I'd avoided the news because I didn't want to learn what the final casualty toll had been from the clumsy, shotgun-blast attempt on my life the previous day on the interstate by the barrel-dropping flatbed truck.

LaBelle was still talking. "Mm hmm hmmm. Imagine not knowing what the hell is going on. Imagine something like that. Mm hmm hmmm."

SIXTY-ONE

The phone from Lizzie's panty drawer started ringing when I was less than an hour from Ridgway driving across the expansive land of the high-country plateau that yields the always-worth-celebrating annual bounty of Olathe Sweet.

I could almost taste the buttery, savory sweetness of the legendary local corn. I shed a tear knowing that "almost" was as close as my lips would ever get to tasting it again.

My associations skipped from Olathe Sweet to butter to lips and then on to Thea and the girls. From the road to the horizon, I saw nothing but a sky full of lips I'd never kiss again.

But I ignored the phone.

The panty-drawer phone disturbed the quiet again a while later as I was cutting through Grand Junction to catch I-70 eastbound over the Rockies.

And I ignored it again.

Just outside the small town of Rifle, the phone began to chirp at me every minute or so. I considered turning it off. Instead, I answered it. Why? Maybe boredom. The stretch of I-70 between Grand Junction and Rifle is not exactly Colorado's most scenic chunk of road. But mostly I answered because of the tantalizing possibility that Lizzie had indeed found Adam.

"Yeah?" I said.

"Where are you?" Lizzie asked in an enthusiastic voice, as though she thought I'd been waiting all day to talk with her.

"Rifle," I said.

She recognized the irony and laughed. Her laugh made me smile. My smile was as involuntary as her laugh.

"Are you on your way to Connecticut?"

"Why should I tell you that? Why should I trust you?" I said.

"Because I found your son. I know where he is."

"I would have found him on my own."

"Maybe."

"They tried to kill me."

"Don't be so surprised. You hired them to kill you."

"A lot of people died."

"It's not an ideal result. But to them, it's sometimes necessary. I guarantee that they consider the carnage your fault."

"My fault?"

"You are being ... difficult. From their point of view, you're interfering. You could have chosen to overreact when that first barrel came your way. That cliff was right there, waiting for you to fly over it. Would have killed you for sure. Who knows, maybe no one else would have died."

I wanted to scream at her. I told myself it wouldn't help. The urge passed, like a swallowed belch.

A word she'd used was bothering me. "You said 'them.'"

"Us," she said. She said "us" reluctantly, I thought. For a transient moment I was tempted to grant her the benefit of the doubt that was linked to that reluctance.

But that impulse passed, too. I broke the connection and shut down the power on the phone. I wished I had killed it before I'd made the mistake of answering the call near Rifle.

*

She called me back on my own phone a couple of minutes later.

I was waiting for it.

"Don't hang up," she said. "You need me. You won't find him."

"Do I? I'll bust down every door in New Haven if I have to. I'll find him by myself."

"You don't have time to bust down every door in New Haven."

"My luck has been holding." I could have told her about skiing steep slopes in the woods, about my uncanny ability to keep both skis on the same side of every tree. But she probably already knew.

"Your luck isn't the variable in question. Adam needs you."

"Why?"

"Trust me, damn it. He needs you."

"Is he okay? Is he sick? Hurt? What?"

"Sick" for me used to mean the flu. A cold. Strep throat. With the kids, it was ear infections, or fifth disease, which was Cal's latest malady. On a bad day, sick meant pneumonia. Not anymore. Now, "sick" was a toxic word. Sick was a killer.

"You need to hurry."

"Why? Tell me what's going on?" My question was a demand. The most futile kind. The kind I couldn't enforce.

"Adam needs you."

"You said that. Tell me why."

"Take me with you," she said.

My son needed me and she wanted to bargain? My rage finally blew out from my core like magma spewing from a lava dome. I yelled, "What the fuck is wrong with my son, Lizzie?"

"I'm in Glenwood Springs. I'll be sitting in the Wendy's

374

near the off-ramp. You can see it from the highway. Knowing the way you drive, you should be here in fifteen minutes."

She hung up.

As promised, she was sitting in the fast-food restaurant with her back to the door and to the road. She was so confident I was coming to join her that she didn't even bother to monitor my arrival through the windows that faced the highway.

All that was on the table in front of her was a bottle of water. The brand was BIOTA, an acronym that stands for blame-it-on-the-altitude. It's a natural spring water bottled by a company in Ouray, a couple of spectacular valleys and passes away from my Ridgway home. Was there a message there? I didn't know.

But probably.

I sat down on the plastic bench across from her. She was wearing a hat that almost, but not quite, covered her bald head.

No wig. Not a whole lot of makeup. Lizzie was officially outing herself as a chemotherapy patient.

"It's not exactly Papaya King, is it?" she said from behind a pair of opaque sunglasses.

I didn't have to look around to know that the Glenwood Springs Wendy's—or any Wendy's for that matter—bore little resemblance to the Upper East Side Papaya King where she and I first had lunch. "No," I said. Unable to wait a second longer, I said, "Tell me about my son. What's wrong with him?" I surprised myself with how level I was able to keep my voice.

"I want to go with you. If I tell you what I know you'll leave me behind."

I was grateful that she didn't pretend that her motives were anything different. I said, "I won't leave you behind."

"You've ditched me once already."

"I had to say good-bye to my girls."

A moment later, I watched a tear sneak out from below the rim of her sunglasses. She let it migrate to the corner of her mouth and caught it with her tongue. I imagined the salt she was tasting.

"I accept that. But I have to go to New Haven with you. It's as important to me as your visit to Ridgway was to you."

It was beginning to get dark in the mountains. Time was tight. On clear roads the drive from Glenwood over the Divide to the metro area was almost three hours, even at the speeds I planned to be motoring. I glanced at my watch, looked at Lizzie, and said, "We should go."

"Can I get you something to eat for the road?" she asked.

"Not a good idea," I said, imagining the inevitable nausea. And then the inevitable vomit.

Out in the parking lot, I said, "I have to climb in from your side. The driver's door doesn't open."

She examined the mangled metal and scratched paint on the driver's side of the Porsche. "I'm sorry," she said. "About your car. You've had this for a long time, haven't you?"

What, I wondered, *do they not know about me?*

I patted the German girl on the hood. "Yeah, a long time. But it's just stuff," I said. "Though there was a time not too long ago when all this damage would have broken my heart."

"Yes," she agreed. "It is just stuff." She kept a hand on the sheet metal as she ambled around the back of the car to the passenger side. After one last affectionate caress on the German girl's flesh, she stepped back and allowed me to lower myself onto the passenger seat and contort myself over the gearshift to the driver's side. She joined me and I started the car.

"Wait," she said.

I looked over. She was pulling a small nylon pouch from her shoulder bag. "What?" I asked.

She zipped open the bag and pulled out the familiar tools of a phlebotomist. "I need to check your blood."

I was beyond surprise. "For what?"

"Toxins. They—my colleagues—may have decided to . . . poison you. They're very good at it. And you've gone on record as preferring drugs to bullets."

Jesus. "How the hell do—" I stopped myself. *What difference does it make?* "And if you discover they did?"

"Depends what agent is involved. I may be able to administer an antidote if I can identify what they used. I know their favorites."

"How will you get the blood analyzed?"

She pointed across my chest to a guy sitting in a white van across the parking lot. "He's a messenger. He's going to deliver it to the lab for me. I should have some of the results before we get to Denver."

"No bullshit, Lizzie?" I asked. "You're taking my blood, not injecting anything into it?"

"I don't know how you made it so far in life not knowing whom to trust. But, no. No bullshit. If I was going to kill you—"

"I know. I'd already be dead." I held out my arm.

"So you've decided to trust me?" she asked me a moment later as she tightened a tourniquet around my bicep and swabbed the crook of my elbow with an alcohol swab. Berk called that particular part of her anatomy her "elbow pit." That little memory, and what it represented, caused a plume of vomit to rise in my throat.

I involuntarily winced in anticipation of the poke. I said, "I've decided to be vulnerable to you."

She filled three rubber-stopped tubes with my blood and pulled the catheter from my vein before she turned up

377

to face me and lowered her sunglasses so that I could see the linear patterns in her irises. "What's the difference?"

"It's a long story," I said.

She stuck a bandage over the tiny wound, dropped the vials into a small, pre-printed envelope that she'd already marked, and honked the horn. The guy from the white van walked over. She handed him my blood. She said, "Stat" as she held out a hundred-dollar bill. He took the encouragement, but he didn't say a word. Lizzie pulled the shoulder belt across her body and clicked it into place. She slid down on her seat and pulled her floppy hat low over her eyes.

"We can go now?" I asked.

"Sure. We have a long drive," she said. "Plenty of time for you to tell me all about the difference between trust and vulnerability."

My palm found the familiar orb of the gearshift. I popped the Porsche into first, eased back on the clutch, pulled out of the lot, and accelerated up the ramp onto the interstate.

The engine was thundering before I dropped the transmission into second. I said, "And then you can tell me why I didn't find any magazines in your apartment. But that's after you tell me what the fuck is going on with my son."

SIXTY-TWO

The drive east from Glenwood Springs on I-70 toward the Continental Divide is, intermittently, glorious. Lizzie wouldn't reveal anything more about Adam while we drove. Nor would she tell me how she'd made it to Glenwood from Boulder after I'd left her behind at Dr. Gregory's office, but her fresh, wide-eyed wonder at the marvels of Glenwood Canyon and the rushing Colorado River below the highway clued me in that she had made the journey either at night on the highway or by airplane.

We were zooming past Eagle when I started to share with her all the details I could remember about Dr. Gregory and my epiphanies about intimacy and openness and vulnerability. I was still going strong as we flew below the ski areas at Arrowhead and Beaver Creek, and then Vail. We both grew quiet as she absorbed the beauty of the highest reaches of Vail Pass and the White River National Forest. It seemed to take us only minutes to slice through the ravines between Copper Mountain and Frisco in the shadows of the Tenmile Range. Seconds later we were on the bluff above Dillon Reservoir. A temporary electronic warning sign had been placed on the shoulder a half mile before the Keystone/Highway 6 exit. The sign warned, TUNNEL REPAIRS AHEAD. EASTBOUND ONE LANE ONLY. TRUCKS EXIT AT HIGHWAY 6.

I hesitated for a moment, considering whether I wanted

to be in line with a thousand cars waiting to squeeze through one lane of the tunnel, or whether I wanted to be in a convoy with a few hundred big rigs trying to climb the treacherous, curvy route over the Divide on Loveland Pass. It wasn't a tough call. I downshifted into fourth and began the final, long, determined climb that would take us up and over—well, through—the Continental Divide.

I'd chosen the tunnel approach.

As we climbed the steep hill I kept at least one eye focused on the side of the road, watching for men with cell phones, solitary scouts with binoculars, or even the glint of reflected light from a scope atop an assassin's rifle in a sniper's lair. Every van I passed I marked off as a potential adversary already vanquished.

Lizzie remained assured that the Death Angels would not kill us while we were together.

I didn't share her confidence.

She'd nodded off to sleep moments after we started up the obscene grade to the twin tunnels that cut through the Divide. By then the mountain canyons below us were completely dark. I'd spotted nothing that worried me. And we were making good time.

Traffic slowed about halfway up the long climb to the tunnels, near the point where the final few trees before timberline were nothing more than stunted, pathetic versions of their downhill forest cousins. I was neither alarmed nor surprised by the slowing traffic, but I was disheartened that the construction backup might extend back this far. Although the uphill highway was blessed with a climbing lane for overburdened trucks, it wasn't uncommon for drivers to underestimate the grade, or overestimate their vehicles—or both—and for the slowest sloggers to clog two of the three uphill lanes. When that happened, traffic could back up far in advance of the tunnels. But not as far as it was backed up that day.

I estimated we'd lose at least half an hour to the construction delay. The only alternative to waiting in the two-mile-long line to make it through the narrowed tunnel passage would have been getting in an almost equally long queue on Highway 6, the pre-tunnel route over the Divide that led across Loveland Pass some twelve thousand feet above sea level. The pass was a twisty, panoramic, exciting two-lane roller coaster lined with sheer drops and hairpin turns. But clogged with lumbering eighteen-wheelers that had been detoured from the tunnel, it was certainly no panacea to the delays that we were facing on I-70.

I tried to be calm and tried not to look at the clock. Instead, I watched Lizzie sleep. We inched our way up to the tunnels. I fiddled with the controls on the radio in an attempt to pull in a radio station that would tell me that the sniper had been caught.

Didn't happen.

The Porsche's valves continued to ping in protest whenever I got careless and allowed the rpm to migrate too low for her tastes.

Some things never change.

And some things change so fast I can't keep my eyes in focus.

It didn't take long in that traffic—three minutes, five?—for me to start feeling like a sitting duck. My planned defenses against a Death Angel sniper rifle on the drive east to the Front Range were going to be the Porsche's speed and maneuverability, and my willingness to exploit both. Those advantages were eliminated by the bumper-to-bumper uphill crawl. I tried to compensate by staying in the middle lane on the interminable climb to the tunnel, doing everything I could to keep the little sports car in the shadows of someone else's oversized vehicle. I pulled in behind a small UPS van in the middle lane, and adjusted my speed to try to always keep an SUV flanking me on the right. To the left, though, was my greatest vulnerability. That's where the cliffs were; that's where the sniper's best angle would be. For the first time in my life, I was thankful that so many Colorado drivers preferred big, hulking SUVs and pickups. I was taking some comfort whenever I could linger in their figurative shade.

I was wrong by half in my estimation about how long it would take to snake up to the eleven-thousand-plus-foot elevation of the tunnel entrance. It took us forty-five minutes, not thirty, to dodge and merge and inch up the hill to the final stretch of the tunnel approach.

Known locally as the Eisenhower Tunnel, the twin bores through the Continental Divide are officially named the Eisenhower/Johnson Memorial Tunnels. The original Eisenhower bore now carries only westbound traffic. The newer, two-lane eastbound passage that Lizzie and I were about to enter was the Edwin C. Johnson Bore, named after a state politician who'd long advocated mountain highways and ambitious tunnels, including this one.

Edwin C. had gotten his wish; the tunnel bearing his name is ambitious, and long. It shoots just shy of two miles through the hard granite wall that divides the North American continent down its geographic center. Anyone who drives the route regularly knows that two lanes in each direction no longer provide sufficient capacity. And when one of the two lanes in either direction is closed for some reason, the resulting backups can leave vehicles bumper-to-bumper for miles.

Lizzie woke up to the blare of a big rig's air horn. The truck was on the other side of the highway, coming downhill. It seemed to me that the trucker was signaling to another long-haul driver who was heading off the road to a paved area where he could check his brakes prior to the steep descent that awaited him on the road toward Dillon.

"Are we there?" Lizzie asked, dazed from her doze.

"Wishful thinking. We're still in traffic. There's only one lane open through the tunnel. Things should free up as soon as we're on the other side."

"How long will it take after that?"

"I've been known to do it in well under an hour," I said. When she didn't respond I asked, "I've been wondering something. If they poisoned me, what should I be watching for? How would I know?"

"I don't want to suggest anything to you. I'm watching you for symptoms. Leave that to me."

"And?"

"So far I don't see anything but paranoia." She laughed.

I didn't.

A minute later I pulled, finally, into the tunnel portal. Orange cones blocked off the left lane. A series of tall rolling scaffolds had been erected so that workers—I guessed electricians—could do something with the overhead lighting. Coils of Romex snaked out of exposed circuit boxes above our heads. I thought the workers were replacing the fixtures.

With the tunnel lighting intact above the right lane, along with additional lighting that had been mounted on the scaffolds to assist the workers, and with the headlights of the slow-moving vehicles inside the bore, the tunnel was almost as bright as an overcast day.

"How long is this thing?" Lizzie asked.

"The tunnel? A little less than two miles."

She shuddered. "So we're in the middle of a mountain? I don't like tunnels. I especially don't like not being able to see the other end. I feel trapped when I'm in them. In the city, I can't use the tunnels under the river anymore; I always take the bridges. Always."

"What about the subway?"

"Until what happened in the Tube in London, it didn't bother me."

"That makes no sense," I said. *Except,* I thought, *for the part about London.*

"I didn't say it did."

"A few minutes, we'll be out," I said, touching her on the wrist.

"You promise?"

"Yeah."

But a minute later I wasn't so sure. We hadn't made it far and the line of cars in front of me had come to a complete stop.

Lizzie tolerated the lack of progress for about thirty seconds before she asked, "What's wrong?"

"I don't know. Construction, I guess."

"Why aren't we moving? We were moving before."

"Maybe they're shifting the position of one of those scaffolds and they're temporarily blocking both lanes."

I noticed that she'd moved her left hand onto my thigh. I felt pressure through her fingertips. She was anxious.

I considered the likelihood that I was with a claustrophobe in a stalled elevator.

My own fear was, as she had suggested, much more paranoid than phobic.

Lizzie's difficulties aside, my mind started playing with the variables. She and I were trapped a little over halfway into an almost two-mile-long tunnel. The left lane was closed for maintenance on the overhead lighting. On the outside of each lane was a raised pedestrian pathway intended for use during emergencies. Traffic was stopped dead in the open lane in front of us and behind us. A parallel tunnel, over a hundred feet to the north through solid granite, carried traffic back in the direction we had just come. The only links between the two bores were occasional pedestrian passageways—built for use by maintenance personnel—that ran perpendicular to the roadways. The entrances to the cross tunnels seemed to be at least a quarter of a mile apart.

The question I was pondering was: *Would this be a good place for the I-70 sniper to take someone out?*

How would he, or she, avoid detection? How would he, or she, escape?

I quickly decided that avoiding detection was impossible. The lighting in the tunnel was brilliant, there were a thousand possible witnesses, and a surveillance camera system covered every square meter of the interior.

Getting away? Immediately, I recognized that those maintenance passageways between the two bores might allow a relatively uncomplicated escape. The sniper could wait just inside one of the connecting passages, shoot someone—like me or Lizzie—while we were stalled in the eastbound bore, then turn and run thirty or forty yards through the pedestrian connection to the adjacent west-bound tunnel. There, a car would be waiting, the assassin would jump in and be out on the Western Slope side of the mountain in a minute or less.

But—*but*—the whole episode would be monitored by the tunnels' surveillance cameras. The Colorado State Patrol would know within seconds exactly which vehicle to chase coming out of the tunnel on the Western Slope. Since there are no highway exits for miles on the western descent from the tunnel, the troopers would certainly be able to apprehend the sniper within a short time.

That's as far as I'd gotten in my musing when the overhead tunnel lights flashed off.

No flicker, just—*poof*. Off.

My pulse jumped.

Seconds later—five, maybe—a smaller pattern of lights came back on. The tunnel was noticeably darker than it had been before the power failure.

Emergency generators, I thought. *Backup lighting. Much lower wattage.*

"What was that?" Lizzie said. "What just happened?" Her voice was tight with concern. I could tell that the pressure was tunnel phobia. She hadn't made the logical leaps I was making. Yet.

Before I could answer her question the work lights on the scaffolds began to die. Not all at once. But haphazardly, one here, one there. The workers must have been following instructions to kill the lights in the event of a power failure so as not to tax the tunnels' backup generators. Priority would undoubtedly channel most of the auxiliary energy to power the huge fans that were necessary to suck poisonous exhaust gases from the two tunnels. Overhead light was a luxury.

"I'm not sure," I said. "Power failure, maybe. It's no big thing. The car headlights provide plenty of illumination for us to see our way out."

She was examining my face and I could tell that she could see that I was trying to solve a puzzle. If this were a chess game, and not life and death, this would be like a mate-in-four exercise. This time, though, I knew it wasn't a game, and I wasn't on the attack; I had to see the future to avoid getting mated.

Because this time getting mated meant dying.

And dying meant not seeing Adam.

"What are you thinking?" she said. She was dead calm. I didn't know what to make of the sudden change in her demeanor.

"I'm thinking that you may not be right about your colleagues' reluctance to take us out together."

She sat up straight and focused her attention out the windshield. "Tell me what you're thinking. Exactly."

"About fifty yards up on the left there's a pedestrian passageway that leads over to the parallel tunnel, the one that carries westbound traffic. Workers use it, not the public. See it? That opening in the tile? It's a dark shadow."

She nodded. "Yes, I do."

A horn honked someplace in front of us. Some other idiots echoed the noise.

Above our heads, the emergency lights flickered for a few seconds. Then they, too, died. The upper reaches of the bore went from shadowy to dark. The only illumination left in the tunnel came from the vehicle headlights.

Lizzie's temporary placidity evaporated. She was breathing heavily, through her mouth. "Go on," she said.

"You know about the sniper who's been working in Colorado?"

"Yes."

"Is it one of yours?"

"I don't know. I've wondered. It's not out of the question. It wouldn't be a primary plan. But it might be a backup. Kill a few people at random. Then kill you. Your death will look random, too."

I growled, "Fuckers." Then I refocused. "For the sake of argument, let's say the sniper's a Death Angel, and they've decided it's time to kill us. If someone takes us out in here, that pedestrian tunnel could be their escape route. Two quick shots, then a short run down the passageway. It would be choreographed so a car would be waiting to pick them up on the other side. The only thing I can't figure is how they would avoid the surveillance cameras."

Without a moment's hesitation, Lizzie said, "Smoke."

"Where?"

"No, no, I don't see any. I'm saying they'll use smoke to mask what they're doing from the cameras."

"How will they see us?"

"They'll identify us before they create the smoke, and then if they need to, they'll track us with infrared. The tunnel surveillance cameras need visible light; they won't be able to see a thing."

Her confidence in the tactical plan told me that the strategy she was imagining wasn't a novel one for the Death Angels. Lizzie had seen smoke diversion used before. I was curious to learn more about the previous tactical details, but wasn't sure I had the time to pick her brain.

In front of us, drivers began shutting off their engines. People climbed out of their cars. They began to huddle together; strangers started chatting with strangers. Lots of fingers were pointed down the tunnel. At what? I didn't know.

"Should we get out of the car?" I asked.

"Yes," she said. "Definitely. If they already have us identified—and they know this car, so I'm sure they have—then they have an infrared scope on us by now. We have to move out of their line of sight so they can't identify us so easily when the smoke starts. We have to put something between us and them to block the infrared signature. Otherwise we're just . . ."

I silently finished her thought: *Sitting ducks.*

She got out of the car first. I thought of lowering the window on my door and pulling myself out of the opening like a stock car driver. Instead, I fumbled my way over the gearshift and climbed out in a more conventional manner on the passenger side. We were both still trying to act casually.

"Should we get behind the car in front of us?" I asked, my voice low.

Far down the tunnel somebody yelled, "Fire! That car's on fire! Smoke, look!"

Someone else yelled, "Ruthie? Look! Let's get out of here. Run! Run! Shit! Fire!"

I hopped forward and pulled myself up on the bumper of the Suburban that was stopped in front of the Porsche and used the perch to peer as far down the tunnel as possible. I couldn't see any smoke at first.

Then I could.

White smoke was billowing out rapidly from the line of cars in big puffs, like thunderstorm clouds, or like steam bursting from a smokestack. My eyes moved left across the blocked-off lane and found the rectangular opening in the tile wall. The source of the smoke was just beyond the passageway. The cloud was moving in our direction.

"Smoke, Lizzie," I said, without turning. "Almost exactly where the cross-tunnel passageway is. You were right." When I turned to see why she hadn't answered me, she was gone.

SIXTY-THREE

I dropped off the bumper and fell into a crouch in the space behind the Suburban. I wondered what I looked like in the sniper's infrared scope.

Green, I decided. I looked green.

The panic in the tunnel in reaction to the smoke was predictable, and almost immediate.

People not already out of their cars jumped out and everyone began scrambling up the short ladders on the outside tunnel walls to get to the raised emergency pedestrian passageways, but since we were stuck somewhere close to the middle of the tunnel the throngs couldn't decide which way to run. Some were pushing back in the direction from which we had come, away from the smoke. Others had apparently decided to try to sprint through the smoke to get to the eastern portal.

Tempers were flaring. People hurrying became people shoving. Yells became screams. Fear became panic.

Within thirty seconds the visibility in front of me was less than two car lengths. The smoke continued to thicken.

I dropped to all fours and hugged the roadway to try to stay below the worst of the smoke, and I searched for Lizzie. As I crawled back toward the Porsche I heard the retort of a rifle, and the metallic *phhhfft* of a slug piercing metal.

Before the volume of the screaming grew even louder, a

second shot impacted the fender of my car just above the front tire on the driver's side. That second shot had missed my head by no more than a foot.

I dove back for the relative safety of the shadow of the SUV.

I hissed, "Lizzie!"

"I'm under here," she said. I felt fingers on my ankle.

"They'll come for us," I said.

"Yes," she said. "They will. Soon. Any ideas?"

"Come on," I said. I took her hand.

We crawled, we crouched, we hopped, and we sprinted, trying desperately to stay in the shadow of the single line of vehicles as we made our way up the far right side of the roadway in the direction the cars were heading. In the direction of the smoke. In the direction of the sniper.

Despite the fact that traffic was at a dead stop, most of the people who were emptying out of the cars continued to fight for space on the emergency pedestrian walkways. Lizzie and I stayed on the tunnel roadway, using each sequential vehicle to shield our body heat from the infrared sensors in the Death Angel's rifle scope.

She stopped in front of me seconds after it became clear we weren't fooling whoever was shooting at us. Another slug whizzed between us as we skipped between two cars. The bullet chipped off a two-square-inch piece of subway tile from the wall behind us.

Lizzie sat on the roadway, her back against an old Dodge pickup. I did the same. The sniper knew where we were, and was obviously in a terrific position to intercept us before we made it to the pedestrian passageway.

"He can't be on the walkway on either side. There're too many people around," she said. "He has to be up on—"

"One of the scaffolds," I said. "You're right."

By then Lizzie and I were only about two car lengths

away from the pedestrian tunnel that ran between the two bores. The smoke had become a thick, still fog. The light in the tubular beams from the parked cars' headlights bounced right back at them. I knew that the stillness of the smoke cloud meant that the tunnels' ventilation fans had failed. If enough drivers had left their engines running, carbon monoxide poisoning would be a factor.

We had to act.

"I have an idea," I said. I told her what I was thinking.

"Why not?" she said. She turned around, reached up, and opened the door of the old Dodge.

I crawled in first, staying low in the foot well as I wormed my way to the floor on the driver's side. Right behind me she did the same, but she stayed on the passenger-side floor. As I'd suspected, the keys to the truck were in the ignition. I forced the gearshift into neutral before I used one hand to turn the key, and the other to put slight pressure on the gas pedal. After a couple of plaintive turns of the starter motor, the engine kicked to life.

"Ready?" I asked. "On three. One, two—"

The last number got lost in the flurry of activity that followed. I pulled myself up onto the driver's seat, pounded the clutch and popped the gearshift into first. Lizzie jumped up onto the passenger seat. The weight of the clutch threw me for a moment and I almost stalled the truck as I turned the wheel hard left and begged the thing to begin to accelerate. But the truck was all torque, little acceleration. Once the transmission finally accepted what I wanted it to do it became apparent that the truck had plenty of low-end power. After a short initial roll, we jumped out of our lane and began to devour the series of flimsy orange cones that were cordoning off the work space in the left lane.

Lizzie reached over and kept pressure on the horn with her left hand so that any stray pedestrians would have a fighting chance to get clear of our path. I could see occasional glimpses of the tile wall off to my left, just enough to keep the truck going relatively straight as I built up speed and shifted into second gear. The smoke made it impossible for me to know how far it was going to be until the truck collided with the first scaffold.

It wasn't long. The interval between my first sighting of the scaffold and our impact with the metal frame wasn't more than half a second, barely enough time to brace myself, not enough time to get a "hold on" warning out of my mouth for Lizzie. The metal-framed structure was more substantial than I'd suspected, and at first I thought it was actually strong enough to slow the truck's momentum. But I floored the gas pedal at the initial contact and within another half-heartbeat, it was clear that the pickup was shoving the reluctant structure down the left lane of the Edwin C. Johnson Bore at significant speed.

Three seconds later, maybe five, we cleared the worst of the smoke. Lizzie was leaning forward on her seat, looking straight up at the top of the scaffold. She screamed, "He's still there! I can see him!" The truck slowed, but the scaffold kept moving. I could see it begin to rock forward, but it didn't appear that it was going to tip enough to fall over. Gear teeth grated as I pounded the transmission back into first and floored the accelerator. The second impact with the truck rocked the unstable scaffold hard.

Lizzie and I both stared upward as the tower leaned toward us, tottered for a second on two wheels, and finally began to tumble back on top of the truck. The sniper's balance couldn't adjust to the rapid rocking. As the scaffolding fell he went flying over the safety rail in the opposite direction, flipping backward off the far side. We instinctively slid low in our seats to brace for the impact of the heavy frame on the roof of the passenger cab. But the concussion was minor; most of the frame missed the part of the truck where we were sitting.

A secondary shudder followed a second later. It came from below. The sniper's body had passed under the truck's frame.

I hit the brakes hard, and screamed, "Now!"

Lizzie and I had already choreographed our next move. The moment the truck stopped moving, we jumped out and starting running forward toward the eastern portal, making a rapid perusal of the inventory of available abandoned vehicles so that we could pick one for the next leg of our escape. Without consulting me, Lizzie sprinted ahead four cars and jumped into the right seat of a BMW M3.

It was a great choice. The car was a little rocket. I followed her onto the driver's seat, found the key in the ignition, started the engine, popped the gearshift into first, turned the wheel hard left, and squealed through a gap in the orange cones into the closed lane. I accelerated through the remaining length of the tunnel, slowing once to dodge a terrified pedestrian, and once more to do a nifty slalom around the final scaffold.

By the time we were approaching the eastern portal I was already doing about eighty.

SIXTY-FOUR

At the first sign of electrical failure the tunnel administrators had undoubtedly closed both bores to traffic. Once smoke started to fill the eastbound lanes and drift out the exit portals, drivers stopped at the eastern slope entrance must have recognized that their wait to get through the tunnel was going to be a long one.

By the time Lizzie and I exited the eastern entrance to the westbound bore in the stolen M3, a couple of cops were already in place diverting vehicles that were lined up to enter the tunnel from the east into a U-turn that would permit them to go back down the hill and exit onto Loveland Pass, the sole alternative route in the vicinity over the Divide to the Western Slope. Seeing what was going on in front of us, I braked hard, slowing the M3 so that I could sneak into the orderly procession that was heading back down the hill. I feared a cop would stop us and ask how we'd managed to get out of the tunnel, but the one who saw us coming gave me a thumbs-up and waved us on. Most of the other cars in the queue joined the slowly crawling line to exit at the Loveland Pass off-ramp.

We didn't. Lizzie and I had a different destination.

I moved into the left lane and maintained an approximation of the speed limit until we reached Silver Plume.

At that point, I let the M3 stretch her legs a little and I

attacked the decline of the Georgetown hill as though I were still in the Porsche.

We were going to New Haven.

Initially I surmised that we would enjoy at least an hour's cushion before the owner of the M3 realized that her car—the insurance card in the glove compartment identified the owner as Carrie Belvedere of Littleton—had been stolen. Before Carrie would be allowed back into the tunnel, at a minimum, power had to be restored. The source of the tunnel fire would need to be identified. The exhaust fans would need to be checked, and rechecked. The air quality might have to be sampled. The reports of sniper shots would have to be investigated.

The puzzle of the toppled scaffold and the battered Dodge pickup with the body trapped below it would need to be solved.

Lizzie disagreed with my assessment about the time all that would take. "The owners of those cars aren't going to be allowed back into the tunnel to retrieve them for a long time. The whole tunnel's a crime scene. The cops are going to shut down access for hours. Maybe all night. They might use the other side for two-way traffic, but the side we were in? It's closed for a while."

"So no one's looking for us?" I said hopefully.

"No one in law enforcement," she said.

The Death Angels are still looking for us.

That's what she meant.

"Oh."

"They're not accustomed to taking casualties. To my knowledge, it's never happened before. It will complicate things."

Lizzie had said "they."

"For them?" I asked.

"Yes. For us, too."

"Will they try to hit us again on the way down?" I asked.

"They didn't expect to fail in the tunnel. That was a complex op."

"That means no?"

"If we're lucky they don't know where we are right now."

"They did before? They knew where we were?"

"All of your vehicles are GPS'd," she said. Her tone conveyed her disappointment that I hadn't figured that out myself.

Of course they are. "The plane, too?"

She nodded. "Planes are easy to track. Anyone can do it on the Web. They're angry at you now. You stated a clear preference not to be shot. Those kinds of preferences are typically honored. That they were planning to take you out with a bullet is a clear indication that their patience is exhausted. Anything goes now. Anything."

"My home?"

"Maybe not your home."

"My plane?"

"Even your plane. My advice? Don't fly it over water. If they bring it down, they'd much prefer that it go down in the water."

SIXTY-FIVE

Lizzie found a cell phone in Carrie Belvedere's purse. As soon as we were close enough to the city of Georgetown to be in reliable contact with a cell tower, I used the phone to call Mary's mobile.

"Hey, it's me. Did you capture this number when I called?"

"Yes."

"Call me back on a land line." I hung up.

Twenty seconds later, the tiny phone burst into the opening melody of "Material Girl." We were a half mile down valley from Georgetown by then. I had just started trying to coax Lizzie's eyes to see through the natural camouflage so she could spot a small cluster of bighorn sheep that was perched halfway up the almost vertical cliff face above the other side of the interstate.

Even with my help Lizzie couldn't find the sheep. Picking out bighorns in their natural habitat is like solving a perceptual puzzle. The first time it's almost impossible to discern their still shapes out of the rocks and grass and dirt. But after that first time it gets easier. You quiet your eyes, do some concentration/perception thing that's a combination of Zen and gestalt, and suddenly—there they are.

The harsh canyon habitat where the sheep thrived made the cell signal crappy, but I was grateful for any coverage at all on this stretch of I-70.

Mary asked, "What's up?"

"Are you at Centennial?"

"Yes," she said. "The plane should be ready in about an hour. I'll take her wherever you want, whenever you want. But you know I can't fly into Telluride at night. That will have to wait until morning."

"No problem. There's a change in plans. Ready?"

"Go."

"Good. This is what I'd like you to do."

Lizzie never found the sheep. I wondered if she'd have a second chance. Ever. I assumed I wouldn't get another chance to coach her through it.

I waited until we were passing the Highway 40 exit that led toward Berthoud Pass and Winter Park before I said, "You were going to tell me about the magazines."

"I was?" she said. "It's funny, I've never told anybody about the magazines. Not that anybody's ever asked."

I touched her leg. "The magazines are your Adam," I said. "Aren't they?"

She inhaled in a little gasp.

"I did my oncology residency in Texas. At Baylor," she said as we were entering the canyons west of Idaho Springs. "That's where I met my husband."

Those mundane revelations seemed to exhaust her. I waited almost a quarter of a mile for her to continue. I had to bite my tongue to keep from saying, "Tell me."

"We married. Had two kids. Two girls."

Had. Two girls.

"My husband is, was, from Jordan. He is a not-too-distant relative of the royal family."

"Yes?" I said.

"That's important, that he's from . . . overseas. And that he's . . . connected."

"Okay."

"We moved to Dallas. A lot happened between us. Most of it wasn't good. But none of it was particularly unusual. It was a marriage that was dying in one of the normal ways that marriages die. One week in the fall, when the girls were four and two, I went to New Orleans for a short medical conference. When I came home, they were gone."

"He took your girls?"

"He took my girls. He took them to Jordan."

"To Jordan?" I repeated her words so I could buy time to look ahead. To anticipate where she was going.

"Initially, yes, I think. He never contacted me again, so I don't know for sure. But later, after I joined the company, I was able to get hold of records showing that the girls went through immigration that week in Amman."

"There aren't any treaties with Jordan? To bring them back here? What about custody and—"

"Shhh," she said gently. "I'm thorough. I checked every avenue five times in five ways. It doesn't matter what the law says or what the treaties say; Roger wouldn't have stayed in Amman. Never. Not even for the girls. He hated it there. Despised his parents. Where he took my girls next, I don't know. But he got them new passports; I'm sure of that. New names. Maybe even a new mother. Remember, he's connected. Me? I've spent the last eight years of my life looking . . . for my girls."

I slowed as we approached the speed traps in Idaho Springs. The combination of the memories and the intrusion of civilization seemed to quiet Lizzie. Not too far away on the other side of town was the steep hill where I'd encountered the flatbed with the oil drums.

I told myself to focus.

She said, "The magazines?"

It felt like a non sequitur. I said, "Yes?"

400

"In my work, now, I get a lot of free time. It's important to me, the free time. I use it to travel. I imagine places he would like to live, places he dreamed aloud about when we were together. He was a restless man, never satisfied, always felt that happiness was waiting for him someplace else. Maybe with someone else. So . . . I travel to places where I can picture him. Warm places. By a pool. At a golf course. In Scottsdale. Las Vegas. Austin. All over Hawaii. Palm Springs. Ojai. You know Ojai? It's a long list. Places in Europe, too. But only southern places. Provence. Sicily. Barcelona. Northern Africa, too. Tunisia. Mexico. I've been to Costa Rica looking for him. All over Australia. Thailand, too. I went there after the tsunami and looked at the faces of all the dead children."

"God," I said.

"When I get someplace where I can see him living, I'm ready with a list of the good schools, the private schools, the best schools—the man I married is a snob—and I wait outside for the kids to go into the school, or later, to come back out. I take pictures. Back in my hotel, I examine every face of every little girl. Trying to find mine. Trying to find my girls."

"What are their names?"

"Andrea and Zoe." She smiled. "A to Z."

"I'm so sorry," I said.

"The magazines I get all have pictures of children in them. Mostly girls. Pretty girls. Happy girls. Girls on horses. Girls at the beach. Girls dancing. Girls dreaming of being pop stars. I turn pages every night, hoping . . ." Her voice became almost inaudible. "Hoping."

I downshifted to begin the climb up toward El Rancho.

"Each day when I leave my apartment, I toss the previous night's magazines into the trash chute. If I let them pile up, if I let them remind me of the futility, I get

401

hopeless. So I throw them away. I start fresh again each night. New girls. New hope. New faces."

She fell asleep as we crested the ridge at El Rancho.

I wanted to wake her and comfort her and cajole her into telling me what was going on with my son. I didn't. I consoled myself that I'd know within a few hours.

There's no highway to carry traffic north along the Front Range of the Rockies after drivers on I-70 exit the foothills onto the high plains. The closest northbound freeway is I-25, which snakes through the heart of Denver about ten miles east of the mountains—too far away for my purposes that night. Although I would have preferred to stay on a freeway, my best choice from the bad alternatives was to take Wadsworth Boulevard north toward my destination.

Traffic was tolerable, traffic-light timing was acceptable, and Lizzie and I pulled onto the access road to Jefferson County Airport exactly fifty-eight minutes after we had exited the tunnel.

We were early.

I stopped the stolen BMW in the lot of the fixed base operator where I had arranged to meet the plane. Lizzie stirred, saw where we were, and asked me if I had any change. I gave her the coins from my pocket. She jumped out of the car, peeled away, and found a pay phone near the corner of the building. I followed her and eavesdropped. She knew I was listening but she didn't seem to care. She was calling the laboratory to get the results of my blood work. I watched as she jotted down numbers for most of a minute. All I heard from her end of the conversation was "yes, go on," "okay," and "got that."

"Well?" I asked, when she hung up.

"For now everything looks okay. There are no anomalies in your liver functions. That would be a big concern.

But some of what I asked them to look for isn't done yet. I'll have to check back with them again in the morning."

"Why not use your cell phone?"

"You may have noticed that my colleagues are pretty well connected with the mobile-phone network."

I nodded. "What's going on with Adam, Lizzie? Please."

She shook her head. "You'll leave me behind. I can't let that happen."

The Lear from Centennial didn't land for another ten minutes. I recognized the familiar green spiral on the plane's tail as it rolled past the midpoint on the runway during its landing.

As the plane taxied to the FBO, I could see through the windshield that Mary was in the right-hand seat.

"That's our ride," I said to Lizzie.

She didn't hear me. She was beside me on the lounge sofa, curled up into a fetal ball. Again, sound asleep.

Mike came out to meet us and got us settled; Mary stayed in the cockpit. The Lear's nose wheel went aloft at 10:54. Not too long after takeoff Mary came back to the cabin.

She seemed to be focusing an unusual amount of attention on Lizzie, who was on the couch in the back of the cabin.

I gave Mary a big hug and asked her about her cousin. We spoke in whispers.

"She's doing some deep-sea fishing in the Gulf for a few days. The boat is chartered in my mom's name. I think she's safe."

I liked the plan. "Thanks. Thanks for everything."

"It's nothing."

"Flight time tonight? Any idea?" I asked. "How are the winds?"

"Jet stream's not going to be much help. Weather's going to be a problem over the Great Lakes. Five hours and change is my current estimate. Could be more if we have to dodge a storm or two. With any luck we'll get in just before dawn. Given the hurry, we didn't have a chance to get any catering on board. Are you hungry? I can check the galley for you, see if there's anything left in there."

"I'm good," I said. "I'll try to sleep." I motioned for her to sit down across from me. "Do me a couple favors? Don't worry about turbulence. And avoid the Great Lakes."

She frowned. But she said, "Okay."

"How did it go at Centennial?" I asked.

She glanced, again, at Lizzie. "When you called the generator was already installed, and we were just about to run tests on the electrical system. After I talked to you, I told everybody your plans had changed and that we could finish up the next day. If anyone outside was watching us it looked like we were giving up for the night. We locked up the hangar, turned off the lights. Mechanics drove home, none the wiser."

"How did things go with Jimmy Lee? Any trouble getting the Lear?"

She made a dismissive face. "You kidding? With the offer I made? Jimmy jumped at it. Mike was cool about doing the extra night flight when I told him that there was a thousand-dollar bonus for each leg in addition to a generous layover allowance. I assume you don't mind."

Mike was a pilot friend of Mary's. The Lear, Mike's baby, belonged to the insurance company that my friend Jimmy Lee worked for in the Denver Tech Center. Mary had arranged to trade flight hours in my Gulfstream for some hours in the Lear. The Lear was slightly faster than the Gulfstream, but my plane was bigger and had better range. I'd told her to offer one and a half G-IV flight hours for one Lear flight hour to sweeten the trade.

It was a great deal for Jimmy's company. I knew he'd go for it.

"I don't mind at all. You'll get the same bonus Mike gets. Tell LaBelle. No one saw the two of you go back to Centennial?"

"When I left the airport I drove over to Mike's condo in the Tech Center. He lives in one of those high-rises off Belleview, keeps his car in the garage downstairs. You can't see it from the street. We used his car. I didn't show my face again until we were in the hangar. If someone followed me, they probably think I'm doing a . . . sleepover." She smiled.

"You trust Mike, Mary?"

"Mike's . . . good people. Yes."

"Flight plan for tonight?" I asked.

"The FAA thinks we're heading to Hartford. It's one of Mike's usual routes—all those insurance company headquarters that are there?—so if anyone's tracking this plane, it shouldn't raise any suspicion at all; they'll assume he's carrying an exec to a morning meeting. In a few hours, we'll file an amended flight plan. Are you sure you don't just want us to go into Hartford or one of the New York airports? You can drive to New Haven pretty quickly from some of those fields. I can have a car waiting."

"No, there's no time, unfortunately. It has to be New Haven. I don't think anyone will be able to figure out what we're doing. There's no reason for anyone to be watching this plane, right?"

My question was rhetorical.

Her answer—"No, I don't think so"—wasn't. She added, "Mike and I will wait for you in New Haven. You know, in case you need to get someplace fast."

"Thanks, but no. I want you back in Denver. Refuel and then head home. Stay in touch with LaBelle." I was thinking that Thea might be needing the G-IV.

"Mike and I will have to get some rest before we can head back."

"Then drop us off and take the plane someplace close by to catch some z's. Don't stay in New Haven, okay?"

"Okay." Mary looked once again at Lizzie, still asleep on the sofa. The hat was off Lizzie's bald head. "You know, the whole time I was following her I didn't know she was wearing a wig."

"Me neither," I said. "Good wig."

"Breast cancer?"

I nodded.

She touched me on the face until I looked her in the eyes. "This is still about family, boss? Right?"

At that moment, I realized that Mary may have seen something while she was tailing Lizzie for me. What? I didn't know.

"I'm looking for Adam, Mary; he's still missing. She's helping me. That's what this is. And that's all that this is about. I have some information that he might be in New Haven and that he may need me."

"Gotcha," she said.

She kissed me on the cheek and walked back toward the cockpit of the Lear. Before she got to the door, she tilted her head toward Lizzie and said, "What's her name? What should I call her?"

I said, "Lizzie. Call her Lizzie."

As Mary disappeared from the cabin, I realized I hadn't heard from LaBelle about the results of her research into Lizzie's true identity.

I pulled out my cell phone and checked to see if I'd received a text message.

I had one. The time stamp indicated that it had come in

during the chaos of escaping the tunnel. I wasn't surprised that I'd missed it.

"Your data's in. Short list. LB," was how it read.

I stared at the tiny screen for a long time before I picked up the cabin phone and dialed LaBelle's home number.

SIXTY-SIX

It took LaBelle a minute or so to pretend to get over the fact that she was still so far out of the loop she couldn't even detect the curvature of its arc. Why was I on Jimmy Lee's company's Lear? Where was my plane? Where was Mary? Where the hell was I going in such a hurry?

I didn't tell her any of it. But I didn't try to stop her from asking. Why? I loved hearing her talk. She comforted me in basic ways. I knew she'd eventually get around to telling me what I wanted to know: the names of any physicians in the U.S. who were board-certified in both neurology and oncology.

"Girl doctors or boy doctors?" she asked me with an exasperated sigh, finally accepting, or at least acknowledging, defeat.

"Girl doctors."

"There're three girls on your list. Only two boys, though. What do you make of that? Think about it. Number one among the clan of the overeducated is Antoinette Fleischer. She's on the faculty at Northwestern. Numero dos is Priya Micezevski; she's in Tallahassee in private practice. She just does neurology these days, no oncology." After a pregnant pause, she tacked on, "I'm assuming that's a married name. Priya Micezevski?"

I didn't bite. "And three?"

"Jolie Borden. Med school, UCLA. Residency, Baylor.

But I can't find any current professional activity for her going back five years. She may be retired. Probably burned out from all that schooling."

Jolie? Her parents had graced her with the French word for "pretty."

"Age for her? You have it?"

"Dr. J? She's, um . . . let's see, thirty-eight. Yes, thirty-eight."

I looked down at Lizzie. *Thirty-eight?* The medical records I found in her apartment were for female patients who were thirty-seven. Close enough.

The day at Papaya King? I would have bet she was no more than thirty-five.

"Last known address?"

"Highland Park. It's a suburb of—"

"I know." *Dallas.*

"So is Miss Jolie your girl?"

"You're my girl, LaBelle. Have I told you you're terrific lately? Well, you're terrific. One more thing, though. Please find out everything you can about number three. Spend some of my money if you need to. We'll talk soon. I have to run."

I pulled the phone away from my ear to hang up. But LaBelle continued talking, her distinctive voice easily bridging the space between the phone and my ears. "You notice there're no sisters on that list. Antoinette? Priya? Jolie? Those aren't sisters' names. You notice that? I did. We may not go to school as much as some other girls do, but at least we know when to stop."

I smiled as I placed the receiver into its cradle.

SIXTY-SEVEN

I watched Lizzie sleep for a while before I moved to the aft end of the sofa. In my mind, I was trying to transform her from a Lizzie to a Jolie. But before I succeeded I dozed off, too.

I awakened to find her straddling me, her lips only inches from mine. She was pinning each of my wrists with one of her hands.

Her strength surprised me, and it didn't. I could've freed myself.

But I didn't want to. I wasn't even tempted.

"Hi," I said after I'd taken a moment to assure myself that I wasn't dreaming.

The "hi" I used was my charming "hi," my seductive "hi," a variation on the same tune that I'd played almost two decades before in the Buckhead McMansion with Bella on that pre-Halloween night outside Atlanta. And on a few score other occasions before that night, and since.

"This is important," she said.

"Okay."

"I mean it," she said. "It's important."

"I said okay."

"Have you wondered?"

What? "About?" I asked.

But I thought I knew.

"You know," she said.

"I don't know," I said.

I thought I knew.

"This whole time? Since that day I kidnapped you on Park Avenue? The ride in the back of the Town Car? Have you wondered about . . . me? About . . . us?" With that last word she shifted her weight so I felt pressure below my waist.

She had my attention. With the exception of the part of me that couldn't stop thinking about my son, she had every last bit of my attention.

"About you?" I said, acting unfazed. Not feeling unfazed.

She moved her lips even closer to my face. "Have you wondered? What my skin feels like to touch. How I taste. Here"—she kissed me, tracing the tip of my tongue with the tip of hers—"and . . . there. How good . . . I am . . . at . . . what . . . I . . . do."

"Yes," I said. "I've wondered about those things. All those things. And a few others." The words came out in staccato bursts. I was trying to sound cavalier. I was failing.

If flirting is about amusement and advantage, seduction is about . . . What? Was I being seduced?

Yes.

Why?

"Have you wondered if"—she stressed the "if" unnaturally—"we were going to do it? Did you wonder about that?"

"Do what?"

I knew, of course. But I was enjoying the game. I didn't want it to end. And then, I did. I told myself to play along with her, that her game might bring me closer to Adam.

Amusement. Advantage.

Right.

"Fuck," she said, at once answering my question and turning the word into something that didn't even begin to resemble a profanity. "Did you wonder . . . if you and I were going to . . . fuck." As a final punctuation, she stretched out her legs so that all her weight was on top of me. I felt the pressure of her groin focused against mine, and the supple weight of her upper body on my chest.

"Don't you mean, 'when'?" I said. "Not 'if.' "

She sighed and backed away a fraction of an inch.

"This is important," she said again. " 'When' means certainty. I'm talking about something else. I'm talking about the loveliness—the allure—of not quite knowing. The bounty of . . . anticipation. The optimism of . . . hope."

"I thought—"

She put a finger to my lips. "Shhhh. Now, honestly, did you wonder?" she asked. I thought I detected a little frustration in her voice that time, as though she was disappointed at being forced to start all over from the beginning. She rotated her hips just the slightest bit, grinding herself onto me. One clockwise revolution. One counter-clockwise revolution.

She repeated, "Did you wonder?"

Then she said it again, the pressure of her softly spiraling ass framing the repetition.

"Yes," I said, trying to recover my focus. "I wondered."

"Has it been good?"

"What? Has what been good?" I wasn't playing any longer. The new question confused me.

"Has it been good? The wondering? The *if*."

"Great. Beyond good. It's been great."

"Do you really mean that? Or has it all been prelude for you? Are you just hanging around with me waiting for the washing-machine moment?"

The reference to Bella and Buckhead was all tease. But

412

her words stunned me from my trance. How could Lizzie know about that?

She locked her eyes onto mine and waited for my answer.

"You know about Buckhead?" I said. "How do you know about—?"

She shook her head, redirecting my attention. "Tell me about the wondering. About the 'if.' I want to know. All of it. Everything."

"I love anticipation. I love the 'if.' "

Her eyes told me she was skeptical.

"More than you love the 'when'?" she asked.

I moved my hips to echo her grind. "I'll be able to tell you that . . . in a few minutes."

"You're married," she scolded.

More teasing? I wasn't as sure as I had been. *What is going on here?*

Suddenly—as though exhaustion had taken her hostage—she lowered her bald head onto my shoulder. One of her hands began to caress the muscles of my neck. The fingers of the other hand snaked into my hair, and settled there.

The one in my hair was her off hand.

I could feel her jawbone tracing lines on my chest as she began, again, to speak. "Have you ever noticed that life, like death, is mostly about the if, not about the when. When we—"

"They."

I'd interrupted her because I sensed she'd changed direction and I guessed where she was going. She had stopped talking about sex and had started talking about the Death Angels.

I didn't want her to be part of that team. Not right then.

"They," she said. "When *they* fulfill a contract, when

413

they provide end-of-life services, they take away the *if*. What they leave behind is only the when. And the window of when that they leave behind is minuscule. Days only. Sometimes weeks. But not long, never long."

"Yes?"

I almost said "go on." But I said "yes."

"They don't merely hasten death by what they do. What we—*they*—do is take away the most essential part of living."

"Which is?"

"The part that we can't know."

"The if?"

"Yes. The if."

"When we'll die? That's part of the if?"

It was a guess on my part.

"An essential part. But there are other ifs that fill us, that keep us yearning, that keep us putting one foot in front of the other. That get us out of bed in the morning."

"Like?"

"Who we'll love, for instance."

"Adam?" I said, seeing the tracks in the sand. *Andrea and Zoe,* I thought. This is about Adam and Andrea and Zoe.

"Yes, yes. But for you? Berkeley, too. And Haven. They were once ifs. But the ifs go on and on. Once you love, how long will you get to love? And Thea. The wife."

I said, "And how? How will I get to love?"

My hips were moving involuntarily by then. Less provocatively. More affectionately. The result? At that moment I was more focused on the how than the if.

"How?" she said. I felt a chuckle shudder through her body. She murmured, "Yes. How? That, too. That's one of the ifs."

Her hips had stopped moving. I suspected they'd been quiet a while, but that I'd just then noticed.

Her voice descended a couple of octaves into the gravelly range of a lounge singer after a night at the piano. "If I stripped off my pants, and pulled down your trousers, and I slid you inside me right now—right now—all of those things would fly away. All the wondering. All of it. A thousand ifs would become a single, fleeting when. Hope would die. Wonder . . . would die. All for a solitary when."

"Maybe a terrific when," I said, trying to hold on to the enticing mirage before it vanished.

"Maybe. But maybe not. Maybe a most pedestrian when. There are no guarantees in love. Or in life. The if doesn't always become the when. And the when isn't always worth the wait."

"What are you saying, Lizzie?"

"I'm telling you about you. I'm telling you about me. About us. I'm telling you why I'm helping you. With Adam."

"You are?"

Still prone on me like a spent lover, Lizzie said, again, "This is important. It is so, so important."

"Okay."

"Hold me," she said. I did. Within a dozen heartbeats, she'd fallen asleep on my chest.

Her delightful, distracting little seduction had certainly left me wondering about the if. Which was, after all, where we'd started. And where it always should have ended.

My heart with Thea.

As her breathing leveled I realized I'd been outplayed. Any advantage from our mutual infatuation was now hers, not mine. What I didn't know was why she felt she'd needed it.

SIXTY-EIGHT

Outside the FBO at the Tweed New Haven airport, Lizzie asked me to stand back while she gave a yawning taxi driver our destination. Only then did she allow me to get into the cab.

She was all business. The quasi-erotic episode on the sofa in the plane had, apparently, never happened.

"I'll know soon enough where we're going," I said, pretending patience, as I settled onto the seat beside her.

"Yes. Soon enough."

"We're going to see Adam, aren't we? Right now?"

"You are. Adam isn't one of my ifs," she said. "My girls aren't in New Haven. Roger hates snow. But, yes, you'll find out . . . about Adam."

There was enough sadness in her words to fill Long Island Sound.

I was quiet for a few miles. I spent the time rehearsing what I'd say to Adam, how I'd make him understand the ifs that I had tried to avoid, the when that was coming.

The mistakes I'd made.

"They're not far behind us, you know," she said, jolting me from my reverie.

I knew. To keep her talking I said, "You mean the Death Angels?"

She nodded.

"How far behind us do you think they are?"

Lizzie answered me with a question. "When—exactly—did the pilots amend the flight plan to bring us into New Haven?"

"Forty-five minutes out, maybe fifty. Why?"

"You got the plane we were on from Jimmy Lee, right?"

Her question stunned me. "Yes, I did. From his company. How do you know about Jimmy?" Had she overheard me talking with Mary in the car? Or during the flight? She must have.

No surprise.

I stared at her face and saw a different truth in her eyes. The pieces tumbled into place for me. The puzzle came together; it was like watching Adam solve the Rubik's Cube.

My God. Lizzie was telling me that Jimmy Lee didn't just *know* a guy.

Jimmy Lee was *one* of the guys.

Jimmy Lee was one of the Death Angels.

"They already know we're in New Haven," I said, digesting the news, accepting defeat.

"It will take them a short time to mobilize, but yes, they know we're in New Haven."

"Jimmy is one . . . of them? One of you?"

She shook her head. She wasn't denying that he was a Death Angel. She was telling me that she wouldn't divulge anything about the roster. In a perverse way, I understood her loyalty. Still, I couldn't keep another question to myself.

"Is he involved in . . . end-of-life services?" I was wondering if my old friend's body was crumpled beneath a Dodge pickup truck in the Edwin C. Johnson Bore.

I was wondering if his sweet kids were orphans.

If I'd made his sweet kids orphans.

She touched my hand. Once again, she shook her head. She wasn't going to go there, either.

"Did I kill him in the tunnel?"

"You'll never know. It's better that way. If he was there, he would have killed you."

"Yes, but I hired him to kill me. There's a difference."

"It's not that simple," she said. "Not really. I once thought it was. But it's not."

"How long before they're here? In New Haven?" I asked. "The Death Angels."

"Maybe a few minutes. Maybe a few hours. No more than that. Our—their—resources are astonishing. The reach is, at times, breathtaking."

"Could they be ahead of us?"

"They could be," she said. "Depends where the closest resources were available when they got word. Certainly no farther than New York. If it turns out that they're ahead of us, we're going to be walking right into their trap." She turned toward me on the seat. "Is that okay with you? To walk into their trap?"

"If I get to see Adam first, yes."

She squeezed my hand. "Well, that's still the plan."

SIXTY-NINE

The taxi took us into the city, but not toward the familiar territory of the Yale campus. Lizzie still wouldn't reveal our destination. My heart plummeted from my chest to my toes when I realized that the cab was rolling to a stop on York Street outside a building I recognized from a previous visit I'd made with Connie back when he was—barely—ambulatory. We'd stopped by to visit a philosophy department friend of his who was recovering from prostate surgery.

Involuntarily, I said, "No."

Lizzie threw some bills at the driver and pulled me out of the cab onto the sidewalk. Outside the front entrance. She held my face in both her hands and said, "I said he needed you. I wasn't lying. What do you know about acute liver failure?"

Above her head I could read the sign on the outside of the building. YALE–NEW HAVEN HOSPITAL.

"Oh my God. Oh my God. Where is he? He's here?"

"What do you know about acute liver failure?" she repeated.

"Nothing," I said.

"I'm going to call you 'Doctor' once we're inside. Do you understand?"

Inside the Yale–New Haven Hospital.

"Yes," I said.

"You're a physician, a colleague of mine from out of town. It's natural for you to feel out of place."

"Okay."

"The less you say, the fewer mistakes you'll make."

"Yes," I said. I was having trouble putting one foot in front of the other. Falling on my face would certainly be one of those mistakes.

We'd arrived near morning shift change and the elevator lobbies were full of staff waiting to head up onto the patient floors. Lizzie held me back from the group. She said, "Wait." Two cars arrived simultaneously a moment later. The lobby emptied. "I think we're about to get lucky," she said. "It's a good sign."

I wasn't feeling lucky.

A third elevator arrived. We stepped on alone and waited for the doors to close. Ever so slowly, they did. We had the car to ourselves.

Little-known fact: Hospital elevators are the slowest moving vehicles on the planet. They are the sloths of vertical travel. Usually I found their torpidity frustrating. That day, though, the languid pace gave Lizzie time to tell me a story I was desperate to hear.

She said, "Adam was dropped off at the emergency room two days ago by a Hispanic man. I'm guessing that it was your brother's friend, Felix. He told the triage nurse that the kid's name was Adam, that he'd been sick for a couple of weeks but had gotten much worse in the past twenty-four hours. He said that he was going back out to his car to get the kid's papers and things. He never came back inside. Adam had no ID with him, no insurance info. Nothing. He presented with fever, obvious fatigue, nausea, vomiting. Severe confusion. It took the ER docs a few hours to identify what was going on. Your son is suffering from acute liver failure."

"From what?" I asked. I was baffled. And I was argumentative. I tried to counter her words, to change the reality. "He's never had liver problems."

The truth was that I didn't really know that. I'd never asked about my son's medical history. *God.*

She recognized the desperation of my tactics and lowered her voice to slow my escalation. "I don't think they know the cause. It's not always simple to identify the etiology. Most likely it's something infectious—maybe viral hepatitis. But it could be toxic—an overdose of Tylenol could do it. Or it could be something idiosyncratic and metabolic. It could even be a complication of something cardiac and chronic that's previously gone undiagnosed."

"What's your fear?" I asked. I could tell she had one.

"Worst case? If it's fulminant viral hepatitis, it could be . . . critical. Very serious."

Some of her words made sense. Some didn't. "Fulminant" was one of the words that didn't. My medical-technology background failed me; all I could manage was to ask her for some variation of the same assurance I'd asked for three times since she held my face in her hands outside the cab: "He's okay, though? He'll get through this?"

She answered the same way she had the other times. "He's very sick. Prepare yourself. He won't look well."

"It might not be him up there," I said. "There are lots of Adams in the world." I wanted it not to be him.

I want it to be him.

"It's him," Lizzie said.

It's him.

Seconds before the elevator doors opened, she said, "We don't have hospital IDs so this is going to be tricky. Improvise with me. Confidence and arrogance. Ready?"

"Yes. Where are we?"

"Intensive care."

"Oh shit."

"Some advice?" she said.

"Anything."

"If confidence fails you, rely on arrogance. Double up if you need to."

Lizzie marched to the sprawling nursing station that was separated from the patient rooms by a wide corridor. She stepped behind the counter as though she'd been there a hundred times.

After perusing a chart rack, she selected a plastic-jacketed chart with the name "Adam Doe" written in block letters on a piece of tape on the front.

"Those labs back yet?" she asked the unit clerk, who was gazing back at Lizzie over her shoulder. The look from the clerk was tired and mostly bored, but partly curious. She was wondering if she knew Lizzie. But it was the end of her shift and she wasn't sure if she really cared if she knew Lizzie.

Finally, in an uninterested voice, not a suspicious one, the clerk said, "The blood just went down ten minutes ago." Left unsaid: *You should know that, bitch*.

Lizzie sat down at a computer and went online. Within seconds the screen was covered with columns of lab values. She sent a couple of pages to the printer, picked up a phone, and punched some numbers. "This is the ICU. I need an ETA on the new liver numbers for Adam Doe . . . Yeah . . . I know they'll be in the computer when they're done. The problem is they're not . . . Okay, you'll do that now? . . . Promise? . . . Great, thanks."

She grabbed the pages out of the printer tray, stuffed them into her bag, and said, "Come on, Doctor." After a momentary brain cramp, I realized she was talking to me.

I followed her from the nursing station across the hall into a vestibule that led to Adam's room.

"Gown and gloves. Do what I do," she whispered. She was pulling a pale yellow gown over her clothes.

I started to do the same. But I couldn't take my eyes off a teenage boy, suddenly visible through the window in the center of the door.

It was Adam. *My Adam.*

He was yellow. Not the same yellow as the gown I was holding. His yellow was more mustard, less lemon. God, he looked sick.

Lizzie grabbed my wrist. "Focus," she insisted. "Do what I do. Come on. Act like you've been here before."

Somehow I managed to pull the flimsy gown over my clothes and snap some latex gloves onto my hands.

She handed me a face mask. "Just hold the mask up to your face. Don't bother to tie it." She modeled how she wanted me to do it.

I did what she did.

"You're his doctor, not his father," she said.

Wrong.

We walked into the room and stood beside Adam's bed. She picked up the clipboard hanging at the foot of his bed to check his ins and outs, and then started checking the labels on the infusion bags hanging above the IV pump. I read his blank, yellow face. It took every bit of self-control I had not to crawl into the bed and hold him.

He was hooked up to fifty leads, surrounded by a dozen monitors.

Lizzie said, "They're giving him neomycin to treat encephalopathy. The chart said there was no edema so far. That's good."

What? "Edema?" I whispered, parroting her. The word was, of course, familiar, but I couldn't put a definition to it. *I should know what that means,* I thought. *I should.*

"Swelling in his brain. It would be a serious complication."

Shit. "Can he hear me?" I asked.

"I doubt it. No." She paused. "Maybe."

"I need to tell him things."

The intercom sounded from a location near the door. I almost jumped out of my shoes.

"Doctor? Those labs are back," the unit clerk said in the exact same bored voice she'd used earlier.

"Thank you. I'll be right out," Lizzie said. To me, she whispered, "I'm going to go look at the labs. You stay here while I do. Remember, you're a doctor, not a father. People don't know you; they'll be watching."

She took a step toward the door before she stopped and turned back toward me.

"What I was fearing? It's happening. Adam needs a transplant. Without it, he could die. They're looking for a donor liver."

"What?"

What?

"He could die without a new liver."

"When?"

"Soon."

"What soon? Next week? Next month?"

"Sooner," she said. She stepped from the room.

SEVENTY

Did I know right then?

Not in any complete sense. Not really. I couldn't have explained it. I couldn't have choreographed the next few steps. But I had a premonition about what was coming and I could have predicted what the set, absent a few props, would look like when the curtain finally came down.

I thought I knew the "if" even if I didn't know the when.

Or maybe I knew the when, but I didn't know the if.

Everything was backward.

My son was dying.

That was never part of the plan. That was never part of the deal with the Death Angels.

Not at all.

But I was suddenly serene. For the first time in a long time, I was serene.

Adam listened, or he didn't, as I told him everything I could squeeze into the three or four minutes I had alone with him in that hospital room. I told him about the Death Angels and about intimacy and about cowardice—mine—and about love and Thea and Cal and Haven, and about Lizzie and about me and how I thought I'd changed and how he was a big part of how I'd changed, and why

I'd changed, and I tried to explain why I'd been able to change.

I told him I was sorry and I asked him for forgiveness.

I told him that there was a psychologist in Boulder named Alan Gregory who would fill in all the details I would never get a chance to tell him.

I told him I loved him.

"You have to live," I implored him. "None of it makes any difference if you don't live."

"We should go."

Lizzie was behind me. Her voice was at once firm, and soft. I hadn't heard her come back into the room. "It's too risky to stay here any longer. As soon as shift change is over or one of his docs shows up, we're screwed. We have to go."

"Can I kiss him?"

"No."

"Shield me," I said to her.

She stepped forward. I leaned down, pulled the mask from my face, and kissed my son on his yellow cheek and then once, dodging tubes, on his chapped lips.

His lips tasted of glycerin.

"Good-bye, Adam," I said.

Lizzie was in tears as we left the room.

Me? I was a wreck. I was the man I thought I would be had I hit one of those two trees at the bottom of that chute in the Bugaboos. Lizzie could've transported me back out of the ICU in a thermos.

I felt pain unlike anything I'd ever experienced in my life.

But I was serene.

SEVENTY-ONE

We took the stairs down to the lobby.

"I'm sorry," she said. "I'm so sorry."

She said it more than once. How many times? I was crying too much to notice.

I wiped away some more tears and nodded.

"I want to find Felix," I said. "Maybe he can tell me something. You know, what happened."

"Sure," she said. We were almost down to the first floor. "That shouldn't be too difficult."

It was all so banal. It was just conversation. We both knew that Felix had no answers that would make any difference.

I turned toward the main exit, the one we'd used to enter the building. She tugged me in another direction. "No, this way," she said.

I followed her down some corridors to the Emergency Department. "Let's go out this way instead," she said. "Just in case."

In case the Death Angels are waiting. Watching.
Aiming.

I felt no fear at the thought. None.

Outside, the morning air was chilly. Not Ridgway chilly. Connecticut chilly, with a biting wind off the Sound, which was Ridgway chilly to the *n*th. Twenty yards or so down from the ER door, but still under the long overhang that protected the entrance, Lizzie hopped ahead of me and sat on the wide rear bumper of an ambulance that had backed up earlier to deliver a patient. She patted the space next to her on the bumper. I sat, too. Instantly, I could feel the cold steel through my trousers.

"They may not get him a liver in time," she said. "You have to know that. He's very sick, and it's hard to get organs on short notice. He could get too sick, too fast. Acute liver failure can be a runaway train."

I tried to use logic as a salve. "He'll be a priority, right? He's young, healthy. That's how it works? He'll be a priority, won't he?"

She pulled out a cell phone and punched in a number. Seconds later she said, "ICU ward clerk, please."

A moment later I heard the sound of the clerk's bored voice. She said, "ICU."

"I'm about to give you the identity and contact information on Adam Doe, the teenager with liver failure. Ready?" Lizzie stated Adam's name, Bella's name, address, and phone number, and then my name, address, and phone number. She provided his student information from Brown and dictated his health insurance coverage information. She surprised me most by then reciting a concise version of my son's medical history. She knew his vaccination status and knew he'd had pneumonia when he was eight. She knew he was allergic to sulfa. I didn't know any of that. "You get everything? Good. No questions? Now you need to call everyone stat, starting with his docs, and then his parents, and let them know what's going on. Get someone else to alert the New England Organ Bank, and the United Network, and make sure that they're up to speed on all this. Give the transplant team a heads-up, too. Get an OR ready. Do you understand what I'm saying? This kid needs a liver. Go get him one. He's out of time."

She hung up.

To me, she said, "He was already a priority. Maybe he's more of one now. But there are no guarantees. None. A lot depends on how fast he gets sicker."

"The hospital will call Thea and Bella?"

"Yes."

Thea would call LaBelle. LaBelle would call Mary. Mary and Trace would fly Thea to New Haven. They'd pick up Bella in Cincinnati on the way east.

Lizzie hugged me. I held her.

We both cried.

But the tears didn't chill my flesh.

I was feeling the if.

It was warming me like a hot wind blowing from the south.

PART II

His Story

SEVENTY-TWO

Did either of them—my patient, or the woman he called Lizzie—know they were being recorded on a surveillance camera as they sat side by side on the back bumper of that ambulance outside the Emergency Department of the Yale–New Haven Hospital?

I've wondered a lot about that. Maybe she knew. Lizzie.

I doubt that he'd given it a thought. By then he had too many other things on his mind.

But the surveillance camera was there, capturing all the events of the next few minutes.

I saw an edited version of the clip for the first time that same evening on CNN. I didn't see the entire footage for another couple of days. Not because it wasn't available. It was available everywhere, had been downloaded a gazillion times on the Web.

I didn't see the entire footage for another couple of days because I couldn't bring myself to watch it.

Their embrace on the bumper of the ambulance lasted for a long time. It was hard to tell who was more thirsty for comfort, but the poignancy of them holding each other, their bodies occasionally shaking from swallowed tears, was so intimate that it was painful to watch.

It was as though a camera had surreptitiously caught

lovers coupling, and the footage was being played for all to watch on the evening news.

When they pulled apart—she let go first, not him—she reached up and held his face in both her hands and pulled him within inches of her. She spoke to him for most of a minute. As she spoke her right hand caressed his face, her fingertips edging up into his hair. Her left hand stayed perfectly still on his cheek, holding him.

At one point, she said, I think, "Now . . . is when."

He didn't say a word in reply. He nodded, though.

I've watched this part of the video at least twenty times, most of those times in slow motion, trying desperately to read the words her lips were forming. Dozens of Web sites blossomed with translations of her subtle lip movements. Each interpretation was a little different.

Talking heads argued about her mouthed words on cable news. Hearing-impaired specialists debated the esoteric art and science of lipreading.

I'm still not sure exactly what it was she said to him after she said, "Now . . . is when." But whatever else it was that she was saying, he was nodding in reply.

Agreeing.

I'm certain, a hundred percent certain, that he was agreeing.

Enthusiastically agreeing.

When she was done speaking, and he had nodded one last time, I think she asked him, "Are you sure?"

And I think he said, "Yes."

She sighed then. It's easy to tell that she sighed. You can watch her fill her lungs with air—her mouth opens, her chest expands, her shoulders rise—and then she expelled all the spent gases out of her body at once.

She smiled just the slightest bit before she reached into her shoulder bag and lifted out an envelope, a legal-size envelope. She removed one sheet of paper from it—it's apparent there were others that she had left behind—and handed it to him. He took the pen she was offering and he began to sign it without reading it.

"No, read it," she said.

I hope I've made it clear that lipreading isn't a reliable skill of mine, but I'm confident that's what she told him. For what it's worth, most of the bloggers agreed with my assessment. The "no, read it" translation wasn't controversial.

He did what he was told. He read the page, signed it, and handed it back to her. She signed it, too, and returned the paper to the envelope, which she handed to him.

He stuck the envelope in his jacket pocket without even a glance at the rest of its contents.

I could read his lips—everyone could—as he said, "Thank you. Thank you."

They stood up then, holding hands. Left to right, right to left. Their lips were so close together that the steam from their exhales fused into one little cloud.

This part of the tape is charged, almost erotic.

Okay, not almost erotic. Definitely erotic.

She's the one who made the next move. She opened the back doors of the ambulance, but he climbed up inside the vehicle first. She stepped up right after him.

Behind them, she left the door open about three inches.

I think it was intentional. Leaving the door ajar.

A hospital resident, a husky young black woman wearing baggy green scrubs with her hands stuffed deep into the pockets of a quilted down jacket, walked into view at the bottom of the screen as Lizzie was climbing up into the ambulance. The young doctor turned her head and opened her mouth as though she was going to say something. I imagined her saying, "Hey, you can't go in there."

But she didn't say anything. Her shift was over; she was heading home. She probably didn't want the hassle. She probably wanted to forget the last twenty-four hours of her life. She wanted a bed. She wanted a dream. The resident didn't even break stride. She put her head down.

She kept on walking.

The surveillance video has no sound.

No sound.

The way that the camera was positioned, most of the action I've described took place on the upper part of the screen, in the right corner. The geometry of the boxy ambulance was slightly distorted by the angle, as though it had been drawn for use in a cartoon that exaggerates perspective.

"Keep on Truckin'."

Like that.

Once the young resident passed by the ambulance and exited the frame, the camera lens captured no movement at the top of the screen, nothing, not a bird flying through the sky, not a squirrel in a tree, not a stray cat darting below the vehicle chassis.

Nothing, for a full ninety seconds.

On the bottom of the screen, where the ER door was visible, there was some motion. A little over halfway through the time that they were together inside the ambulance, a nurse rushed out the ER door, appearing startled. She looked around, left, right, then back to her left.

She saw what we saw on the video.

She saw nothing. A parked ambulance. That was it.

Did she notice that the back door of the ambulance was slightly open? She didn't appear to. If she did notice, she didn't care.

On the video we can't tell what had startled her, what drew her outside, what caused her to look around.

Whatever it was, though, she didn't see any more evidence of it.

She stepped back into the hospital and, we suppose, returned to her post in the ER.

The next motion we see on the video is the woman he called Lizzie as she pushed open the doors and climbed down from the ambulance. She straightened her jacket, tugged at the cuffs of her sleeves, and pulled off the floppy hat she was wearing, revealing a surprising, glossy bald head. She tossed the hat on a concrete bench that sits against a wall, below a window. She began to stride, purposefully it seems, her hands swinging by her sides, toward the emergency room doors.

She was heading back inside.

SEVENTY-THREE

Watching someone being assassinated by a high-powered rifle—without sound—is an eerie, terrifying thing.

Oddly, it was more terrifying watching the assault the second time and the third than it had been the first. The first time I was more shocked. The other times I was more horrified.

The hypersonic slug stunned Lizzie when she was about halfway to the ER door. That part is clear: She was stunned by whatever it was she felt as the metal slug sliced into her, then instantly, through her. In an odd, ironic way, the impact initially straightened her up as though she had just been ordered by someone—a teacher? her mother?—to correct her posture and she was instinctively trying to comply. But the fix to her carriage lasted for less than an eye blink.

Before her right foot could reach out to complete another step she collapsed into a clumsy U-shape on the concrete, a dark stain immediately spreading onto the walkway from an even darker spot that was visible on her throat.

High on her throat. An inch and a half below her ear.

The U-shape of her body on the concrete was open toward the camera. Her legs were splayed unnaturally, her left knee folded back.

After a couple of seconds her right hand moved once,

as though she were grabbing for something that she had dropped.

Every time I see that hand move now—on the screen, in my dreams—I wonder if it was her off hand.

Then she was still.

She was dead.

On the video, the sniper shot that killed her made no sound.

In the reality of New Haven at a few minutes after seven o'clock in the morning, the shot must have made a terrible sound. But viewers of the video are left to imagine the abrasiveness and insult of that report.

The same nurse who had edged outside the ER moments before responded by rushing back out the door again. We can guess why this time: She must have heard the bark of the shot. This time she spotted Lizzie's fallen body and the spreading pool of blood near her bald head. The nurse turned and she screamed back inside.

We see the nurse scream. We assume she screamed for help. But we don't *hear* her scream. For one long moment, mouth open, eyes aflame, she is as silent as one of Munch's tormented.

The paramedics from the ambulance were the first to make it out the door in response to the nurse's wail. One of the two EMTs, a woman, rushed up and knelt over Lizzie's inert body. Her partner dashed instinctively toward their rig to retrieve some equipment, or their stretcher.

We watch him jump up inside the ambulance and reemerge, in shock, twenty seconds later. He yelled something toward his partner. She looked up at him and mouthed, "What?"

He said something into his radio before he repeated his words to his partner.

In the next chaotic minutes, whatever forensic treasures law enforcement authorities might have mined at the two crime scenes were obliterated by emergency medical personnel doing what they were trained to do.

Since my patient's body was, conveniently, already waiting for them on a stretcher in the back of the ambulance, they transported him into the ER first.

Lizzie's body was lifted from the sidewalk onto a gurney only seconds later.

All the remaining docs and nurses and EMTs who had rushed outside became part of Lizzie's escort; each of them took a spot leading the gurney, flanking it, or chasing it back inside the door.

The last images on the surveillance video are poignant.

Everyone was gone.

A light snow had started falling.

At the top of the screen, the ambulance doors stood wide open. On the left side of the picture, mid-frame, the dark stain of blood from Lizzie's neck had spread into a pond that was about the size of a watermelon but had the asymmetry of an eggplant. Remarkably, no one had stepped in the puddle.

Once again, the video was still. There was no motion.

Suddenly, a cop—New Haven? Hospital security?— rushed out the ER door in a crouch, a gun in his left hand.

After ten seconds of tension—the pistol barrel going this way, then that—he realized there was no one to shoot.

He straightened himself up and exhaled. He lowered the weapon to his side.

It's pretty clear that what he said next was "Fuck."

SEVENTY-FOUR

Most of what I know about what happened later I learned from simply watching the news.

There was plenty of news. For a few hours the Yale hospital tried desperately to maintain the illusion that Adam Doe was just another patient. But because of the tantalizing video from the surveillance camera the story quickly became a national obsession.

My patient's body had been discovered on its side on the stretcher in the back of the ambulance. He'd suffered a single gunshot wound to his head. The entrance wound, surrounded by powder burns, was behind his right ear. The slug had almost obliterated his brain stem.

Blood loss was minimal.

That had been Lizzie's plan all along, of course: to minimize blood loss. The aim of her shot, one ER doc said in an interview a couple of days later with Diane Sawyer, had been "surgically precise." He added that his patient—my patient—"was a dead man before he heard the shot."

Valiant efforts inside the ER didn't change that. Resuscitation efforts didn't last long.

My patient stayed dead.

The envelope Lizzie had given him was stuffed into the waistband of his trousers when he was wheeled into the ER. On the outside of the envelope, he had written READ

THIS FIRST. Inside was a printout of laboratory results of blood work that had been analyzed only the night before at a Colorado facility. The pertinent values, highlighted in fluorescent orange, confirmed a number of things.

Among them, that my patient's liver was healthy.

More important, the numbers confirmed that he was a reasonably compatible organ donor for his son, Adam, who just happened to be upstairs in the ICU suffering from acute liver failure. Fulminant hepatitis, to be precise.

The piece of paper that my patient had signed was in the envelope, too. It was the sheet that Lizzie had made certain that he read before he climbed into the ambulance to die.

That document was an organ-donor directive that specifically bequeathed his liver to his son. Whatever other of his organs turned out to be useful, he donated to anyone else's son or daughter who might need them as desperately as Adam needed his father's liver.

The ER attending read the letter and digested the laboratory data within moments of my patient's arrival. Immediately, the doc ordered his team to take the necessary steps to preserve and prepare the body for organ and tissue harvest.

After some contentious too-public arguments in the Emergency Department between the transplant team and the homicide detectives who had shown up to investigate the two deaths that had happened just outside the ER, surgery to harvest my patient's organs and tissue began promptly.

Nine different people ultimately received tissue or organ donations from his body.

Adam received his father's liver. The surgery, by all reports, was long, but uncomplicated.

A hospital spokesperson said that once Adam had

recovered sufficiently he planned to go back to Cincinnati to recuperate with his mother.

My patient's wife, Thea, refused to deal with the media. Like a vocal part of the public, I was curious about her reaction to her husband's murder, and particularly curious about her reaction to the circumstances around her husband's murder. But Thea stayed silent. Adam's mother, Bella, on the other hand, liked to talk to reporters. Too much, it seemed to me. Even the media tired of her quickly—rumors of an imminent appearance on Dr. Phil's show evaporated once she'd done a two-day marathon that included all the network morning shows and any of the cable news shows that would have her.

Twenty-four hours after the shooting, the New Haven police still hadn't been able to identify the location where the single sniper shot that had killed Lizzie had originated.

A vehicle, some theorized. Something large enough to allow a sniper room to move. A witness came forward who said he'd seen a black Hummer on York Street just after dawn.

The Humvee never showed up on any surveillance video.

No one stepped forward claiming to have witnessed the shot. No evidence was discovered to identify the location of the sniper's lair.

The same was true after a week. No progress.

And after two.

The doorman at Lizzie's New York apartment—a man named Gaston Rezzuti—called one of the national newspaper tabloids and offered them a peek inside his infamous tenant's apartment for two hundred thousand dollars. He'd ultimately accepted seventy grand for the little tour and walked away from his doorman job before he was fired.

The tabloid photographer he'd led inside Lizzie's home discovered a bubble-wrapped trove of family memorabilia secreted away in the door-less credenza of her tiny office.

The photographer displayed some of the dozens of photographs he found in the stash on Lizzie's teak desktop and took pictures of the photos for his publisher. Most of the images were of two small children. Girls. Andrea and Zoe. Some were of the same two children with their parents.

There were also love letters from a man named Roger.

The two small children were hers, and Roger's.

I never saw a single mention anywhere in the news about the Death Angels, not even an allusion.

The juicy parts of the story, as far as the national media was concerned, were the dual provocative murder mysteries. Both had to do with Lizzie. One mystery had her as victim—a young woman with advanced breast cancer who had been shot to death by an unknown sniper on the sidewalk outside the ER at Yale–New Haven Hospital. The other mystery had her as perpetrator—fingerprints and gunshot residue seemed to establish that she had shot a man in the head in the privacy of the back of an ambulance that had been parked outside Yale–New Haven Hospital. Like herself, her victim—a man she'd apparently barely known—wasn't too far from natural death at the time of his murder.

She'd shot the man, a wealthy medical-technology businessman, the story went, so that his gravely ill son could have his liver.

But why?

I heard a lot of theories. None of them was even close to the truth.

How could they be close to the truth? I wondered. *Who could have guessed the truth?*

A stolen BMW M3 recovered at an airport in suburban Denver, and interviews with a couple of pilots, seemed to tie the pair murdered in Connecticut to an abandoned, beat-up old Porsche 911 and a wrecked pickup truck with a body beneath it in the eastbound bore of the Eisenhower Tunnel, and to other still-perplexing events that had taken place the evening before in the long hollow that traversed the Continental Divide in Colorado on I-70.

Once again, I heard a lot of theories. A few of them tried to link my patient to the sniper murders that had been terrifying drivers in Colorado in recent days. The fact that the sniper took no more victims after the day of the New Haven tragedies only fueled that speculation.

But nothing really made sense.

Unless I added in the Death Angels. Only then could I make it all make any sense.

But I never mentioned the Death Angels to anyone. I didn't tell my wife, a D.A. Or my best friend, a Boulder cop. My patient's caution—*"They know you have a daughter"*—continued to resonate in my head like a loop of lyrics from the most irritating pop song ever written.

I learned a lot about the woman he called Lizzie from the news. But everything I learned stopped almost five years before her death.

Her real name was Jolie Borden. Her husband, Roger, it turned out, was actually a Jordanian American who had been born Raja and had originally come to the United States on a student visa. He was an anesthesiologist currently making his living as an "investor and developer." He surfaced at a news conference at his lawyer's office in Rancho de something, California, a week after the events in New Haven. Roger's lawyer did all the talking to the press.

Her client and his two daughters, the attorney maintained, had been abandoned eight years before by the woman who had been killed by the sniper outside the emergency room. After looking for his wife for a few years, her client had started a new life with his kids. He hadn't spoken to his ex-wife in ages.

I observed Roger's silent performance with jaded, psychologist's eyes. I was, I was certain, watching a man who lied with the same facility that I breathed. A man who could lie without saying a single word.

The lawyer asked that the press allow her client and his children privacy so that they might grieve.

Ha, I thought, watching him clinically. *If that is grief, I am a unicorn.*

A correspondent for CNN, also of Jordanian descent, revealed that Roger's given name, Raja, roughly translated, means "hope."

The reporter didn't seem to recognize the irony.

SEVENTY-FIVE

I attended a public memorial service in Denver that was held for my patient five days after his death. Had anyone at the service asked me how I knew him, I was prepared to make something up.

Adam was still convalescing in New Haven and wasn't at the memorial, but I did see my patient's two lovely daughters. I also laid my eyes on Thea for the first time. His description of his wife had been so accurate I felt as though I already knew her. She was accompanied throughout the long service by a man about her husband's age who stayed within whisper range of her. Some part of his body seemed to always be in contact with some part of hers. He had bright eyes and a quick, engaging smile. I could tell she felt safe with him. During an upbeat gospel song I whispered a question to the woman sitting next to me. "Do you know who that is? With Thea?"

She told me it was a family friend. His name was Jimmy Lee.

SEVENTY-SIX

A little less than three months after the events in New Haven, my partner, Diane, stuck her head into my office at the end of a long Tuesday. She told me that a young man in the waiting room wanted to see me.

I was wary while I made the short walk out to the front of the building. I had no more appointments scheduled that evening.

The person who was sitting in the waiting room engrossed in *Scientific American* was a tall, thin kid with an unruly mop of hair. He wasn't dressed warmly enough for January in Colorado.

"Dr. Gregory?" he said.

I thought, *Damn,* and figured I was about to get handed a sheaf of unwelcome legal papers by a process server. It wouldn't be the first time it had happened under almost identical circumstances.

"Yes," I said.

"I'm Adam," he said. "You wrote me a note about . . . my father."

"I did."

I'd handwritten the note on my professional stationery about two weeks after Adam's father's death and mailed it to him at his mother's house in Ohio. I'd marked the outside of the envelope CONFIDENTIAL. In the letter, I introduced myself as a psychologist who'd been working with his father and stated clearly to Adam that, if he was interested, I had his father's permission— encouragement, actually—to share information from his father's psychotherapy. I suggested that he might find what I had to say interesting and asked him to get in touch with me when he was feeling better.

I wished him a speedy recovery.

I hadn't heard back from Adam, but based on what little I knew about him I wasn't surprised by his silence. Nor was I surprised that my first contact with him, when it happened, came in the form of an ambush in my waiting room.

I shook Adam's hand—his handshake lacked not only character but also enthusiasm—and invited him back to my office.

He dumped a heavy daypack on the floor next to the sofa and sat down.

"It's a pleasure to meet you," I said. "I've heard a lot about you."

He nodded as though he was agreeing with something—perhaps that it was, indeed, a pleasure to meet him. Whatever I might have been thinking about why he was there, he was letting me know that he wasn't in Boulder as a supplicant.

He looked like his father. Their eyes were so similar that it was hard for me to look away from Adam's gaze, even for a moment.

"So what do you got?" he said.

His question was a theatrical version of bored. It was also obviously ungrammatical, a smidgeon provocative, and just a tiny bit disrespectful. I assumed that every last bit of the package was intentional.

Adam wasn't going to make this easy for me. I reminded myself that he hadn't made it easy for his father, either, that first day that he'd shown up unannounced on his father's porch and asked if the little girl trying to escape her father's legs was his sister.

As I recalled hearing about Adam's first visit to his father, I relaxed.

The ground, unsteady from the moment I spotted Adam in the waiting room, stopped shifting. Therapeutically, I suddenly knew where I was.

I was sitting in my office with a young man who had to be wondering what impact losing an uncle, two step-fathers, and a father might have on his life.

I was sitting in my office with a young man who had been running away from a father who'd loved him, a father he was certain was doomed to leave him.

A young man who had to be wondering what it was going to be like to have every molecule of his blood filtered through the tissue of his dead father's donated liver.

A young man who had to be wondering—had to be wondering—about the nature of his dead father's cowardice, and about the nature of his dead father's sacrifice, who had to be wondering about the betrayals and the benevolence that had played out that day in New Haven.

A young man who was brilliant about many things but who, like his father, probably lacked wisdom about the inviolate link between intimacy and vulnerability.

I didn't know much about the Death Angels, or the work they did, or about the great thinkers' take on the ultimate value of life.

Nor was I an expert on the psychology of transplant recipients.

But I knew something about young men. And about young men like Adam. Young men who were searching for perspective and understanding about the bizarre things that happen between fathers and sons, the odd things that happen within families.

I was on solid ground there.

"News from your father," I said in reply to his question about "what you got." "I have news from your father. Things he wanted you to know."

"Yeah?"

"Yeah," I said.

Adam had come a long way. And although he didn't know it, he'd come to hear a long story.

"Tell me," he said.

I had to clench my jaw to keep from smiling.

ACKNOWLEDGMENTS

The concept for this book, and some of its vignettes, were inspired during the small window of time I spent with a man named Peter Barton. I befriended Peter while he was experiencing his rapidly approaching death, and our time together taught me invaluable lessons about one special man's ability to continue living until he took his last breath. Peter faced the end of his life with a measure of courage and grace that was a wonder for me to behold. I strongly encourage interested readers to take a look at the chronicle of Peter's life, and death, that he co-wrote with Laurence Shames—*Not Fade Away: A Short Life Well Lived*. You'll find an inspiring, lovely story most unlike the one you just read. Thank you, Hawk, for one more gift.

The circle of gratitude spirals back one additional beat; Peter and I were introduced by our mutual friends, Don Aptekar and David Greenberg. Along the way Dave unwittingly provided some of the raw material that became part of this story. My thanks to them both.

I already owed Kern Buckner a lot. Now I owe him a little more. I don't think it would have been possible for me to imagine the events I describe in the Bugaboos were it not for the mesmerizing tale Kern shared about his own escapade on the slopes above Steamboat Springs.

When I presented the concept for this book, first to my agent, Lynn Nesbit, and later to my editor, Brian Tart, I was prepared to meet resistance. I received encouragement. Six months later, when they saw the result, I feared even more resistance. But the good fortune that has followed me throughout my career—the good fortune that has placed me in the hands of publishing professionals who have allowed me to take so many liberties with the conventions of series fiction—held fast. As this project has evolved, Lynn and Brian have been supportive and enthusiastic every step of the way. I can't thank them enough.

Brian's astute editing made this a much sharper story. His is one of the many names of people behind the scenes who help turn manuscripts into books. Claire Zion, Neil Gordon, Kathleen Matthews Schmidt, Lisa Johnson, and many other fine people at Dutton, as well as Hilary Hale at TimeWarner UK, all played essential roles in helping this project find its way into bookstores. They've earned my gratitude.

Early readers have to hurdle over the biggest flaws. Al Silverman, Elyse Morgan, Doug Price, Jamie Brown, Terry Lapid, Jane Davis, and Laura Barton walked point on this one. I'm grateful for their critical efforts, but I'm more grateful that I get to call them friends. Nancy Hall put her indelible mark on things later in the process, after my eyes had begun to blur. My thanks to all.

For the long months each year that I write and edit, I live in two parallel worlds. One of them ends up on these pages. The other one is real. Anyone with the (mis)fortune of sharing a house with a novelist will tell you that the demarcation isn't always crystal clear. Xan and Rose? Thanks for tolerating, supporting, and believing. My mom, Sara White Kellas, remains my biggest fan.

Fifteen years ago two strangers, Jeffrey and Patricia Limerick, had an enthusiastic response to my first manuscript. They certainly didn't have to, but they talked an old friend of theirs at Viking into taking a look at it for me. It turned out that he liked it, too, and he passed it on to a senior editor. The end result? The Limericks kickstarted my career, and I gained a couple of wonderful friends. Sadly, Patty—and about a thousand friends and loved ones—mourned Jeff this past year after a sudden illness took his life. Thank you, Jeff—there will always be a little bit of your spirit on every page I write. You are missed.